CHARLINE'S SOLSTICE

MOONS OF MYSTERY BOOK 2

S BOLANOS

Paperback: 978-1-956128-06-2
Ebook: 978-1-956128-07-9

MOONS OF MYSTERY

Sara's Moon

Charline's Solstice

Diana's Eclipse
(Coming Soon)

CONTENTS

This is for all those who believe in love forever, but know HEAs take work.

I love you, Michael, and I don't ever plan on stopping.

WEEKEND PLANS

A high-pitched giggle startled me out of a delicious daydream about a certain werewolf and all of the naughty things I wanted him to do to me. I shifted in my supposedly ergonomic office chair that clearly wasn't designed for anyone with an actual ass and refocused my attention on the email I was supposed to be finishing. Not sure how many times I'd read the damn thing and not seeing any glaring errors, I checked to make sure the appropriate Human Resources signature was in place and hit send. A second later, tiny pings chimed around the office as every person in Raleigh Marketing Services received the memo.

My microscopic sense of accomplishment disintegrated faster than soggy pie crust as I noticed the self-appointed department head making the rounds. I quickly leaned forward and ducked my head, allowing my curtain of giant curls to hide my face and hopefully my current lack of productivity. Sadly, the red veil of obscurity did absolutely nothing to prevent Beatrice from stopping at the entrance to my cubicle.

"How's it going over here, ladies? Finish those severance reports yet?"

I chanced a peek through my hair and winced as Beatrice raised an overly manicured eyebrow at me.

"Charline?"

Before I could come up with a suitable platitude for why the reports due yesterday were still sitting on my desk, Alyssa from across the aisle rolled out with a smug grin. "I wouldn't pin your hopes on it. *Someone* has been a little distracted of late."

I sent up a silent prayer for her to drop it, but too late. Beatrice smelled gossip.

"Distracted, you say?"

Alyssa nodded enthusiastically. "Don't tell me you didn't see the absolute treat who was coming around a couple weeks ago. I have to admit, I'm both jealous and a little impressed. From Ted to Mr. Hot Stuff like that." She snapped her fingers and I barely checked my groan.

Beatrice swiveled to face me, her blonde bob swinging about her face, hazel eyes wide with shock. "Honestly, Charline, I don't see how you couldn't make it work with Ted. He was so wonderfully reliable."

I gave the woman my best fake smile.

Actually, you nosy cow, Ted was a fucking psychopath AND an honest-to-God werewolf, because turns out those are real. So yeah, not reliable, not even nice really, and fucker tried to murder my best friend...twice.

My cheek twitched with the effort of keeping the truth to myself, that even beyond *all* that, he'd also been a cheating son of a bitch.

"Men aren't handbags, you know." Beatrice placed a hand on her hip, drawing the eye to her ridiculous pink pantsuit. "You can't just switch them out with the seasons."

Far as I was concerned, the fact that Ted was quite literally buried in a ditch in the middle of nowhere served him right, but that didn't erase the doubt or pain he'd left behind. Not just the physical scars on my body, but the ones to my confidence. How could I not have known? Six months. Six *months* we'd been together, been intimate... Who in their right mind couldn't tell they were dating a literal serial killer for that long? Or a werewolf for that matter?

This girl, that's who. The one who'd had bright shiny stars in her eyes about love and family and happily ever after.

"Oh, you know how it goes, Bee." Susan spun around from her own desk to join the fun. "Sometimes you can't seem to find the one that goes with every outfit."

I subconsciously smoothed my navy pencil skirt over my thighs. Since when was it a crime to want to look nice? And when did it become Make Fun of Charline Day? These women were supposed to be my friends. They'd come to my house, eaten food I'd painstakingly prepared, and brought me cupcakes from the little bakery I adored for my birthday. Why were *my* life choices suddenly up for ridicule? Had it always been like this and I simply hadn't wanted to see it? Apparently having your boyfriend turn out to be a psychopath was a real eye-opener when it came to perceiving people clearly.

Elise popped up from her own cubicle. "Hey, Suzie, how's your little one doing?" Elise, at least, I could rely on not to pass judgment on my choices in companionship *or* attire. Of course, that could have been due to the fact that Elise only cared about babies. Full stop.

"Any new pics?" Beatrice asked, latching onto the change in topic.

I groaned to myself, suddenly unsure if it hadn't been better when they were focused on teasing me. Now I'd have to endure the endless parade of baby pictures from all four of them. Being the only unmarried woman in HR came as a special burden. Perhaps that was why their remarks stung so much now. Before, I'd truly believed I'd been close to, as Beatrice said, "making it work" with Ted.

My chest ached at the blind optimism I'd had and my self-esteem crumbled a little more. Apparently, stubborn determination did not a Happily Ever After make. I stared down at my empty hands and gave voice to the despair. Unfortunately, *this* groan did not go unnoticed.

"Don't worry, Charline, someday someone will stick around longer than a couple of weeks." Beatrice gave me a simpering smile before returning her attention to the plethora of baby pictures.

As if I needed a reminder that my luck with boyfriends was less than stellar. Not just Ted, but all of them. The gaggle liked to refer to my attempts at a love life as "the flavor of the week," which while insulting, had unfortunately also proved fairly accurate. Every man I dated ended up having a personality deal-breaker, cheated, were losers from the start, or simply disappeared. Ted had actually been my longest relationship after an impressive line of less than great options, and he'd managed to tick all those boxes and then some.

My thoughts flashed to the terrifying memory of a half-man-half-beast dragging me into the woods, his voice reduced to guttural sounds that raked down my spine while fingers twisted into claws wrapped around my arm.

I absently tugged on the elbow-length cardigan hiding said arms. Normally I wasn't self-conscious of my arms, even if they were a tad larger than the other women's, but the jagged silver scars running down my left tricep were a different matter. A lovely little memento from my supremely awful breakup.

The only bright light out of all of it had been meeting

David, the cavalry that had ridden in to help save the day and the delicious hunk of man the women of HR didn't think I was capable of hanging onto. The fact that he was also a werewolf probably should have given me pause, but considering how upside down my world had become recently, it felt like par for the course. The supernatural was real, but just because one werewolf was a monster didn't mean another would be. Villains came in all forms and so did knights in shining armor.

If only I knew when said knight would be returning from his impromptu trip.

I inched closer to my bag and the phone it held only to pull up short. Calling David when I knew he was busy with something important screamed needy and insecure. Despite feeling exactly that way after enduring this afternoon's teasing, Mama hadn't raised a wilting daisy. I could already hear her voice in my head, simultaneously encouraging and berating me.

Chin up, sugar. You'd think the sun comes up to hear you crow.

I sighed again, making sure it really was to myself this time while the geese around me steadily honked over the pictures of Susan's new baby. A cute baby was one thing, but Susan's looked more alien than human. The ghost of a smile pulled at my lips as I thought about what my grandmother would have said. Ever a woman of proper Southern etiquette, she never would've come right out and said that the poor thing looked like the cat had coughed up a dead lizard. No, she would've gotten inventive as only she could. I could almost hear here trying to be polite amidst the gaggle. "My what a clean baby."

I snickered.

"You say something, Charline?" Beatrice asked, barely taking her eyes from the pictures.

"I should get these reports over to Accounting." I scooped up the severance reports that had actually been done for quite some time, then stood and straightened my skirt.

Three faces looked up.

"You're finished already?" Elise asked.

"You're taking them yourself?" Susan asked at the same time. Right, because Ted had worked in the Accounting department, and I'd been avoiding the area like it was a mosquito-infested swamp since we'd broken up.

"You two haven't heard? Ted quit." Beatrice's ironically chipper statement set off a tizzy that only amplified my desire to get the hell out of there. "Couple weeks ago as a matter of fact." She pretended to inspect her equally ostentatious pink nails and slid a less than subtle glance my way.

What did she expect me to say? That I'd been the reason he'd stopped coming to work? Or maybe confess to filing his fake resignation? I certainly couldn't tell them I'd watched my best friend snap his neck. Rather than stick around for the inevitable prodding, I made my exit.

My route took me past the Marketing department, which ironically was where Sara's werewolf boyfriend worked. Clearly the inter-office policy of not dating at the workplace wasn't doing its job. You send mixed messages when you simultaneously publish contradicting memos to avoid inter-office dating *and* that it's required to report your inter-office dating status. I laughed to myself as I turned the corner that would take me to my destination. I'd filed Sara and Michael's status myself.

The folders made a sufficiently loud smack when they hit the receptionist counter of the Accounting department. I was relieved to see that the skinny blonde that I was sure Ted had cheated on me with wasn't there. I may have been over him by this point, but that didn't mean I was eager to come face to face with his infidelity.

"Good afternoon, Laurie," I said with a genuine smile to the older woman with gray at her temples seated behind the desk.

"Hey, Charline!" she responded enthusiastically as she slid the papers around to get a better look at them. "How's your day going?"

"Eh, ready for it to be over."

She glanced up from thumbing through the stack. "Got plans this weekend?"

"Maybe."

"Oh, you devil. Please tell me it's with that hunk I saw you with a couple weeks ago."

"It might be," I said, playing it up, though I had no hope of it being true. Laurie loved gossip almost as much as she loved her cats, sweet darlings that she doted on without measure.

"Hey, Laurie, what happened to Stacy?" I asked, gesturing at the empty chair beside her, not out of spite, but out of concern. While I may not have appreciated her role in everything, I knew from first hand experience how dangerous being involved with Ted could be.

She leaned forward conspiratorially. "Wouldn't you believe it, she just didn't show up a few weeks back and hasn't been in since. I think she might be in the family way if you know what I mean."

Bless her heart, Laurie had no idea about the rumors concerning Stacy and Ted, so could have no clue how much that particular strain of gossip would hurt. Ted had told me he never wanted kids. Ever. I reminded myself that Ted was the last person on Earth I would ever want a family with, but even that didn't soothe the sting completely.

"Did she ever turn in a notice?" I asked, already knowing the answer. If she had, I would have seen it.

"No, not so much as a post-it. Just disappeared."

My heart sank with fear that her disappearance was more of the permanent variety. I felt guilty for every mean thought I'd ever had about the woman. I wanted to ask if she had any family—someone should know their loved one might never be coming back—but I was worried it would cause Laurie to dig into things she had no business getting involved with.

"Don't look now, but I think you have a visitor." Laurie's words brought me out of my dark thoughts and it took me a moment to register what she'd said.

"Wha—?"

"Hello, little fox," a deep voice whispered in my ear. Goosebumps sprang up across my entire body and I whirled around to see its owner.

Easily six-foot-four, with broad shoulders defined by drool-worthy muscles, and a kind face filled with piercing blue eyes, David was every inch the archetypal knight right out of a fairytale. Even his sandy blond hair looked like he'd just pulled off a helmet. Not to mention, he was gallant down to his toenails and probably had a heart the size of Georgia.

"You're back!" I just barely contained my excitement enough not to squeal with delight. I wrapped my arms around his neck before releasing him, mindful of where I was and the scene I was making. "How did you find me?"

"Well, I did stop by your desk first."

A triumphant smile flashed across my face. "Ha, that'll teach them."

His deep laugh turned my insides into goo that could rival fresh pie filling. "Teach who what?"

I shrugged, aiming for coy. There was no way I was going

to admit that almost all of HR believed I was a flighty airhead incapable of serious commitment.

David let out another low chuckle and shook his head. "Anyway, they told me where to find you. But..." He leaned forward and nuzzled my neck with the tip of his nose. "I'm pretty sure I could find you anywhere."

Heat coursed through me. I couldn't have said the last time I'd ever felt such a strong connection with another person. It didn't even matter that we'd only known each other a couple of months, or that he'd waltzed into my life a scant week after Ted had broken up with me.

I also had zero doubts that my grin was borderline goofy. My suspicions were confirmed when I glanced over at Laurie, who sat fanning herself. I giggled and she waved me off.

"What's so funny?" David pulled away to a safer distance.

"David, we're in the middle of the office..."

"We don't have to be."

His words sent another wave of heat rushing through me. Okay, yeah, I was more than ready to switch from pseudo-dating to full on relationship.

"Well." I stopped to clear my throat while Laurie looked like she was going to die right there with her headset on. Determined to regain control of the situation if not my hormones, I forged ahead. "I thought y'all were going to be gone at least through the weekend if not the next couple weeks." I took a step away from him in an attempt to get some cooler air between us. After a moment to gather myself, I smoothed my skirt and blouse one more time and turned to head back to my own department.

"I thought about it, but I missed you," David said as he fell instep beside me. I almost stopped dead in my tracks. "I can always go back," he added.

I didn't take the bait. Instead, through some previously unknown force of will, I kept my eyes straight ahead and kept walking. Back in my modest cubicle, I took a seat and spun to face him as he leaned against the desk. In the background, three heads ducked out of sight. I had to smother a smile at the inevitable gossip that would spring up in the wake of his timely appearance.

"You don't already have plans, do you?" Doubt laced the question and made a line between his eyebrows.

My heart softened. I wanted nothing more than to reach out and smooth the worry from his golden face, but as Mama always said, no one would buy the whole ice cream truck if I was giving away popsicles for free. I might not have believed in waiting 'til marriage like she did, but that didn't mean I was easy either.

"What makes you think I have plans?"

"Because, Char, you are the kind of woman who has plans." David leaned down and stopped just short of kissing me.

I looked up at him through my lashes and fought the urge to steal the withheld kiss. Instead, I smiled wickedly and tilted forward a fraction. "Nothing that can't be rescheduled."

One of my coworkers choked on something. The noise caught David's attention. I stole the moment to glare in the direction of its source.

"What do you say you come over around eight? I'll cook." The last bit went without saying, but it re-captured his attention.

"Hmm, a night in with your incredible cooking? I could be persuaded." The swift kiss he brushed across my lips lasted less than a second, but it was more than enough to blow all my efforts at constraining my hormones to smoke.

When I finally gathered my wits back about me, he'd

gone. I slumped in my chair and fanned myself much like Laurie had done earlier. David put all my skills to the test and then some.

I quickly pulled out my phone and fired off two texts. One to Sara to fuss at her for not giving me a heads up that they were back and another to let David know that dinner would be ready at seven. Eight o'clock was too far away.

2

WOMAN ON A MISSION

I looked around at the disaster that had developed in my wake. Pots, pans, measuring cups, spoons, and spatulas dominated the beige counters. At least the food was confined to its respective serving dishes and sitting on an otherwise pristine table. Normally I was much better about cleaning as I went, but David's unexpected arrival this afternoon seemed to have put me into a tizzy in more ways than one. I tsked to myself and whipped free a dishcloth, not realizing it held a light dusting of flour.

"Hell's bells!"

Never in all my years had I ever been so distracted by a man. My sigh of frustration blew around the hair that had fallen free of its clip and into my face. I carefully secured it and set to work finishing dessert so I could devote my energy to cleaning.

Pie in the oven, I switched the beater on the mixer out for a whisk and got busy on the final touch. When the contents of the bowl became mountains of fluff with perfect white peaks, I turned off the machine and dipped a finger to taste the sugary goodness. A positively sinful moan rolled out of me at the decadence that exploded on my tongue. Even half distracted, it was delicious. Nothing could beat my homemade whipped cream and I dared anyone to say otherwise. I safely secured the confection then turned to conquering the chaos, starting with the disaster of flour.

While my hands were busy tidying, my mind chose other entertainment. I fully believed David had long-term potential. We certainly had what my nana would call "the spark," but I'd been burned before. In the short term, though, I had an entirely different problem: David was holding back.

I'd had a friend in college who followed what they called the "three-month rule" before pursuing anything past second base, the general idea being that it took three months to really learn who a person was. At the time, I'd thought she was a bit off her rocker. Yet, as time continued to pass, I couldn't help but wonder if David was following a similar rule.

Arguably we'd been thrown together in unusual circumstances. One's ex being a serial killer was bound to put stress on any blossoming romance. Not to mention I was still struggling to really understand the ramifications of dating a werewolf...twice. The fates clearly worked in mysterious ways.

I paused to appraise my progress. True to form, everything was sparkling once again. I caught my reflection in the tile backsplash and did a double take. Flour dusted my face while my hair looked like I'd been left out in a hurricane. I frantically sought out a clock, but the one on the stove had been reset by a recent brownout and the microwave had never been set properly in the first place. At last, I spied my phone poking from beneath a yellow hand towel. The screen came to life and I yipped at the time. I bolted to the bedroom to straighten up as best I could, hoping like the Dickens that I'd be presentable before David arrived.

While the kitchen may have been immaculate, my bedroom was not. I shoved a pile of discarded clothes into the closet before dashing into the bathroom. My hair really was everywhere, the beautiful red curls having become a frizzy disaster. One of these days I'd remember to do my hair *after* cooking.

I finger combed it, hoping for the best. When success was not forthcoming, I pulled it into a messy bun, teasing out a few tendrils so the haphazardness looked intentional. I tossed my apron aside in favor of a flirty sundress not covered in spices. I took a moment to appreciate the bright teal as it flared out over my full hips. Then I touched up my lipstick and dashed out.

A knock came at the door just as I skidded into the living room. I quickly undid the lock and stepped back as I opened the door, simultaneously trying to smooth the fabric of my dress and check my hair.

"Come on in," I said, only a little out of breath.

My hands paused their frenzied movements when David stepped inside. Damn, he was glorious, a real showstopper. As usual, I was overdressed compared to him, but his casual attire didn't come close to diminishing how delectable he looked. His jeans fit well, a darker shade of denim which paired beautifully with the light gray polo that did absolutely nothing to hide his decidedly masculine physique. It stretched over his chest, gripping his defined biceps in a way that made me want to jump on him faster than Granny's pecan pie at a family reunion.

"Good evening, Charline." The greeting came out a sultry purr even though he was supposed to be canine. Just the sound of his deep voice was enough to spike my hormones and turn me into a quivering schoolgirl, something I'd never been before I'd met David Bringer. "You look stunning as ever, and of course whatever you have magicked in the kitchen smells divine."

His eyes never left me despite the reference to the food in the other room. Having now fed no fewer than three friendly werewolves on multiple occasions, I could attest that the draw of food for them ranked up there with oxygen.

I really hoped I wasn't preening. "You're punctual."

His eyes clouded a moment with the same doubt that had enveloped him at the office. "Is that okay?" Damn man was gallant almost to a fault. The idea that he'd somehow transgressed by showing up on time was laughable.

I took advantage of his brief distraction to steal a kiss. "Perfectly."

David's resulting smile lit the room and quite possibly my heart. I grabbed his hand and he let me drag him over to the set table in the kitchen. He laughed at my giddy enthusiasm that I doubted I could have quelled even if I'd wanted to. I released him and stopped just short of performing a ta-da.

"How do you always manage to outdo yourself?" He admired the set up a moment before returning his attention to me. He wrapped an arm around my waist and pulled me close.

I giggled at the sudden embrace, the ridiculous schoolgirl nerves getting the best of me as he placed a lingering kiss on my lips. It made my toes tingle and my breath catch. It wasn't at all like the moments stolen over the last several weeks, though there'd been plenty of them.

Maybe I was right and this could be more. I wanted it to be more so badly it terrified me, but I'd been wrong in the past, so epically, tragically wrong. I wasn't sure how many more misses I had in me. My giggles turned more nervous as I placed my hands on his chest and tried *not* to think about how thin the layer of fabric between our bare skin was.

"Dinner will get cold," I attempted to scold him, though my voice was barely a whisper. Typically such a thing would infuriate me to no end. Allowing a meal that someone made for you to cool was downright rude. My mother would be scandalized and I didn't want to think about what my nana would have to say. But at that particular moment, staring into eyes so blue they could make the sky envious while my heart pattered away, I couldn't care less if it froze.

"We can't have that." He shifted his arm, threatening to release his hold. "It would be a crying shame to waste such a masterpiece."

"You're such a tease," I said before capturing his mouth with mine. His hand re-tightened around my waist, bunching the fabric, while his other drifted up to cup my neck with a delicacy that belied his true strength. When I finally released him, our breathing was ragged. My eyes opened to see his half-lidded with pure lust.

He rubbed his thumb over my now swollen lips, his voice husky as he said, "You taste amazing." His tongue flicked out to trace the path of his thumb across my bottom lip before catching it with his teeth. My breath hitched. "I could just eat you up."

It should have alarmed me that a werewolf was so casually commenting on how he would like to eat me, but it had quite the opposite effect. My insides turned to liquid as excitement thrilled through me.

Suddenly, his eyes caught mine and the intensity was almost too much. "I bet all of you tastes this good."

Waves of desire crashed over me so hard I thought I might faint. Maybe I did, because as if on cue, an arm encircled my legs, and lifted me to a cradled position where he stole a savage kiss. It wasn't until we were almost to the bedroom that my senses returned enough to wonder how he knew where to go. I also became increasingly concerned about going along with this unexpected—albeit amazing—turn of events. I was a proper Southern lady and didn't put out for just anyone. If we'd been in a serious relationship the whole two months we'd known each other, that would be one thing. Never mind that I'd been worried not an hour ago that we'd never get to this moment. Now that we were here...

As my mother would say, I was nothing if not a lesson in contradictions.

While my mind whirled in a hundred directions, David stole another molten kiss that had me doubting whether my legs would hold when he set me down. By some miracle, I didn't fall on my face when he set me free. So few men in my life had ever had the ability to make me feel small and delicate, characteristics I'd striven for as long as I could remember without any hope of achieving, but David treated me like the world's most treasured porcelain.

He lightly held my chin and tipped it up so our gazes could meet. "Is this okay?"

I blinked in surprise. When was the last time I'd actually had a date check in with me? David waited patiently for my answer and I *knew* if I said no, he would stop, take my hand and lead us back out to the dining room where we would sit down and proceed to have a wonderful evening. No questions. No guilt. My racing heart squeezed as I stared back at him. How was it possible for anyone to be so *good*? Any lingering reservations melted away and I nodded.

He placed a soft kiss on my lips, then gently turned me so that my back was to him. The heat of his fingers burned through the layers of cotton as he slowly unzipped my dress.

"Mm, I missed you," he murmured against my already flushed skin.

I consciously took deeper breaths and willed my heart to slow down, lest I pass out. David's breath warmed my back as he traced the curve of my neck with his nose and placed kiss after steamy kiss in the opening left in the zipper's wake. The makings of a beard scratched lightly on my increasingly sensitive skin, adding to the sensations threatening to overwhelm me. He slid the straps from my shoulders and down my arms until the bunched material caught on my hips. Undeterred, he hooked his thumbs in the flimsy fabric and guided it to its inevitable pool around my feet. He made a sound deep in his throat, a bit like a choked growl, that I hoped was a good thing.

My body gave an involuntary shiver as I stood there naked but for lace. David's hands glided almost reverently over my goose-pricked skin, deliciously warm as they paused to appreciate the delicate fabric where they found it. I bit my lip to hold back a moan as his wandering touch melted me. When he finally turned me to face him, he gave me such a look of heat I was sure I'd have sunburn in the morning. In one smooth motion, he reached up and expertly pulled my hair free.

The slightly tamed curls fell in a wave around me. A touch of insecurity fluttered in my belly as his gaze wandered over me. Did he think my breasts were too large? Maybe too small? Did the fact that my tummy was more round than flat bother him? Were my hips too wide? Did he wish I had slimmer thighs? This time when I bit my lip, it was to hold back the tide of questions.

David's gaze finally made it back up to mine, holding just as much heat as it had a moment ago. He thumbed my lip free and pressed his mouth against mine before shifting to run his fingers through my released tresses. Then he cradled my neck and tilted my head back so he could resume his languid trail of kisses. My fingers dug into his forearms as I braced myself and arched back, encouraging his sensual exploration, fully trusting that he wouldn't let me fall. A sound deep in his throat that was definitely a growl vibrated through my core as he guided me back.

The second my flushed skin made contact with the cool sheets of the bed, my repressed moan slipped free. Once I was fully on the bed, his hot touch vanished and the rustling of clothes filled the quiet. It took a second to realize what was likely happening. I pouted in the dark that I couldn't see enough to appreciate the show. David gave a throaty chuckle and I realized that he could probably see just fine.

Finally the rustling stopped. The night seemed to still as the air between us thickened. We stayed like that for a moment, David standing at the end of the bed and me stretched out before him.

"By the moon, you're beautiful."

It was cruelly unfair that he could see the flush spread across my body while I saw nothing but shadows. I didn't have the chance to sulk for long. He resumed his journey across my flesh, starting at my calves and working his way higher until he paused at the junction of my thighs. He gently pushed my legs to place a trail of kisses along the tender flesh. His fingers teased the seam of my panties, the only barrier between his moist breath and my now molten core.

Heat burned across my cheeks as he kissed along the thin straps that kept the undergarment clinging to my hips. Then he guided them down my already quivering legs. I bit down on my lip and prayed he couldn't see how hot my face had become as he settled back between my legs. I needn't have worried, as David seemed completely distracted.

His hands glided up my legs as he sucked lightly on my inner thigh. Then he shifted his attention to my aching lips. I gave a sharp cry as he swiped with the flat of his tongue, then licked at my swollen bud like he was trying to get the last bits of frosting off a cupcake. I writhed in tortured delight as his slow, methodical exploration drove me to the edge more times than I could count.

It was a special kind of miracle that I didn't instantly combust when he dipped a finger in my wetness and stroked my g-spot with confidence. My fingers twisted in the sheets as I arched into his hand and his eager mouth.

"D-David," I panted, on the verge of turning into a puddle.

He gave one more decisive stroke of his tongue and the finger I'd been clenching slipped free, leaving me empty and wanting. The bed shifted as he sat up on his knees. Then he scooped me onto his lap, his mouth closing over mine once more while my breasts pressed against his chest.

I hungrily devoured the kisses, tasting myself on his tongue, and tangled my hands in his hair desperate for something to hang onto. He pulled my body tighter against his, lifting me with thrilling ease. The head of his cock teased my entrance and my breath caught. Then he froze.

I let out a small cry of frustration. Unlike the appreciative pause earlier, this felt like hesitation. Fear lanced through me that he might be second guessing this. Had I pushed him too fast? Was he not ready for this?

Was it me?

The shadow of David stared at me, his eyes glinting yellow in the faint light drifting through the curtains. I hated that I couldn't clearly see his face, couldn't tell what he was thinking. After what felt like an eternity of waiting, his firm grip on my thighs gentled and he lowered me down. He thrust up slowly to meet me and I gave a deep moan as he buried his length inside me. I wrapped my legs around him and his hands shifted to cup my ass and guide the roll of my hips. He captured me with a kiss that effectively banished the doubts that had started to take hold, leaving nothing else to do but completely melt into him.

3

BREAKFAST & A SHOW

The sun shone in a crystal blue sky while the early birds sang their chorus, the promise of summer just around the corner. It wasn't that there was anything particularly *wrong* with spring—flowers were nice and all—but I *lived* for summer. I loved the freedom it promised, the lazy afternoons, the cold lemonade, feeling sun-kissed...

Thoughts of being sun-kissed brought memories of other kisses. A giggle bubbled up as I spun into the kitchen, feeling more weightless than I had in weeks. *Okay, months, give a girl a break.*

I didn't even care that we'd forgone using protection; the pill had served me well in similar heated moments and I had every faith it would now. However, if I'd *known* how the evening would end I would've prepared better. But that was neither here nor there. Besides, wasn't that the whole point of birth control—for when you were with someone you trusted? And I did trust David, more than I'd trusted any man in a long time. Maybe it was his endearing humility, or his generosity, or maybe how he had a way of lifting everyone around him. Most likely, it was the way he made me feel cherished, like some priceless treasure he'd do anything to keep safe.

I pulled the curtains back with a flourish. Sunlight streamed unhindered into the space, lighting up my outsides as much as my insides. I gave the sky a triumphant smile and turned back to the inexplicably pristine kitchen. *Someone* had put away the abandoned meal and cleaned up...and it hadn't been me. My grin made a rebellious return as the only possible culprit came to mind. A quick peek in the fridge confirmed my suspicions and I let out a muffled squeal of joy.

I'd never had a lover like David before, so thoughtful, so attentive. *Absolutely* worth the wait. Once he'd finally crossed that imaginary line, it was like a dam had broken. If stamina was something that came with dating a werewolf, I was one hundred percent on board. My stomach gave an impressive growl, reminding me that while I might be bright eyed and bushy tailed this morning, I'd also skipped dinner.

"Cool your grits, I'm working on it," I said to myself as I snagged ingredients from the fridge and pantry. I went to grab my usual apron from its designated peg. When it wasn't there, I looked around, curious where it could have gotten off to. Then it clicked.

Crap, it's still in the bedroom.

Tempting as it was to tiptoe back in to retrieve it, I had a strong suspicion that if I did that, breakfast would go the way of dinner. I shook my head and grabbed the frillier apron that I usually reserved for hosting. It didn't offer much protection, but it would suffice. The strings brushed enticingly against my still sensitive skin and I sighed appreciatively. It would have been easy to spend the morning reliving the night, but breakfast wasn't going to cook itself.

I was elbow-deep in flour when I heard a low whistle behind me. Even after all of the lavish attention the night before, my cheeks still burned. Making love in the dark and being cat-called in the day were very different things. My shy smile refused to be schooled as I spun to face my appraiser maybe a little too quickly, creating a cloud of white dust that drifted around me as he approached.

"Now that *is* a sight first thing in the morning."

I hungrily devoured the deliciously sexy sight of David in nothing but jeans. Heaven help me, I had no idea why a barefoot man in my kitchen was so flippin' hot. The sculpted planes of his broad chest made my mouth water more than watermelon on a hot day.

He gave me a knowing smirk as he eliminated the last of the distance between us. I stood on my tiptoes to give him a kiss good morning. His impressive height made my formerly daunting five-ten seem downright short. The kiss was relatively tame—more sweet than anything—but when his hand landed on my naked bottom, I realized I'd completely forgotten pajamas.

Oh my God. I must look like a brazen hussy.

A flush burned across my face and down my neck to dip below the frilled edge of the inadequate covering. I pushed down my sudden rush of embarrassment—there was nothing to be done about it now—and shimmied a bit between his arms.

My movement elicited that delicious throaty chuckle. "You're quite the vixen."

Before I could respond, he scooped me up to straddle his waist. Reflexively, I locked my heels so I wouldn't slide while I marveled at the ease with which he performed such a feat. It was new and quite frankly hotter 'n hell. I wiggled again for good measure.

"Charline," he growled, shifting us to one of the few clean counters and conquering me with a kiss that was far from tame.

Merciful heavens, he's going to have me right here, flour and all.

Then he pulled away. And there it was again, that hesitation.

"What?" I sounded breathy and that chafed. He gave me a more chaste kiss that was both tender and unnerving. "David, what is it?"

The mischief from a few moments ago had vanished, replaced by obvious anxiety that put a line between his brows. His eyes searched mine as if *I* somehow had the answer to my own question. I tightened my jaw, refusing to repeat the question.

At last, he let out a heavy sigh. "I have to go out of town for a while—a long while. I won't be able to visit like I have been."

There it was—the other shoe. As my daddy would say, anything too good to be true usually is, and David definitely qualified as too good to be true. My sinking heart fell the rest of the way to my stomach, the impact almost enough to make me physically sick. Anger and hurt swelled up inside to replace the void it had left.

Not again. Why does this always happen to me? Just once, couldn't I be enough?

I pushed him away, putting as much distance between us as my position and arm span would allow. It wasn't feasible to storm off, so I settled for touching as little of him as possible. The pain in my chest spread and the stinging behind my eyes intensified. I mustered up all of the fire I could to stamp it down.

I will not cry. I won't give him the satisfaction of seeing what he's done to me.

There was only one question in my mind and it was ricocheting so hard in my skull it had to come out. "Are you really breaking up with me?" There should have been holes in the counter from the acid that dripped from the words.

David's nervous look gave way to abject horror. He reached for me, but I pulled back as much as I could without falling backwards. There wasn't a snowball's chance in hell I'd keep it together if he managed to touch me.

All the tenderness and passion of last night felt like a slap in the face. I would *not* be jerked around and treated like some floozy. Was this why he'd hesitated before, because he'd known he was leaving? I bit the inside of my cheek in a vain attempt to refocus. Despite everything, I was pretty sure the effort of keeping it together showed on my face.

"Char."

"Do not 'Char' me," I snapped, unable to keep the hurt from coating the words. I felt used and I hated that he could tell how much pain he was causing me.

"No, Charline, you don't understand. I'm doing this all wrong." David ran a hand through his hair as if he was more musing to himself than talking to me. I crossed my arms both as a barrier and as a way to hold myself together. "Charline, I don't *want* to leave you. I *have* to go..."

I opened my mouth to cut off whatever contrived excuse was coming, but he beat me to it.

"I have to go back to the House. I want you to come with me."

The words washed over me, but one of them caught my attention: House. That was where he'd taken Sara to meet the pack. Then the last part registered. *I want you to come with me.* But neither of these things made any sense together, they were just random ingredients thrown on a table.

Beyond confused, all I could manage from my fortress of hurt was a blank "What?"

"Charline, I want you to come with me. I want to take you to the House."

"But...but you said you had to go for a long time. I have a job, you know."

He gave me a shaky smile and I realized every muscle in his body was taut. "You have the time."

It was true. I never went on vacation, so I'd probably accrued enough rollover time to take a sabbatical by this point. I narrowed my eyes suspiciously. I may have been an HR nightmare in regards to time off, but how did *he* know that?

A timer went off, startling me out of my thoughts. "I...I need a minute to think." He let me push him farther away so I could remove myself from the counter. It was a less than graceful maneuver since I'd started to stick to it. "Can you turn that off?" I called back, already halfway to the bedroom, having given up all pretense of finishing breakfast.

Safely in my room, I closed the door and leaned against it. Alone, I could think more clearly.

So he's leaving, but not leaving me. Quite the opposite.

I ripped the apron off and tossed it in the corner to join its companion while my thoughts spun. I was so distracted that it wasn't until I was done dressing that I realized I'd put on jeans and a plain tee instead of the dress I'd planned on. I briefly considered changing again, but I didn't have the energy to primp.

My mind was still struggling as I made my way down the hall.

Do I trust that any of this is genuine? How long is 'a long while'? The whole summer? Longer?

The concept was pretty enough. I'd always wanted someone to whisk me away for an extended lovers' holiday.

But this was different. There was more to all of this. I could feel it.

Back in the kitchen, I was shocked to find that it was clean. Even the floor bore no traces of the flour explosion from earlier. I searched the barren counters for some sign of the meal I'd been making. At last, I spied the breakfast table covered with the missing food and a rather sheepish looking David standing next to it.

"You finished breakfast."

"Yeah." He rubbed the back of his neck, still shirtless of course. "I'm sorry about the lack of biscuits. You don't really follow a recipe."

Of course I don't follow some third-rate cookbook recipe. What kind of cook does he think I am?

It was tempting to snap as much, but I bit my tongue. As my mother would say, I was 'in a mood.' Being contrary was not liable to help our current situation. So instead of saying exactly what I was thinking, I took the proffered chair.

"I, uh, noticed some of the cabinet hinges were loose," he said as he took a seat. "My tools were in the truck, so I tightened them up and set all the clocks while I was at it." He paused as if waiting for me to say something, which I didn't. "Did you know the drawer pull by the stove was held in place with wall putty? I mean, it's not now, but yeah..."

Curse this man and his thoughtfulness. Not only had he cleaned last night and this morning, now he was *fixing* things?

The silence grew strained while we poked at breakfast and I tried to get a handle on my thoughts. I scooted congealed grits across my plate, finding no success and not trusting myself not to lose my temper again.

"Charline, please talk to me." David sounded so forlorn that for the briefest of moments I almost felt sorry for him. It passed.

"What would you have me say?" I quirked an eyebrow at him. "You kind of sprung that on me—none too delicately, I might add. It's a lot to take in."

"I know. I'm sorry. I can be terrible with words. I've been trying to work up the nerve to tell you for weeks."

Weeks! He's known about this for weeks!

I could feel the flush returning and by the look on his face the fire must have been burning in my eyes as well.

"And you chose the morning after we, after we..." I was turning apoplectic and had to stop before I choked myself.

He looked like I'd slapped him. "I want you to come with me." At least he had the decency to sound ashamed.

"To the House." I barely remembered to add the emphasis, but it was there. "That's like taking someone to meet your parents, except it's only a thousand times worse. It's your whole, whole—" I floundered for something that encompassed everyone ever.

"Family," he supplied, though it was almost a whisper.

"Exactly, but it's not a regular family. It's a family of werewolves. A *large* family of werewolves." I rubbed my temples, though it did little to assuage the blossoming headache.

"I know it's a lot."

"A lot? No David, *a lot* is showing up to dinner with an unannounced relative. This? This is more." He shrunk a bit and I finally decided to extend a modicum of mercy. "Maybe if you filled me in on more of the particulars, like why do you have to leave? Why for so long? How long have you known you'd be leaving? Were you planning on coming back? Why take me?" I could have listed plenty more, but I restrained myself. The tide of questions already looked to be drowning him.

He waited a full minute before taking a deep breath. "The pack, my pack, is about to undergo a change of leadership. Our Alpha has decided to step down and there are already people vying for a chance to fill the vacuum. This is an unusual situation and it's going to be a tough time for everyone. Some are supporting the current Alpha's son to take his place, but there's no such thing as succession for wolves. Xander will need all the support he can get if wants to truly fill the role and..." David trailed off.

"And?" While this was proving to be an interesting story, it had yet to answer any of my questions.

"And there will be a complete changing of the guard. The entire infrastructure will be redone," he elaborated. "I want to be part of that."

"You obviously don't want to be Alpha since you've already said you need to support this Xander as the next Alpha. What role are you hoping to get?"

"I want to be his right hand. I want to be the Beta."

I didn't have the energy to tell him I had no idea what that meant. Whatever it was, it was clearly important. I searched all my knowledge concerning wolves until at last I stumbled across something that might match the emphasis he gave it.

"Is that—?

"The second in command. So it's vital I be there for as much of everything as possible. While the transition is still a little ways off, the politics have already started. And this summer the Solstice falls on a full moon, meaning virtually the entire pack will be at the House at some point in the next three months."

"Sounds like a hell of a party." He perked up a bit at my enthusiasm, but, life-goals aside, that didn't answer the important question. "Why take me?"

He deflated instantly. "Because I don't want to leave you."

"That's mighty selfish." The words whipped out. He flinched as if they'd actually struck him.

"I know."

"Seriously. Stringing me along then tossing out an invitation you know I can't accept." My voice rose as I worked myself up, but I didn't care. It was my house; I'd yell if I wanted. "All because what? You don't wanna lose your side piece?" Is that what I was to him? Was there someone else? It wouldn't be the first time I'd been in the dark about being the other woman. The pain and hurt I'd stamped down so savagely earlier threatened to swallow me once more.

A frown darkened David's usually bright face. "No, Charline. It's not a pity invitation or some misguided sense of male ego. I really do want you to come with me. You don't get it. I *have* to go, but I *can't* leave you."

That brought me up short. I had absolutely no idea what to make of the statement, so I focused on the things I could understand. "What about your pack? How will your Alpha feel about you bringing home a human? I doubt any of your pack cares for the likes of me being part of such a delicate time."

"I cleared this with Alexander weeks ago."

I let that information sink in for a moment. So he'd known he was leaving for a while and had been planning on taking me. I'd hoped reevaluating what he was saying would bring enlightenment, but I was still at a total loss. Why had he waited to say anything to me? He could have dropped hints, or...or...I didn't know what else, but *something*. All I knew was that it bothered me that he'd waited until after we were finally intimate to bring this up.

I'm missing something. Something really important. But what?

We cleared the table in silence. Although most of my anger had fizzled, there was still tension between us. David did his best not to press, but it was clear my radio silence was making him nervous.

Deep down, I wanted to truly consider the possibility of going, but one thing was holding me back.

I devoted too much attention to straightening the dish towels, stalling for more time. How could I put into words what was bothering me? Finally I gave up on eloquence and went for it. "If you really do want me to go, then why did you hesitate last night?"

To his credit, he didn't act like he didn't know what I meant. "What if you said no?"

I blinked. The words sounded like they had a deeper meaning, much like everything else he'd said.

"Charline, I don't know what I'll do if you don't want to come."

A vindictive part of me was curious to find out. Would he leave anyway? Would he stay? Would he truss me up and drag me along? Tempting as it was to find out, it was pointless to continue mulling it over, since I'd already decided.

"Then I guess I'm going."

He looked surprised at the response. All the doubt I'd been restraining surged up with renewed vigor.

"David, I swear if this is some sort of elaborate scheme, I'm gonna kill you and I don't give two figs if you *are* a werewolf." I expected him to say something either to confirm my fears or at least backpedal a bit. So I was completely unprepared when he rushed me.

He caught me in a bear hug and spun me around. I couldn't help but giggle at the ardor of the kisses he showered all over my face. At last he set me down and I had a chance to catch my breath. David looked down at me and there was so much hope and happiness in his eyes. A worm of guilt wriggled in my chest for doubting his sincerity.

"Do you really mean it? You'll spend the summer at the House with me?"

At least that answered the question of how long. "I have to clear it with work first, but what the hell, why not? It'll be an adventure."

The rain of kisses before had been lighthearted, but there was absolutely nothing silly about the kiss he captured me with next. I gave a muffled cry of surprise. The small sound only seemed to encourage him. He pulled away just enough to let me steal a breath and whisper a shocked, "David."

At the sound of his name, he resumed the kiss with a passion. While his tongue tasted my lips, his hands slid around my waist pushing my shirt aside to reach the bare skin beneath. I draped my arms around his neck, pulling us closer. This was much more like what I'd hoped this morning would bring.

His kiss became almost methodical in its determination to squeeze every ounce of passion I could give. Fingers deftly drifted up my sides to brush my unhindered breasts. He was completely undeterred by my resulting gasp and took advantage of the brief break to pull my shirt off. He spared an appraising look at my exposed torso, already flushed from the heat of our exchange, but then his attention was all on my face. He kissed me deeply, pressing against me. The feel of skin on skin created tiny sparks at each point of contact. I nipped his lip and could feel him smile against my mouth.

While I lost myself to the passion of the demanding kisses, he conquered my jeans. They put up substantially more resistance than my usual dress, but he persevered. David worked the stubborn fabric all the way down and over my calves before I was free. On his way back up, he grabbed my legs, lifting me as he stood. I placed my hands on his shoulders for balance and leaned down to kiss him again. While his eyes were full of lust, there was also something else I couldn't quite name, something tender and almost beseeching. The counter was sharply cold where he deposited me, but the roving warmth of his hands helped to keep the chill at bay.

He nibbled his way along my jaw until he could whisper in my ear, "I believe someone was less than pleased about making love in the dark."

The tickling words instantly turned my insides to mush. He stepped back, abandoning me to the mercy of the early morning air. David's eyes never left mine as he mimed his lack of a shirt in a true showman style. I smiled wickedly while my gaze roved across his body as if my look alone could feel the muscles that wrapped over his shoulders and across his chest to work their way down to a defined taper. When he was sure I'd had enough time to soak in the top he moved lower.

David might have only been wearing jeans, but he made it count, even turning to add a little shake. I couldn't help but laugh. It seemed to be the desired response so I didn't try to stop it. Draw it out as much as he liked, though, it was still only a short while before he stood before me without so much as a stitch. He was fantastic, all of him golden and defined. David was by no means a small man, but muscle covered every inch of him and he clearly appreciated me looking.

He slowly advanced, re-closing the distance between us. My heart hammered so hard I thought for sure his enhanced hearing could make it out. Gently he pushed my knees apart to settle between them. My breathing turned shallow as he wrapped his hands around my thighs and scooted me to the edge of the counter. His eyes held mine with an intensity that spoke of a deeper need. Time seemed to stretch around me. This wasn't a hesitation. More like he was waiting for me to tell him to stop.

When my only response was to continue to look at him, he leaned down. He captured my mouth at the same time he captured my body. I was already so close that it pushed me right over the precipice. Ecstasy pulsed through me as I tightened around him. We molded together, two pieces of some elaborate puzzle, our bodies moving together in time.

We remained locked in each other's embrace well after both of our passions had been satisfied. He nuzzled my neck and purred my name, "Charline."

"Mm, yes?" I hummed while my fingers searched out each line of detailed muscle on his back and traced it as far as my reach would allow.

"I think you might be cold."

My hands halted in their ceaseless wandering and I placed them on his chest, pushing him back far enough to look him in the eye. "What makes you say that?"

"You have goosebumps." He rubbed his hands over the tops of my thighs for emphasis.

"Oh. I suppose clothing wouldn't be completely uncalled for." I moved to get down, but he stood in my way, refusing to budge. I tried again to shimmy my way off of the counter to no avail.

He scoffed and once more effortlessly scooped me up. I giggled with unrestrained delight and clung to his neck as he carried me back to the bedroom.

4

SEEDS OF DOUBT

Turned out, getting a whopping three months off of work was the least of my troubles. If I hadn't been so determined not to look a gift horse in the mouth, I might have been suspicious at how easy it had been. But, I had bigger issues to contend with, like what in blue blazes did I need to *pack*? If I was going by the rejected options littering the bed and floor, the answer was simple: I had nothing to wear, not a damn thing.

I groaned as I stared at the empty suitcases that should have been packed yesterday. I was a heartbeat away from saying to hell with it and calling the whole thing off when the doorbell rang. In my eagerness to answer it, my foot caught on the handle of a wayward leather duffel and I stumbled on my way to the bedroom door. I spared the offending bag an indignant glare before rushing off again.

"It's about time," I said while Sara stood frozen mid-knock.

"Um, hi."

I grabbed her upheld arm and dragged her inside. "No time for pleasantries. We're in the midst of a crisis." I swung the door shut and hauled her to the disaster zone.

"That's a little dramatic. Surely it's not that—" She pulled up short. "Oh."

"I know—it's bad—but, I don't know what to do. I'm worrying myself sick over all of this. And David is no help. You'd think we were going to summer camp." I flopped on the bed, causing its resident shirts, skirts, and slacks to jump into the air, not all of which fell back on the bed.

Sara's relaxed laugh offered a mild reassurance. I couldn't help but think for probably the millionth time that being turned into a werewolf had been the best thing to ever happen to her. While she was a far cry from being a boisterous extrovert, she was no longer the wilting wallflower I'd met almost three years ago. Suddenly, I realized she'd been talking this whole time.

"—overthinking this. They really are a laid back bunch. Overwhelming at times, but not at all high maintenance." She blinked as if regretting her choice of words and I could practically see the unspoken addition printed across her face.

"Sara Shepherd, are you saying I'm high maintenance?"

"I, well, I didn't, I mean..."

I let her flounder for a bit. It was nice to see that being bitten hadn't *completely* changed her. She was still wonderfully awkward at heart.

"Well, I am, so you might as well come right out and say it." I smiled and shoved some clothes aside to make space. "Here, come sit with me."

She frowned before settling beside me. "If you're done teasing me, what's going on with your packing dilemma?" She gestured at the chaos surrounding us and I deflated.

"Honestly, it's not the clothes, although that certainly isn't helping. The real problem is..." I stalled.

"What?" She placed a gentle hand on my shoulder and I let out a sigh.

"I don't know what to expect. This isn't like when you went. I'm not…"

"A werewolf. You can say it, Charline, it's okay." She offered me a small smile which I returned. "I mean, maybe don't say it *everywhere*," she added with a good natured laugh, "but when it's people who already know, I don't see the harm."

"You got it, doll. But yeah, I'm very much a lowly old human. Why would he want to take me to the House, of all places, and at a time like this?"

"Maybe because he likes you?"

"I like him too, but…"

"But what? Is this about Ted?" Sara asked without so much as a flinch. I envied her that, and still felt immensely guilty for how I'd brought that wretch into her life.

"No, it's not about Ted, not entirely." I chanced a glance at her while I fiddled with the hem of my dress. "Are David and I moving too fast?"

She wrapped an arm around my shoulders and gave them a gentle squeeze, ever aware of her newfound strength. "Do *you* think it's moving too fast?"

Very helpful, Sara.

I bit my tongue. But if I was honest with myself, it was a fair question. The thought of starting something new made me nervous. Was it actually amazing or doomed to fail like all the others?

"Yes. I mean, no. Oh, I don't know what I mean. On the one hand, I feel like it took us forever to be intimate, especially given our chemistry, but on the other, this is huge. What happened to baby steps? It's more than just meeting your boyfriend's family on a weekend trip. It'll be like going to a giant family reunion with all of the extended relatives— and for the whole summer! And another thing…" I straightened up., "When he asked, it was like he'd been planning it for a while."

I left the floor open for her to admit knowing about it, since she was the only one outside of my own department who could possibly have told David how much vacation time I'd accrued. When she didn't take that bait I surged on.

"I can't shake the feeling that there's so much more to all of this, like I'm missing something."

And there it was, a hint of more in her eyes. She *did* know something.

"What should I do?" I pressed. Admitting I needed help rankled, even with Sara, who'd always been supportive no matter what I threw her way.

She plucked at a fraying edge of the bedspread and seemed to choose her words carefully. "You should trust your instincts."

I could have screamed. Instead I stood, nearly toppling her off of the bed. "And what is that supposed to mean? I don't need wolfy logic. I need real, practical advice. I need answers!"

She sighed and spent a few moments readjusting herself. "What I mean is, if you feel like there is more to what's going on, then you're probably right. You have good instincts, Charline."

"Obviously I don't, seeing as how my last boyfriend was a serial killer," I snapped. My anger drained out of me at the look on her face. "Oh no. Sara, I'm so sorry." My shoulders slumped. "I'm a horrible human being. I shouldn't have let my frustration out on you. You're just trying to help." I flopped back down beside her, regretting my outburst.

She took a few minutes to visibly gather herself. Clearly my assessment that she'd moved past everything was ill-founded. I should have known better. Even with greater confidence, Sara was still very much a private person and no amount of super healing could erase the memories of someone trying to rip you apart with their teeth.

Reflexively, I felt the thin scar on my neck. As bad as my nightmares were, they were nowhere near as savage as the ones that must torment Sara. No, the worst for me had been knowing that her would-be-killer had been my unassuming ex. Even though I'd watched his lifeless form go from vicious animal to mutilated man, that knowledge still felt unreal.

At last, she looked back up at me, the shadow of horror having faded from her features. "What I *can* tell you is that most *weres* take dating very seriously," Sara said. "David's no exception. If anything, he might take it more seriously." I got the impression she wanted to add more, but instead, she shifted gears. "Now what on earth do you need with so many suitcases?"

"What makes you think it's too many? It *is* for the entire summer, Sara." I slid back off the bed and began rearranging the mess. Apparently, my answers wouldn't be so easy to come by. It hurt to think that she might be holding something back, especially after all we'd been through together, but I had to trust that she had her reasons.

Sara watched me flurry about for a moment and didn't comment until I'd regrouped all of the suitcases and bags, even the one that had tried to kill me earlier. "I'd say it's at the very least two too many." I looked from the collection to her and back again. "They do have a washing machine you know," she added, cracking a smile.

I froze mid fluster at the unexpected and *obvious* statement that had not once occurred to me. An irrepressible giggle bubbled up.

"What? What's so funny? They do."

Her sweet sincerity only made me laugh harder. I fell to the floor surrounded by clothes, clutching my sides. Already a sharp pain was starting to spread across my middle, but my giggle fit refused to let up until I was gasping for air, tears streaming down my face.

"Right..."

"I'm sorry. I guess I've been winding myself up so tight about this that I was bound to crack eventually." I sat up and wiped the wet streaks from my face. "I've got a question for you."

"Shoot," she said, holding up a frilly top.

"How did David know I had so much vacation time available?"

She looked like she'd been goosed and gave me a nervous smile. "Well, um...you see, David just kind of casually asked while we were on the way to the House how you would feel about taking a vacation together and how much time you could take. I might have made a crack about you never taking any time and that you could probably skip out for a few months, no big deal." She immediately held up her hands as if to ward me off. "Please don't be mad. If I'd had any idea what he was planning, I would have told you."

I gave her a hard stare.

"I'm pretty sure I would have told you."

I didn't blink.

"Okay, I would have at least dropped hints." She squirmed in the hot seat I'd deposited her in. She really did make this too easy.

"Alright, enough of that," I said at last, and her shoulders sagged with visible relief. "Time to get back to the task at hand. What does one wear to meet the pack?"

Her mousy hair swung from its ponytail as she shook her head. A smile played about her mouth. "Like I said before, the pack is really laid back. I mean, jeans and a t-shirt would suffice most of the time."

I leveled a fresh stare. "Do I look like a jeans and a t-shirt kind of girl to you?" She laughed and shook her head.

Now that we'd covered the dangerously complicated topics, packing became a surprisingly simple endeavor, I even let Sara convince me to include several outfits that did in fact consist of nothing more than jeans and a tee. I doubted I would wear them, but she was insistent for versatility's sake.

"Are you ready?" David asked as he entered the house and stopped dead. He ran a hand through his short blond hair, accentuating the sizable muscles in his arm, as he took in the image of me standing between the oversized pair of patterned luggage as well as several extra bags of varying sizes. "It's only a few months, Char."

I threw up my hands. "Look, I've already been through this with Sara, and believe it or not, this is half of what it could have been." His face twisted into a doubtful scowl. "See here, a girl has needs and some of those require an additional bag or two. Besides, the shoes wouldn't fit," I finished with a huff.

He chuckled as he pulled me into an embrace, but I refused to cave even when he tried to kiss the pout from my lips. He cupped my face with his gloriously warm hands. "You can bring whatever you want. I just want you to enjoy yourself and…"

I looked up at him, curious about the hesitation.

"And I'm just so glad you're coming."

I debated pressing for whatever he'd obviously *meant* to say, but before I could, he suddenly looked around.

"It just occurred to me. What're we going to do about your house? We can't exactly leave it vacant, that's like inviting trouble."

"Way ahead of you. I've already talked to Sara about house-sitting *and* I made her promise no funny business, at least not in my bed."

"Stars, you're smart," he declared with a beaming smile, then swiped a quick kiss.

"I don't know about smart. It's common sense really."

He stole another kiss. "Whatever you say. Alright, let's get everything loaded up." He smacked me on the rump for emphasis. I let out an indignant squeak, but he was already out the door with most of the bags.

Left with only one suitcase, I grabbed the handle and rolled it out to join him. I took a moment to step back and appreciate the fact that I wouldn't see this place again for the next few months. Buying my little yellow house three years ago had been a moment of immense pride and I'd devoted so much time and energy to making it a welcoming space. This was my refuge from the world, my pillar of independence. Though after so much time, I'd hoped there would've been more in it than just me. Alas, those were not the cards I'd been dealt.

I let out a wistful sigh and finished locking everything up before making my way over to where David was watching me.

"How long will it take to get there again?" I leaned against the bed of his white pickup as he loaded the bags. He very intelligently did not simply toss them in the back.

David finished securing the last bag before turning to answer. "Only a few hours." He took a step closer, invading my personal bubble. "But I plan on taking my time." The hand that slid beneath my skirt left little doubt to his true meaning. "We probably won't get there until nightfall," he added, his voice husky with a promise that he fulfilled when he captured my mouth.

Tingles sparked in both directions from where his hand

rested on my thigh, dangerously close to my already pulsing core. I nipped his bottom lip hard enough to get his attention and he pulled back, eyes wide with surprise. I gave him my best coy smile. "We should get going, then, if we plan to make it there at all."

He flashed me a wicked grin once we were settled in the cab. In direct contrast to the excitement practically making me vibrate, a tiny worm of nerves wriggled through my chest. I was really doing this. What if his family didn't like me? What if he changed his mind about us halfway through the summer? What if, what if, what if?

I shoved the jumble of doubts into a box that I promptly kicked to the dark recesses of my mind where it belonged, then flashed him a smile. Being with David felt right. I would simply refuse to worry myself sick over it. He flashed me another beaming grin as he draped an arm over my chair and shifted the truck into reverse.

The drive itself was peaceful. We enjoyed the radio and scenery until we lost the third station. I reached over to turn off the offending static then sat back at an angle so I could look at him.

"Tell me more about what to expect."

He glanced over at me. "What do you mean?"

"I want to understand more about what I'm walking into. I know we've been over some of it, but I want to go over it again. Tell me about the people, where we're staying, what all this adventure actually entails." My hands fluttered before me as I listed each question.

"Hmm, let's see...the people will be tricky." He gave me a look out of the corner of his eye and winked before smiling and continuing. "They're pretty much like people anywhere." I huffed a pout and he laughed. "It's not like you don't already know a few *weres*, Char. At the end of the day we're people just like anyone else."

Except they weren't. They were *were*-people.

I tried to recover by being more specific with my question. "Will everyone be a werewolf? Will I be the token human?" *Oops. Probably should have asked that sooner.*

He frowned slightly and a seed of anxiety planted itself while he thought about the answer. "I guess that's fair. The town itself is mostly human. Many are families that have been in the area about as long as the pack, though some are newer."

"Really? How long have y'all been there?"

"Somewhere in the vicinity of a couple centuries."

Talk about a major plus. I loved history. I'd been to my fair share of old towns and always found them fascinating. It never ceased to amaze me how much could stay the same despite the persistent march of time.

"The House itself will mostly be *weres*, but there are a few mixed couples. Even then, you won't be the 'token human' as you put it. Not that it really matters."

"Why do you say that?"

"Because Alexander already extended the invitation, and his word pretty much trumps everything."

Maybe he'd never spent time in a prejudiced community, but Georgia had been full of them. It absolutely mattered beyond what one man said, even if he was the boss. "That sounds...progressive."

"Alexander is to thank for that. He never wanted to be stuck in the past like some of the other Alphas." David's smile exuded pride. Sadly, he seemed to have missed my very real concern altogether. "Most of the more modern practices you'll see are because of him and only started about twenty years ago."

I swallowed. Twenty years was nowhere near enough time to undo a century or more of backward thinking.

"Who exactly is Alexander?" I was almost positive he'd

told me before, but I didn't want to dwell on the fact that my seed had started to sprout. "What kind of practices?" Okay, not dwell *too* much. I tried to stamp out the growing concern that I might be stepping into a pit of snakes instead of a den of lovable fur balls.

"He's the Alpha. Basically, he's in charge."

Man-splaining at its finest. "I know what an Alpha is."

"Duh, of course you do. Anyway he's great." The way his eyes shone when he talked about the man, it seemed 'great' was an understatement. "But he's started to put it out there that he's ready to step down. Which, come to think of it, is actually a pretty modern thing on its own. Alphas don't generally retire, at least not by choice." His tone implied that forced retirement was more gruesomely final. "Then there's Maria, his wife—you'll love her, everyone does. And of course, Xander, their son. He's the young hopeful that is primed to fill Alexander's shoes. Let's see, other new practices…"

He tapped the steering wheel as he thought. At last, he exclaimed, "Oh! There's an exchange program now with other packs. It's only been going for a few years, but that was *huge*. In the past, packs never mingled unless they were defending a territory boundary. Those are strictly maintained. Now *that* was a battle." I couldn't tell if he meant the program or whatever boundary dispute had led to it. "And I don't think I've ever mentioned it, but the company I work for was actually started by the pack."

That last nugget of information barely registered as my thoughts swirled with the information about *other* packs. It made sense that there would be more than one, but just how many werewolves were out there? Had I met some and not known? I technically already knew the answer to that and it was a resounding yes. I shuddered and David glanced over, worry in his eyes.

"I'm fine, just a chill," I said before he could ask.

He reached out and adjusted the air. "Anyway," he continued uncertainly, "you'll get to meet everyone. There should be a good turn out for the Solstice celebration this year. What with everything that's going on and the full moon. It'll be a short run that night, but the party should be pretty sizable."

I held up my hands. "Whoa."

"What?" Fear blossomed in his eyes as his gaze darted to me.

"You failed to mention anything about a giant party. I'm pretty sure I didn't pack anything for that."

The doubt clouding his features melted into a warm smile. "You're always stunning, my little fox. I'm positive whatever you brought will blow everyone away."

I couldn't stop the blush that burned across my cheeks. Then something dawned on me. "What exactly am I supposed to do while everyone is out for a run during the full moons?" By my count, I'd be there for at least three of them.

For the briefest of moments David appeared totally stumped. To his credit, he recovered quickly. "I guess that's really up to you. You're welcome to come out with me or you could spend some time in the village or stay at the House. Whatever you want." Something told me that joining him wasn't really as viable an option as he made it sound.

We passed the time going over simple topics like work or silly stories. As we drew closer to our destination, however, I couldn't escape my growing worry about the reception I'd receive. It didn't help that twilight had started to creep in on the horizon by the time we turned and the trees opened up.

"We're here," he announced.

5

———

THE HOUSE

The House was every bit as grand as Sara had described. Six enormous columns rose up from a wide front porch, stretching up the exaggerated two stories. A multitude of chairs and swings graced the front porch while large windows looked out over the front lawn. A lawn that currently held a noticeable lack of people. Apparently, we didn't warrant the kind of welcome wagon Sara had received.

"You look confused." David's words snapped me out of my scouring search.

"Where is everyone?" My gaze continued to rove over all of the windows for some indication of life within. Old houses could be creepy without anyone in them and the encroaching darkness was not helping. "I thought we were staying at your place?" I'd been eager to see what kind of home he kept.

"We are."

I glanced back at him as he pulled out the last of the bags from the bed. Completely laden with luggage, he resembled a pack mule, but neither the number nor the weight seemed to bother him. "It's still a little early in the

48

season for too many people to be here. Don't worry though, this place will be packed before you know it." He maneuvered the items to sit better then walked towards the main entrance.

"I'm sorry." I shook my head and peered at the grand facade. "I'm having a dense moment. This is the House?"

"Yes," he replied as he pushed open the door.

"Where's your place? Is it around back?" Plenty of older estates had other houses on their grounds.

His face clouded briefly with confusion before his eyes brightened with understanding. "Char, I live *in* the House," he clarified, and stepped inside.

I stared blankly at the square of darkness he'd disappeared into, then scurried to join him. A small click filled the quiet and flooded the space with light. My eyes took a second to adjust, then my jaw fell at the wonder before me.

This was an absolute mansion, complete with antebellum staircase, sconces that looked like they'd been installed during the introduction of electricity, and vintage wallpaper. The furniture was a funky mix of modern and vintage arranged on antique rugs that covered what had to be original hardwood. Despite the unusual combination, the place radiated an air of warmth and hospitality. If any of this was the famous Maria's doing, I was definitely looking forward to meeting her—woman had style.

"It can be a little overwhelming." David gave me a knowing grin. "I'll let Maria give you the grand tour. She'll kill me if I beat her to it." He looked around as if just now realizing that we were the only ones present. "Hmm, they must have gone out. They should be back soon enough. In the meantime, let's get settled upstairs."

I continued to stare at everything in awe as we ascended stairs that seemed to stretch on for an eternity. Art covered virtually every inch of available space, from old-fashioned portraits to landscapes and even recent photos, making it almost impossible to see the patterned paper beneath. "How long have you been in the House?"

His voice drifted back from an equally decorated hall. "I don't know, feels like forever. I'd say recently it's only been a few years?"

I tore my gaze away from an exquisite painting of the Appalachians to find I'd fallen behind. My steps quickened as he expanded his explanation.

"Let's see… I started living here full-time shortly after I got promoted to Chief Construction Officer. I was spending so much time in the field on lengthy projects it just became a hassle to keep the apartment. So when the lease was up, I let it go. Though lately it feels like I'm hardly ever here either." He dropped the bags in front of a door that looked like all of the others we'd passed. The white wood swung open into yet more darkness. "Man it feels good to be home."

As I followed him into the room, it occurred to me that the reason he hadn't been here was because he'd been with me. I flicked the switch on the wall to see better. He might be able to see in the dark, but I couldn't.

A soft yellow glow illuminated light blue walls and yet more crown molding. At first glance, it had the appearance of a standard guest room, but upon closer inspection there were little touches that were all David. Books referencing building codes were stacked casually on a chair. An open set of plans lay on a small desk. What looked to be a baseball rested in the corner. A single shelf with a small collection of framed photographs graced the far wall along with an over-sized ceramic mug with his initials.

I did a double take. On the nightstand was a framed photo of the two of us. It looked to be a candid shot of us at a fair.

"Hey, David, where did you get that?"

"Hmm?" he responded without turning around from organizing the bags in the closet.

"That picture on the side table."

His head whipped around so fast it gave me whiplash. "Oh," he cleared his throat, "that one. Um, Mike took it. He was teasing, but I liked it, so I kept it." The affected nonchalance would've been more believable if he hadn't also been beet red.

I picked up the picture to get a better look while I mentally went through what I'd packed, curious if the yellow dress I was wearing in it had made the cut. Most of that day had been amazing. I'd turned into a gibbering mess the second we'd been introduced despite having been madder than a hornet at Sara for inviting some random guy along not five minutes before. I smiled to myself.

This must've been right before the fun house.

"It's a good picture of us," I said aloud, willfully ignoring what had transpired later that afternoon.

David's arms snaked around my waist and he propped his head on my shoulder, presumably to get a better look. "You're beautiful."

I fought the heat rising in my cheeks. "I wish I'd known about this. I didn't think there were any pictures of us."

"We'll have to rectify that this summer," he said, punctuating each word with a feather light kiss on my neck.

I squirmed in his grasp as he continued to lay a sensual trail of tickles. Abruptly, he stopped and lifted his head as if something had caught his attention. I strained to hear anything, but came up empty.

"Sounds like they're home," David declared and I couldn't help but marvel at werewolf hearing. He placed one last kiss on my cheek and released me. "Ready to meet some people?"

I stole a minute to smooth out my dress and pat my heated cheeks. Satisfied they were a little cooler, I raced out the door to join David who was already halfway down the stairs. My gaze skipped past him to settle on the woman standing at the entrance, speaking with a young man.

They both turned at the sound of our approach. "David!" they exclaimed in unison.

"You're early!"

"When did you get in?"

"How was the drive?"

"Hey guys!" David bounded down the remaining steps and swept the woman up in a hug before turning to the boy. They shared what looked like a secret handshake, complete with hand slapping and fist bumps. *Boys.* I mentally shook my head and continued at a slower pace as David asked, "Where's Alexander?"

The woman gave a dismissive wave to the back of the house. "You know him. He's already sequestered himself in the study."

"He's been stressing about everything," the youth added.

The woman let out a long-suffering sigh and pulled her long, dark hair streaked with silver over her shoulder. Her gaze flitted past David and landed on me as I neared the bottom steps. A warm smile spread across her dark face that reminded me of the rich clay that had been prominent where I'd grown up. "You must be Charline."

"Hi," I offered with a small wave.

"David, don't be rude. Introduce everyone," the woman scolded David.

"Oh, right." He positively beamed when he turned and extended a hand to lead me down the last few steps. While visually gallant, it made me feel awkward. I self-consciously tucked a rogue hair behind my ear and prayed the heat burning my face wasn't visible to everyone. "Guys, this is

Charline Montgomery. Charline, this is Maria Wolfsbane and her son Xander."

"It's a pleasure to meet you both. Thank you for having me in your home. It's lovely."

Maria's smile shone in her eyes and Xander looked like someone had told him an amazing joke that he was too polite to laugh at out loud.

"Honestly," Maria said, "I was beginning to doubt whether David was ever going to bring anyone to the House." She waved away my extended hand and pulled me into an embrace. The hug reminded me of hugging my own mother and I instantly relaxed, momentarily forgetting my nerves at meeting such an important person in David's life. "And don't let this lug fool you. We don't stand on much formality here. I expect you to call me Maria and make yourself at home."

She pushed me to arm's length and I gave her a steadier smile than my earlier one. I could understand David's comment about everyone liking Maria. She was an absolute gem.

"David, she's lovely." A savage blush heated my cheeks at the praise. "You must be tired from your trip, so I wont keep you. How about we do the full tour in the morning?"

"David mentioned you'd want to do that yourself," I said as she released me.

"And he was absolutely right. I'll show you the kitchen for now and we'll convene there when you wake up."

"Okay Missus—" she gave me a look and I quickly altered what I'd planned to say. "Okay, Maria."

"Hey, Maria," David asked, "do you think it would be alright if I popped in and said hey to Alexander?"

She shrugged slim shoulders, accentuating the voluminous rope of hair still draped over her shoulder. "I don't see why not." David barely waited for her reply before he headed down an adjacent hall.

"Hey, wait up!" Xander called after him. "I'll come with you."

Maria showed me the kitchen, a quaint intimate space that I itched to explore every nook and cranny of, but I didn't want to appear overly nosy in front of the statuesque matriarch. She bid me goodnight, reiterating her promise of meeting up again in the morning, and we went our separate ways.

A short while later, I'd unpacked what I could, changed into pajamas and crawled into bed. A smile stretched my cheeks as I traced our happy faces in the picture of me and David. Never in a million years would I have expected to stumble upon someone like David after what I'd gone through with Ted. With a contented sigh, I replaced the frame right as the door opened.

"Sorry I took so long," David said, shutting the door. He pulled his shirt over his head and ditched his jeans, kicking them in the corner to join the renegade baseball. My smile returned as I shamelessly appreciated this gorgeous specimen of a man.

"Maria seems really nice," I said as he got under the covers where my eager fingers could appreciate the thick coat of blond hair blanketing his sculpted chest.

"She thinks much the same of you." I gave him a quizzical look and he elaborated. "I ran into her on the way up. I see you've managed to get comfortable."

"I hope it's alright. I hung up a few things," I added, ducking my head.

He chuckled. "Of course it is. I don't expect you to live out of a suitcase the entire summer. I was actually referring to the jammies." His hand burned against my cooler flesh as it slid up my thigh.

"David."

"What?"

"You're incorrigible." I shimmied deeper under the covers, which had the unintended effect of moving his hand even higher.

"Fine, you win. Rest first." He pulled me closer, effectively cocooning me with his body. He shifted my hair and nuzzled my neck.

"That doesn't feel like sleeping," I teased.

"Curse you, woman."

6

THE GOOD STUFF

Shortly after dawn, I found myself quietly padding down the stairs to the kitchen. Thin rays of light illuminated the lovely farm-style layout that I suspected was original to the house. Mercifully, the appliances at least had been updated.

I took the time to familiarize myself with the space like I'd wanted the night before. As I explored, my nerves about being in an unfamiliar place settled. The beautiful thing about kitchens was that no matter how big or small, at their heart, they were all really the same. It took hardly any time to determine where everything was kept, but the true object of my quest remained elusive.

I placed my hands on my hips with a frustrated huff. "Maybe they don't drink tea."

"It's behind the filters."

I jumped at the unexpected voice and turned to find Maria in a dusty pink robe that brushed the floor. She might not have been a tall woman, but she certainly had presence. Once more, her long hair was twisted around to fall over her shoulder. I checked where she'd suggested and sure enough found an old tin box housing the most wonderful smelling herbs.

"I stock the good stuff, but I have to hide it because the others never want any until they see I have some." She smiled and pulled down two mugs while I filled the kettle and put it to boil.

"Thank you. I hope I wasn't too loud." I relocated the kettle to an iron trivet right before its shrill whistle could pierce the air. "Are you sure you don't mind?" I asked, indicating the tin box.

"Like I said, make yourself at home. I'm just glad I'm not the only one who prefers tea to that tar the rest of them drink." Her "them" sounded like it encompassed quite a few people. "Don't worry too much about the noise. Most of the House has updated insulation, though sound does carry if the doors are left open." She took a seat at the intimate kitchen table as I poured the water. "I see you're also an early riser. Did you sleep okay?"

"I'm usually up by five most days, so adjusting to a summer schedule will be...interesting." I set the steaming mug in front of Maria and joined her. "Though I confess, I typically don't sleep well when I'm somewhere I haven't been before." The rude honesty popped out before I could stall it. My mother would be ashamed.

Maria seemed unphased by what *I* at least considered a major faux pas. She took a sip of the scalding liquid. "That's to be expected, but I'm sure you'll adjust in no time. David tells us you're an amazing cook." I had to smother a grin. Maria segued as gracefully as my own mother.

"He does, does he?"

"Truth be told, we likely know far more about you than is probably decent. David talks about you virtually every chance he gets."

"That's pretty impressive considering we haven't actually known each other that long and he's only been back—what —once since then?"

"True, but he calls regularly. It's actually been a little strange not having him around all of the time these last couple months. Though it's nice that he's finally found a reason besides work to get out of the house."

I sipped my own tea now that it had had a chance to cool. "I don't mean to sound rude, but it seems odd that he would need to check in with Alexander so frequently."

Her laughter bubbled out. "Oh sweetie, David's not calling *him.* I mean, they talk occasionally, but usually he's calling me." My confusion must have been stamped on my face. "He's my nephew, after all. We became quite close after his mother passed."

I took another cautious sip of my tea. David's mom was dead? He was related to Maria? Why hadn't David ever told me any of this? How long ago had she passed? What about his father?

Maria reached out and patted my hand. "Don't be sad, dear. He doesn't like to talk about it. Her illness wasn't wholly unexpected, but expected or not, losing a loved one is never easy." Before I could absorb this new information, she removed her hand and shifted gears again. "Now, onto more pleasant topics. I would love it if you'd show me a recipe or two. I'm always looking to expand our usual routine. It can be a bit tricky to get fancy with the spices around here when all anyone ever wants is meat."

"It would be a privilege, Maria." I hid a smile behind my warm mug. The meat battle was one that I'd become intimately familiar with.

She glanced behind me out the window. "Good, the sun is officially up. Why don't you go get dressed and I'll meet you in the front? Then I can give you the official tour."

I smiled in agreement and rinsed my cup before heading back upstairs where I ran into a now awake and apparently frisky David.

He swept me up into an embrace that threatened to topple us onto the bed. "Good morning, my little fox."

"Cool your grits, Romeo." I giggled as I extricated myself. He swiped at me as I danced out of reach and stepped into the closet in search of something to wear on my first real day.

Unperturbed, he dove into the closet after me. "Who's this Romeo?" With nowhere left to run, I was at the mercy of his energetic efforts to wish me good morning.

"Maria is waiting for me downstairs, you silly goof," I finally managed to squeak out between kisses.

"Why didn't you say so?" He nipped at my nose and left me to my efforts.

I fanned myself and grabbed something at random, not really caring anymore beyond hoping that my internal temperature would cool before I had to see Maria again. David treated me to a self-confident snicker before I dashed out.

As promised, Maria was at the bottom of the stairs. She gave my blue sundress an appraising look before launching into full tour guide mode.

The rest of the mansion proved to be just as impressive as the entry. Each space we entered provided a new set of marvels. We ventured down halls that became formal sitting rooms and walked through narrow entrances that could have easily been secret passages at one point. My eyes must have been the size of saucers as I soaked up the lavish decorations and history that seemed to saturate every square inch. I got to see the study to which David had disappeared the night before with Xander, as well as a library full-to-bursting with books, equal parts new paperbacks and dusty tomes, and no fewer than three formal sitting rooms.

"Good morning, my dear," a man's voice drifted out from a sudden opening in the hall.

Maria turned at the welcome and stepped into a surprisingly sunny parlor. I followed. Like the library, books covered the walls and even more were stacked on tables and chairs. But unlike the formal area, almost all of these volumes appeared to be ancient. Even to my human nose the room smelled of age.

When Maria stepped away from the source of the voice, I finally got my first view of who could only be the Alpha of the North Carolina werewolf pack. Like Maria, his jet black hair was peppered with silver, making him look distinguished, though his skin was a shade or two lighter than hers. Much like a military man, his face carried the hard lines of command, but if you looked a little closer you could just make out the ghost of a smile waiting to be freed.

"I hope you slept well, love." The concern in Maria's voice further softened the man's features as he graced her with a look of tender adoration. The private moment continued in silence and I debated slipping out so I wouldn't intrude further.

He traced a finger delicately down her cheek and she leaned into his hand. "I'm well. Just tired," he said, then without ever taking his eyes from hers added, "I see you've coerced our guest into joining you this morning."

Maria let out a small "Oh," and turned back to see me standing awkwardly in the doorway. "Alexander, this is Charline. She and David got in last night. And for your information, she was already awake when I got up."

"Was she now?" His considering gaze finally shifted to me and it was hard not to feel like I was being weighed and measured. "Welcome, Miss Montgomery. I hope you'll make yourself comfortable in our home. If you need anything at all, please don't hesitate to let one of us know." I took his extended hand. The shake was warm and firm. Maybe not such a salty general after all.

At last I smiled. "Thank you both again for having me, Mr. Wolfsbane."

The smile I'd guessed at earlier made an appearance along with a hearty laugh. "Please don't call me that. Others think the name is ironic. I just hate it. I insist you call me Alexander."

"Maria, you beat me to it," a familiar voice echoed behind me.

"Oh hush, David," Maria scoffed. "It wasn't intentional. We ran into him on our tour."

"A likely story," David said as he stepped up beside me and placed a large hand on my shoulder, gently rubbing my exposed neck with his thumb.

"Hey, what's all this?" Xander asked as he stepped into the room as well. "No one tells me anything. Why wasn't I invited to this morning gathering? Don't suppose there's breakfast?" His scowl brightened with hope.

"Probably because you never seem to wake up before noon," David said, mussing the boy's hair with his other hand.

Xander batted him off, fixing the mess to no clear difference. "Haven't you heard? Since I started college, I've been waking up at reasonable times. Sometimes the little hand is even before the ten," he joked.

"You decided to do the school thing after all, huh?" David patted the substantially slimmer youth soundly on the back.

"Eh," he shrugged. "A little more knowledge never hurt anyone." He looked at his father who in turn appeared quite proud.

"What are you studying?" I asked.

"A couple things. Government, sociology, and history. I can't seem to decide. I'll see what the fall semester brings and maybe I'll have a better idea for narrowing down my major."

I was about to ask more when Alexander cut in. "Xander, why don't you take Charline to see the orchard?"

"Sure, Dad. Come on, you'll love it. There should be some fruit ready." Xander had a decided bounce in his step as led David and I out of the room.

"David," Alexander called after us, "before you go, I'd like to talk something over with you."

"Yes, Alpha. I'll catch up with you guys later." David gave me a chaste kiss on the cheek and returned to the room, leaving me and Xander to wander out the back of the House.

As we made our way up a short hill beneath a perfectly blue sky, I tried not to dwell on what Alexander could possibly need to talk to David about right now. Alexander's seamless shift from open and friendly to shuttered and serious took me aback, but no one else had batted an eye. I glanced over at my young guide and wondered if it would be too untoward to pump him for details.

No sooner did the thought occur to me than I dismissed it. I didn't know any of these people well enough to start digging for particulars simply because I was uneasy. Only way to fix that was to get to know them.

"So, Xander, what school are you going to?"

"I'm over at Blackwell Hollow. Most of the pack goes there."

"That's pretty close," I said, dredging what knowledge I had of North Carolina geography. "Most of the pack?"

"Yeah, we've made some pretty large contributions over the years. Actually, it was Dad's idea to buy a house on campus."

"Like a fraternity?"

"Kind of. It gives people a safe place to be around other

weres and not have to worry about maintaining appearances."

"Your dad is really smart."

Xander's gaze settled on the ground. "I just hope I can live up to the standards he's set."

"I'm sure you will," I said as we walked through rows of apple trees.

He glanced at me, a glimmer of hope in his eye. I was suddenly struck by just how young he was, far too young to be taking on his father's mantle.

"Who else is over there?" I asked when he didn't say anything further.

"A few of us. There are twenty wolves in the house now. As a matter of fact, my best friend is still there. Jennifer decided to stay for a couple summer classes."

"Jennifer, eh?"

"No, no, no." He waved his hands emphatically. "It's not like that," he added with a laugh. "She's my cousin, more like my big sister. Way too weird."

David pulled up to join us in our mindless meander. "What about Jenny?"

"Xander was just telling me she's still at school." I forced a bright smile despite the sudden stab of hurt. I'd told David a lot about my family and yet the most I'd learned about his had come from two virtual strangers in the same morning.

"She taking extra classes again?" He scoffed and shook his head then went on without waiting for an answer. "Some day she's gonna realize there's more to life than books."

A mischievous smile curled Xander's lips and sparkled in his eyes. "Actually, I think she's trying to avoid a certain someone at the House."

"No..."

Xander simply nodded sagely. I watched the exchange, clueless as to what on Earth they were talking about.

"Oh, what did Dad want you for?"

I perked up at the question that echoed my own burning curiosity.

David waved away the question. "Nothing much, just logistical stuff about the summer. Jenny gonna make it to the Solstice?"

"Like she could miss it." They shared a laugh at a joke I clearly didn't get and I deflated a bit. It would seem my curiosity would go unquenched.

<hr>

"Alright, that's it. There are officially too many cooks in this kitchen."

I laughed as Maria shooed all three men out of the tight space. It had only been a few days, yet the time we'd spent together had easily convinced me how fantastic the Wolfsbanes were. Every last one of them may have been a werewolf, but they were really no different than any other family.

Xander moped his way out of the kitchen, proclaiming the vast unfairness of it all while Alexander swiped a taste of the sauce simmering on the stove before Maria smacked his hand and finished shooing them out. David, on the other hand, was obediently waiting in the hall. He gave me a wink before leading the others to finish setting the table.

"They're quite the handful," I said as I stirred the abused sauce.

Maria stood with her hands on her hips. "Don't even get me started," she huffed, blowing hair out of her face. "Forget what I said about it being nice to have him home, take David out of here. He's nothing but an instigator, and with Jonathan away, there's no one to keep Alexander in check."

"Who's Jonathan?" I asked, draining the pasta. It was still

a little al dente for my taste, but it would continue to cook in its own ambient heat.

"Oh, um, David hasn't said?"

I wiped my hands on the apron she'd lent me and shook my head in the negative, now even more curious about this mysterious person.

"Yes, well, Jonathan...Jonathan is Alexander's best friend." Her evasive tone made it seem like that sentiment wasn't as solid as it once had been. Perhaps the two had recently had a falling out.

"I'm not sure him being here would actually improve our nosy-cooks situation. If they're anything like David and Michael, I suspect they're worse trouble when combined."

"They were at that," she said almost so low I didn't catch it. Louder, she added, "Now that we have some breathing room, let's wrap this up. It smells divine and I'm ravenous. Are you sure we made enough?"

With her petite stature, it was easy to forget that Maria was also a werewolf and had an appetite to match. "I promise you, there will be plenty—maybe no leftovers—but at least enough that everyone will feel full. I've had practice feeding the wolves." A short while later, we carted out the last of the food to join the others at the dining table.

"Let me help you with that, my love." Alexander stole a tray and a kiss before resuming his seat. Sometimes their sweetness was almost too much to bear. Apparently, I wasn't the only one who thought so, because Xander was rolling his eyes and making classic signs of gagging.

"Mock all you want, scruff. Your day will come," Alexander said without ever glancing toward his son. Xander stuck his tongue out while he took another tray from his mom and placed it on the deep chestnut table.

"You know he saw that." David elbowed the lad as he

relieved me of my platters and gifted me with my own kiss on the cheek.

"Like you have any room to talk," Xander replied, once again looking like he knew a joke he wasn't allowed to laugh at. Maria leveled a motherly glare at him. "What? I didn't say anything."

Maria's glare traveled to David.

He shifted in his seat and refused to meet her stern gaze. "I don't know about everyone else, but I'm famished."

She refrained from comment, instead rolling her eyes and handing a serving spoon to her husband.

I'd half expected that they would all wait for him to start. Not so. Everyone tucked in with a relish. Silverware chimed against porcelain serving platters, which thankfully weren't antique. Ice clinked in glasses of lemonade that might or might not have had an extra boost of something stronger. The mood overall was congenial and relaxed. Everything about the meal was normal aside from the quantities that disappeared, leaving little evidence they'd ever been there.

"What's so funny?" Xander asked after polishing off the last bite of his second helping.

"I just love how food brings people together," I answered with a pleased sigh.

"Around here, that's kind of a given." Xander gave me a cheeky grin and David rolled his eyes.

"No, she has a point. When was the last time we all sat together and just shared a meal?" Alexander asked no one in particular. He sounded pleased, but the look he gave Maria was wistful.

She squeezed his hand. "We'll make sure to make more time for it."

"I'd like that." The soft way Alexander looked at Maria spoke of a lifetime of love and devotion. Xander straightened up, going from carefree teenager to responsible adult in the blink of an eye. "Charline, this meal is lovely. Thank you," Alexander said, without seeming to notice his son's impressive transformation.

"Oh." I blushed, feeling like I'd been caught thinking about all of them and he knew. He had an uncanny knack for addressing people while they were distracted. "It's nothing really, and I had a lot of help."

"Too much help," Maria said, smacking the hand she'd just been holding. Alexander pulled it back in mock injury and the light-hearted atmosphere reasserted itself.

"It's almost impossible to get her to take credit for her incredible works of art," David said with a broad smile and a distinct note of pride. My face burned hotter. "But this? This is nothing. Dinner is one thing. Dessert though..." He trailed off looking into the middle distance as if he could see some imaginary morsel.

"It's really not... I'm not that..." My mother had always said I was too prideful and here these people were claiming I didn't take enough credit for myself. I floundered another moment then said to hell with it. If they thought I was overly proud, so be it. "Okay, you've got me. I may or may not be a pastry genius."

They all laughed and I relaxed a little more. Xander brought back another round of drinks. I didn't want to be rude, so accepted it, though I wasn't sure where I was going to put it given how full I was.

When the meal was over, we made short work of the dishes, then convened in the front room. I giggled as David almost sat on me on a floral patterned couch. Like most of the furniture in the room, it was older and creaked at our combined weight. He gave no sign of concern so I didn't say anything.

I looked around and realized that everyone was holding another fresh glass. How many was that? I eyed my own which seemed suspiciously fuller. *Oh dear.* David caught the look, slyly finished his and switched the glasses. I curled my fingers around the empty glass and did my best not to beam over his thoughtfulness.

"You know, I could get used to this." Xander plopped into a wingback chair reminiscent of those found in the study his father frequented.

"Easy there, pup," Alexander chided, that playful smile I'd grown accustomed to back in place as he settled onto another couch across from us with Maria.

"Besides, chairs by yourself are no fun," David added, squeezing me until I squeaked.

Everyone laughed and then Maria produced a binder that bore a striking resemblance to my mother's event planner. "Now that we're all settled, we can go over the details of the Solstice."

David and Xander groaned in unison while I perked up at the mention of party planning. I'd been trained by no fewer than three generations of Montgomery women on how to throw a party that could knock your socks off.

"David mentioned the Solstice fell on a full moon this year. I take it that means things will be a little...wilder?" I finished for lack of a better word.

Alexander snorted into his cup. "That's a mild way to put it."

"I'll take none of your nonsense this year." Maria smacked the binder open on the coffee table and glowered at her husband. "If you don't like the way I plan a party, you can do it yourself."

Alexander laughed and waved his free hand. "I wouldn't dream of it, my love. I know better than to get in your way. Just tell me what you need, and I'll see it done."

"That's what I thought." Maria sniffed and straightened up. "I know we normally have the main festivities in the east fields, but with the attendance we're expecting, I don't think that will work."

I set my spiked lemonade down on a side table. "Oh? How many more are you expecting?"

"We normally have a good half to two-thirds of the pack come to the House at some point during the summer. Typically the younger ones. But I don't expect anyone to want to miss the Solstice this year." She studied the planner for a moment then gave a sharp nod. "Yes, I think the west woods will do nicely."

"The clearing in the west woods is so small, though, there's no way it can fit all three hundred of us," Xander interjected. "The bonfire will set the whole forest ablaze."

Maria gave him a smile I'd seen many times on my own mother's face. "That's why you and David, and whoever else you can snag are going to clear an extra fifty meters."

Xander choked and I did a double take at the size of the bonfire she proposed. Sure, I'd survived meeting the intimate circle of family, but three people were much easier to manage than three hundred.

Rather than give voice to my increasing anxiety, I burrowed into David's shoulder and focused solely on the details. Come hell or high water, I'd find a way to make myself useful.

7

———

SUMMER VACATION

The following days passed in a wonderful compilation of family meals, adventures in the woods, party planning, and even a movie night. When David and I weren't getting lost in each other, we spent hours exploring the historic house, much to the merriment of Maria who was quickly becoming an idol to rival my nana. Xander also turned out to be a pretty neat kid, even if he was a little wet behind the ears. Alexander, however, remained a mystery to me, secluded as he often was in the library.

I smoothed my skirt as I stared out at the strict lines of apple trees that made up the orchard and wondered again why someone as young as Xander wanted to take on a position that weighed so heavily upon his father.

Maybe it'll become clearer when more of the pack starts showing up.

I pulled up my wavy tresses into a high pony to keep the hair off my neck and turned away from the picturesque scene. "What would you say to another tour?" I asked David. "I'm sure it'll only take a couple more before I can find my way around this place blindfolded." My arms fell back by my sides as my gaze landed on him propped up on the pillows, his glorious chest with its thick layer of blond hair on display for my hungry eyes.

"I think you've seen enough of everything around here." David stretched his legs out and crossed his ankles, the ultimate picture of summer ease straight out of a naughty calendar. "Besides, why would you need to find your way around in the dark?"

Spoken like a man who could *actually* see in the dark. I shook my head and my hair swung in a wild arc. Then with complete disregard for my pressed dress, I pounced on him and smacked a big kiss on his lips. "You're. No. Fun," I said between smaller kisses that traveled from his jaw to his collarbone and onward. He purred a low growl of appreciation and slid his hands beneath the edge of my skirt to grip my thighs.

"I'm plenty of fun. But I do think it's time we got you out of the House."

"So the orchard then?" I popped up from kissing his chest.

He tightened his grip and yanked me forward, pulling me deeper onto his lap. His mouth closed over mine, effectively silencing any argument I might have concocted. "No. No more orchard. If I eat another apple, I'll turn into one."

My happy smile flipped into a pout and I settled back on his thighs. "You didn't seem to have a problem eating apples last night when you were eating my apple pie."

His gaze lidded dreamily. "Mm, that was delicious." He placed a hand on each side of my face and gave me a purposeful kiss. "It was really great of you to do that with Maria." He teased my bottom lip with his teeth. "I know she appreciated it. Shame there were no leftovers."

"Yes, but if we go to the orchard, then we can get more apples and I can make another one," I tried to say in between more kisses.

"Nope. Not happening."

"Please," I crooned, pressing my chest against him.

He growled and gently pushed me back so he could extricate himself from the bed. "You're insufferable."

I immediately hopped up and grabbed my basket for the apples while he started to get dressed.

"Still not going to the orchard."

"But..." I glanced down at the empty basket that would apparently be staying empty.

"Don't worry, we're going out, just not there."

"Then where?" I asked, up for the possibility of a new adventure. "You've already nixed the House. The woods?" We'd only made a brief foray there. Apparently the endless stretch of trees was more interesting on four legs than two.

"We, my little fox, are going to Stone Creek," he said, tipping my chin and planting a small kiss.

I cocked my head as I struggled to place the name. Then it dawned on me. "The village! Christ on a cracker, I totally forgot there was a village nearby."

"I gathered as much." He sat back down to pull on his worn work boots while I danced impatiently from foot to foot. "It's easy to forget. It's such a small place and, much like the House, tucked up in the hills." He stood and clapped his hands. "Now let's get you out of here before you burst with excitement."

I spun on my heel and zipped for the door, only to hover at the threshold. "Is this going to be okay?" I indicated my dress of the day.

He covered the distance between us in two strides and pulled on my hips, causing me to lose my balance and fall into him and a waiting kiss. "You're perfect."

That wasn't what I'd asked, but I suspected it was all I was going to get. He opened the door and we stepped into the hallway. In no time at all we were on a country road headed to Stone Creek.

I filled the short drive with rapid fire questions about the town, buildings, and people. Due to his work restoring old buildings, David knew quite a bit about the history of the architecture. His knowledge of the actual people, however, was surprisingly lacking. Odd, considering the pack and town had been neighbors for generations.

I couldn't help but gape as we drove down the main road of a town that looked more like the set of a Hallmark movie than a real place.

And I thought where I grew up was quaint. How's it possible I've been here a whole week and we're just now *getting around to the town?*

The plan was to do a full circuit so David could point out the highlights and then park. Or it would have been.

"Wait! I wanna get a closer look." My seatbelt whizzed as it recalled and I tried to exit the moving vehicle.

David laughed and pulled into the nearest parking spot. The truck was still settling when I launched out the door like a greyhound at the races.

"Stars above, woman. At least let me put her in park first," David chided me as he did exactly that then joined me on the sidewalk. "See anything you like?"

I turned to stare at him with wide eyes. "Is that a real question? Because I absolutely freaking love everything." He laughed again and went to grab my waist, but I was already gone.

I bounced between aged storefronts with chipped paint and renovated marvels that sported deep red bricks. Stone Creek had all the makings of a quintessential small town—a local butcher, a small hardware store, and even a flower shop. Positively picturesque. None of the buildings rose above three stories with the exception of a converted bed and breakfast that reached up a whole extra story.

Joy filled my chest and tingled in my fingers as I soaked up the sights and friendly locals, all of whom went out of their way to welcome me and introduce themselves. Occasionally, we bumped into folks who recognized David, but there weren't as many as I would've thought and almost none of them were human. He'd even pointed out a mixed couple sweeter than strawberry and rhubarb pie.

"David," I began as we took a table at what appeared to be the largest eatery in town. The Lunar Cafe had retained its historic charm with only a few touches of neon and some plastic coated menus to show that it was in fact part of this century.

"Yes?" He pulled up his chair after helping me into mine.

"The couple we saw..." I glanced over at the bar top and debated whether or not I wanted something more substantial than sweet tea.

"The Turners? What about them?" he asked, not bothering to look at the faded menu.

"Well, they're married, right?"

He chuckled. "Yes."

I pulled my hair free and toyed with a curl. What I really wanted to ask was how the pack had taken that, but I wasn't sure how not to sound like I was putting the cart before the horse. Instead, I chose an alternatively awkward question.

"If they have a baby, what'll it be? Before you get smart, I don't mean gender." It was a huge assumption that they even could have children. The question felt like I'd dropped a bag of down feather on the table as muffled silence drifted up to encompass us in a cocoon.

After what felt like an eternity, David reached out to take my hand, forcing me to set my menu down. He peered at me thoughtfully while his thumb rubbed circles on my hand. I got lost in his eyes and for a moment forgot that we were sitting in a very public restaurant talking about something that almost definitely was not common knowledge.

"The child would be a wolf," he said at last. I looked around at his blatant use of the word, conscious of prying ears. He noticed my caution and answered another question I'd been wondering. "Don't worry, no one is paying us any mind."

I took my hand back and tucked my hair behind my ears. "How do you know?" My impression had been that interspecies relationships were relatively new in the grand scheme of things, but maybe I'd misunderstood. Had there already been children? How many? How long had that been going on?

The string of unasked questions might as well have been written on my face. David sat back and considered me in a silence that felt heavier by the second. Not for the first time, I wished I could at least pretend to think before I blurted out whatever I was on my mind.

"My father wasn't a *were*." He might have said it matter of factly, but to me he might as well have casually declared the bar would blow at any minute. "He was in the army and stationed at a base near my mother's hometown."

I frowned. "I thought your whole...family," I waved generally in the air, "lived here."

He shook his head. "Not everyone chooses to live so close to the House and pack territory *is* quite extensive. Anyway, they married young, and it wasn't until after he was deployed that my mother discovered she was pregnant. She knew the moment I was born that the gene had carried over. As for my father, he died in action before my first change. I still don't know if he ever knew what we are. So, to answer your question, history has shown that the *were* gene is dominant, and that's how *I* know, personally."

I leaned forward to place my hand on his. "I'm so sorry, David." He straightened up and rolled his shoulders as if to shrug off the condolence.

"I was too young to remember him." Be that as it may, it couldn't make that loss hurt any less. I was about to say as much when he shook himself and glanced over my shoulder. "Oh, look, here's the waiter. Do you know what you want?"

It seemed best to give the moment a chance to finish dissipating, so I gave him my order and excused myself to the ladies room. I wasn't sure what broke my heart more, that David had grown up without his father or that he didn't even know if his father had died with the knowledge his son was a werewolf. Add to that, this was the first I was hearing of any of this and I definitely needed a moment to compose myself.

David probably knew everything and then some about my family, right down to what size dress my Aunt Rita thought she wore, yet I knew hardly anything at all about his. My instincts had been right, though. If I was patient, he would eventually open up, though the waiting might actually kill me. As my mother said, patience wasn't a flower that grew in my garden.

I weaved my way around bucket seats to get to the narrow hallway that held the restrooms. I'd nearly cleared the exceedingly tight space when I knocked into a rail of a woman as she came out of the very place I sought.

"I'm sorry," I said, worried that I might have hurt the petite creature.

All I caught was a short curtain of black, glossy hair and the faintest "It's fine" before she slipped past and vanished. The door closed behind me and I pushed the rude encounter from my thoughts.

When I returned, the menus were gone and the drinks

refilled. In record time, our food was delivered by the same waiter that had taken our order.

"Thank you, Henley," I said as the young man set our plates down. He smiled and left us to our meal. I was all set to tuck in when I caught sight of David's raised eyebrow. "What?"

"Nothing. Leave it to you to be in town less than a day and already making it your business to learn who everyone is."

"I do work in HR. It's kind of my thing."

He shook his head, but kept smiling. "I think it's great how easy you get along with whoever you meet." I shrugged noncommittally and took a bite of my shepherd's pie. That wasn't always true, but it was a nice thought.

We continued to chat amicably without mentioning anything from the previous conversation. I was perusing the dessert menu and trying to decide if I could just make it better myself when I felt an itching sensation between my shoulders, almost as if someone was watching me. I looked around in search of a likely culprit. Usually the sensation was accompanied by a leering man, but I saw no suspects. The cafe was virtually empty but for ourselves and a handful of other patrons, none of whom were looking our way.

"You okay?" David asked.

"Yeah..." I shook my head and returned to the task at hand. "I think I'll skip on dessert. We both know I can make all of it better anyway," I added in a conspiratorial whisper. No need to offend the chef.

David gave me a wolfish grin. "Of that, I have no doubt."

8

ALL GROWN UP

"Looks like the first wave has finally arrived," David observed as we rounded the final bend to the House.

I snatched my gaze away from the distant mountain peaks to stare out the front window. Sure enough, almost a dozen people milled about in front of the grand entryway. David flashed me an excited grin before maneuvering the large truck up the last stretch of drive. My desire to make a good first impression tempered my own excitement to finally be meeting more of the pack. The gathering casually moved aside as we approached to allow us to park and get out. We'd scarcely cleared the cabin when names went flying.

"David!"

"Marc."

"David."

"Isabel. I see you dragged Kaleb along." David wrapped a young woman with brown hair in a fierce hug and winked at the guy beside her before stepping back. "And Lucas, I thought you weren't going to be able to make it?"

"Eh, I made room on the calendar."

"You rascal. Daniel, Keith, couldn't get your dad to come?"

"I'm right here. Still as blind as ever I see." An older man with more gray than brown at his temples wrapped David in an embrace that probably would have broken me in half.

"It's good to see you, Randy." David clapped him on the shoulder and turned to a pair of younger men walking up. "Carl, did you and Matt carpool or take the long way?" They laughed and shook hands with the eager David. "Now wait a minute, I could have sworn there were more of you. I may be blind, but I'm sure I can still count."

"I'm right here."

David spun around at the soft voice and his eyes immediately widened as they fell on its owner. "No. Vicky? Is that you?"

"In the flesh," she said, holding her arms from her rail thin form.

"Stars, I haven't seen you in ages. What's it been? Ten years?"

Her asymmetrical bob swung in a perfect black sheet around her petite face. Recognition dawned as she said, "Something like that."

"Wow, you've grown up," he said, giving her an appraising once over. An ember of jealousy glowed in my chest. "I can't believe you're here." He scooped her up in one of those epic, bone crushing hugs that seemed so popular among the wolves and a fan blew across my ember. I diligently reminded myself that David was a substantially better man than Ted had ever been. He'd never cheat on me, and certainly wouldn't flaunt it in front of my face.

At last he set her down and her laughter at the over-the-top greeting subsided. A broad smile stretched across her narrow face as she placed her hands familiarly on his muscled chest and crooned, "I'm not the only one." His cheeks turned a deep crimson and the ember burst into flames. I mentally chanted *He's not Ted* over and over, then cleared my throat and took a step closer.

"Oh." David pushed the slip of a girl away and turned to indicate me. "Everybody, this is Charline. Charline, this is *some* of everybody." Everyone laughed except for Vicky who stepped closer to David. "Come here, Charline, I want you to meet Victoria." He grabbed my hand, pulling me more firmly into the mix. "Vicky and I grew up together. Gosh, we've been friends practically forever."

Relief washed through me. They were old childhood friends reunited, that was all. I took a deep breath and extended a hand, excited to meet someone from David's past. "Nice to meet you, Victoria. We actually bumped into each other earlier at the cafe."

David immediately turned to her. "Why didn't you say anything? You could've joined us."

"I would've loved to, except I just got here. Haven't been to town at all," she said with a smile as she took my hand. My cheek twitched as she did that insufferable thing where she only accepted the tips of my fingers then released my hand almost instantly.

I diligently worked not to, as my mama would say, "make that face out loud." While I hadn't gotten a good look at the woman's face earlier, I was *positive* this was the same person. What I didn't get was why she would lie about it.

"Charline." Victoria rolled my name around in her mouth. "That's an interesting name. Where are you from? You don't...sound like you're from around here." She eyed me up and down. While I was used to comments about my accent, I didn't think that was what she was referring to and judging by Isabel's face, I wasn't the only one.

"I'm from Georgia. I'll be joining y'all this summer," I said with the brightest smile I could muster.

Her eyes tightened and her thin lips slanted down. She looked over at David who was still beaming at her, having completely missed the veiled slight. A vile smile transformed her frown into a menacing grin and I flashed back to the same vicious smile Stacy in Accounting had given me when she'd all but admitted to having an affair with Ted.

"Oh? How long have you two known each other?" she asked.

Before I could find my voice, David said, "We actually met a few months ago when I was working a job in Raleigh."

"Hey, isn't that where Michael lives?" A man—Keith maybe?—asked.

"Yeah," Daniel added. "That's where y'all caught the mutt."

"Did any of you get to meet Sara? The *turned* wolf?" Matt asked, though I wasn't sure if the emphasis on "turned" had any more relevance beyond general distinction. Victoria wrinkled her nose, but kept her peace.

"Oh, yeah. She's a pretty thing," definitely-Keith said.

"Shame she's already taken. The women around here are a little more trouble than I'm up for." Carl nudged Isabel.

"If memory serves, you're not *up* for much," she said without missing a beat. He feigned an arrow to the heart, staggering back.

"Actually, Sara is my best friend." All eyes turned to stare at me. They'd completely forgotten I was there.

Victoria placed a hand on David's arm which he didn't seem to notice. "That must have been hard on you," she said and pointed with her free hand at the scars on my left arm. I subconsciously reached to tug on the non-existent sleeve, then dropped my hand and looked away.

David stepped away from Victoria and pulled me into a substantially gentler side hug. "Nah, Char was amazing."

Victoria raised an eyebrow at the unusual shortening of my name, but didn't comment.

"Right, I'm going inside," Randy said. "The rest of you lazy louts are welcome to stay out here, but *my* trip at least was long. I could use a sit down and some of Maria's lemonade." He hiked an abused duffel onto his shoulder and wandered into the House. Some of the others followed, but many stayed chatting outside, including David, who turned to ask Matt and Carl more about their drive.

Released, I spun on my heel and made my way to the strip of woods that skirted the orchard without a word, "He's not Ted" playing on repeat the whole way. I gulped down air as insecurity burned through my veins, jealousy blistering at the edges.

Thankfully, no one remarked upon my sudden departure. I walked faster, eager to escape the doubts that had roared to life at meeting David's childhood friend. It wasn't that I missed Ted, or would have taken him back if he hadn't turned out to be a sociopathic killer, but he'd done a real number on me, the reminder of which would be forever emblazoned on my skin.

I'd just stepped into the woods proper when David caught up. I couldn't help but wonder how long it had taken him to realize I'd left.

"Hey, Char, where are you going? I thought we'd all hang out so you could really get to know everyone." When my only response was to keep walking, he added, "Don't mind them. They didn't mean anything about Sara. Honest."

I stopped. This wasn't about Sara, though them talking about her like that hadn't exactly been great either. I opened my mouth to tell him what I thought of his childhood friend and choked on the words. Even if I could say what was bothering me without sounding like some stage-five clinger, I doubted he would understand. I'd met the woman once for all of five minutes. He'd known her practically his whole life. I glared at the gnarled bark in front of me and diligently worked to conquer the unreasonable inferno my ember had become.

He's not Ted.

"Char?"

At the entreaty, a strong overwhelming urge to claim what was mine surged through me. My dress flared as I spun to catch him with a fierce kiss.

"Charline," he laughed, kissing me back.

I worked my way to his collar, almost snapping off the tiny white button that held it closed. Need burned through my veins, consuming me from the inside out. I would not be put on the back burner by some porcelain twig.

"What's gotten into you?" he chuckled, not stopping me.

I tasted the skin of his chest and his laughter took on the edge of a growl. Better, but I wanted more, needed more. I continued to work my way down, freeing buttons and trailing my fingers through his chest hair as I went until my knees kissed the ground.

"Char-*line*." His voice hitched as I made short work of his fly and pulled him free. Already his length was hot and hard in my hand. He let out a low moan when I wrapped my lips around him, and tangled a hand in my hair. I pulled him deeper, and nestled the hand not wrapped around his base in the hair on his stomach. Another groan rolled out of him. "Char—Charline, they're still out here."

He came free with a muffled pop. I looked up at him and gave a firm stroke. "Then I guess you'd better be quiet."

He let out a strangled moan and I reclaimed my prize. "For the love of the moon," he gasped, his fingers flexing in my hair.

I hummed at my victory, then in a move that defied human speed, found myself pressed against a nearby tree, my skirt pushed up around my hips. David's mouth mashed down on mine, the force of it pushing me harder against the tree while he pulled my panties aside. Pieces of bark broke into my hair and scratched the exposed skin of my back and shoulders as he buried himself deep in one thrust.

My breath caught and I fought the urge to cry out at the punishing tempo. I arched my hips forward desperate for more and followed my own advice, biting down on my knuckle to hold the traitorous sound at bay.

"Shit," he hissed, his fingers tightening on my thighs as he pumped faster, pushing both of us toward the edge.

My release exploded like a firework on the Fourth of July. His mouth closed over mine just in time to catch our dual shouts as his body tensed with his own climax. When he finally stopped moving, I leaned my head back against the tree that I was now pretty sure I was a part of, painfully aware of the shaking in my legs as he kissed the sweat from the top of my breasts.

I panted for breath and finally managed a cracked, "We should go."

He trailed kisses along my collar and nuzzled into my neck. "You're right. There's just one problem."

"Huh?"

"We smell."

"I beg your pardon."

"Sex, we smell like sex." His throaty laugh buzzed where his lips touched my flesh and my insides quivered in response. "We need to get to the House," he said in a low growl.

"How? I'm pretty sure my legs don't work." Mercifully, he didn't laugh again; I wasn't sure my body could take it.

"We'll have to go around the side and sneak in the back." He very carefully lifted me free of his already re-hardening length and gently set me down. I smoothed my abused dress as best I could while he tucked himself away. "You go first and I'll be right behind."

Shaky legs or no, I didn't really have a choice. I moved as quickly and quietly as I could manage in the direction of the House. Unfortunately, there ended up being people by the back entrance. The last thing I wanted was for anyone I'd just met to see me in such a state, so I switched gears and made my way to the front. I waited until a straggler finally walked off then padded inside. I prayed for everything I was worth that I wouldn't run into someone as I ascended the stairs with all the stealth of a drunk ninja.

"So much for going around back," David said as he stepped through the door a scant minute after me, closing and locking it behind him.

"Oh my God," I gasped. "I can't believe we just did that." I let out a nervous laugh and fanned myself to bring the persistent flush down. His smile was somehow shy and wolfish all together. "I've...I've never...I don't know what came over me." I reached up to hold my head before it fell off, and found loose bits of nature. I systematically started pulling them free.

"Your dress."

At the apologetic tone, I looked down. Oh yes, the dress was definitely ruined. "To hell with the dress."

That deep laugh of his that never failed to make my insides jelly filled the room and he started stripping down.

Need to change, right.

I fumbled for the zipper of the destroyed garment, hoping it still maintained enough of its integrity to work.

"Here, let me help. Turn around." David twirled a finger and I gave up my efforts.

"I just hope we don't need scissors." Even as I said it, my gaze wandered around the room in search of a pair.

David delicately lifted my hair and placed it over my

shoulder. "Stars, I'm sorry, little fox. Does it hurt?" A pressure no more than a feather touched my back and I hissed. I'd completely forgotten about the scratches I'd accumulated.

"No," I lied. I wouldn't trade our dalliance for anything. An even softer touch of lips brushed the sensitive skin. I sighed as the moisture from his breath drifted over me like a caress.

"I think we have some antibiotic ointment around here somewhere. These look superficial, but that will help." With that same delicate touch, he pulled the zipper down.

"Mmhmm," I hummed as his warm hands glided down my sides to free me from the shredded fabric. What was left of my undergarments followed in its wake and I shivered beneath his exploratory caresses. Rough fingers slid up my legs, over my thighs and stomach to cup my breasts. He placed a sweet kiss on the side of my neck as he rolled my nipples between his fingers briefly, then returned to his roving appreciation.

I was so absorbed with the feel of his touch that I cried out when he pulled my hips back into him and buried himself deep once more. A needy moan fell out of me as I caught myself on the wall to keep my body from folding in half. David's primal growl as he drove in and out set me alight and I tightened around him. He groaned and pressed kisses into my back that stayed feather soft with no more pressure than a breeze. Fingers dug into my sides, adding to the bruising from earlier. I didn't care. I pushed back harder until we climaxed in tandem.

My entire body shook from our passionate lovemaking and I sagged against the wall. We stayed like that a moment, catching our breath, then David tugged lightly on my hips and guided me over to the bed. He stretched out beneath me, gently maneuvering me until I straddled his hips. "My beautiful fox," he said with a reverence no one had ever directed at me before as he held me up and I let out a quivering sigh. "Take what you want. I won't interrupt this time."

"I...David I can't."

"Yes, you can." To help me do just that, his hands slid down to angle my hips to take him again. My sensitivity defied logic. I gasped as he finished setting me right. "Charline," he whispered like a prayer and proceeded to glide his hands across my skin in a fluid motion from my thighs to cup my breasts.

I looked down at him and placed my palms on his chest, then ever so slowly I rocked. His eyes lidded, yet he never looked away, never stopped watching me. Gradually I picked up my pace, adjusting my angle until every roll of my hips stroked just right. My breath stuttered as I rocked harder. David's groan vibrated through my core and he abandoned my sides to twist his hands in the sheets. Pained need played across his face, but he still didn't intervene.

My release danced just out of reach and I let out a small, desperate cry of frustration. "David," I moaned, digging my fingers into his chest.

His hips flexed up once and I shattered around him. He thrust up again and grunted through his own release.

I collapsed onto his chest too exhausted to even shake, his ragged breathing loud in my ears. We didn't say anything, just lay there wrapped in each other. Eventually, he pulled out a blanket to cover us and that's how I drifted off, snuggled deep in his embrace.

When I woke up, the dark auburns of twilight glinted through the window and David was gone. My usual disgruntlement at sleeping away the afternoon could scarcely be found as I stretched my exhausted and exceptionally satisfied body. I gave myself a good shake and didn't bother schooling my cat-got-the-cream grin as I cleaned up and donned fresh clothes.

Halfway down the grand staircase, my self-consciousness reasserted itself. What would the others think of me storming off like that and then reappearing hours later? I frowned to myself and walked faster. My good first impression so far was not off to a great start.

At the bottom of the steps, I looked around for any sign of where everyone had gone. A quick glance out the front window revealed the lawn in its usual empty state and a perusal of the front rooms proved no more illuminating. The more I looked, the more concerned I became.

Surely David wouldn't have left the House without letting me know, not with new people having just arrived.

After scouring practically the entire downstairs I discovered the missing people sitting around on the back patio. As I walked up, I caught snippets of their conversation.

"I don't know how you do it, Keith. I couldn't move from town to town like that," Isabel said, pulling her wavy brown hair out of her face.

"We can't all be homebodies," Matt supplied in Keith's defense.

Marc leaned forward. "It's no different really than what David does."

"Yeah, but we all know David is the ultimate homebody," Victoria's voice joined the mix.

Rather than give into my unfounded insecurities again, I squared my shoulders and marched straight into the wolf den. Victoria lay draped over the back of David's chair like some sort of oversized house cat. Consequently, this also meant she was draped over a good portion of David. He was looking up at her, laughing while she rubbed his arms.

"Hey, Charline." Lucas waved in greeting. David transferred his smile to me, but Victoria's fell into a glower. Her eyes narrowed when he bounded to his feet and raced over.

He placed a gentle kiss on my lips that I turned far less innocent. "Well, good evening to you too," he whispered. Whispered or not, the others clearly heard, as sly smiles sprung up around the gathering.

My cheeks burned as my own words of advice in the woods drifted back to me. Curse werewolf hearing.

He squeezed my hand and said louder, "I'm glad you're awake. I didn't want you to miss dinner." He led me to the oversized picnic table easily large enough to seat twenty, equipped with several benches.

We all clustered at one end as Randy and Maria brought out trays of food. I got up to help with drinks out of habit and when I resumed my seat David had already served me a plate. I put down his drink, silently thanking him with a smile.

"Are you sure that's enough food for her?" Victoria's words vaporized my good mood.

David's brows pinched together. "Charline's not a *were*, Vicky. She doesn't actually eat that much."

"Oh. My mistake." The look she gave me said that the comment had nothing to do with a *were* appetite. My cheeks burned at the double-edged insult and I sank as deep as my wooden seat would allow.

David continued on, completely oblivious. "Wait until you see, my little fox is an amazing cook." My appreciation at the proud comment died an agonizing death at Victoria's response.

"Is that so? I guess she samples her own creations."

Carl choked on something, and bless David, he just kept going. "Who wouldn't? You haven't lived until you've had her homemade whipped cream." Some of the guys snickered.

"What?" he asked, then immediately frowned. "Y'all are so immature." He threw a roll at the other side of the table which Keith caught with ease while I tried to spontaneously die.

"What's so funny?" Maria asked, finally joining the rest of us.

"Nothing, Maria," they chorused, sobering up.

She scowled at the group. "I hope y'all aren't being inappropriate at my dinner table."

"No ma'am."

"When did you get back from school, Xander?" Victoria asked as she stabbed a small potato. I blinked in surprise at the question and glanced over at David. How had she known about that when David hadn't even heard?

Xander took a seat near his mother. "A couple weeks ago. Actually right before David and Charline arrived."

"You've been at the house that long?" Victoria asked David, pointedly not including me in the inquiry.

"After I finished the Mason Project, there really wasn't much reason not to and once I convinced this lady to join me," he bumped my shoulder for emphasis, "all that was left to do was pack up the truck and head over."

Marc nodded. "Will you continue your job with the firm after the summer?"

"I guess it really depends on how things shake out. The rest of the year is going to have a lot going on. Not sure if running off to different jobs will really be doable." The diplomatic answer did literally nothing to assuage my own curiosity.

"Oh quit dancing around it," Xander snapped, instantly snatching everyone's focus. "We all know Dad is stepping down."

Maria spared him a look of motherly concern, but didn't reach out.

"No matter who comes out on top, things will change," Xander said, making a point to look at everyone. "The only way we get through these next few months is to keep in mind that we're still a pack, still a family." He reached out to take his mother's hand. The look in her eyes spoke of more than just a mother's pride and I could see why David believed Xander was up to the task.

9

CAREER FAIR

Bold swaths of gold cut across the room and I hummed in contentment, not giving two figs that I'd slept late. My body still felt like it was mid ecstasy, with delicious tingles dancing along my skin and stirring a hunger deep inside me not even remotely decent for a proper Southern Belle like myself. The magic of memory intensified until I gasped and my eyes flew open.

"Good morning, sleepyhead." David's deep timbre worked its own special kind of magic and I moaned as my body arched into his embrace. He stopped kissing along my collarbone to capture my mouth while his fingers curled inside and sought out more toe-curling pleasure. Stars exploded behind my eyes that rivaled the morning light in brilliance and I let out a silent scream that stole all the air from my lungs as I tightened around him.

My breath came in stuttering gasps as I sank bonelessly back into the sheets. "Jesus, David. That's one hell of a wake up."

His fingers slipped free to rove in gentle caresses around my thighs. He placed a sedate kiss on the side of my neck.

"Moans are wonderful, but I think that silent scream just shot to the top of my favorite things."

Rather than play into his teasing, I tangled my fingers in his hair and pulled him close to press my shaking body against him. His hand drifted around to grab my hip and pulled me even tighter so I could feel how much he wanted me too. I moaned into his mouth and shifted beneath him. To my disappointment, he did *not* take the invitation to keep going. Instead, he released me altogether.

"We'll have to pick this up later," he said with a sad smile. My bottom lip jutted out and I tightened my hold on his hair. His eyes sparkled with humor as he kissed my pout and continued stroking my side. "I can hear more people arriving."

The weight of my disappointed sigh did little to persuade him. At last, I admitted defeat and released him. He chuckled as he stood and started gathering the necessary articles of clothing for decent society. I bit my lip while I appreciated all the glorious nakedness before me. Catching my appraisal, he very intentionally wiggled his bare ass into his jeans.

"Tease," I admonished.

"You're welcome," he said, leaning down to kiss me where I still lay tangled in the sheets, pajamas askew. For a shining moment, it seemed like he might tumble back into bed with me, but he straightened up and looked toward the door.

I was about to call him a tease again when he reached down and pulled the sheets back to blast me with cold air. I yelped and made a grab for the dissipating warmth.

"You too, lazybones," he said, being sure to keep the covers out of reach. I gave him my best scowl which had convinced even the meanest of church ladies to step off, but

David simply turned around to continue getting dressed. With an indignant huff, I followed suit.

"Who do you think is here?" I asked, plucking out a pink dress with pockets.

He sat on the bed and cocked his head to the side as if listening. I giggled at the sight and earned myself a roguish grin that did little to quell my still dancing hormones. "Sounds like just a couple of people, though I wouldn't be surprised if more arrive later in the day."

"That'll be nice." I slid on some sandals and turned to face inspection. "Well?" I prompted, with a flourish that encompassed the outfit. The beauty of dresses: roll out of bed and toss one on, maximum effect with zero effort.

David flowed off of the bed so gracefully it hurt and wrapped his arms around my waist, careful not to mess the fabric I'd just laid flat. Looking into his crystal blue eyes felt like falling through the sky. He leaned down to kiss me and I went from falling to drowning.

"You look good enough to eat, as always." He released me and opened the door, gesturing for me to lead the way.

"You really are a horrible tease," I said, walking past him. We ventured down the stairs, but no one could be found in the foyer. I glanced over at him, more than a little perplexed. "I thought you said more people had arrived?"

"Sounds like they've moved to the sun room."

I shook my head. "You know, I'm beginning to think this place isn't as insulated as I was led to believe."

"Who told you it was?"

"Maria."

David choked on air and coughed to clear his throat. "I'm not even going to ask when she told you that. I don't want to know."

My face scrunched in confusion as I tried to figure out what he meant. After all, he'd been the one to point out the silent scream. The only time I'd really made any noise was after we'd returned from the woods. My face flared with heat that could fry an egg.

"David Bringer." I smacked him as hard as I could, which admittedly didn't hold a candle to werewolf strength.

"Ow." He laughed, not in the least bit phased.

"Does she always beat you?"

The suspiciously monotone question cut through our playful moment. We looked up together and my happy smile faltered at finding Victoria in our path, thin arms crossed across her flat torso, looking about as friendly as a wet hornet.

"Good morning, David," she crooned, blatantly ignoring me.

"Yes, it is." He waggled his eyebrows at me and I smacked him again for good measure, momentarily forgetting our audience. "Alright, alright. Hey, I see Alexander. I want to check in with him about the clearing and a few other things. I'll meet you there." He kissed me on the cheek and disappeared down the hall that led to the study, leaving me alone with his childhood friend who seemed resolved not to like me.

Determined to right this teetering ship, I smiled brightly. "Lovely morning, isn't it?"

She shrugged her lean shoulders and continued to openly stare at me, taking in the dress with its frills and embroidery. "Are you always this abusive or do you save it for special occasions?"

My mouth fell open and I had to consciously snap it shut. Surely she could recognize that we were just fooling around. Right? David was a werewolf, for Christ's sake. I'd have to hit him with a truck to even make a dent. She raised an eyebrow at my clear shock.

When I still failed to respond, she answered for me. "I

suppose it makes you feel like you're on more even footing among those so much...more than yourself," she said, dead serious.

What the actual hell?

Maybe she didn't mean it the way it sounded.

Her lip curled as her gaze proceeded to pick me apart from head to toe. "A little high maintenance, don't you think?"

Or maybe she did. Before I could tell her and her unwanted opinion to shove it where the sun don't shine, Victoria spun on her heel and walked towards the back of the house. To my utter dismay, she walked into the same sun room where I was meant to join David.

I followed with faltering steps. What in the world could I have done to make the woman dislike me so much? David would have mentioned if they'd had a thing, I was sure of it. Maybe it had been unrequited. Maria had said David had never brought anyone home...

"Charline..."

I blinked to find Xander standing in front of me and finally registered the warm glow filling the sun room and the small crowd of people gathered there. "What?" I asked, out of sorts.

"Welcome back to Earth," he said with a cheeky grin that made him look even younger. "Like I was saying, this is Marissa and her daughter Rosie. They live a couple towns over. And that's Joseph. His girlfriend Lisette is on assignment in New York so she won't be here for a few more weeks."

Joseph waved from his position on the back of a wicker chair, while Marissa tried to coax a little girl with a golden halo of hair to say hi. The moment in the hall fled my mind. It had never occurred to me that kids would be here. Which, now that I thought about it, was a little daft.

Without a second thought, I knelt down to be on the child's level. My skirt flared out and drifted back down in a cloud of pink to settle around me. Rosie's eyes widened to the size of saucers as she looked at me, her tiny thumb still in her mouth. "Aren't you precious? Hi Rosie, my name is Charline. It's nice to meet you."

She briefly took her thumb out and said, "You look like a princess," before popping it back in her mouth. She made a face at the adults' good-natured laughter and hid in her mother's skirts.

"Sorry, she's really shy. Though I can honestly say that was a first." Marissa looked down at the mass of curly blonde in wonder.

I stood back up, straightening my skirt. "That's alright. There are a lot of people here and I'm a stranger. She's pretty as a peach though." Rosie's golden ringlets bounced as she stole another look at me. I gave her a wink and she buried her face again.

I glanced behind me where Victoria was leaning against the door. With her black pants and navy crop top, she looked more like a punk reject than a princess. *See, some people appreciate a little maintenance and pretty things.* She affected an air of nonchalant boredom and resumed looking out the large glass window.

"Are y'all from around here?" I asked, making my way deeper into the room toward a stand laden with lemonade. I grabbed one and made myself comfortable.

Joseph answered first. "Mostly. Majority of us grew up either in the House or were here practically every summer." He smiled, as did most of the others. I couldn't even begin to imagine what that must've been like. I was close with my extended family, but not *that* close. "Lisette and I travel a bunch though. She's a vacation journalist for Travel, so we go where they send her. I just edit the articles."

"That sounds like fun," I said, taking a sip.

"Actually, it's not much different than what Vicky does. You're a photojournalist right?" Joseph asked.

She pushed herself off of the wall and sauntered over to sit on a vacant arm of the couch. "Yep, but I specialize in wildlife."

"I just have a boring desk job." Marc glowered into his almost empty glass.

"What about you, Charline? What do you do?" Marissa asked, now cradling the tiny Rosie against her chest.

"Oh. I confess, I'm with Marc in the boring desk job category. I work in HR at the same firm that Sara and Michael do."

I anticipated questions about the two of them. I did *not* expect the snide comment from Victoria.

"So, you basically get paid to sit around and gossip all day. Must be sweet. I wish my job could be so relaxed. Between deadlines and grizzlies, I can hardly catch a break." She sipped from her newly acquired glass and leaned back.

I shrugged, refusing to let her goad me into making a fool of myself in front of all these people. "It's nice to know I'm at least good at something. I don't suppose you brought any of your work with you? I think a candid shot of a grizzly would be fascinating," I said with a smile sweet enough to melt sugar with shame. Of course, I'd love it even more if said grizzly was chasing her.

The guys leaned forward eagerly.

"Oh yeah!"

"That would be so cool."

"What about hawks? Got any of those?"

"I totally saw a bobcat the other day."

"Liar."

"I did too."

"There aren't any bobcats in North Carolina, doofus."

"Says who?"

My over-the-top grin relaxed in triumph. They'd completely lost track of the original conversation and I had no intention of putting them back on it. Victoria, however, glared daggers at me as I took a seat.

10

BOUNDARY LINES

I picked up a tray of lemonade and meandered my way to the front room. The door swung open with a well placed hip bump, revealing people strewn about the room like a bunch of house cats. Not that I would ever express that particular observation aloud. A few people offered me a friendly wave before resuming their conversations as I set down the tray. I took a glass for myself and assumed the same seat I had with David almost three weeks ago. It was hard to believe so much time had already passed and that I'd met so many werewolves, all of whom had been incredibly welcoming.

All except one.

I immediately flipped my frown upside down.

I'll win her over eventually.

Confident in my eventual success, I smiled and lifted my lemonade. I'd scarcely taken a sip when the adorable Rosie boldly walked over. I wasn't sure if it was my dresses, my smiles, or what, but the dear had taken a shine to me.

"What's so funny?" she asked as she stopped in front of me. Little thing had to be the most precious creature I'd ever beheld.

I passed her a child-sized lemonade and encouraged her

to join me on the love seat. "Nothing sweetie, I just love lemonade. Don't you?"

She eyed the glass skeptically before taking a sip. Her eyes lit up with wonder like she'd never had it before, which I seriously doubted, and she promptly gulped down half of it.

"That's tasty, Miss Foxy," she said with all the gusto her tiny body could muster. I shook my head and chuckled at the unfortunate side effect of small children parroting what they hear.

"Where's your mom, sugar?" While it wasn't uncommon for the children to be found wandering sans parents—there were plenty of watchful eyes around— Rosie was still young enough for me to expect her mom not to be too far.

She wrinkled her nose. "Mama's in the field with Oscar."

I laughed to myself at Rosie's obvious distaste at her brother getting to do something she couldn't. The "field" as she put it was reserved for the children closer to their first change, a safe place they could play and learn control of their evolving forms. I ruffled Rosie's hair and she giggled before taking another sip.

"That sounds nice. What's wrong with that?"

"Oscar's a butt and he gets to do everything." Her bottom lip stuck all the way out in the most heartbreaking pout.

"You sound jealous."

She made a sour face like she'd taken a particularly tart sip. "Mama says I'm still too little to play with the others." Bless her heart. Even at a surprising five years old, Rosie was on the petite side, and I could see Marissa's concern about letting her play with the older children.

"Well, I for one am glad you're not in the field."

She looked up, her sorrow momentarily eclipsed by curiosity. "Why?"

"Because then you wouldn't be here with me," I said, tickling her.

A riot of giggles erupted out of her and she nearly spilled her drink all over her smart frock. I quickly snagged the wayward cup before we could have an accident. No sooner did I set it down, though, then she was off to chase a fellow youngster. She'd just careened around the corner, her cheeks flush with sugar and glee, when a new person entered the room. My smile faltered, but I fought to shore up my flagging confidence.

Victoria's gaze roved the small gathering, her eyes narrowing when they landed on me. She sauntered across the room in my direction and I let out a relieved sigh when she didn't take Rosie's now vacant spot. I wracked my brain six ways to Sunday for something to say that could endear her to me, but came up empty. I debated going after Rosie as an excuse to leave.

Victoria must have caught my lingering gaze, because she asked, "Looking to snatch a little one of your own?"

"I love kids and Rosie is a sweetheart." I smiled and gazed after her wistfully. "I'm glad to see she's warming up to me."

"Just be careful not to get too close. I'd hate for her to be heartbroken when you leave."

Before I could ask what *that* was supposed to mean, Marissa ran into the room, her eyes wide and face flush with panic, David hot on her heels.

"Has anyone seen Xander?" David asked.

Rosie chose that moment to return and her mama swept her up, clutching the tiny girl to her breast like she might vanish at any moment. Rather than soothe the child, the motion only served to upset her and the poor thing immediately burst into tears.

"I think he's in one of the studies. Here, I'll take you."

Victoria stood up and stalked with determined purpose out of the room.

I frowned after them and moved to follow without thinking. David didn't need anyone to lead him to the only study I'd ever seen Alexander occupy, which was undoubtedly where Xander was. So why in tarnation would Victoria appoint herself as a guide?

Inches away from my destination, the door to the study slammed shut. I jumped back before it could smack me. Rather than stand around like a nosy goose, I wandered down the hall in search of a different way to discover the source of the commotion. When I conveniently spotted two of the latest additions to the House, it seemed my quest would be accomplished in no time.

"Hey, Agnes, Camille." I looked at each of them, surprised when neither acknowledged my greeting. "Um, I don't suppose you've heard what's going on? David dashed off before I got a chance to ask."

Camille flicked a glance in my direction while Agnes's gaze remained fixed on her phone. "Nothing for you to worry about."

Camille bumped her companion. "We should get going. Leroy is expecting us in town." Agnes nodded and offered me an absent wave before walking toward the front of the House.

"Okay..." I said to absolutely no one, since they'd walked off without so much as a see you around. "Maybe someone else will have the time to talk to me." As it turned out, they did not.

After a solid two hours of being politely ignored, I opted to wait for David in his room. He surely would fill me in. My fingers had just settled on the stair railing when the distinct sound of gossip reached my ears. After a quick glance around, I slowly backpedaled toward the half-closed door of the parlor.

"Can you believe it?"

"The nerve."

"I hope Alexander does something about this."

"The little ones must have been terrified out of their minds."

"What happened?"

"Haven't you heard?"

"Humans from town were in the Eastern field. A whole crew of them."

I immediately clapped a hand over my mouth to stifle a gasp. If anyone of the youngins had been practicing their control, the whole pack could be in danger.

"They know that's trespassing, right?"

"Way I hear it, they think they had a right to be there."

"No..."

I strained to hear more, but the sound of approaching footsteps obscured the rest of the response. Thwarted in my eavesdropping, I straightened and resumed my trek up the stairs.

An agonizing twenty minutes later, the door swung open on silent hinges and David ghosted into the room. His shoulders hung heavily and shadows darkened a face beyond weary. He trudged over to the bed and sat on the edge.

I chewed my lip and continued organizing the closet to give him the space he clearly needed and keep my hands busy. Finally, I couldn't take it anymore. I joined him on the bed and wrapped my arm around his shoulders.

"David, what's the matter?"

His gaze flicked up to me, hesitation written in every line of his troubled features. Then he let out a giant sigh and seemed to deflate before my very eyes. "There are issues with the town council in Stone Creek."

"Okay. Why does that sound like there's more to it? Surely the pack is on good terms with the village, considering how long y'all have been neighbors."

His mouth twisted much like Rosie's had earlier. "Apparently, there's a boundary dispute."

"Oh." Over a century after settling the region struck me as a strange time to start arguing about fences.

"Ultimately, all of this land is pack territory, but of course they don't see it that way. They're bringing up some old agreement with the original settlers and owners of the House. The way *they* tell it, the Southeast woods are considered common ground and they're pushing to develop it."

"That doesn't sound so bad."

"That's where the young ones play."

"Okay, maybe not so great. That explains Marissa's reaction earlier."

He nodded and fisted his hands on his knees. "The whole thing is ridiculous. If it was just wolves infighting the solution would be simple. But humans require so much—diplomacy," he spat as if the word had an unpleasant taste. "Both Alexander and Xander are determined to find a peaceful solution and I'm trying to help, but the council isn't backing down. All this talking is getting us nowhere."

"Talking not really your strong suit, eh?" I nudged him playfully, to take the sting out of it. David had many admirable qualities, but diplomatic acumen was not among them.

"You know I'm terrible with words." He leaned on me and I squeezed his shoulders. "Besides, it's typically the Alphas that are the diplomatic ones. Betas are..."

"The muscle?"

"Well, yeah."

I snuggled a little closer. "Speaking of Betas. Where's Alexander's? Johnathan, right?"

David tensed. "No one's seen him since Alexander announced his intent to retire."

Well, fiddlesticks. I'd gone and made David more anxious. I pressed a kiss to the side of his head and stroked his arm.

"Why do they think the property is theirs to develop?"

"They say they have documents proving their right to the land." Defeat coated his words and he leaned more heavily against me.

I recalled the ancient tomes I'd seen in Alexander's study. "If that's true, surely the pack would have a copy of that agreement."

"You'd think, but Alexander has been scouring the histories for weeks and nothing."

So the boundary dispute *wasn't* a new issue as of today. "What about their copy? Has anyone reviewed that one? It may not even be legitimate under today's laws."

"They say they have it, but no one seems able or willing to produce it."

"They can't really expect Alexander to honor something they refuse to share."

David shook his head. "They're threatening to take it straight to lawyers and Alexander wants to avoid that at all costs."

I scoffed. "Sounds like a bully tactic to me."

"Definitely, but the risk of exposure is too great to ignore. Xander is already looking into the real estate laws, but so far what they're quoting seems like it would hold. If we can't find the pack copy or get ahold of theirs, I fear..." He trailed off . We both knew the rest. Alexander would do what he had to in order to protect the pack. If that meant ceding land to stubborn developers to avoid the law getting involved, he would do it in a heartbeat.

I'd sensed enough of the tension in the House to know how well *that* would be received. Alexander caving to the village would likely start a mutiny. The odds of him being forcibly retired instead of stepping down like he'd intended would grow with each day this went unresolved. If Xander backed his father's play, he'd likely lose any support he'd gained, thus destroying any chance he had of stepping into his father's role. I didn't want to imagine how all of that would affect David's goals.

"David, why did you want to be Beta in the first place?"

"Xander asked me."

"Why do you think he asked?" I pushed.

"I hadn't really thought about it." He shrugged. "I just assumed he wanted me for the typical reasons. Don't get me wrong, I love the kid to pieces, but as far as Alphas go, he's a little on the scrawny side. The traditional Beta role is to be the enforcer, or even the champion when needed. Betas uphold pack law."

"Does Xander strike you as the kind of *were* who plans on needing an enforcer?"

David shifted. "Well, no."

"Then why do you think he asked you?" Understanding brightened his eyes and I nudged him. "He wants you because you're a good leader. You're honest, sincere, kind—people trust that. Have a little more faith in yourself. "

He looked at me out of the corner of his eye. "You really are wonderful. You know that?"

I waved away the compliment. "It's just putting the pieces together. Sometimes you have to take a step back and remind yourself what puzzle you're trying to solve."

He caught the hand I'd been waving about while his other rose up to cup my face. My cheeks gradually heated as he continued to stare at me with open appraisal. After several moments, he placed the tenderest kiss on my lips. My heart skipped and my breath vanished as he gave me another that was the barest brush of his lips against mine.

"Thank you," he whispered, staring into my soul with those crystal blue eyes.

At a complete loss for words, I blinked back at him. I needed something to diffuse the tightening in my torso where my heart stubbornly refused to remember how to beat. A silly quip, a more aggressive kiss, *something*.

Ask and you shall receive. Right on cue, *something* banged out in the hall, most likely someone running into a wall or maybe a frame. We both turned toward the door.

David let out a sigh and dropped my hand. "Back into the trenches. Not that I don't love seeing everyone, but there are way too many people in the House." He stood and gave himself a good shake as if tossing off the funk from earlier, and glanced down at me. "I'll see you later?"

"Uh-huh," I replied, still in a daze.

He smiled and marched through the door with renewed purpose. I reached up to tentatively touch my lips where a sense of more seemed to tingle on them. Another loud noise filled the hall, shortly followed by a firm reprimand from David. Then the feeling was gone, no more than the memory of a dream.

The story of townsfolk being found on pack property spread like wildfire and grew more outlandish by the telling. The latest exaggeration had a surveyor smacking one of the kids with the equipment. Needless to say, the tall tales were only increasing tensions between the people of Stone Creek and the House. Meanwhile, summer itself promised to be sweltering and the humidity climbed daily as if trying to keep pace with the thermostat.

I braced myself for the scalding ninety degrees that awaited beyond the cool embrace of the air conditioning and ventured out back laden with a bowl of freshly cut apples. Many of the pack, including David, had been hard at work getting the clearing expanded to Maria's specifications. Personally, I believed watermelon to be a superior reward for hard labor, but the apples were more plentiful.

The sun hovered in a cloudless sky and I squinted against the brightness. When my vision finally adjusted, I found a whole lot of exposed skin that put my airy sundress to shame. At first, I thought someone had set up a sprinkler or popped up a pool for the kids, then I realized no one was wet. A group of *weres* walked past without noticing me and I realized they also weren't wearing swimsuits. I stood frozen taking in the sight of over a couple dozen werewolves wandering around the lawn practically nude.

"Yes! Maria put ice in the apples."

"What?" I turned to look at who was talking and was greeted by Kaleb in skimpy boxers that left nothing to the imagination. My cheeks burned as he promptly relieved me of the bowl and triumphantly marched it over to a group equally lacking attire.

"You seem shocked."

I startled at the unexpected woman's statement. The owner giggled at my obvious discomposure.

"I take it David didn't warn you that *weres* aren't exactly bashful?"

I swallowed. Sara had made a comment before, but I'd no idea what she meant until now. A look around confirmed my fears. I spied David across the way by Daniel and Keith. He waved me over, causing the muscles in his chest to shine in the light.

Oh no, not you too.

It wasn't until the person who'd addressed me stepped forward to go towards David that I realized it was Victoria. My stomach swooped unpleasantly as she stepped in front of me, wearing the shortest shorts I'd ever seen in my life and a sports bra, if it could even be called that. It was the first time I'd seen her without her trademark skin-hugging pants. Her pale skin positively glowed in the sunlight.

"Aren't you hot?" she asked as she pulled her dark hair back, exposing a narrow neck and even more porcelain skin. "Good grief, I'm itchy just looking at you. Maybe you're just too..." she looked me over, "shy to join the rest of us. But then again, if I had that much to fill out a dress, I wouldn't want to strip down either."

She didn't give me a chance to come up with a witty retort. After catching my eye to make sure I was watching, she bounded across the yard and jumped on David's back. I couldn't hear what he said to her, but the group laughed and he tossed her off. She sailed through the air, landing with ease and looked back at me as if daring me to do something. Flames danced across my vision as pure unadulterated rage pumped through my veins.

That bitch.

It took every ounce of my etiquette training to shove down the seething anger and plaster a smile on my face. I took my time joining them, making sure to add a little extra sway with each step. David's gaze lingered on my curves and a heat that had nothing to do with the temperature burned in his eyes. When I arrived, he casually slid an arm around me and I had to bite my tongue before I could stick it out at Victoria. I didn't know what game she thought she was play-ing, but she was going to lose.

"Hey Daniel. Keith," I said with a more sincere smile. They each raised a hand in greeting. "I had apples, but

Kaleb commandeered them." I hiked my thumb to show where he and another group were now throwing ice cubes at each other.

Keith nudged Daniel. "Come on, let's get him." The two brothers instantly left to pursue the prized bowl of chilled fruit, leaving David, Victoria and me standing there awkwardly. I was running through options for small talk when Keith shouted, "Vicky! Give us a hand. He's a slimy bastard!" She spared me a scathing glance before racing off to answer the summons.

David's rich laugh rolled out of his broad chest, so unlike the rest of his packmates as he took in the spectacle of Kaleb trying to defend his stolen goods. "They'll lose all of the slices before they get that bowl."

I put a hand on his arm and took a moment to appreciate how much smaller and more fragile it was compared to him.

He looked down at me, still smiling. "What's up, little fox?"

A part of me wanted to demand he put on a fucking shirt, but as mama always said, pick your battles. "David, what was that about?"

His brow furrowed. "What was what about?"

My tempered anger flared hot a second before I could get it back under control. "She jumped on you."

"Oh, that?" He laughed and I almost lost my composure. "That was nothing. A childhood game. I wasn't always this big, you know. It was cute of her to try though."

"It didn't seem cute to me," I snapped. Not my most diplomatic effort, but I was still shaken at coming outside to see a yard full of half-naked werewolves, one of whom was my boyfriend.

"Come on, Char, it's just kid stuff. Nothing there." He released his hold on me and crossed his arms over his chest, accentuating his exposed physique as he turned his attention back to the chaos of frivolity. The dismissive reply only got my ire up more.

Over by Kaleb, the fruit was indeed everywhere, though that didn't seem to discourage anyone. David chuckled as Marc made a dive for Daniel who was running with the now empty bowl. He missed by a mile, but Daniel's victory was short lived as Camille launched from all fours to tackle him. Mercy swiped the bowl and held it up victoriously only to be tackled herself by Keith. One of the children walked over and picked up the forgotten container as the other two continued to wrestle.

If David's reaction was any guide, this was a typical day in the life of the pack and I...wasn't pack. The weight of that realization doused my anger with a heavy dose of depression. No matter what I did, that would never change. I could help plan every Solstice from now until the end of time. I could make the most decadent meal ever eaten. None of it would make a difference.

No longer in the mood to be social, I turned to go seek something inside that would make me feel less like an outsider. Before I could make it three steps, David snagged me and swung me around. I let out a small squeal of surprise as I went airborne. I reflexively wrapped my arms and legs around him for fear of falling despite the impropriety of it. The moment I realized I was safe, I squirmed to be set down and restore decorum. Then I caught sight of Victoria watching us and squeezed tighter instead.

David's large hands palmed my ass as he gave me a brazen kiss that would have made my mother *and* my grandmother faint. I couldn't help but giggle at the mental image of all the dutifully proper women of my family keeling over all at once.

"There's that smile."

I looked up at him. How could this man be so damn impossible? I'd never met anyone so capable of pulling me out of a funk as fast as David could. My grin stretched from ear to ear as I tightened my arms around his neck. "Thank you," I whispered.

"For what?"

"Nothing," I said, letting him go.

He set me down and laughed with me as we straightened my dress, then we rejoined the others in the hope of snagging the fresh batch of fruit.

11

PROVOCATIVE WHISPERS

As more people arrived, the feeling of being pushed aside increased. What contributions I *had* been making toward the Solstice party planning were slowly being delegated to others, regardless of if I wanted them to be or not. At first it made sense—these people had way more experience organizing this particular event—but when I learned that meal-prep had also been taken off my plate so to speak, I despaired.

Tempting as it was to whine to David about my lack of occupation, one, he had his own troubles to deal with and two, I wasn't that sort of woman. I'd faced equal if not greater odds when I'd moved away from home and started my life in Raleigh. As Mama would say, it was time to put on my big girl panties and show these people I was not a woman to be left on the back burner.

Invigorated by my micro pep-talk, I walked into the front room, bearing a couple glasses to share with the handful of people I'd befriended. My day immediately brightened when David stepped through the other entrance from the main foyer. His intense gaze wandered the room until it settled on me.

He stepped closer with a smile on his lips, but the heaviness in his shoulders stayed. "Hey, little fox."

"Hey yourself, stranger," I replied with a wink. I set the glasses down and wiped my hands on my skirt. "Missed you this morning."

He winced and tucked a loose curl behind my ear. "I know. I'm sorry. Things have been…"

I placed a gentle hand on his arm. "I was only teasing. There's a lot going on right now. You warned me the summer wouldn't be all play. I'm a big girl." His shoulders relaxed a fraction and I wanted nothing more than to scoop this big bear of a man into my arms and squeeze until the rest of him relaxed.

"What are you up to today?" he asked, trailing a finger along my cheek. My silly heart skipped and I wondered if it would ever stop doing that when he touched me.

"Nothing much. Relax, maybe read a book, see if I can make myself useful with dinner."

"Maybe you should make a run to town," he suggested as he stuffed his hands into his jeans. Behind him, the people I'd come to spend time with started filing out.

"I…uh…I suppose I could. But I don't really need anything," I finally said, dragging my gaze away from everyone leaving.

"I think it would be a good idea. Get you out of this place for a while."

I narrowed my eyes. "You're being oddly persistent." All the tension that had lifted from him returned two-fold. "What? What is it?" I asked, my skepticism lost in my concern.

"Alexander's called a meeting."

"Okay…"

"Now," he deadpanned.

I glanced back at the now empty room, reevaluating the

silent way everyone had left, and looked back at David at a loss for what to say. "Oh." I fought valiantly to school my hurt and disappointment, but clearly failed miserably.

"Please don't look at me like that." His shoulders tightened as he fisted his hands in his pockets. "It's a pack meeting."

I shook my head. "You could just tell me that instead of trying to manage me. I'm not a child."

"Of course you're not, I just didn't want you to get... upset," he finished, having the decency to look abashed.

I raised an eyebrow. "If I'm upset, it's because you assumed that I wouldn't understand and you believed you needed to convince me to make myself scarce. Have a little faith, David. I'm fully aware there are aspects of pack life I can't participate in."

He winced. "I'm sorry, you're right. Truth be told, most of the time I forget that you're not actually part of the pack."

As much as that sentiment warmed my heart, not to mention what sounded an awful lot like an unsaid *yet*, he'd said the meeting was now. "Right, let's have 'em." I held out my hand for the truck keys. His face relaxed into a relieved smile and he graced my cheek with a kiss as he dropped the keys into my waiting hand.

"I'll fill you in later. Drive safe."

"You better." I winked then made my way out the front of the House.

I wasted some time adjusting the seat and mirrors, then drummed my fingers on the steering wheel as I tried to determine how exactly to occupy my time. Not finding inspiration on the lawn, I shifted the truck in gear and made my way to Stone Creek. Thankfully there was really only one way into town, so I wasn't in any danger of getting lost, though I did almost miss the turn off. Tucked in the hills was really just a nice way of saying in the middle of nowhere.

I pulled up to the local grocery. Despite my best efforts, my parking was abysmal. I doubted that trying again would make it better so I left it and went inside. A blast of air hit me, instantly transporting me to another world.

Fluorescents illuminated an intimate grocery that easily could have been plucked out of my hometown. Bins of fresh fruit and produce dominated the right side while short, precise rows filled the rest of the space. The sheer mundanity of people navigating the aisles and chatting in a neighborly way with each other put me off kilter in a way I hadn't anticipated. A sudden surge of homesickness rushed through me. I'd been so eager to get away from small town life, I'd left the first chance I had. Never in a million years did I think I'd actually *miss* the quaint homeyness of everyone knowing my business.

I blinked away the stinging in my eyes as I grabbed a buggy and guided it toward the nearest aisle. I started by adding a couple miscellaneous items because they struck my fancy. Like I'd told David, I didn't really *need* anything, but I also had no idea how long I needed to make myself scarce. I looked around, unsure what to do now that I was here.

Well, when in Rome, do as the Romans do. When in a grocery store, go grocery shopping.

I made my way down the aisles with renewed purpose. While the limited selection nixed some of my typical choices, the buggy gradually filled with items that would have graced my own pantry.

A sense of accomplishment filled my breast as the attendant helped me to load the last of the bags into the bed of the truck. Upon further examination of the full space, maybe I'd gone a little overboard. I glanced at the time, hoping that three hours would be sufficient.

"Anything else, ma'am?"

I extended a hand to the young man and smiled. "Charline Montgomery. Thank you so much for your help, Brian." Confusion flashed across his face before he realized his name was on his shirt.

"Not a problem, Mrs. Montgomery."

"Miss," I corrected as I passed him a tip. There really had been a lot of groceries; the poor place was going to need to be restocked.

"Oh no, I couldn't, Miss Montgomery."

I leveled a look at him. "Brian, you can either take it yourself *or* I can stick it in your shirt. But I don't think the lovely lady at the register would appreciate that too much."

He blinked wide-eyed at me like I'd goosed him then glanced back towards the store where you could clearly see the young woman in question very pointedly not looking at us.

"If you're not already going out, you should ask. I have a good feeling she'll say yes." I gave him a wink and ducked into the cab of the truck. He continued to stand there, waving me off with a lopsided grin as I carefully backed the truck up. Once clear, I shook my head as I shifted gears. If only the pack was as easy to read as a couple of teenagers.

Thankfully, my timing was spot on and a slew of helping hands materialized to take the bags inside when I pulled up. I grabbed the last couple myself, pocketing the keys, and strode inside. I couldn't help but glance curiously around, but there was no hint that some super-secret pack meeting had been held. Everything was the exact shade of normal I'd become accustomed to: kids ran around playing tag, people lolled about like giant house cats, and far as I could tell, everyone was still accounted for.

I dropped off the bags in the kitchen where the same helping hands made short work of them, then went in search of David. Unsurprisingly, that was easier said than done. I'd ruled out all of the front rooms and was making my way down the hall when voices caught my attention. I slowed and peeked into the nearest room only to quickly flatten myself against the wall when I discovered Victoria and a few other women I'd noticed were always near her.

"This isn't right. Why should we stay out of Stone Creek just because *they* have issues?" The voice sounded like it might be Ally.

"It's not fair." That was definitely Carrie, judging by the whine.

"The village is crawling with humans. Why would you want to be there in the first place?" Victoria asked, her voice filled with scorn.

"It's not that I *want* to be there," Carrie argued. "I just don't appreciate Alexander ordering the place off limits. What right does he have?"

"He's the Alpha," Ally replied.

"Not for long," Victoria said. I checked my gasped shock at the contempt. "Far as I'm concerned, the whole pack should avoid *all* humans. I still don't understand why David allows *her* to stay." The statement stabbed into my heart and brought a clarity I'd been actively avoiding.

"That's a bit harsh. I mean some of the other wolves have human partners as well. Why can't he?"

"Because it's disgusting, that's why," Victoria growled. "He can't expect to be Beta when that's the example he's setting. If the fringe want to fool around with humans, that's their business, but I wouldn't be surprised if a lot of that changes when Alexander steps down."

"But Xander supports his ideals," Ally argued. "There's no reason to expect that to change."

"Who says he'll be Alpha?"

The words dropped like a stone and silence followed. Someone bumped a chair in another room and the bang of it hitting a wall echoed. I held my breath and sent up a silent prayer that they'd keep talking. No such luck.

Victoria stalked out of the room, minions in tow. I gulped and pressed harder against the wall as her withering gaze settled on me, now fully aware of just how much she didn't like me.

"Listening at doors now?" She posed the question calmly enough, but rage burned in her eyes. Suddenly, I had a very good understanding of fight or flight instincts. I wanted nothing more than to run and find David, but scurrying off would be tantamount to admitting defeat.

I straightened up to my full height, a move that only made her eyes burn brighter, and squared my shoulders. "It's not eavesdropping if you're talking loud enough for *anyone* to hear," I said, then promptly turned on my heel and walked away as calmly as possible, a decided itch between my shoulders the whole way.

Once around the corner, I took a deep breath and chanced a glance back to make sure she hadn't followed me. Did David have any idea that she wasn't rooting for Xander? He'd been so staunch in his support it had never occurred to me that Xander might face serious opposition.

I meandered aimlessly toward the stairs as I picked my brain for any memory of someone mentioning who else might be on the docket. For the first time, I realized I actually had very little understanding of how the Alpha and Beta process worked.

"Good, you're finally back." My head snapped up from it's study of the carpet at the sound of David's voice. "I feel like I've been waiting up here forever. Come on." He grabbed my hand and pulled me into the nearest room.

David swung the door closed at the same time he wrapped me in an embrace.

"Da—"

He captured the exclamation with a kiss, one of his hands tangling in my hair. "I'm so sorry about my behavior earlier," he apologized between deeper and deeper kisses. "It was rude and stupid. Of course you get it. You're smart, and amazing, and thoughtful."

When I finally had enough room to breathe, I squeaked out, "This isn't our room."

"Yes, it is," he mumbled, still refusing to release me.

"No, it's not."

He spared a quick look around and growled. Before I could protest, he snagged my hand again, dragged me out of the room and a little further down the hall to his room. This time, the door hadn't even finished closing when my shoulders pressed into the wall and all of him pressed against me.

I arched into him and dug my fingers into his biceps. If I'd known this was waiting for me, I'd have returned sooner. Through the slim opening I saw people making their way down the hall. I fumbled for the door, finally closing it with a thud.

David's adamant kisses landed hot on my mouth and neck, diverting my focus and making my skin burn with need. He squeezed my waist and let his hands rove deliciously over my body while he continued to steal my breath. I gasped as he pushed my hair away to expose my shoulder and sucked out a bruise.

He palmed my ass and pressed me against the hard bulge in his jeans, then spun me around, moving my hair once more so he could get to my zipper. His teeth grazed against my shoulder and I clenched in response. He pulled my hips back against him and I let out a low moan, because yes that, *all* of that. He finished pushing the dress down and turned me back to face him.

"Remember your own advice, little fox," he whispered roughly in my ear. My thoughts flashed to the people in the hall and I whimpered. His mouth closed back over mine as he dragged my arms above me. I arched into him, having completely forgotten what was so important to tell him.

I jumped as the door shook with sudden banging. "David, you in there?" a young voice asked from the other side.

Nothing about the growl that vibrated through my chest sounded friendly. "Go away," David said, the words barely distinguishable from the sound.

"Alexander is asking for you," the young voice insisted. David's second growl held noticeably more frustration. "Hey, don't shoot the messenger. He's waiting in the study."

"I'll be down in a minute." The hand that gripped my thigh said he had every intention of making that minute count. Without thinking, I rubbed against him, seeking friction, and dragged another growl out of him.

"I'm kind of supposed to wait. So yeah..." The unfortunate messenger trailed off.

David blew out a stream of air through his nose that felt like steam against my already flush chest. "I'm gonna need a second."

"Right... I'll wait at the end of the hall."

I half expected David to steal a few more kisses. Instead he pushed himself away from the wall, releasing me. He gave my still shaking body a look filled with regret.

"This is just not my day." He ran his hands through his hair, then redid his pants, though I was flabbergasted as to when he'd undone them. "I'm sorry, Char. I guess I'll have to fill you in later," he said, cupping my face.

I leaned forward, hoping for at least one more kiss. To

my dismay, he placed it on my forehead. When the door opened for him to slip out, I caught sight of said messenger looking very much like he wished someone else had been sent to retrieve David. They made their way to the stairs and I pressed my forehead against the cool wood of the door as I closed it. It wasn't looking like my day was any better.

Now that it was no longer held down by the crush of desire, what I needed to tell David floated back to the surface. "Well, shit."

I snagged my robe from the desk chair and took a seat. After a few indecisive moments, I opted to call Sara to fill her in on the unnerving pieces I'd started to accumulate. When she didn't answer, I shot off a text and slumped in the chair.

Restless energy had my hands exploring every nook and cranny of the utilitarian desk. Most of the time I tried not to be too nosy, but left to my own devices in the room and unwilling to go back downstairs, I couldn't help myself. Except, there really wasn't much to nose about; David was an honest, open person who lived a simple life. The desk only held work items and the nightstand was virtually empty. The only other things to explore were the closet and chest of drawers.

After obsessively organizing the clothes, I turned to the shelf of pictures I'd yet to study. The small frames seemed to encompass years, from his childhood to some that were more recent. The first one was a picture of a woman who looked vaguely like him except with dark hair. If Maria was David's aunt, perhaps this was his mother.

Curiosity piqued, I scoured the display for images of others who looked related. I found another one of the woman, this time with a person who was obviously a younger Maria, confirming that theory. My gaze settled on one of David very young, maybe five or six, with another little boy. They looked almost identical except the smaller, pudgy one had David's eyes. A smile tugged at my lips as I pulled the frame down to get a closer look. He certainly had grown.

I replaced it and resumed my perusal. There was another picture of David, older this time with a different boy, but they looked nothing alike—in fact, the new boy looked suspiciously like Michael. Thoroughly enjoying my peeks into David's past, I pulled down another frame that was set farther back. It was of David in his teens, this time with a group, standing next to a slip of a girl with long dark hair. She was so small in comparison to the others in the photo it took me a moment to recognize her. Victoria. I set the picture down, not relishing the conversation to come about what I'd overheard or the fact that his childhood friend seemed to hate me on principle.

Looking at the rest of the images, I longed to know more about David's life. How he'd grown up. What his dreams had been. Who the boy was that looked so much like him. More than anything though, I wanted to know why he hadn't already shared any of this with me.

It was with a sad heart that I finally crawled into the bed determined to stay awake until he returned.

He didn't. Not that night or the following morning.

I woke up having fallen asleep reading on my phone, which was now dead. Sighing, I plugged it in, dressed, and headed downstairs. The whole day passed without so much as a passing glimpse of David. If everyone hadn't been so calm, I would've been worried.

I tried to go about my normal routine, but it was difficult since I was also trying to avoid Victoria. I had no idea what she would do after catching me listening in on her and I had no desire to find out. Us going at it wouldn't do anything to help David's stress, so I made a concerted effort not to get into a situation that might end badly.

I managed to pass some of the time making nice with a few of the *weres* who had straggled in the past fews days, but when I tried to spend time with the ones I'd gotten to know a little better, they were conveniently nowhere to be found. Finally, I threw in the towel and went upstairs for the night with no ambition of trying to stay up. I had no idea how long I'd been out when a noise startled me out of a dream.

I felt around in the dark for the lamp switch. A soft yellow glow invaded the space and I blinked against the intrusive light.

"David?" He looked terrible standing there. Exhaustion etched into every line of his body. His shoulders slumped, and while it may have been a trick of the light, I could see the bags under his eyes from here.

He let out a sigh. "I'm sorry, I didn't mean to wake you."

"That's fine. Where have you been? Are you okay?" The two questions seemed to only add to the weight pressing down on him. I let them go and instead slid out from under the covers to help him undress, and pulled him back into the bed with me. He must've been more tired than I imagined, because he didn't resist.

Once back in bed, his arms slid around me, holding me close as he buried his nose in the back of my neck. My mind screamed at me to tell him the news before I lost my chance again. I flashed to the sight of him looking so defeated. It could wait a little longer. The way he held me felt like a child holding their favorite stuffed critter for comfort.

If this is what he needed then I could be that for him. I fell back asleep with the lamp still on. By morning, I felt more refreshed than I had in days. I eagerly sat up to tell David everything, but he was already gone.

12

PACK BUSINESS

In spite of my early success, it took all of a week to see me completely cut out of everything. My new friends scarcely spared me pleasantries, Maria point-blank refused to acknowledge anything was wrong, and I couldn't even find David half of the time. Worse, nothing I did seemed to make any impact. The strengths that had helped me ingratiate myself in a new city simply weren't applicable here.

Thanks to Alexander's standing order to avoid the town, the influx of people arriving daily had nowhere to go. If I'd thought things were tense in the House before, it was nothing compared to having what I imagined was every werewolf in a two hundred mile radius crammed into a building designed to hold fifty at best. I never did get a chance to tell David what I'd overheard from Victoria, a sentiment that now seemed shared by several other whispering voices. Add to that the pending full moon, and the place was a powder keg ready to explode.

What I needed was an ally. Someone who knew me and wouldn't leave me to the wolves. I'd hoped that would be David, but between Solstice preparations and helping Alexander maintain some semblance of order, he understandably did not have the time to spare. As much as I missed our cuddles and late night chats about everything from movies to the cosmos, I also didn't want to add to the stress that seemed to cling to him like a second shadow.

I walked over to the nightstand, plucked my phone off the charger, and hit the quick dial. Two rings later, Sara's voice poured through the line, a balm to my frayed nerves.

"Hey, Charline."

"Remind me when you're coming," I demanded as I flounced on the bed. Talking on the phone always made me feel like a teenager. All that was missing was a cord to twirl around my fingers.

"For the millionth time," she began with a laugh, and I could practically hear her rolling her eyes as she repeated what she'd told me several times already, "we won't be able to get there until the actual Solstice."

"I know, I know, I just…" I trailed off. What could I possibly tell her? That her buoyant friend had taken to staying out of the way, all but hiding at times? Or that my whirlwind romance had taken a backseat to pack politics?

"What's the matter?" Sara's immediate concern brought the sting of tears to my eyes and I pinched my nose to stave them off.

"I don't know. I can't seem to get my foot in the door here."

She scoffed and I couldn't really blame her. From the backwater town I'd grown up in to the bustling city of Raleigh, I'd never had a problem fitting in, not until now.

"I'm serious, Sara. No one wants to talk to me about anything—it's all pack business. I didn't realize it would be so hush hush."

"They're just anxious about Alexander. This is apparently very different from the usual way, even Michael is a little wound up over it. I personally don't see the big deal, but what do I know? I've been a werewolf for all of five months."

"Fair point. But what about the little things? Like pleasantries? Since when is small talk too much to ask for?"

"Wolves can be a pretty tight knit bunch. They're really social once they open up, but it might take some convincing."

"You know, that kind of information would have been useful *before* I got here," I griped.

"I'm sorry. I didn't really think. There are some things you just take for granted when—" She halted mid-sentence.

"Say it."

"I didn't..."

"You were gonna say 'when you're one of them,' weren't you? Open-minded my ass. I've never felt so fucking human my whole life." I groaned, immediately regretting lashing out. "I'm sorry, that was uncalled for."

"No, I get it. You're dealing with enough of that nonsense without me adding to it. To be fair, outside of werewolves, you're kind of a wonder woman."

"Tell *them* that." I let out a frustrated huff. Aside from the darling Rosie, I couldn't think of a single *were* in the House that believed I was in any way special—and she was five, so that didn't really count. "It's more than that though. There's a woman—a *were*—named Victoria. Apparently she and David were 'besties' back in the day."

"Victoria... Can't say that name rings a bell. I don't think she was there when we came."

"Wouldn't surprise me. David seemed surprised to see her...and enthusiastic."

"We've talked about this. You know David is totally into you."

Maybe *she* knew that, but my little seed of doubt and insecurity was threatening to grow into a full grown oak at this point. "You haven't seen them, Sara. She's always hanging on him, always touching him, and whenever he's not around, she makes...comments."

"What sorts of comments?"

I chewed on my nail as I considered how to go on. I'd avoided mentioning anything before because I didn't want to come across insecure, but I needed help and maybe a heavy dose of perspective. "It's hard to explain, nothing outright mean, but right at the edge." I flashed back to the latest incident. "Like she said I couldn't keep up when someone suggested going for a morning run."

"Well, Charline..."

I quickly cut her off. "They weren't shifting, just jogging, speed-walking more like. She was calling me out of shape."

"I don't know about th—"

"And when she bumped into me in the hall, I hit the wall so hard I broke a picture. *That* went over real well. Plus, she keeps managing to whisk David off for some supposed wolf-related nonsense. I feel like I've hardly seen him at all since she showed up. Oh, and get this, everyone walks around with hardly a stitch on. I mean, I know it's hot, but *come on*."

"Really? I guess the temperature hadn't risen enough when I was there, but I can't say I'm surprised from what I've heard from Michael. Besides, we don't exactly get to keep our clothes when we change. It makes sense that *weres* who've been running together for years wouldn't be phased by a little skin showing."

"It's not a little. Okay, maybe it wouldn't be *so* bad, except for the hanging all over David part."

"I'm sure it's not that bad."

"It definitely is. She keeps making digs about how I don't fit in here and how happy David is to be surrounded by his own kind, and she's constantly ridiculing me."

"What does David have to say about this?"

"She makes sure to never do anything beyond two-faced remarks in front of him. I'm worried he'll just think I'm being the jealous girlfriend. He grew up with Victoria. He's only known me for a handful of months."

"If it bothers you so much, you should talk to him about it."

"I know you're right, and I have tried…sort of." Her silence told me exactly what she thought about that. "You don't understand. Everything she does *seems* fine on the surface, but there's this undertone. And the looks. And need we revisit the touching? She's trying to ruin our relationship, I know it. Plus, she's up to something, I just can't figure out what."

"Not *everyone* is out to get you, Charline." I hissed at the sharp rebuke and she cursed. "Shit. I didn't mean it like that."

"It's not all in my head," I insisted.

"I didn't say it was," she argued.

Except she kind of had, just like I expected David would. "I can hear Michael in the background. I'll let you go."

"Charline, wai—"

I ended the call, pulled my hair back, then went to find David. If he couldn't see what was going on right under his nose, then I'd make him. I stalked through the house, determined not to be derailed. David was a smart man. If I laid it all out, he'd understand, he'd *do* something.

All my gusto faltered as I stepped out into the backyard. The summer I'd been so eagerly anticipating had been rolling along without me as I hid upstairs and out of sight. Even when I'd been young and mercilessly teased about my squishier body, I'd never let anyone keep me indoors on a beautiful day. How had it come to this?

My gaze wandered over the damn-near naked *weres* littered about the yard until I spied David and several others mid-game of touch football. He wore a carefree smile without a hint of stress lining his shoulders or his face. A tightness in my chest eased at seeing him relaxed for the first time in what felt like weeks.

Being raised in the South, I was no stranger to any form of football. I quickly surveyed the scene to make out where things were at. Only, there didn't appear to be any rhyme or reason to the teams or the game. Still, everyone looked to be having a good time. David smiled when he caught sight of me and I waved in return, forgetting for a brief moment that anything was wrong.

"I wouldn't if I were you," someone said behind me.

"Wasn't planning on it, Victoria," I said, missing neutral by a mile and landing squarely on deadpan.

"It must be hard standing on the sidelines," she said as she stepped up beside me, scrutinizing her nails as if she didn't have a care in the world. "I guess you're used to that though. After all, I'm sure it's not the only contact sport you can't really participate in."

Red fury blazed through me from the soles of my feet to the tips of my hair. I clenched my hands at my sides before I tossed my last give a damn into the wind and tried to strangle her.

A cruel smirk twisted her lips. "Well, if you're sitting out, then you won't mind if I take your place."

I choked on my rage and watched helplessly as she slid into the game. My gaze darted from where she'd set up in direct opposition to David. I wanted more than anything to close my eyes so I wouldn't have to see what I knew would happen. They refused to obey and stayed sadistically open so I couldn't miss a single second of the horrible scene that unfolded before me.

The ball snapped and David lunged off the line. He wasn't even aiming for her, yet somehow she magically manifested in his path. They went down in a tangle of limbs and grunts. My stomach turned. I could hear her giggling like some obnoxious preteen from here. He lay atop her, laughing while she pretended to try and push him off. Bile crawled up my throat at how close their faces hovered. Finally, he stood and reached down to help her up.

As she found her feet, Victoria tossed me a sinister look that belonged more on a cartoon villain than a living person, then placed a hand intimately on the small of his back. He left it there as they continued to chat. She played with her hair, still giggling. He reached up and tucked a stray strand behind her ear and I had to pinch my lips together to stop everything I'd eaten in the last week from coming out.

I tore my gaze away and shuffled back toward the house, careful to keep my gaze fixed on the ground. I'd nearly made it back to safety when someone grabbed my arm.

"Hey, where are you going?" My stomach swooped unpleasantly at David's question. "I feel like I haven't seen you in forever."

"Probably because you haven't," I snapped and stupidly looked up.

His handsome face crumpled in confusion, the clear blue of his eyes turning overcast. "What's that supposed to mean?"

"Nothing. You've just been...busy." I waved in Victoria's direction, which conveniently encompassed a healthy portion of other *weres*.

"You knew this wouldn't just be a vacation, Char."

"Well, maybe I didn't know how much time you'd be spending with...others." I still couldn't bring myself to say it outright. Giving it voice would make it real. "Whatever. I'm going back upstairs," I said with a finality I'd learned from my mama.

"Hey, this isn't like you. What's up?" He followed me inside, grabbing a towel by the door.

I kept walking without responding, but was admittedly impressed when he made it all the way upstairs without getting sidetracked.

"Talk to me," he insisted after closing the door in a mockery of privacy.

I watched him continue to towel off and tried to get a handle on my growing bitterness. Somehow my gorgeous specimen of a man had lost some of his shine now that I knew every wolf in North Carolina had gotten to appreciate the view.

"I...I don't really know how to say it."

"Then just blurt it out," he said, plopping on the bed and vigorously toweling his head.

"I think Victoria is out to get me."

The towel stopped and fell down. He looked at me incredulously. "What? Why would you think that?"

"It's lots of things." I took a deep breath and let it out slowly as he waited patiently for me to continue. "For starters, she's mean to me."

"I've never heard her be anything but nice to you. She compliments you all of the time."

"You're not hearing her right." He made a face. Rather than argue the nuances of insulting someone with an insincere compliment, I jumped to my next point. "And she's always touching you."

"No she's not. That's all werewolves, we're a touchy bunch." He laughed at his own joke. When I didn't, he added, "You're seeing things. I've told you, we're friends. That's all."

"Why are you spending so much time with her then?"

Storm clouds darkened his sky blue eyes to gray and his brow lowered. "We were really close growing up. I haven't seen her in years. I don't understand why this is a problem." He grabbed a shirt and pulled it over his head. Considering he hadn't bothered to wear one in days, there was no mistaking it for what it was—armor. Pushing my hurt aside, I squared my shoulders and played the one card I'd hoped could open his eyes.

"She doesn't support Xander."

"Of course she does."

"Actually, neither her nor any of her cronies do. I overheard them talking about it days ago. Right after that first meeting, as a matter of fact." Suck on those eggs.

His jaw set and fire blazed in his eyes. "You are above this."

"Above what?"

"Making up lies."

"Are you serious right now!" It took an active force of will to bring my volume under control. "What reason would I have to lie about that?"

"Because it's obvious you don't like Vicky and for some reason that I cannot understand, you're threatened by her."

"Did you just try to wolf-logic me?"

His bravado visibly faded, but he wasn't backing down and neither would I.

"You're right, I don't like her. I have no reason to pretend otherwise. She's made it her mission to single me out since she got here. And any minute she's not finding some fresh way to ruin my day, she's clinging to you like white on rice."

"This is absolutely ridiculous. I can't believe this is a real conversation we're having."

"David, we haven't had a real conversation for over a week," I countered.

He shook his head. "That's not right."

"No, it's not. You've been too busy—which I totally get, I do—but I guarantee you're talking to Victoria."

"Why should that matter?"

"Because you talk to her about things you won't talk to me about."

"I can't help pack business, Charline." To hear the very phrase that had come to haunt my waking moments fly from his mouth sent me soaring right past the realm of reason.

"Do you talk to *her* about your mom?" I clapped a hand over my mouth, but it was too late, the damage had already been done.

The fire that had been burning in his eyes shuttered, leaving them a dull, lifeless gray. His shoulders fell from where they'd been bunched up by his ears and his arms hung limp at his sides. He pushed up from the bed and walked out of the room without another word.

I sat hard in the spot he'd vacated and cradled my head in my hands. "What have I done? One of these days this temper of mine is going to get someone killed." Considering what kind of creatures I was surrounded by, it would probably be me.

13

FULL MOON

I mentally calculated how to multiply my chicken casserole dish as I made my way to the kitchen. I'd just rounded the corner when Victoria's voice launched into the hall as if thrown.

"I'm telling you, Alexander, they're getting out of line."

"A misunderstanding, I'm sure," Alexander replied in that remarkably calm tone he had.

I hesitated and debated taking a different route, my latest argument with David fresh in my mind. Adding charges of eavesdropping wouldn't go over well in my continued efforts to get him to see Victoria's true character. I dithered another moment, then squared my shoulders and kept going.

I'm not doing anything wrong. It's not my fault they're talking loud enough for anyone to hear.

At Victoria's abrupt snort, I missed a step. "Not likely. Look, I don't know what rumors you've allowed to sprout over the last few years, but the city council directly snubbed us."

"How do you know it was them?" Alexander asked,

exhaustion edging the question. My heart went out to him, I didn't envy his seat on this powder keg.

"They'd just left a meeting. It was clearly printed on the sign. Not to mention the mayor was there." My steps slowed at her insistence.

Agitation filtered through Alexander's stoic calm. "Why were you in the village at all?"

"I will not be forced to stay away from a place just because the *locals* are a bunch of jumped up busybodies." I quickened my pace at the sound of footsteps coming toward me. I'd almost cleared the hall when Victoria added, "You won't be Alpha forever. What happens when the village decides that we aren't welcome anymore?"

I stopped dead outside the entrance to the kitchen and gasped in shock. In all my time here, *no one* had ever had the audacity to talk to Alexander like that. I knew things were getting bad in town thanks to the rumors flitting about the house like a million firebugs, but openly defying Alexander? What was she on about? There was no way he'd risk exposing the pack to hold onto some land. Did she have some kind of agenda? Maybe one that aligned with whoever she was supporting for the next Alpha since it certainly wasn't Xander. And what *was* she doing in Stone Creek?

"There you are," Maria said as her head popped out of the kitchen.

I squeaked in surprise and clutched a hand to my hammering heart. "Christ on a cracker. You scared me half to death."

She frowned, her brown eyes dark with worry. "Is everything okay? You look upset."

I floundered. Did I tell Maria what I'd overheard? Did I trust that Alexander would keep her in the loop? Did I have any right to butt into any of this? I set the whirlwind of doubt aside and shook my head even as I reached back to loosely braid my hair and keep it out of the way.

"It's nothing. I just don't think the recipe I had in mind will work."

Her eyes narrowed briefly before she disappeared back into the room. I let out a breath I hadn't realized I was holding and followed after, grabbing a spare apron from the wall.

Spices clustered on the counter in no particular order with various cooking utensils sprinkled among their haphazard groupings. Pots dominated the stove while various sized spoons and measuring cups were scattered on every available surface. Expanding the kitchen might destroy the original charm of the House, but I needed to talk to Maria about reconsidering. The tiny space was simply not equipped to handle this many mouths. Even if the House was only ever this packed a couple times a year, it would be worth it.

I took a moment to orient myself then set to work. When it was clear that I'd taken over, Maria took a step back, allowing me more space. The more I moved, the more my turbulent thoughts calmed. This was what I did best.

The chaos quickly became an assembly line staffed by the various children that inevitably showed up when I was in the kitchen. Not that I was complaining. I loved cooking, and the excited shouts of "Foxy's in the kitchen!" warmed my heart. But warm and fuzzies or not, Mama didn't have idle hands in her kitchen and neither would I. If they wanted to be there, they'd be put to work.

"Have you heard anything about something going on in the village?" I asked Maria as I spun to remove another tray from the oven in my culinary ballet.

She waved a hand and took another long drink of iced tea. "Some of the pack have had run-ins. Apparently telling people to stay away is like a hand-written invitation to go there." She sighed and I heard the unspoken addition—it hadn't always been that way.

I paused mid-stir and glanced over my shoulder at her. "Are people starting fights?"

Maria set her tea down and slumped deeper into her chair with a heavy sigh. "Someone sure is. I hear just as many rumors saying the pack is picking fights as people from the town going out of their way to cause trouble. Thus far, I think it's just been name calling—thank the moon—but I confess, this is not something we need right now."

Talk about an understatement. David had explained more than once that things weren't normally like this, that the summers were traditionally more low key and relaxed. But the pending Solstice on top of the unprecedented circumstances had tensions running higher with each passing day.

"Xander seems to be handling it well enough," I said as I put spices back in the cabinet.

"You would think, but I fear that some of the wolves feel like he's too much on the humans' side." She blinked as if realizing what she'd said. "No offense, Charline. Pack is..."

"Pack is family. I get it." The rolls burned my hand as I tested them, matching the pang in my heart at hearing that my last bastion of support held the same opinion as everyone else where humans were concerned. How could I ever hope to get David to understand without looking like a brat when even Maria harbored anti-human sentiments?

Maria looked up at me inquiringly as I repositioned the tray a little too forcefully. "You okay?"

I shook my hand as if cooling it. "Just a little singe, nothing to fuss over."

"Let me help." She shifted to push off the chair and I waved her back down.

"No, I'm fine, really. You rest, you've done so much already."

She sagged back in her seat, wariness radiating off of her. "Are you sure?"

"Absolutely. Plus, we're all but done." I passed a bowl of buttered potatoes to another scamp who had entered too far into my domain. He looked forlornly at the fridge before dutifully taking the bowl outside.

"You do well with them," Maria said with a smile.

I grabbed a relatively clean spoon to stir a pot in danger of boiling over. "They're good kids. Honestly, I wish all kids I met were so helpful in the kitchen." I mussed the hair of little Rosie who'd snuck in to grab the rolls. She giggled and hot footed to the patio where the masses of food were being relocated as ready. She and Maria had to be the only *weres* in the entire House who openly still liked me. My happy smile faltered and I hid it behind tucking a loose curl behind my ear.

"Still, you have a natural instinct. Maybe someday...?" She let the question hang.

Yep, Maria reminded me very much of my own mother. Mama also pumped me about marriage and a family every chance she got and ever since she'd learned about David, it had gotten a million times worse. I didn't have the heart to tell her that things weren't going well. Much as I loved my mama, she could also be pretty critical and *that* was a guilt trip I didn't need.

"I guess time will tell," I replied with forced cheer.

A glance around the cramped space showed mostly clear counters; as impossible as it seemed, all of the food had managed to make it out of the kitchen. Everything was turned off and pots were soaking in the sink in preparation for whoever pulled dish duty. There was really only one thing left. I dusted my hands clean and placed them on my hips as I turned to face the main entryway. Sure enough, my battalion of mini sous chefs clustered in the doorway.

"I suppose I know what all of you are here for." Their little faces lit up in anticipation. I opened the doors of the fridge to a chorus of expectant coos. "Alright, everyone grab a tray and we'll all go together."

They rushed the tiny space, then practically carried me off with them. I could almost forget my own troubles surrounded by their smiling faces. As far as I was concerned, they were the best part of the pack, untainted by politics and back-biting. Outside, we set the several trays of fudge down and I held up their prize—a small batch made extra special just for them.

"Easy now," I laughed, "you don't want to spoil your appetite."

"Yeah, you wouldn't want to spoil your appetite."

I straightened from giving Rosie's brother Oscar the last piece, licking my fingers of the clinging sugary goodness. My joy died when I saw Victoria. I covered my discomfort by grabbing a nearby glass, heedless of its contents. A glance behind her revealed two of her minions and, of course, no David in sight. I schooled the frown threatening to take over my face.

"Hello, Victoria." I took a sip of my stolen beverage. "Jealous?"

She snickered. The bitch could probably eat an entire fudgery by herself and still not weigh more than a hundred pounds soaking wet. She eyed the numerous trays with something akin to revulsion.

"Some of us enjoy...meatier things," she said with unnecessarily pointy teeth.

"What's the matter, Victoria? You seem upset. Lose an argument?" I asked, taking a gamble. A storm cloud passed over her face only to be replaced with a snarky grin.

"What makes you think I'm upset about anything? I mean, it's not like *my* boyfriend has gone off and left me to fend for myself among a bunch of strangers—a fox among wolves."

Indignant fury blanketed me from head to toe. "Listen, you skinny bitch-"

"Hey, babe." The vindictive comment dried on my tongue at David's sudden arrival. "Save me any?"

I shot Victoria, who didn't look the least bit surprised, a withering glare.

"Please don't tell me you two aren't getting along." He rubbed a hand through his hair in clear exasperation.

"Of course not," she crooned, her harpies miraculously nowhere to be seen. "I was just asking Charline if she'd saved any of her special batch for the rest of us."

"That's good," he said, clearly not paying attention. "Stars above, looks like Destiny and Tyrell are going at it again. I'll catch up with you later, little fox. Save me some." He didn't wait for my response, just gave me a swift kiss, then vanished as abruptly as he'd arrived.

I turned back to face Victoria and could have crowed with delight at her mottled expression. "What's the matter, Vicky? You look madder than a wet hen."

Amy, minion number two, laughed as she rejoined us. "That's a silly saying. What the hell does a mad hen look like?"

"I'm *so* glad you asked." I reached out and calmly poured my glass of what had turned out to be overly sweetened tea on Victoria's head.

Rage burned in her eyes as she shook the still dripping liquid from her eyes. Before she could find a way to retaliate, I turned on my heel and headed back into the house. My feet wanted to run as fast as they could up the stairs to the safety of David's room, but I couldn't afford to look like she'd gotten to me. At last, I found myself free to exhale and immediately sucked it back in as David burst into the room.

"Oh good, I hoped I'd find you here. I wanted to let you know we'll be running in the North woods for tonight's full moon."

I stood there dumbly, my apron hanging off of me as he continued to stare at me.

"Did you want to come?" he added belatedly.

I shook my head, at a loss for what to say to the offhand invitation. He shrugged his shoulders and once more left as abruptly as he'd arrived. I stumbled a step forward.

One Mississippi.

My palm flattened on the door.

Two Mississippi.

I pushed until it clicked shut.

Three Mississippi.

Numbness spiraled out from my fingers to encompass my whole being.

Four Mississippi.

I staggered back until the backs of my legs hit the bed.

Five Mississippi.

A sob tore through me with the force of a riptide. I gasped for breath as the weight of enduring every slight, every questioning glance, brought me to my knees. The burn of the rug didn't even register as I collapsed in on myself. I could withstand a lot, but not David's passive acceptance of the pack's treatment of me. And now, he was going for a run...with *her*.

I mustered enough energy to drag myself off the floor, then crumpled on the bed, desolate in my sea of isolation. Heartache became my companion as the sun set and the unforgiving light of the moon pierced the curtains to compound my agony. I'd been drifting in and out for what felt like hours when the soft click of the door catapulted me to awareness.

"Hey," I said barely above a whisper, my voice hoarse from hours of crying as the moon rose higher and higher in the sky.

"You're still up?"

I had no idea what time it was, and didn't want to. The bed jumped as David flopped on top of the sheets.

"Oh stars, Char, you should have seen it. Can you believe I almost forgot how awesome it is to run with a full pack?" He folded his arms behind his head as he continued. "There's really no way to describe it. It's just amazing. And we started a howl. A *howl*. Can you believe it?" His tangible excitement rolled over me, each word a fresh thorn. "I mean, the howl was mostly Vicky's idea, but man it was great."

I choked back a raw sob. The traitorous sound instantly caught his attention and his tirade of joy instantly turned to concern.

"Char, are you okay? I'm sorry. I shouldn't have jumped on the bed like that. I didn't hurt you, did I?" His fingers brushed over the healed scratches on my back. It took all of the steel I had not to flinch or make another sound. "I'll let you sleep. We can talk in the morning." He placed a feather light kiss on my shoulder and rolled up to finish undressing. The bed barely shifted when he resumed his spot.

14

PERSPECTIVE

Around five, I slipped out of bed, got dressed in the dark, and padded downstairs into a silent house. For the first time in weeks, noise did not dominate the hall. No loud arguing, no pounding feet, no anything, just beautiful silence.

I drank my tea lukewarm so that the sound of the kettle wouldn't disturb the bubble of peace. It was almost easy to forget that I was really an interloper in these people's lives as I gazed out the kitchen window at the blush of dawn. But the truth was still there. No matter what I did, I wouldn't belong here. I'd never be one of them.

Yes, as David had said a lifetime ago, there were other humans, but what he'd failed to mention was that they were few and far between and they didn't stay at the House. They very wisely left, either with or without their wolfy partners, to pursue more mundane pursuits.

I dreamed wistfully of my little yellow house with its spacious kitchen and cabinets stuffed to the brim with every spice imaginable. Sorrow pulled at my heart as I longed for the escape of baking for hours on end without a soul to disturb me. With a sigh, I set my empty cup down. Getting lost in the push and pull of dough, in the gentle whir of the mixer, in the meticulous measurements and decadent scents weaving through the air... that wasn't an option here.

Perhaps a little space will give me what I need.

I rinsed out my mug, dried it, and put it back in the cupboard. After a final glance to confirm everything exactly as I'd found it, I set out for the front to wait for the cab I'd called. The last thing I needed was them honking their arrival and waking the entire blissfully quiet house. I settled in one of the many rockers and alternated between staring at the drive and the delicate pastels painting the sky.

"You're only hurting his chances, you know." The statement lacked Victoria's characteristic bite, but that didn't stop it from stinging. Engaging her at this ungodly hour wouldn't do any good, so I didn't. "You're holding him back," she continued, nonplussed. "He's a wolf and should be with a wolf. No Beta can be with a human. He deserves this chance. If you really cared, you'd leave."

Despite my best efforts, a tear streaked its way down my cheek. Maybe going into town for the day wasn't enough. Maybe it was time to call this. When she didn't immediately seize upon the traitorous response, I turned to look at her, only to find the expansive porch empty.

I continued to stare at the wide stretch of bleached decking, not sure if I'd imagined the whole encounter, until the crunch of tires on gravel snared my attention. The cab pulled up and I slipped into the back seat without a word.

The House slowly shrank behind us as the cabbie glanced at me through the rearview. "I hear they're a rough bunch up there."

I shrugged and stared out the window at the passing line of red maples. This time of year they were a decided green, but come fall they'd turn a shocking red. It would be a brilliant sight. Shame I wouldn't get to see it.

"I'm told they howl at the moon. Never heard it myself, but others have."

I squeezed my eyes shut at his poor choice of topic.

It was Vicky's idea.

"Hey, don't be too down. I don't know if you've been there yet, but Stone Creek is a nice town. Good people, not like the lunatics you hear about roaming the woods." He squinted at me in the mirror. "You know, it's early, but you should really try Mimi's... Oh wait, no." His face crumpled in disappointment and I found myself intrigued. "I'm sorry, I keep forgetting they shut down. They used to have the best scones. Not that I'm hoity-toity or nothin', but it's hard to beat a good scone. You bake?" he asked, his weathered face once more bright.

"Yes. Quite well actually." I found myself responding despite my melancholy mood.

"Aw shucks." His round cheeks stretched into a warm smile that thawed some of the frost around my heart. "That's great. Ever make scones?" His brown eyes shone with friendly hope.

I gave him a small smile, trying to put some meaning in it. "I can't say that I have."

"Oh." His face fell as he refocused on the road for a moment, then the amiable chatter returned. "Maybe you should try 'em out some time." The car rolled to a stop in front of a vacant shop with age-spotted windows and flaking paint. Even the lettering up top was gone. "Gosh ma'am, I'm sorry. I wasn't even thinking and brought you to the old bakery. I can swing 'round to the cafe if you like, they should be open by now."

"Here's fine." I paid my fare and got out. Before I closed the door though, I called back in, "What was your name again?"

"Eddy, Eddy Martin ma'am."

I gave him a smile that, painful as it was, was mostly genuine. "Thank you, Eddy. I appreciated the conversation." I started to close the door and paused. "Oh, and Eddy? Don't believe everything you hear about the people up there." He tipped his cap and I shut the door. I stared after the cab as it pulled away from the curb and sent swirls of mist spiraling out, not sure why I felt the need to defend people who clearly didn't want me.

The faded yellow cab rounded a corner, taking its friendly driver with it. I turned my attention to the abandoned storefront adjoined to a tailor on one side and a little boutique on the other. My gaze roved over the dust-smeared windows and chipped facade, curious why the place had gone out of business and how the prime real estate had withstood occupation.

I wondered if dear Eddy pulled this stunt with all of his passengers as I took a step closer to peer inside. I could just make out a couple of forgotten chairs and a small table. The counter at the far end certainly looked like it had once housed pastry goods. I squinted, but without more light, I couldn't make out any details. A tad disappointed, I gave up in favor of wandering aimlessly down the sidewalk. The stillness of early dawn lent the town a surreal quality reminiscent of that space between being awake and asleep.

As I meandered, the village gradually came to life. The laughter of children filled the air. People smiled and waved as they passed on the street. Shops pinged as the day's first customers rushed about their business. With each pleasant greeting sent my way, I found it more and more difficult to believe that this town had taken a sudden dislike to the inhabitants at the House. None of the folk I passed struck me as malicious or even mildly perturbed. Then I recalled what Eddy had said. Lunatics, rough, howling at the moon

—some of it held a nugget of truth, but most of it had the distinct ring of hearsay.

Rumors I knew. They'd destroyed my last couple of relationships. Not to mention, I'd somehow acquired the unwarranted title of office gossip queen. What was so wrong about wanting to know what was going on? Working in HR meant that I needed to be able to find the information people weren't always willing to share. Besides, not all gossiping was done with ill intent. I smiled to myself as I recalled hours of sitting around on my family's front porch listening to the matriarchs cluck away companionably about the latest to-do in our small town.

A small tent sign obscured the walkway and I glanced up at the Lunar Cafe neon. On cue, my stomach rumbled and I ducked inside.

"Good morning, miss," the host greeted kindly. "You must be the lady from the mansion on the hill. Eddy said you'd probably be by."

I mentally shook my head. I knew better than most how fast news could travel in a small town. They smiled good-naturedly and gestured to a table.

"I imagine you're wanting to get away from the chaos. Heard there was an epic party up there last night," they added with a hint of envy.

The fog of contentment I'd been aimlessly wandering in dispelled sharply, much like the mist outside with the morning rays. "Actually, just hoping for a decent cup of tea and maybe something to nibble on. Any scones by chance?" I asked with a sudden hankering for the flaky treat.

The host laughed and placed a short menu on the round table. "Oh yeah, Eddy has definitely gotten to you. One of these days he'll convince someone to buy that old place."

"How long has it been closed?"

"Shucks, over a decade at least. The owner got really sick. I think she died."

"That's awful," I said, per social niceties, to the morbid statement.

They shrugged. "Before my time really. No one talks about it much. Well, except for the codgers griping about it darkening the strip. Anyway, what'll it be?" They held up a small pad and pencil and waited.

At a loss for how to respond, I ordered tea and a muffin. While the cup of Earl Gray was decent enough, the dry muffin failed to impress. I was playing with the crumbling mass and watching the sky lighten when someone vaguely familiar and obviously in a hurry walked by the window.

If I didn't know any better, I'd say that was someone from the House.

Frowning, I laid some cash on the table and went outside to get a better idea of what could bring one of the *weres* to town so early and right after a run. Despite my quick exit, I only managed to get the vaguest impression of a thin frame and dark brown hair before I lost sight of them.

"Well, fudge," I said aloud as the crowd swallowed my quarry. A few passersby looked at me askance. I smiled and offered a small wave before continuing on my way.

Now that I'd acquired some breakfast, exploring the town topped my agenda. David and I had made a good run of it last time, but we'd also intended to return. Heartache tightened my chest. Wandering the streets with him had been wonderful fun. We'd played the tourists, taken silly pictures in front of some of the more iconic buildings, and laughed the day away.

My hand drifted to my phone of its own accord. I tightened my fingers into a fist and refused to give in to the desire to scroll through the images. Resolute in my determination to enjoy the day, I focused on window shopping at the numerous little boutiques. I walked past the abandoned bakery where I'd started this morning's adventure and into the boutique next door.

"Good morning," the attendant said as she held the door, having just turned the sign to proclaim that Silver Lining Boutique was open for business.

"Good morning. Misha, right?" I returned in kind, recalling her name from a conversation at the House. Her eyes widened in a surprise that intensified when she reached up to touch her blouse to confirm she wasn't wearing a name tag.

"Um, yes. Please let me know if you need anything, Miss...?"

"Charline," I offered, extending my hand. She seemed relieved to have a name in return. "Thank you and I'm sorry, I didn't mean to startle you. I've heard great things about this place." Her smile relaxed as she released my hand. "I'll let you know if I have any questions." She nodded and stepped aside to leave me to my wandering.

It didn't take long to get lost among the trinkets and intricate stitching on some of the garments. I was debating whether or not the finely embroidered bolero I kept coming back to was worth the price tag when the bell announced that I was no longer the only shopper. Naturally, I looked up to assess the newcomer.

A woman wearing a sharp business suit walked in talking on her phone. In fact, everything about her was sharp, from her angular features to the cut of her mid-length, blonde hair. She gave a passing wave to Misha and started shuffling through racks. I scowled, curious how she expected to find anything flipping through the hangers that fast. The woman snapped all the hangers to one side and proceeded to abuse another rack while her focus remained on her conversation.

"I'm tired of asking. I want the agreement. No, I don't want to just *see* it again. I want it in my hand at the town hall where it belongs." She made an irritated tsk and switched racks. "He's being difficult. You could have warned us how bad it would be. I'm still fielding calls from the mayor about the surveyors' complaints. Those people were downright hostile." Suddenly she straightened up and I shrank behind a nearby display of necklaces. "Now listen here, I know full well that you have your own agenda, just make sure it doesn't fuck up mine." She shot a glance towards the counter where Misha was doing a spectacular job of pretending to be invisible. "Fine." She returned her attention back to the rack. "I'll see you then. And Johnny, Alexander better cave."

My head shot up at the name, bumping the display and almost giving away that I'd been eavesdropping. I fumbled at the clattering necklaces, but fortunately the woman didn't take notice. She stuffed the phone in her purse, gave the shop a last once over, then promptly marched out. I made my way over to Misha who appeared relieved that the woman had left, even without purchasing anything.

"Who was that?" I asked as casually as I could, laying down one of the necklaces.

"*That* was Edith Sharp," she said with an eye roll, and I snorted. "I know, right? If ever a name fit. She's the head of the village council, only next to Mayor Hawthorne himself."

"Is she always like that?"

"Miss Sharp can be...intense."

"Miss, not Missus?" I asked, unable to help myself.

Misha's face pinched comically and I smothered a laugh. "She never married. Personally, I think she likes it that way." Her hazel eyes sparkled with mischief as she glanced behind me toward the door then leaned on the counter to whisper conspiratorially, "They say she used to date the guy who owns the mansion. Hasn't been serious with anyone since."

My jaw hit the floor. "Alexander Wolfsbane dated *her*?"

Misha nodded. I looked back at the exit, my mind reeling, and fought the urge to pump the young shopkeeper for every scrap of detail she could muster. I simply could not reconcile the extreme woman I'd just seen and the warm, motherly Maria. Talk about a complete one-eighty.

I added the debated bolero to the counter and absently thanked Misha. My puzzle had gotten much much bigger. Now if only I could get some of the pieces to finally start coming together. Much as I wanted to scour the village for information about the two newest players to this horrible game that had become my summer, I also didn't want to dally too long in town.

To my surprise, it was once again Eddy who answered the call for a cab. Maybe he was pulling a double or maybe the town really was that small. Either way, the anxiety I'd eluded gradually increased as we drew closer to the House. Several surprised faces looked up from their morning pursuits when we came to a stop and I stepped out. No doubt a cab was an unusual sight here. A beat passed without comment, then everyone went back to what they'd been doing.

I set my bags down and considered what to do next. I was still debating whether or not to while away the afternoon in the orchard or go straight upstairs when my feet vacated the ground. Thick arms wrapped around me, threatening to crack my ribs and squishing all of the air out of me in a strangled squeak.

"There you are. I've been looking everywhere for you. No one saw you this morning and when I couldn't find you..." David trailed off as he finally eased up on the back-breaking hug. I dragged in a pained breath and looked behind him to find his ever-present companion.

Victoria pushed off of the massive pillar and walked towards us, arrogance radiating off of her with each step. Would I never have a reprieve from this vile woman? "Maybe House life is just too much for her. It's understandable, really." She shrugged her slim shoulders and gave me a knowing smirk.

"Vicky, could you give us a minute?" David asked without taking his eyes off me.

Shock exploded across her face like someone had doused her with cold water. I bit the inside of my cheek to keep from snickering. Her face pinched and she left without another word to crawl back into whatever hell-hole had spawned her. My mental celebration was mid-mambo when David's warm hand engulfed mine and gave it a light squeeze.

"Let's go for a walk."

I nodded and let him lead me down a path toward the woods worn smooth by generations of feet. Trees obscured the house as we delved deeper into the forest proper. He glanced over at me and gave my captive hand another gentle squeeze.

"I missed you this morning. Where'd you go?"

"I needed a little space, so I went to the village for breakfast. I didn't sleep well and I didn't want people to keep asking me how I was." Truth be told, no one had once asked me how I was doing since we'd arrived, the man at my side notwithstanding.

"Looked like you found one of the little shops."

"Crap! I left my bags in the yard."

"Don't worry," he said with a smile, "I had one of the others grab it."

"Thank you." He shrugged, and on a whim I decided to

share the nugget I'd learned at said boutique. "Do you know Edith Sharp?"

"Yeah, she's on the town council. Why?"

"Actually, she's head of the council. She came into the shop I was in. She's...interesting."

He snorted. "That's a mild word for it."

"Anyway, she was talking on the phone to someone named Johnny. It sounded like they were discussing the agreement over the land." That caught his full attention. "Don't suppose that could be the elusive Johnathan?" I asked hopefully.

David shook his head. "It's possible—Johnathan did used to go by Johnny back in the day—but there's no *way* he'd be talking to Edith Sharp. Definitely not after everything that happened." He gave a shudder. "Past that, I don't know anyone in the House or village who goes by Johnny. Any chance you heard something that could help us out?"

"I wish. The most I got is that it sounded like he was holding the agreement hostage, though whose copy it is, I have no idea." I hesitated, not sure how the last tidbit would be received. "It sounded like she's really gunning for Alexander."

"Wouldn't surprise me." I raised an eyebrow at the response and he added, "She can really hold a grudge."

A perfect opportunity to cough up some real dirt and that's the best you've got?

I resisted the urge to roll my eyes and I let it drop. My golden piece had apparently been useless. Johnny *wasn't* Johnathan and David was being stingy with the gossip. We walked a little further in silence that thickened until I thought it'd choke us. I was on the verge of feigning exhaustion and insisting on returning to the House when he finally spit out the real reason he'd led me away.

"I heard about the incident with Vicky last night." He'd probably heard the story straight from the horse's mouth.

"Oh?" I didn't trust myself to be diplomatic.

"You can't do things like that, not with everything that's at stake and the issues in the village."

My meager breakfast turned rancid in my stomach. What did he expect me to say? He obviously believed he already had all of the facts. The nauseating silence resumed as I continued on without responding.

"Charline, are you okay?"

I'd been deluding myself to think this stroll would lead anywhere but the brambles. "You're not even going to ask me what happened?"

"I already know what happened. Plenty of people saw."

I shrugged and kept walking. This conversation required energy I didn't have.

"Please talk to me, Char. I know I haven't really been around and I'm sorry. It was never my intent to leave you to fend for yourself." He seemed at a loss for how to continue. "Maria says you're a wonder with the pups."

"Most people like you when you give them sweets."

"That's not what I meant..." When I didn't answer, he fell quiet.

We walked a little farther without talking. I knew my silence was bothering him, but it was the only weapon I had left. I couldn't afford to risk losing the wall I'd started to build. All it would take was one loose brick to send me tumbling down into the same rabbit hole I'd fallen in last night.

Without warning, David stopped, forcing me to turn back and retrace my steps. When I was close enough, he cupped my cheek with one of his callused hands. "Char, I really am sorry. You've been incredibly patient with me. I wasn't expecting the clearing to take so long or...other things, but that should be done soon. I'll try to be better about not running off."

Mention of running brought unbidden images of what had probably happened last night. The wall shook. I desperately wanted to lean into his hand, to seek the comfort I knew I could find there. But it would be fleeting. This moment wouldn't last, and everything would go back to exactly the same the second we returned to the House.

David placed a tentative kiss on my lips and stroked my cheek as he searched my eyes. "You'd tell me if something was wrong, right?"

I barked a cynical laugh and he pulled away. "I *have* told you. You just don't want to hear it."

"Is this the Victoria thing again?"

"Again implies that you've heard any of what I've told you before. Just because you don't want to see it, doesn't mean it's not happening." This conversation was exactly the one I'd been afraid of this morning when I slipped out.

"Charline, she's just a friend, that's all."

"Does *she* know that?" I snapped, putting more distance between us as the remnants of my pleasant morning went up like dry kindling.

"Please, you've got to move past this."

Cold coursed through my veins like liquid ice. "I think you should go back to the House. You found me. I'm alive. The others will be missing you." I struck out from our path in the direction of the orchard without waiting for him to respond.

He didn't follow.

15

TROUBLE IN TOWN

Seemed baking would be in my future after all. I just hoped Maria didn't mind too much that I was commandeering her entire kitchen. I dumped a shirt full of apples on the counter to join the overflowing bucket, snatching one mid air before it could drop to the floor. Then I put my culinary skills to the test as I made every apple dish I could imagine. When I resorted to applesauce, that's when I knew I'd hit rock bottom.

Exhausted, I slumped into a chair, my scant breakfast long since worn off, and snagged a still warm turnover from the breakfast table.

"Think you've got enough sugar in here?" Victoria taunted from the entryway.

"I'm not going to let you ruin this," I said and promptly took a bite that sent golden goodness oozing unhindered out the sides.

"Shoving your face full of sweets won't change anything but your waistline, though I doubt anyone would notice."

I swallowed down the sweet that had turned tart on my tongue and wiped the corners of my mouth. "Clearly you've never had a dessert that could change your whole day."

Before she could launch yet another barb I stood up, grabbing one of the pastries on my way out. As I stepped past her, I tossed the treat. Even with enhanced reflexes, she almost dropped it. "Here, have a fritter. Maybe it will improve that sour disposition of yours."

Over the next couple of days, I did my best to stay out of Victoria's way to no avail. When the House proved to be a minefield of snarky comments and insinuated insults, I turned to the village for sanctuary, even if that did mean Victoria would have more unsupervised time with David. It smarted to admit that she'd been successful in running me out of the House. If I was being honest with myself, though, I wasn't just avoiding her. While I'd known there was no way David could ever keep his promise to spend more time together, it still hurt that he hadn't even tried.

There were some pluses to spending so much time in town. Eddy became my regular ride both to and from the House. I became a fixture at the Lunar Cafe that thankfully did not take offense at my suggestion to improve the quality of their muffins. People started to recognize me and call me by name. And most importantly of all, I finally felt like I could be myself without ridicule.

For want of a real task to occupy my time, I devoted my days to uncovering the identity of the mysterious Johnny and hopefully the real reason the village and the House were at such odds. As far as I could tell, before this summer, there'd never been any issues. Visiting *weres* had always been polite and friendly. Most of them had spent quite a bit of time in town over the years, so it wasn't like they were total strangers. So what had prompted the shift?

As I got to know the people of Stone Creek and they got to know me, I started to pick up on the gossip that inevitably floated around such a small community. It was honestly a relief to know that I hadn't lost my touch for ferreting out the secrets that people seemed incapable of keeping. For instance, I knew that the cafe was planning on renovating and had pointedly not gotten a quote from Wolfsbane Construction. I'd learned that Susan Miller was planning to leave her husband for her neighbor's girlfriend. But most importantly, I learned that members of the pack were still regularly sneaking into town despite Alexander's repeated order to the contrary. What they were doing in town, however, remained a mystery, because I disappeared anytime I saw a group.

I peered through the spotless glass storefront of Silver Linings to ensure the way was clear before bidding Misha a good day. "Thanks again," I said as I pulled the door open to the tinkling of bells. "Let me know if that order comes in."

She gave me a thumbs up and I stepped onto the sun-bathed sidewalk. The butcher down the way caught my attention and I returned Darren's friendly wave as I sidled up to the empty bakery next door. The mystery of the place itched at me and I'd repeatedly found myself peering inside in search of clues.

Finding myself no more enlightened than any of the other half dozen times I'd stared through the grime covered windows, I shook my head and continued on my way. I'd meandered half a block when the shout of angry voices slowed my steps.

"Watch where you're going!"

"You don't own the whole sidewalk."

"It's called decency, but I wouldn't expect you freaks to know anything about that."

I turned the corner to see three teenagers from the House confronting a group of similarly aged townsfolk.

"Don't start something you can't finish," one of the boys from the House growled.

"Oh, I'll finish it. I'm tired of y'all walking around like

you own the place. You like your land so much, stay there! And leave the rest of us in peace."

"It would be easier if you'd stop trespassing," one of the other teens from the House snapped back.

The young man from town pushed his sleeves back as if preparing to fight. "You can't trespass on common land."

I stepped away from the corner to intervene before this could get truly out of hand. Even from this distance, I could see the kid from the House who'd been doing most of the talking had abnormally long nails. There was only one way this could end—badly.

I'd gone all of three steps when a heavy hand fell on the young *were's* shoulder. I followed the arm to its owner, an older man with graying hair and a square jaw. While I'd never seen him before, the others clearly recognized him.

"That's enough, Laurence. They'll get what's coming to them." The boy, Laurence, snarled at the village youth before allowing himself to be guided away by the larger man. The rest of the *weres* fell in line behind them and vacated the area while the remaining youths seemed just as surprised by the man's intervention as I was.

With everyone now dispersed, I looked a bit strange standing there so many paces from the standard path. I quickly relocated and waved to Darren again, having forgotten that I'd already done so.

A couple hours later, I ran across one of the kids that had been in the group from town. Unable to keep my curiosity at bay, I approached him.

"Hi, this is probably going to seem weird, but I saw what happened earlier."

"What of it?"

I bit my tongue at the rude response. Tempting as it was to tell him to learn some damn manners, I needed information and being terse with him wasn't likely to help. "Do you know those kids?"

He narrowed his eyes at me in obvious distaste of my word choice. "Those guys? They're always around. Laurence thinks he's hot stuff and he owns everything he sees, just because he stays up at the mansion during the summers."

"They cause trouble a lot?"

The youth rolled his shoulders and dropped his gaze to the ground. "They didn't used to."

"I'm sorry, how rude of me. My name is Charline. What's yours?"

"Taylor, ma'am."

I shook the proffered hand, pleased to discover he had some manners after all. "Taylor, did you and Laurence used to be friends?"

The boy's shoulders slumped and I knew I'd hit the nail on the head. "I don't know what happened. We've always been friends. But one day, he just started acting like a total jerk, like he was better than me."

"When did it start?"

"A few weeks ago maybe? Right after school got out. We all normally go camping when they come to town, but this year he didn't want anything to do with us."

"That man who stopped the fight, do you know who he is?"

"I don't know his name. Pretty sure he lives at the mansion with the others."

"Don't suppose you know anything else about him?"

He shook his head. "No ma'am, though I've seen him talking to Councilwoman Sharp. She never looks happy to see him. Then again, she never looks happy to see anybody." He snickered to himself then remembered to whom he was talking and immediately looked abashed.

I gave him a small smile and a wink. "Oh, I've met Miss

Sharp." His shoulders unbunched and he offered a tentative grin in return. "It was nice to meet you, Taylor. Thank you for talking with me. I know it's hard losing a friend, but may I recommend just avoiding them until everything blows over? Laurence will come around eventually." I had no idea if that would be true, but the promise seemed to bolster the young man's spirits.

Truthfully, I was more concerned that he heard the warning. If his former friend was willing to attack him in the middle of the street, there was no telling what else he'd be willing to do. I finished excusing myself and moved along, troubled by the day's events and the questions that had emerged from them. What would convince friends to turn on each other so suddenly? Who was the man that had intervened and how did the young *weres* know him?

Day after day the rift became more pronounced between the two factions. Friendly waves and pleasantries gave way to downcast eyes and shuffles across the street to avoid crossing paths. Frightening stories about "the wolves up on the hill" and howling heard at all hours of the night had more than just the townsfolk spooked. Exposure risked everyone. I did what I could to mitigate the increasingly tall tales, but the rumors persisted, leading me to believe that *someone* was feeding them.

But who could I tell? I hadn't seen or talked to David in days and anytime I was in the House for longer than two minutes, Victoria found me. I'd given up attempting to talk to Maria, or anyone else at the House for that matter. What was the point? At the end of the day, I was human and that automatically made me the enemy.

I sat at my usual table in the cafe, drinking a somewhat decent cup of tea, though it didn't hold a candle to the stuff Maria had hidden in the House, and focused on parceling out fact from fiction. But no matter how I arranged the pieces, no connection emerged. I stared into the dregs of tea thoroughly bummed at my lack of results. Mama had always said I could ferret out the truth faster than a coonhound could find a cougar, but it seemed like I'd finally met my match.

"Good morning, Charline," Liza from the shop next door said as she picked up her daily order, dragging me out of my gloomy thoughts.

"Hi, Liza. How's your mother doing?"

"She's doing well."

I smiled and waved goodbye, my thoughts already getting sucked back into my quagmire. Trouble was, I'd all but exhausted the gossip in town. If I wanted the missing pieces, I'd have to venture back to the House. Resigned to my course of action, I called my ride.

"Something going on, Miss?" Eddy asked, directing my attention to the front lawn of the House covered with people.

"I...I don't know."

The arrival of the cab seemed to stir them into a tizzy, much like someone kicking an ant hill. My anxiety at returning prematurely notched up several degrees. Then I saw David marching thunderously down the front steps, his bitch of a lapdog hot on his heels, and it skyrocketed.

Storm clouds darkened David's face as the cab came to a stop and I shrank back against the cushion. Before I could even think to reach for the handle, he yanked the door open. I winced at the sound and slowly exited the cab beneath David's imposing glower.

"Where have you been? You haven't been seen in days."

"I've been in the village," I squeaked, despite my endeavor to sound calm and confident.

"You gonna be alright, Miss Montgomery?" Eddy asked

from the front seat, his hand discreetly hovering over his cell. Bless his heart, the man had a death wish.

I reached back in to reassure my poor, naive cabbie and grab my bag. "I'll be fine, Eddy." I chanced a quick glance at his phone and shook my head slightly. The last thing anyone needed was the cops getting involved. Not one to look a gift horse in the mouth, Eddy waited until the door closed, then drove away as fast as the crowd would allow. He was sweet, not brave. I just hoped he wouldn't call the local law enforcement the second he was in the clear.

At mention of the man's name, David's eyes lit with rage. "And who pray tell is Eddy?"

"H-he's just a cab driver," I faltered. "He's been driving me to and from the village."

"Why have you been spending so much time in the village?" he demanded, the storms in his eyes nowhere near abating.

Because they actually want me there. I bit my tongue to prevent the words from spilling out.

David read the hesitation and a muscle in his cheek twitched. "Are you aware there was an altercation in the village?"

My first thought went to what I'd witnessed between Laurence and Taylor. Maybe someone besides myself had seen the claws. Not wanting to admit I *had*, I asked, "What altercation?"

"Some villagers attacked Vicky and her friends in the street."

I snorted. "No they didn't." I might have been ignorant to the comings and goings at the House, but if something like that had happened in town, I would definitely have heard about it. "She wasn't even there."

"How would you know?" Victoria chimed in.

"Because, I was literally just there." I gestured behind

me where the cab they'd all seen me get out of had vanished. Too late, I realized I'd blindly walked into a trap. Victoria unleashed a tirade the likes of which I'd never seen.

"You probably goaded them to it." The viper took a step forward, wagging her finger in my face. "Don't try to play the innocent, we all know you've been running off with the townies every morning."

Anger simmered in my veins. The *only* reason I'd been skipping into town practically every day this week was because she'd made it abundantly clear I wasn't welcome here. And my so-called boyfriend wasn't doing a fucking thing to disabuse her of the notion.

"Now listen here, you vindictive bitch. You must be out of your damn mind if you think I'm just going to stand here and let you throw these wild accusations at me. Even if you *had* been in town, I'm sure whatever reason the villagers had for knocking you down a notch was probably well deserved."

"See, David? I told you she had it out for me," she simpered. "With that kind of temper, it's a miracle they didn't do more damage."

The temper in question went from red to white hot. "That's it. You want a piece of me? Come and get it. You want to see a temper? I'll give you a temper, and I don't give two figs if you are stronger than me."

I stepped forward only to have my momentum abruptly halted. I looked down in disbelief at the large hand pressed against my chest. David didn't even flinch at the expression of total betrayal that had to be written all across my face when I looked up at him.

"Charline, you have got to stop attacking Vicky," he admonished me, like I was some wayward child in need of a time out.

"You can't be serious."

"Why have you been spending so much time in the village lately?" His stern features melted into worried concern, while Victoria's eyes shone with victory.

Suddenly, I knew whatever story she'd concocted would say a redhead had been spotted near the scene of the alleged attack. She'd set me up and nothing I said would change a damn thing.

"I'm leaving." It took every ounce of willpower I had to only say those two words. Blessedly my hand didn't betray my shaking as I physically removed David's from my chest and stormed into the House. No one moved to stop me and those in my way parted without a word.

I stormed up to David's room to get away from all the prying eyes and immediately called to get another cab back. To my chagrin, it turned out that it would take hours for someone willing to come up to be available. Resigned to waiting, I pulled out a suitcase. The time at least would give me a chance to get everything ready.

I kept expecting David to walk in at any moment to explain away this awful mess. When he failed to materialize, my anger and my resolve doubled.

He's probably waiting until I've had a chance to cool off before mustering up the fucking courage to confront me.

I shoved the few remaining garments from the closet into the suitcase.

Well, joke's on him, I don't plan on still being here when he finally grows a pair.

The remaining cases lay open and empty across the room. The clothes that I'd gathered barely filled one. Everything else was dirty. I could have screamed with frustration.

A couple of hours later I found myself in the laundry waiting on my last load to dry. Since the epic scene on the lawn, no one had so much as looked at me, including David. While the menial chore filled the wait for my ride, it left my hands and mind idle. If I hadn't needed the clothes, I wouldn't have even bothered. Hell, I probably would've started walking to town.

A tiny voice in my head called me on my BS. It wasn't about the clothes at all. I was buying David time, for all the good it was doing me. Whatever tale had been spun must've been a real doozie. Of course, with no one talking to me, I had no idea what it could be.

My mind whirled with all of the horrible possibilities and I still fell short of something that could produce the level of animosity David had shown before. What could she have possibly said to make everyone react so? And David. Part of his anger I could understand, but his attitude about Eddy left me at a loss. It almost sounded like he felt threatened. But that didn't make any sense. The poor cabbie was a squat, balding man of middling age with almost fully grown children of his own.

At any rate, once this load was done, it wouldn't be my problem anymore. I sat with my feet propped up and my back to the door while I glared at the timer and debated stuffing the wet clothes in a suitcase. All of a sudden, the hairs on the back of my neck stood on end. I didn't need to turn around to know Victoria now stood behind me.

"I'm surprised you're still here. I mean, if I'd been humiliated like that in front of half the pack..."

I refused to rise to the bait. Engaging would only egg her on and I simply didn't have the energy for another verbal battle.

"It was easy, by the way. He didn't even question whether or not you'd actually been involved. I just let him make his own assumptions."

I could hear the sneer in her voice. My heart constricted painfully and my eyes stung. I hated that I believed her, but no matter what it took, I wouldn't let her see me cry.

"Fuck off, Victoria."

I jumped at the intrusion of a second voice. It sounded familiar, but it certainly wasn't Maria. A few moments slid by and then someone pulled up one of the spare folding chairs. I looked out of the corner of my eye not sure if I should be concerned, and did a double take. My rescuer was none other than the shy Isabel.

"I'm sorry, Charline." She shuffled in her chair, setting free the curtain of hair she'd pushed out of the way. "You're a good person. You don't deserve this." She paused as if unsure how to go on. "I wish I could have done more. It's all gone too far."

I held my tongue and mentally went through the countless times she could've stepped up to intervene or at least speak out like she'd just done.

"Anyway, I just wanted to say I'm sorry." She stood, leaving the chair where it was.

She was almost out the door when I finally turned to look at her. "Thank you, Isabel."

She gave me a weak smile, then left as quietly as she'd come.

16

BED & BREAKFAST

After Isabel's intervention I debated trying to stick it out a little longer. Maybe I had more friends than I believed. However, I was definitely sure I wouldn't survive another altercation with Victoria. And if I was being honest with myself, I didn't want to face David again. I shoved another stack of folded clothes so hard into the open luggage that I undid some of the work I'd just done.

The bedroom door opened and closed again with only the change in pressure and catch of the latch to betray David's entrance. An awkward moment passed while he apparently waited for me to say something.

I pretended he wasn't there.

"What are you doing?" he finally asked.

"I told you. I'm leaving." My hands tightened in the mess of fabric. I calmly extricated them and resumed carefully arranging the remaining items.

"But...but you can't."

I wanted to look him in the eye and dare him to stop me. I forcibly shoved my temper down. If I let it get the best of me now this would be so much worse.

"If this is about Victoria, I've already talked to her."

Against my better judgment, hope shimmered to life in my chest. "All you need to do is apologize."

The hope shriveled up and died. So many times, so many different opportunities and he still chose her.

"Apologize?" I asked, my anger uncoiling like a cottonmouth.

"Yes. Then we can all finally move past this." He made it sound so simple.

"Apologize to *her*?" I threw the brush I had been holding in the bag so hard it bounced out. "Why the fuck would I apologize to her?"

"Charline, this is ridiculous."

I rounded on him. "I'll tell you what's ridiculous. That no matter what happens you take her side."

"I'm not taking her side."

"Yes, you are. You always take her side!"

"I do not," he insisted.

"Name one time. One fucking time, David." I placed my hands on my hips and waited.

He didn't think long. "You're still here. I didn't send you home."

I felt like I'd been slapped, probably looked it too. "Well you needn't worry about that any more." I zipped the case so hard I was sure I'd broken the zipper. "Feel free to congratulate her for me."

"Charline, you can't leave."

"Yes, I can."

"No, you can't."

"Watch me." I ripped the door open.

"But Char...I love you."

I froze in the doorway and slowly turned to face him. "How *dare* you," I said, my voice dangerously low.

Pain flashed across his face like I'd stabbed him. It was all the head start I needed. I was at the bottom of the stairs by the time he recovered, but wasn't fast enough to get to the door before he was barring my path.

"Move."

"Charline, please, you have to listen," he pleaded.

"Like you've listened to me?" In the periphery, people filled doorways to see what the commotion was about. "Don't make a scene. I would hate for you to ruin whatever headway you've made in winning over supporters."

"I'll damn well tear the house down if I want!" He reached out to grab my arm, but stopped short when he saw that he was about to grab me where the three pearly scars proclaimed my previous abuse at the hands of a *were*.

Never would I have ever thought I'd be grateful for the unsightly marks. I took advantage of his hesitation to slip out. Much to my surprise, it was Eddy who was already parked with the trunk open, mercifully without a police escort.

David looked like he wanted to tear the man apart with his bare hands. The plump cabbie noticed and quickened his movements as much as he could.

"Thank you, Eddy. We should get going." Saying the cabbie's name aloud was an unnecessary smack, but after the casual declaration that I needed to apologize to Victoria of all people, I couldn't help myself.

I didn't look back as I slammed the door against the assortment of onlookers that had gathered. For a brief moment, it seemed like David was going to block the cab, but he glanced up as someone came outside.

I didn't have to look. I knew it was Victoria.

Any other time I would have been beside myself to stay at the gorgeously historic Stone Creek Bed & Breakfast. Today though, I looked at the colonial beauty without emotion. My bags followed on a trolley to a room on the second floor. Or maybe it was the third. I wasn't really paying attention.

The place should have been booked solid with so many of the *weres* coming from out of town. I'd caught a small break there. Thanks to the issues that had sprung up, many of the *weres* staying in town had moved to the estate, pitching tents if they couldn't find someone to share a room with. As a result, the few remaining guests were purely human and the B&B had rooms to spare.

The porter turned the old fashioned iron key in the lock and I stepped into a lavish suite. I thanked him and he left me to unpack in private. While he hadn't dubbed it the honeymoon suite, it was certainly one of the best rooms in the house. Gauzy fabric drifted down from a frame that sat atop the four poster bed to be gathered at each carved pillar. Prints of flowers and birds covered the dusty rose walls while striped, cream wallpaper rose from the deeper pink of the plush carpet to create a kind of faux wainscoting.

Everything about the room was absolutely stunning—and completely wasted on me. It spoke of love and happiness, neither of which I currently had. I pulled back the curtain, hoping my old friend the sun could help bring some life back to my world. It didn't. A glorious day shone in direct opposition to how I felt.

I looked forlornly up into the sparkling blue sky, longing for a storm that could shake the building, a deluge to drown my sorrows. The squeal of tires broke through my melancholy and I glanced down at the street, fearing a wreck. What I saw instead made me equally sick to my stomach. David's truck lurched over the curb in a haphazard park. He launched out of the driver's seat and scanned the nearby area, not even bothering to close the door. The village folk scurried away from him. He searched their retreating forms, then finally looked up, spotting me instantly.

My heavy sigh carried the last of my strength. I sagged against the sill and pulled the curtain closed. The barrier did little to hide my view of the street and I watched as he marched into the building. I cast a grateful glance at the key still in the lock and returned to the bedside to finish organizing my things.

David's loud bellow pierced the layers of building between me and the foyer. "Fine, don't tell me what room she's in, I'll find her on my own." Guilt tugged at me for having dragged the staff into our mess. They hadn't signed up for any of this. Then again, neither had I.

I'll have to find a way to make it up to them.

In barely any time at all, thundering filled the hall, then he was at the door.

"Charline!" David shouted through the thin wood. "Enough of this."

I walked a bag to the opulent bathroom, taking my time to lay out each item. The handle jiggled and I dropped my toothbrush. I quickly retrieved it and willed the sound to stop. At last the key stopped bouncing and time itself seemed to stretch into silence.

A soft thud hit the door, like he'd rested against it. "Please let me in. We can talk about this. I—"

I love you, that's what he wanted to say. Knives cut across my heart to leave it freely bleeding and struggling for life. I swallowed and returned to the bedside, leaning on it for support.

"I can fix this. You just have to let me. Char, please." The pleading in his voice was almost unbearable.

I held a hand over my mouth to help hold back the sobs. If he heard them, he'd never leave and if I caved, neither would I. The door shook in its frame from an impact on the other side. The key rattled alarmingly in the lock. Renegade tears streamed in silence down my already stained cheeks.

Different voices filtered through the door. "Sir, I'm going to need you to vacate the premises."

I could just make out David's responding growl.

"Either you can leave on your own or you can be escorted in handcuffs. Your choice."

The door wiggled in the frame as David stopped leaning against it. "Alright. Alright. I'm going."

Bless my caring townspeople, doing what they could to protect me from my terrifying werewolf boyfriend—ex—my terrifying ex-werewolf-boyfriend. I had two now. At the realization, my heart cleaved clean in two. I fell on the bed wracked with sobs that seemed determined to hollow out every feeling I'd ever had. I didn't care if he could still hear. I couldn't deny my hurt any longer.

Hours passed by in a haze of misery until a small, tentative knock came at the door. I pushed up from the pillowtop and slid with a muffled thump off the bed to my feet. An ornamental gold mirror conveyed my current appearance—a hot mess. A nearby robe would suffice to cover my disheveled clothes, but there was no hiding that I'd been crying.

Too exhausted to care, I cracked the door open and peered out. One of the girls from the front desk stood behind a tray laden with the makings of hot tea, a stiff drink, some bath salts, and if my eyes didn't deceive me, a first aid kit on the bottom tier.

"Good evening, Miss Montgomery, I...We thought you could use something to drink and..."

I opened the door the rest of the way. "Come on in, Carly." The wheels squeaked as she rolled the cart into the large space. "Thank you."

"Miss Montgomery, are you, are you alright?" Carly was

a small mouse of a girl not a day over seventeen, probably working a summer job.

"I'll be fine, sweetie." She glanced down at the bottom tier and it physically hurt to think these people believed David was abusive. "Don't worry, that won't be necessary." Her eyes narrowed with disbelief, but she didn't argue. "The only thing that hurts is my heart. These," I indicated the scars that poked out past my sleeve. "These are from a different break up."

The reassurance seemed to comfort her, then she took me by surprise as she suddenly wrapped me in a tight hug. Of all the things she'd brought, I needed that hug the most. I held her tight and fought back a fresh tide of tears.

"You're going to leave, aren't you?" she asked when she finally stepped back, her own eyes misty.

"I don't really have a choice."

"We're going to miss you."

"I'll miss all of you too. Y'all have been wonderful and I've loved getting to know you. I'll be here a little while longer though. Eddy says it will take a while to find someone who can take me all the way to Raleigh."

She gave me another quick hug and dashed out of the room, surreptitiously wiping something from her face before the door clicked shut behind her.

The sympathy in the eyes of everyone I saw confirmed my suspicion that the entire town had heard about David's visit to the B&B. Tempting as it was to stay in my room and wallow in self-pity, I needed to repay the kindness that had been so generously extended to me. No thanks to unfortunately timed engine repairs, I had plenty of time to come up with something.

The only silver lining I could find on my otherwise supremely shitty week—more like month—was that David hadn't made a reappearance. Not that I planned to sit around to see how long that would last. There was a perfectly hospitable village beyond my sanctuary and I aimed to soak up every second of it.

While I didn't feel much like primping, it did help take my mind off of things, the usual routine of doing my hair and makeup comforting in its normalcy. I walked over to the suitcase propped open on a luggage rack. So many dresses and none of them appealing. I glanced over at the discarded jeans laid over the back of a chair.

No. I have not been reduced to settling for jeans without a good reason.

A sunny yellow number appeared defiantly in my hand. Just because I felt miserable, didn't mean I had to look it. Wardrobe dilemma solved, I marched down stairs determined to fake it 'til I made it. Poor Jimmy didn't know what had hit him. Perhaps I should have settled for the sevens instead of the whole nine.

"Good, good morning, Miss Montgomery," he stammered.

"Good morning, Jimmy." As I walked up to the counter something occurred to me—eventually David *would* make an appearance and I didn't want to be caught unawares. "Can you do me a favor?" I spun a notepad around and jotted down my cell. "Give me a call if anyone shows up who maybe shouldn't." He looked dumbfounded as he took the paper.

Maybe I should have asked Carly.

At last he nodded. "S-sure thing, Miss Montgomery." That settled, I whisked outside. As it happened, Eddy was dropping another person off next door. He sure stayed busy for such a small town.

"You're looking in better spirits," he said with a jovial grin. "It's nice to see you out away from… It's just nice to see you out. Can I take you anywhere?"

"No thanks. I could do for a walk." He tipped his cap and continued to help his passenger.

Confident the episode at the House would keep the *weres* sequestered there, my walk became a leisurely stroll and I gradually relaxed. I hadn't lied when I told Carly I would miss this place. Stone Creek really was wonderful.

A familiar chip in the sidewalk caught my attention and I glanced up, surprised to find myself in front of the old bakery yet again. It seemed about time I got to the bottom of at least one mystery. With a sense of purpose, I altered my trajectory to speak with the butcher a few doors down. Darren noticed my coming and smiled, waving me over.

"Good day, ma'am," he said with a cheeky grin as he leaned against the frame of his establishment and crossed his arms to emphasize the hard-earned biceps straining against his sleeves.

The nerve. Ma'am-ing me. I checked my eyeroll and stepped closer. "Really, Darren? How old do I look?"

He gave me a once over that stopped just short of improper. "In that? I'd put you at twenty-three."

"Cute," I said, following him into the empty shop.

Ten o'clock was a strange time of day for him. Most of his commercial customers had come and gone hours ago and the regulars had yet to make the rounds. He walked through the pass-through open on the counter while I took a spot on the other side. "What can I do you for?"

"I've been meaning to ask about the vacancy next door."

"I was wondering when you'd get around to that. You certainly come by often enough." He slid another surreptitious gaze over me and offered a rueful smile.

"I'm sure it's been painful."

"You have no idea," he said, bracing his forearms on the counter to face me. I frowned at him and turned to inspect the cuts on display as he changed the topic back. "Mimi's Bakery used to do really well back in the day, but when the owner got sick, there was no one left to keep it up."

"Who was the owner?"

"Funny you should ask. I think it was actually one of the people from the mansion." I whirled around and he held up his hands defensively as he laughed. "I'm not sure if you want me to tell you or avoid anything to do with that place."

I forced myself to relax and assumed an air of nonchalance. "I could care less about the House. The old bakery, though, is a different story. I've learned practically everything else about this town. It's the only mystery I haven't unraveled." Well, one of.

"If you really want to know, I'll tell you what I can. It's not much. I was pretty young when all of this happened."

"I'll take what I can get," I said, which seemed to be my personal theme these days.

"Right, so the owner went by Mimi. I have no idea if that was her actual name. As I'm sure Eddy has told you, the scones were legendary. And...that's it."

"What? Come on, you have to give me more than that."

"I'm serious. That's all I've got. One day she got sick out of the blue and no one's heard a peep since. Consensus says she passed away, but honestly, she just disappeared. But people come and go from the mansion all the time."

I could certainly understand that. What still puzzled me was who it could've been. Admittedly, my information on pack members was scarce, yet surely there was a nugget somewhere that could point to the identity of the mysterious owner.

"What was her last name?"

"Bright? Singer? I don't know, it was a long time ago." He passed me some jerky from the sample of the day display.

I leaned against the counter and bit off a piece as I mentally tossed the names about. It wasn't much to go on and they were completely different.

Singer and Bright. Sight? No. Star? Ugh, that's worse.

Come on. I can do this. Just need to think about how people remember things.

Then it hit me. Pieces I'd had no idea I'd been missing suddenly manifested. "Did she have a son?"

"Uh, maybe?"

"He would have been about your age. Blond. Full of energy."

Darren snapped his fingers. "You know what? There *was* always a boy there. He never snuck any treats," he added more to himself.

"Bringer. Her last name was Bringer. And her son David is...was my boyfriend," I corrected.

"Was, huh?" he asked hopefully.

"Darren," I scolded, smacking him on the arm, then thanked him for the story and bid him farewell.

My feet wandered while my mind tumbled like dough in a bread machine. Once more, complete strangers gave me more information about someone who should have been willing to share these things with me.

So much for my distraction.

I looked up at the facade of an old theater that had been renovated several years ago. I knew it had been one of David's first jobs, and the offices across the way also had his hand all over them. I let out a stifled scream of frustration, startling some passersby.

An elderly woman stepped away from the group and approached. "Are you okay, dear?"

"I'm fine, Letty, just...just a little lost I guess."

"Oh, sweetheart, that sounds like that special kind of lost. Here, how about this? If you're not doing anything, why don't you join me and the girls for luncheon? We're having our weekly book club meeting today."

I giggled once. Then again. Then an entire series burst out of me. It wasn't that I found her invitation humorous, it was just so gloriously ordinary.

"Oh goodness," one of the other women in the gaggle commented to the sage head nods of the others.

"Don't worry ladies, my cheese isn't quite off its cracker just yet." The phrase only seemed to concern them further. "What I mean to say is, I would love to join you this afternoon." I fell in line and was surrounded by the group of well meaning biddies. "What are we reading?"

"Oh, you'll love it," a woman who was introduced as Ann said.

"It's quite a page turner."

"Speak for yourself, Margaret."

"You're just upset that the heroine ended up with the rogue instead of the gentleman."

"Don't we all choose the rogue?" I stifled my laughter at the succinct counter from Margaret.

"Anywho, it's a steamy one." Letty held up a paperback that boasted the rather risque image of a woman in serious danger of losing her dress and a glistening man that looked suspiciously like a blond Fabio on the cover.

Oh Lord, what have I gotten myself into?

But much to my pleasant surprise, the afternoon ended up being a marvelous adventure. My doubts that a book club concerning a steamy romance novel would only make me relive my own drama proved to be unfounded. The 'girls' as Letty called them were a hoot and a half. Between cucumber sandwiches and chicken salad they picked apart every page without mercy.

If I hadn't been so determined to be on good behavior, I could have easily been rolling on the floor laughing from the comments alone. The birds had no filter whatsoever, but they'd given me the one thing I'd been incapable of procuring for myself: a moment of peace from my thoughts. They were so successful, in fact, that by the end of the meeting I'd even devised a way to repay all of the kindness that had been finding its way to me.

17

ONCE BITTEN

It took surprisingly little convincing to get Lucas to allow me the use of his kitchen at the Lunar Cafe. However, cooking in a commercial kitchen proved to be a lot harder than expected. Thankfully, I had plenty of help navigating the industrial space, though no one would accept any compensation beyond a handful of my own recipes.

The joy of cooking with others sent me right back to the days of working alongside my mama and nana, laughing as mixers whirred and oven timers beeped. A giddiness I hadn't experienced in ages filled me as the chefs and I applauded each other on a job well done when the last parcel left the kitchen. The exorbitant quantities of food may have been more than I'd originally intended, but I wouldn't have changed a second of working with such wonderful people.

I dusted off the residual flour from my hands on a proper chef's apron and made my way to the dining room bursting at the seams with people. My heart swelled at seeing all of the smiling faces. Carly and the porter Jimmy were there. As was Eddy and his family. The tailor, the flower shop attendant, Misha from the boutique, Darren and his apprentice Lance, and so many more. I even spotted Letty and her gaggle of girls.

A cacophony of sound greeted my appearance and my efforts to wave it away went unheeded. Eventually everyone settled down and I found a vacant stool to enjoy the scene. This had always been my favorite part of cooking, not the act itself or even the eating, but the way it could bring all sorts of people together. Sadness fluttered in my chest. *This* is what I'd wanted from my time at the House, to be able to make people smile and forget their differences.

I startled as a plate manifested in front of me along with a rolled set of silverware. Lucas spared me a wink before vanishing into the kitchen, no doubt to pump everyone for as many recipes as they could recall. As I stared down at the beautifully plated food, a tear turned cold on my cheek. My appetite had suffered a major hit the last few days, but it wouldn't do for the chef to refuse her own food. My fingers tightened around the fork as I brought a small bite to my lips. After what felt like weeks of crying, none of it held any flavor for me beyond the spice of heartache, though no one else seemed to have the same issue.

As people left they came by to offer thanks and praise the food. I gave up trying to eat and focused my energy on them. Eventually, my smile gained more feeling and I graduated from waving in thanks to hugging each of them. Somewhere along the line, I'd fallen in love with these people and this town. A different heartache blossomed in my chest. I really would miss this place.

When the last person said their thanks and left the cafe, I hung up my borrowed apron and ventured into the gloriously sunny afternoon. A long walk was out of the question given my current state of exhaustion, but a short one could be just the thing to keep my spirits elevated for at least a little while longer. I turned the corner on White Oak to wander down by the bakery again and ran smack into someone hard enough to make me stagger back.

"Goodness. I'm so sorry," I said as I squinted through the harsh reflecting light.

"Oh, you will be."

My good day shattered. I quickly finished blinking the light from my eyes. Victoria's doll-like features came into focus and I could have wailed in despair.

"Can't you leave me be?" I pleaded. "You won!" That this sorry excuse for a woman had reduced me to begging for peace and admitting defeat made my stomach threaten to reject my tasteless lunch.

"How can I? You ran into me. Remember?" For all I knew, she'd been lying in wait, but pointing that out would accomplish nothing.

"Why are you in Stone Creek, Victoria? I thought Alexander ordered everyone to stay away from the humans." Also wasn't worth pointing out that I fell into that category.

"I have business. Besides, I confess, I was kind of hoping I'd bump into you." Every bit of that sounded sketchy.

I strode forward, but she stepped into my path and pushed me back. "Haven't you done enough?"

"There's always more that can be done," she said with another shove.

"Why are you doing this?"

"Honestly? At first, it was just because a *were* like David has no business being with a pathetic human. But now? Now, it's just fun." She punctuated her words with yet another push.

"Knock it off."

"Or what?" She pushed again, harder this time, and I stumbled back a step before I could catch my balance. "Don't you want to know how David is doing after your... episode?" Her features twisted into a feral grin.

"Not really." I shifted to take a different route. She advanced, cutting me off.

"He needed *so* much comforting after you walked out. Of course, I was more than happy to oblige. He ran right to me the second the door closed."

"No he didn't." Even though I knew for a fact she was lying—he'd followed me to the B&B—doubt spread through me. It was exactly what I'd feared was happening the whole time.

She raised an eyebrow and ruthlessly went on. "You know, I hadn't realized all of the ways he'd grown. He's quite impressive, even for a *were*." I knew she was goading me, and worse, she could tell it was working. My temper flared white hot. She kept on pushing me to emphasize her vile story. "So generous, so passionate. You know it reminded of the night we ran together, he—"

My hand cracked across her face with a mind all its own. Her head snapped to the side with the force of the blow and shock exploded across her face along with a hand print quickly shifting from ruby red to purple.

"You bitch!" she screamed as she pulled her fingers away to find tiny drops of blood from where my nails had broken skin.

Between one blink and the next, she got over her surprise. Her eyes filled with animal fury as she launched herself at my throat. I barely moved in time and nails like talons dug into my shoulders. A shout tore from my throat as we fell back to the ground in a rolling heap.

I looked around in search of a camera or witness or something as I tried to get my feet under me. The street remained bereft of life, oblivious to my need for help. My stomach gave a sickening twist as the reality of my situation settled. Victoria had set me up, had probably orchestrated the whole mess from the beginning. My mind's eye flashed to the image of black hair in a narrow hallway.

"You! I *knew* you were at the Cafe that day." She snarled a response not fit for a human mouth and fear spiked through me at a fresh realization—*She's going to kill me.*

Terror at what this monster planned to do to me powered my limbs. I elbowed her in the gut as hard as I could, buying myself a few precious inches.

People, I need people.

My legs became a canvas of scrapes and scratches from the gritty sidewalk as I scrambled to get away. She kept me pinned. Distantly, I wished I'd worn jeans instead of a dress. She grabbed my ankle as I tried once again to regain my footing, yanking me back down.

I bit my tongue as my knee crashed to the ground with a sickening crunch. My stomach heaved and the metallic tang of blood filled my mouth while hot streams of it ran down my leg. My hand found its way to her hair and I pulled for all I was worth. She growled and easily knocked me loose, causing me to roll a ways.

At last, I stumbled to a mostly upright position only to be immediately slammed into a brick wall. My head cracked against the unforgiving surface and my vision swam with discordant motes of color. I tried in vain to pull her off, but she was latched on in some kind of demented piggyback.

A shout ripped through my throat as pain shot through my shoulder. I spun and smashed her against the very wall with which I'd just been intimately acquainted as hard as I could. Once. Twice. Until her hold loosened enough and I stumbled free a few steps. My shoulder throbbed from whatever she'd done to it and I feared she'd actually taken a chunk out.

Mercifully, I caught sight of people drawn to the noise of the fight and lurched toward them on unsteady legs. Victoria's gaze raked over the gathering crowd and snapped back to me. While she dithered about continuing to rip me apart piece by piece, more people arrived. Another look at the accumulating witnesses and she spun to retreat the opposite direction, forcibly relocating those who didn't jump out of her way fast enough.

Relief bubbled at my lips. I took another shaky step and my leg gave out. Instead of the unforgiving ground, I hit something soft. I blinked through the haze of pain to see Darren over me. The buzz of voices hummed indistinctly in my ears as I struggled to focus.

"No...no hospital," I mumbled in response to the half-heard insistence that something be done. Despite my head throbbing hard enough to fracture my thoughts, I still knew that would be a mistake. I'd been on the losing end of a fight with a werewolf in broad daylight, but the world didn't know about those. I couldn't risk exposing David or Sara.

"At least let us call the local GP," a voice argued. I blinked, surprised to find not Darren, but Jimmy, the red brick of the Bed and Breakfast behind him and no recollection of being moved.

"I'm fine really. Just a few cuts and scrapes, that's all. A hot shower and some rest will put me right as rain." I prayed Jimmy wouldn't press the matter as he continued to scrutinize me for another hot minute then nodded.

"I'll help you up to your room and have someone send up a first aid kit." Relieved that I wouldn't have to muster the energy to keep talking or get my banged-up self to my room on my own, I waved in thanks to Darren in the driver's seat and let Jimmy assist me out of the car.

Finally alone in my room, I took stock of my injuries while the tub filled with steaming water. The goose egg on my head would take time to go down and ibuprofen would have to cover the throbbing headache. Smears of red-tinted dirt covered my legs, but at least my knee had stopped bleeding. I hissed in pain as I brushed away loose gravel from the cuts so I wouldn't take dirt into the tub, then carefully removed the rags of my dress.

The ruined fabric fell in a heap to the tiled floor and I leaned forward to get a better look at whatever Victoria had done to my shoulder. Pain radiated from the mass of bruising and turned my stomach. I gave up my tentative exploration, the area too swollen to make out anything useful, and lowered myself with exaggerated care into the tub.

The superficial scrapes on my knees stung as they submerged in the scalding liquid. I bit the inside of my cheek to keep from crying out. Inch by agonizing inch, I lowered myself until my bottom hit porcelain. I leaned back against a rolled towel, mindful of the talon marks on my back and my injured head. The water around me turned a faint shade of pink as I carefully washed every inch of me, giving special attention to my abused shoulder.

After toweling dry, I put on the lightest dress I could find in my luggage, my movements slow and pained as soreness took hold. I would have preferred the fluffy robe, but my overly-sensitive skin was having none of that. Even the soft down stung where it touched the scratches. Thinking back to the last time I had gotten scratches and how long they'd taken to heal, I did not relish the experience this promised. Now more than ever, I was eager to be safe and sound back in my little yellow house.

Maybe the next town over has a place where I can rent a car.

It wasn't until the door swung open that I realized I'd forgotten to lock it. I looked up from doctoring my knee, expecting to see Carly with some tea or Jimmy with a well-meaning treat from the kitchen. I certainly hadn't expected

David to be standing there, his broad shoulders filling the frame, his face a twisted contradiction of worry and anger.

Shit.

I straightened, doing my best not to put too much weight on the damaged appendage. Once the adrenaline had worn off, the swelling had set in with a vengeance and my insistence on moving around was not helping matters.

"What the hell happened?" he demanded.

"Why even ask? You clearly already know the whole story. I'm sure Victoria gave you a colorful play by play." She must have run back to him as fast as her twiggy legs would carry her.

"I have her story. I want yours."

"What do you want me to say? Yes, I slapped your precious Vicky in her stupid face. Quite frankly, I should have done it weeks ago."

"Damn it, Charline, you can't do that. The humans and wolves are already at each other's throats." He dragged a hand through his hair and shook his head. "Fighting in the middle of the street? Do you realize what you've done?"

"What *I've* done! All I've *done* is defend myself. No one else was going to fucking do it." David recoiled as I threw the antiseptic down on the comforter before I could squeeze the tube into oblivion. "You don't honestly think *I* started that fight?" Doubt flashed in his eyes, confirming my suspicions. "Seriously? How stupid do you think I am? She's a werewolf for Christ's sake!" I barely brought my voice down, realizing at the last moment that the door was still open. On the upside of being totally pissed, the adrenaline pumping through my veins dulled the ache dominating my body.

"Then why did you hit her?"

"I was provoked."

"That's not a good enough reason. What could she have possibly said to goad you into doing something so reckless?"

"You, David, she goaded me about you. About how you ran to her for comfort." His flinch said that was at least partially true. "How she enjoyed having her way with you. That she liked how much you'd changed. About all sorts of horrible things. And that was just today."

"And you believed her?"

"Why shouldn't I?"

"How many times do I have to tell you, nothing is going on between us—nothing ever has and nothing ever will. Why can't you believe me?"

"Because you haven't given me a reason to!" I shouted, throwing my arms out for emphasis and immediately hissing in pain as I tore open the scab on my shoulder. I turned to the nearest mirror to inspect the damage. "Shit. It's bleeding again." I snatched up a nearby hand towel to staunch the renewed crimson flow, but even with the scab gone, the swelling was still so bad I wasn't sure what it was.

"Charline, what's that?" David asked, his voice suspiciously calm, especially after I'd been yelling at him.

I looked over my shoulder. "It's nothing."

"It looks like a bite mark."

"Probably because it is." Of course, once he said it, the pattern made sense. I dabbed carefully at the wound dripping blood all over the bodice of my clean dress.

"Who did that?"

I snorted. "Really, David? Who do you think?"

"Vicky did that?"

"No, I bit my fucking self. What can I say, your bitch fights dirty. No surprise there."

"Damn it, Charline, give me a straight answer. Did Victoria bite you?"

I hadn't heard him step closer and his sudden proximity and intensity frightened me. My quippy comeback fizzled into a feeble, "Yes."

His face paled alarmingly as all of the color drained from it. "No. No, no, no, no." He grabbed his head as if somehow it could stop the truth of what was right in front of him.

"Yes, your evil little pet bit me after tricking me into fighting her in the first place. A fight I clearly lost, in case that slipped your notice."

He continued to shake his head in open denial. "Stop being so flippant. Victoria tried to kill you."

"I know. I was there!" I tossed aside the ruined cloth and administered a fresh round of antiseptic and ointment to the viscous wound.

"Charline, you don't understand. This," his hand engulfed my shoulder coming just shy of the bite. The pressure hurt, but I stood my ground. "This is bad."

"No shit, Sherlock. Hurts like the devil too."

He took a shuddering breath. "This is a death sentence."

"No, it's not." I rolled my eyes. "She barely even broke skin."

"Char, you were bitten."

"Yes, we've established that," I said, though his excessive calm was starting to freak me out.

"By a werewolf," he added for emphasis.

"That's what you're worried about?" I dismissed the concern. "She wasn't even changed." Despite my confidence, a note of uncertainty crept into the bravado.

"That doesn't mean anything."

"So, so I'll turn. Just like..." I trailed off as my mind struggled to grasp the leap in logic and the world gave the faintest teeter. "I'll be..." My chest heaved as it became harder and harder to breathe.

"Charline, you don't get it. There was never a guarantee Sara would turn. It was just as likely that she could have died in that hospital bed. And after..." He trailed off. This part I knew, this part we'd come dangerously close to—after, she could have gone mad and died anyway. My chest spasmed.

"I'm going to die," I whispered as an uncontrollable shaking wracked my body.

"Charline, I'm so sorry," he whispered in my hair as he wrapped his arms around me.

I'm going to die. She's won. She's really truly won.

"I'm right here." He held me tighter and I leaned into his reassuring warmth. I'd missed this, missed him. I wanted nothing more than to give into the longing that ached in my heart, to relax into his strong embrace. But it was too late for that.

I took a trembling breath and pushed myself free. The sadness in his eyes almost broke my resolve as I wrapped my arms around my middle. "You need to leave."

"Charline."

"I mean it. Go." Tears streaked freely down my cheeks.

"Please," he begged as he backed away. "Please don't do this

"Go."

His eyes implored me to reconsider as he reached for the handle. "Char."

"I said get out!" A sob tore through me, raw and visceral, the second the door slammed home. I fell to the ground not even caring if it was locked. My fractured piece of the world gave a final splinter and shattered.

18

TWICE SHY

I rolled onto my side, my body still heavy with sleep, and my stomach lurched into my throat. The comforter tangled around my legs as I struggled to get free of the bed before I could be sick all over it. My feet hit the ground and I swallowed back a fresh wave of nausea as the impact radiated up my leg. I limped to the bathroom as fast as my injured knee would allow and barely made it in time before bile burned my esophagus.

I lost track of time as the cold tile warmed beneath me. Eventually, the convulsions stopped and I crawled my way to the sink to rinse my mouth out with water that tasted vilely of sugar. With the aid of walls, counters, and whatever else I could get my hands on, I stumbled back to the bed where I collapsed, utterly exhausted. I lay there panting for breath until I had the energy to scrutinize my throbbing knee. No sooner did I look, than I wished I hadn't.

Varying shades of purple and yellow mottled the torn flesh that had swollen while I slept. I glanced at the nightstand and gaped in shock. A whole day had frittered away according to my phone and the digital clock on the stand. My gaze shifted to my dwindling medical supplies. I'd have to venture out to get more. I also needed food. My stomach clenched at the thought, but I persevered and pushed back out of the bed.

I discarded yet another blood-stained dress and carefully put on a fresh one of a similar style, then delicately swept my hair aside to inspect my shoulder. Definitive teeth marks shone in high relief against the contrast of red, puffy skin. Having learned my lesson from probing my knee, I refrained from touching the bite. I gently layered my bedraggled hair over the wound and reached for the room phone to call the front desk.

"Good morning, Miss Montgomery," Jimmy said after the second ring with an audible note of relief.

"Hey. I know it's late, but do you think if I came down I could still get some breakfast?"

"That won't be necessary. I'll have something sent up for you."

"No, I don't want to make a fuss. I can come down."

"No fuss, ma'am. Carly will be up shortly with your usual tea. Did you have a preference for breakfast? Yogurt? Oatmeal? May I recommend a croissant? They were excellent today. I'm sure Bart still has a couple."

I frowned at his unusual chatter. "Jimmy, why don't you want me to come downstairs?"

"You should be resting."

"And..." I prompted.

He hesitated before dropping his voice to a whisper. "He's still here. He never left." I could clearly visualize David sitting in one of the oversized red chairs in the lobby. "We called the cops, but they said he's not actually doing anything." That didn't really surprise me. I suspected the cops that had been called either knew better than to mess with people from the House or were actually pack themselves. "He's looking at me."

Because he can hear you.

I gripped the phone until the plastic squeaked in protest. The unmitigated gall of David staking out the B&B and making my young friend anxious. "Tell him to leave or I'm calling Alexander."

"Is that his dad?" Jimmy asked, understandably confused.

"Close enough."

"Yes ma'am." His voice shook, but he didn't argue.

"And Jimmy? He has thirty minutes." I replaced the phone in the cradle and pinched the bridge of my nose to stave off yet another crying fit. I didn't envy the boy.

An hour went by and as promised Carly came and went. My knee hurt like hell as I made my way nervously down to the lobby. I let out an audible sigh of relief at finding the space blessedly empty. While confident in my threat, there'd still been the chance David would ignore Alexander's standing order.

Jimmy looked up at my approach and raced over. "I couldn't believe it, Miss Montgomery. He left just like you said. At first it didn't look like he would, but sure enough, out he went. Imagine a big guy like that afraid of his dad." Jimmy shook his head in disbelief.

When I could finally get a word in, I asked, "Do you know where I could go to see a doctor?" Jimmy's eyes narrowed with unspoken reproach. "I know, I know. Ease up on the guilty stare. You could give my nana lessons."

His mouth twisted to the side, but he dropped the glare. "Doctor Fitz should be in his office. I'll get Eddy to take you and call ahead."

Eddy must have been close by, because in a matter of minutes we pulled up in front of an office that declared its occupant to be Randolph Fitz, General Practitioner. I got signed in and a short while later, an older man, probably in his late seventies, with a kind face, a receding hairline, and soft, wrinkled hands led me to an examination room.

"You must be Charline Montgomery. Jimmy called to say you were coming. Please make yourself comfortable." He gestured to the exam table, but neglected to mention whether or not I'd be changing into the paper dressing gown folded neatly on the stool.

"I apologize about the late notice, Dr. Fitz. I know it's highly improper to basically walk in and expect to be seen."

He waved away my apology and added with a warm smile that crinkled his eyes, "Do we look busy to you?"

I gave a nervous laugh and sat as instructed, disregarding the gown. He waited until I settled, then launched into pleasantries as he began a cursory examination.

"How long have you been in town?"

"Just over a month, almost two. I've actually been up at the House for most of it though. Staying in town is a more recent development." He nodded his head as if none of this was news to him. I let out a puff of air. Of course it wouldn't be news, the way this town gossiped...

"You're from the Raleigh area, right?"

"Yes, but I'm originally from Macon. It's in Georgia," I clarified at his puzzled expression. Another nod.

"Right, so tell me about what happened."

I was a little surprised he bothered to ask. Surely the whole town was aware of what had happened by now. "I was in a fight." When I failed to elaborate he stared at me over the rim of his spectacles. "...with a w-woman." I bit my lip and hoped he didn't notice the stutter, unfortunately his severe expression suggested he'd caught the hiccup.

His fingers deftly probed around my knee, investigating the scrapes and the massive bruising that had developed. "When?"

"Day before yesterday."

"When was your last period?"

I stared down at his thinning hair in shock. True it was a standard enough question at any doctor I'd ever been to, yet under the current circumstances I could hardly see how it was relevant. Relevant or not, though, I had no idea as to the answer, which was downright embarrassing. "Umm...I don't know."

He continued his examination unphased. "How does this feel?" His fingers pressed down into the skin around my shoulder and I cried out.

"It hurts like hell." The pressure immediately lessened. It wasn't until I caught our reflection in the mirror on the door that I realized he was nowhere near the bite.

"What have you used to treat the wounds?"

"Honestly? Whatever the desk had. I'm pretty sure they'll need to restock their first aid supplies." I felt a little bad about going through enough antiseptic and gauze to effectively clean them out. I swayed a bit on the table as the morning's exertions finally caught up with me.

Dr. Fitz narrowed his kind eyes at me over his half-moon spectacles. "How long have you been experiencing fatigue?"

"Does forever count?" He didn't seem to appreciate my flippant response and I wilted. "I...uh...awhile. Hard to say though. A couple weeks. Maybe a month?" It didn't take a genius to see that he found my responses less than satisfactory. Finally, he straightened up and placed his hands in his lap.

"I'm going to prescribe an anti-inflammatory to take care of the knee as well as a heavy-duty antibiotic to combat the infection I can already see taking root on your shoulder. In addition, I'm putting you on bed rest and on a diet of broth to keep your fluids up." He stood from his seat and straightened his coat.

"But I'm leaving soon," I argued.

"Not on that knee, you're not. I'll have Patricia call Eddy to pick you up with instructions to get the prescriptions on the way back to the B&B." He opened a drawer and pulled out a sealed package. "I'll also put in an order for extra strength ibuprofen to help with the pain," he added as he removed a syringe from the protective plastic.

"Um, what's that for?"

"Blood work. It's vital to see how advanced the infection has become so we can take appropriate measures." He gestured for me to rotate my arm so he could tie the rubber tubing around my elbow. I hesitated, then did as he asked. "I'll do what I can to get you the results as soon as they're available."

By the time I was remitted back to Eddy's care, bone-weary exhaustion weighed me down. I made it all the way back to my room and out of my dress, then flopped onto the bed for a well-earned nap. The beautiful darkness of slumber danced on the periphery when a knock came at the door and chased it away. I groaned with disappointment and carefully pushed myself up.

"Who is it?" I asked, swaying beside the bed in nothing more than my undergarments.

"It's Darren."

"Just a minute." I scoured the room for something decent. The dress caught my eye and was quickly dismissed. It had been difficult enough to get out of the first time. Then I spied the robe thrown across a chair. It would have to do. I took a deep breath and slid it on, securing it tightly. My stomach immediately heaved at the unwanted pressure being placed on my shoulder.

"You alright?" he asked through the door.

I opened my mouth to respond and immediately snapped it shut as my stomach threatened again. A few steadying breaths later, I shuffled over to the door and opened it to find Darren standing there with a small bouquet of flowers.

"Sorry, you kind of caught me unawares." Never in a million years would I have thought Darren was the sort of man to blush, but his cheeks darkened nonetheless as he took in the sight of me wrapped in the fluffy robe.

"No, I'm sorry. I don't want to intrude. The lads and I just wanted to see how you were doing. I can come back another time."

Preferable as that would be, deeply ingrained hospitality won out. "No, it's alright. Besides, you're already here. Come in." I stepped aside. "Help yourself." I gestured to an untouched tray of cheese and fruit no doubt left by Carly.

"Are you sure?" He placed the flowers in a cup half full of what I hoped was water. I waved away the question and sat in a nearby chair before I could fall over from exhaustion.

"So the lads, eh?" I prodded. He passed me a plate that consisted of samples from the tray. I set it on my lap, then politely forgot about it.

"Alright, mostly me," he confessed as he took a seat across from me. "To be fair, they were concerned." He popped a cube of cheese in his mouth.

"I appreciate the thought. It's nice to know y'all care." I laughed. The room swam a bit and I stopped. This needed to be a very short visit.

"So I have to ask," he raised an eyebrow, "how does the other guy look?" He chuckled at his own joke.

"I might feel better if she looked worse. Sadly, the only thing to show I smacked her at all is the fact that my hand feels like a cast iron skillet got dropped on it." I held up my hand for emphasis. Already the anti-inflammatory was doing its work in bringing the swelling down.

"At least you got a good shot in."

"Shame it will be gone by now."

"What?"

"Nothing, I'm still a little out of it."

"Then I'm not gonna keep you. You rest. I can come by another time." He went to pat my knee, but stopped short when I flinched.

"That would be great. Sorry I'm not a better host."

"Not a problem. I'll come by again later." He surprised me by placing a small kiss on my cheek, then excused himself.

Once my shock wore off, I shuffled over to the door and locked it, then dropped the robe in an unceremonious heap and crawled into the bed without caring to shut the curtains.

Sleep and mind-numbing boredom consumed the next few days. Darren never did reappear as promised though I did get several calls every time David did. Food went cold as I barely managed to stomach a few spoonfuls before racing to expel the much needed fluids.

I debated reaching out to Dr. Fritz for a house call as the bite got worse and the flush of fever started burning in my veins. Then I got the call that someone was finally available to take me back to my perfect little yellow house, my beacon of salvation.

In blatant disregard of Dr. Fitz's orders, I scurried with manic energy to collect my things. Everything would be fine if I could just get home. A part of me recognized the delusion, but my fevered mind didn't give two figs. I'd schedule an appointment with my own doctor and all of this would become nothing more than a horrible nightmare.

I hummed to myself as I gathered the last few items from

the bathroom, then hobbled back to the main room. Shock slammed into me like a wall at the sight of David standing in the middle of the room. My armful rained to the floor in a horrible clatter of plastic. Shampoo rolled under the bed along with a soap bar. My toothbrush bounced almost all the way back into the bathroom.

A quick look showed the key still firmly in the lock. "H-how did you get in here?"

"The window was open."

"So, what? You let yourself in?" Forget the fact that he'd have to scale three stories up the front of the building. I bent down and angrily began collecting the renegade items. The exertion made me light-headed and I had to steal myself before standing straight. The ones beneath the bed would have to wait.

"You're not taking my calls and I know the front clerk isn't giving you my messages."

"Why should he?"

He wrinkled his nose. "He obviously lets others up. It smells like the guy who tried to bring you flowers."

"What do you mean 'tried'?"

David shrugged his shoulders and refused to answer. I glared at him and considered chucking the few items I'd reacquired at his head, then I remembered I had shit aim and a bum shoulder.

"You don't get a say in who sees me and who doesn't," I said as I shuffled over to my original destination. A wave of nausea and dizziness swept over me and I leaned against the mattress for support. This was not the time for my burst of energy to fail me. David stepped forward, his hand extended to help. I leveled a warning glare then deposited the gathered items unceremoniously in the case.

"Where are you going?" he asked softly like I was some

kind of skittish animal. To be fair, if I could have bolted, I probably would have.

"Home. I'm going home." I took a sip of water to try and mask my growing unsteadiness.

"You're not well."

"And whose fault is that?"

David turned a faint shade of green. I couldn't tell if it was because he blamed himself or Victoria; either way, he was at least partly to blame for my current state.

"I don't want to be here anymore."

"At least wait until the moon. Please."

"I won't turn, David. I just want to go home, to *my* house." My hand started to shake from holding the heavy glass.

"You don't know that. You need to rest."

"I'm fine and I'm going home. Nothing is going to happen. I'm sure work won't mind if I come back early." Water sloshed onto the nightstand.

"You can't leave."

"Yes, I can. I've already lined up a ride."

"Please, Charline," he begged, his voice cracking with desperation.

I squeezed my eyes shut, so I wouldn't have to see the pained expression on his face. "No, David. I can't do this anymore. I just want to go home."

I flipped the top down on the case and fanned myself. Only a few more things and I'd be done. Without thinking, I moved the hair plastered to my skin to get some cooler air on my neck. Before I could blink, David was on top of me, moving the hair even more to the side.

"This looks infected," he said as his fingers stirred the air above the gruesome bite. My stomach heaved. I didn't have to see it to know that it was oozing a greenish substance.

"Bitch probably doesn't brush her teeth," I snapped, but

the barb lacked feeling. "I'm fine. I have antibiotics." I moved to push him away and the world tilted and blurred like I'd had three too many shots of tequila. His hands wrapped around my arms to steady me. I drew in a sharp intake of air and he instantly released me.

"You're burning up," he gasped.

I fumbled for words as the room got fuzzier and fuzzier. "You...you lost all rights to touch me when...when you chose her." I took a step back with my bad leg and crumpled to the ground hard enough to make the lamp rattle.

"Charline!"

The shout echoed in my head like a timpani. I struggled to focus, blinking bleary eyed at my surroundings. Why was I on the floor? Who was shouting? Someone grabbed at me and I recoiled.

"Leave me alone," I mumbled, unable to do more. Then, as if by magic, my body rose into the air. I'd always wanted to fly. However, the room spun violently when I tried to see how I was managing it and my current state of weightlessness disagreed immeasurably with my stomach.

A door clicked open, which didn't make a lick of sense, because the damn thing was locked. Vague patches of pink turned to streaks of green. I opened my eyes wider to gain a better picture and found a distorted Jimmy walking on the wall.

"Sir—"

"Move."

"I'm afraid I can't let you take Miss Montgomery." Bless his heart. He's such a sweetheart. He'd make some girl very happy one day. "She needs a hospital."

"She's coming with me."

"I..."

"Look kid, you can either get out of my way or I can push you over the banister. Your choice."

"I'm going to have to call the cops."

"Do it."

My head lolled to the side in search of the source of the rude threat. The image of David on the ceiling sharpened as my eyelids fluttered only to blur back out.

The world around me continued to fade in and out. Brief flashes of clarity came like a snapshot, then dissipated. I was floating—no, I was in a car. No, that was wrong too. A truck? I floated for a while and then the flying sensation returned along with a massive white pillar that dominated my view.

"Maria!"

I winced at the harsh sound.

"Get her upstairs," a softer voice said. I caught a glimpse of a woman with silver in her hair. She reminded me of an angel I'd seen in church once. "Mac, Lucia, help me with the ice. We need to cool her down."

"Is she going to be okay?"

"I...I don't know."

19

RETRIBUTION

Sleep and wakefulness wove together, a dark tide punctuated by an all-consuming fire and a pain in my middle that
refused to relent. On the occasions I managed to crack my
eyes, the world moved disjointed beyond me, like scenes
from a movie with inconsistent sound.

I willed my heavy lids to part and a sliver of vision
emerged. David sat in a chair designed for aesthetics rather
than comfort. Golden scruff covered his gaunt and haggard
face. Shadows danced beneath sunken eyes, emphasizing
the unhealthy hollow of his cheeks.

I should tell him to eat something.

My stomach lurched violently at the thought of food.
The vision became awash with pain and faded into nothing.

Blink.

Something hit the surface I lay on and I jolted awake. I
wanted to close my eyes against the increasing noise that
came with awareness, but also wanted to see the source of
my sudden discomfort. The world spun in a blur of color as
I continued to be jostled.

I struggled to focus enough to provide identities for the
multitude of people crowding the small room. The bed

seemed to pitch beneath me. I squeezed my eyes shut and pinched my lips together to ward off the resulting nausea.

A small tube swam in my vision. I looked past it to its bearer and squinted at the indistinct face.

"Sweetie, you have to eat something." The angelic voice registered, but no amount of want could bring their features into focus.

"Please, baby, just a little bit," a sad voice implored me.

I groaned, the effort of stringing words together too much. That voice, I knew that voice. I didn't want to hear it sad, but between the pain and exhaustion I couldn't remember why. The straw pressed to my lips again. I moaned at the intrusion and turned away. I didn't want food, that only made it hurt more. Didn't these insistent voices know that? I slid back into darkness to escape.

Blink.

Light swirled like mist in the room, surreal and insubstantial, while agony saturated me from head to toe. I peered through the gloomy veil at an empty room. Recognition danced at the fringes of awareness as my gaze settled on an empty chair. I struggled to figure out why its vacancy bothered me and dragged my attention to the next nearest thing in my limited field of vision.

Thirst clawed at my insides and turned my tongue to sandpaper. I desperately sought out water, but found a framed photo instead. Bright colors smudged together and I had to blink a few times to bring the image of two people into focus. Happiness radiated from their smiling faces and the crushing weight of loneliness settled on my chest.

I gasped, strangled for air, and someone came into the empty space. A small cry filled the room, then darkness.

Blink.

Pushy hands jerked me out of my hollow of nothingness into a sharp reality of sensation. My body fluctuated wildly between freezing cold and burning hot. Panicked questions shot through the contradiction of pain.

"Why is she bleeding? What's wrong? How do I make it stop?"

I latched onto the frenzy of concern and everything else fell away. Who was bleeding? Lost in my sea of darkness, I wondered if it could be me, except it couldn't be, because I couldn't feel anything, not anymore. Concern stabbed through me as I realized even the pushy hands barely registered on my suddenly numb body. I focused harder on their touch and the world blasted into painful color.

"Hold her down."

"I...I..."

"This is not the time to be squeamish. Help me. She'll hurt herself."

Someone screamed and kept screaming. I wished they would stop.

Blink.

Near perfect night encompassed the room, disturbed only by the soft yellow light of a lamp sitting on the floor. I longed to escape the heat of too many heavy blankets weighing me down, but couldn't convince my body to move. Frustrated, my eyes rolled in search of help and found a woman who vaguely resembled a porcelain doll standing in the open door.

My gaze shied away from the unpleasant figure and lit on the man with golden scruff. He sat in the same uncomfortable chair and stared at me. No, stared through me.

"You're not welcome here," he said without turning to acknowledge the woman, a hint of danger edging the flat declaration.

The woman said something I couldn't make out, then turned to leave. The man's frozen gaze shifted to follow her and she hesitated.

"If she dies, you will never run with the pack again. I'll make sure of it." The woman blanched and left without another word.

I wonder who's dying?

Maybe it's me.

Blink.

The man with golden hair gestured emphatically as he shouted at a young man with black hair and the angel that kept trying to feed me. "I'm telling you I saw her eyes flash yellow."

The boy looked over at me, doubt clear in his own eyes. "David, I understand that this has been really stressful."

"You don't understand anything."

"You're not sleeping. You need food and rest. You're no good to her like this," the angel added.

"I can't sleep, not until I know."

"Then change at least."

"No, the last time I left... No, I won't leave her again."

"You stubborn boy, if you don't take care of your own wounds, how do you expect to help her?"

"I'll be fine." He turned back to address the youth. "They were yellow. I didn't imagine it."

The young man hesitated. "I know it's not easy to accept, but I think you're just seeing what you want to see."

David turned to face me and the light shone on a nasty bruise on his face along with deep gashes running the length of his arm. "I know what I saw."

Blink.

An older version of the boy stood in the room with what looked like a pair of bodyguards. "You will *not* turn in this House."

"I won't leave her." David's weary face crumpled as if the mere act of saying the words hurt. Gashes still ripped across his flesh, though the bruise on his face had paled to a disturbing yellow.

The man gestured to the others with him and they stepped towards me. "Then she'll have to go with you." David moved to intervene when two more guards came in from the hall and restrained him.

"Alexander, please. Alpha."

The older man remained unmoved by his pleas. "Take him." David's panicked gaze fell on me as he struggled in vain against their hold and they dragged him from the room.

The original pair lifted me with a care that contradicted the rough treatment of David. The room transformed into a hallway, then a large room that bounced. When I found David again, he sagged defeated between the two guards while his worried gaze searched me. A door opened behind him.

Blink.

Trees rose up all around me. The men from earlier were gone and a clear patch of sky studded with stars winked at me through a distant canopy. Suddenly, David's face, clouded with shadow, obscured the sight.

"I'll only be a moment. I'm coming right back." He placed a kiss on my forehead that burned like a brand then was gone.

I moaned into the night as heat continued to radiate out from where he'd touched me. Pain pulsed through my shoulder in time with my heartbeat. I vaguely recalled something biting me. A woman's face flashed in my mind, pale and cruel.

Agony ripped through my shoulder as I arched off the ground only to have my body try to fold itself in half the other way. My eyes flew open as pain flooded my senses, erasing the feel of heat with a new torrent that defied description. I choked on a call for help as I stared straight up at a perfect white sphere that eclipsed everything else. For a single microscopic second, the world froze, then splintered into a million pieces.

My cry hit the canopy and bounced back as the bones in my fingers twisted and broke. Bile crawled up my throat as my shoulder punched into the ground hard enough to dislocate. I rolled to the side and vomited pure acid onto the earth through twisted lips. My hand rose shakily to my face to inspect the wrongness and I screamed as my arm bent at an unnatural angle. Agony dominated my existence, it went on and on without any hint of subsiding, and then—it stopped.

Aches twitched in my muscles as I ventured to stand, but the torture didn't renew. I took a ragged breath that didn't burn, didn't *hurt*. All around me, the torn earth stood testament to my violent seizure, while each panted breath brought more strength. I took an unsteady step and details launched out of the darkness. Cracked bark, fuzzy moss, the scrabble of tiny feet high above. I struggled to get my thoughts to focus and the last memory before the pain floated to the surface: Victoria.

A howl rose up in the darkness.

Ash, oak, and pine flew past without touching me. I weaved around roots and rocks, leaping over the obstacles that couldn't be avoided. Faster and faster I ran, zeroing in on the sound, until I burst into a large clearing lit by the full moon above. The shrill note cut off abruptly as the gathering of wolves turned to look at me.

Confusion curled around my mind and I took a wary step back. None of them seemed familiar. I searched the faces for the one in my mind, but they were all wrong. Not one had a doll's features with a curtain of black framing it.

Then I saw her. She looked nothing like what my mind said, but I knew without question it was her.

My backtrack ceased and I rushed where she stood frozen, eyes wide in alarm. I barreled into her full force, heedless of the pain, and sent her smaller frame flying. Dirt flew as I skidded to a halt and searched for where she'd landed. Everything swiveled into painful clarity only to fuzz out again as my gaze swept the area.

Several yards away she pulled herself up, her sleek canine form scrawny and insubstantial compared to mine. Her feet back under her, she turned and growled, her lip curling over viciously sharp teeth. My own threat rolled through me and fear flashed in her eyes as I charged again. This time she moved aside, snapping at my foot as I skidded past. Claws dug into the earth and I snapped back, catching her tail. She let out a loud yip and claws tore into my side.

I snarled as a wave of pain washed over me. My growl turned savage and I bucked her off, kicking out with my back legs. The other wolves stood by as my teeth sank into her collar. She squealed in pain, yet still none of them moved to intervene. Blind rage blocked everything else out as I shook her violently from side to side. My hold loosened and I bit again harder. She wiggled free and made it half a step before I grabbed her leg and dragged her down. Claws and teeth flashed in the moonlight. Red shone wetly in the white light. At last, she gave a final whimper and rolled over, exposing her pale belly to the night.

I stepped back, my sides heaving from exertion, and surveyed the damage I'd wrought. A look around the clearing showed the other wolves now seated. Not a paw moved in aid of my adversary. I looked over at the crunch of underbrush, the first true sound that had registered since the fight had stopped. Out of the same undergrowth I'd flown through, stepped a wolf much larger than the others.

Even half out of my mind I could recognize David.

He stepped into the clearing and his sandy coat shone beneath the moon. The eyes of the onlookers swiveled to follow his progression. Another step.

I lowered my head and growled, my teeth dangerously close to Victoria's exposed belly. Her eyes rolled with fear, but the rest of her remained perfectly still.

David paused, but kept his gaze riveted on me as he let out a low whine. He ducked his head ever so slightly and whined again, still maintaining eye contact. Surprised, I stopped growling and raised my head. Another step brought him into my bubble and I craned my neck back, not sure if I wanted that. Slowly he reached forward until his breath stirred my hair.

I relaxed and lowered my head to touch his. The moment we met, clarity burst into life. The world sharpened into almost blinding focus. I hadn't died, I'd turned…and I'd almost just torn Victoria to pieces.

Shame spread through my chest. This wasn't me, this wasn't who I was. I danced a step back and David shifted to follow. My head swung wildly side to side as the reality of what I'd almost done hit home. I spun on my back legs and bolted.

Blurred foliage raced past as I dove deeper into the forest to escape the others. I wasn't safe to be around. I was a killer. I may have survived the change, but who would survive me? My rage from earlier had abated, yet I could still feel the potential waiting deep inside. I stumbled through the woods, crashing into trees and getting caught on thorns. A tree root rose up and I tripped, rolling several feet, until I came to a final stop completely exhausted.

No sooner did I cease moving than David appeared right behind me.

No. You have to go away.

My whine only seemed to encourage him to come closer. I staggered to my feet, desperate to find some way to tell him I wasn't safe, and the world around me broke in two. I fell back to the ground, my body convulsing. David's approach faltered as I writhed on the ground. I urged him to run while he still could, but the warning came out as a scream. He looked around nervously then raced past me. Another wave of pain swallowed my relief, retribution for what I'd done to Victoria.

Time twisted in on itself until the agony stopped as abruptly as it had begun. I forced myself to stand on wobbly legs and looked around at the dense clearing while the breeze lightly caressed my sweat-soaked skin. David. I had to find David. He needed to know I wasn't safe before I lost control again.

I shuffled through dirt and broken twigs to follow the path he'd taken earlier, my legs threatening to buckle with each unsteady step. Fortunately, he hadn't gone far. I emerged from behind an exceptionally large white oak to find him still on all fours panting, his golden skin glistening in the night. He looked over at the sound.

"Charline!"

I stumbled towards him, my legs gaining strength with each step, not caring that we both were naked, covered with the exertion of the change. He matched me and we came together in a bone-crushing hug that forced all of the air out of me. We remained locked in our embrace for a minute, then he pushed me back. Words poured out of him like a river as his hands glided over me in search of any damage.

"Thank the moon you're okay. You can hate me all you want. I don't care. I'm just glad you're alive. The clearing smelled all wrong. I didn't know what to do. And when I couldn't find you..." He trailed off as he wrapped me in another hug that sent the air whooshing out of me.

"David."

"I'm so sorry. I never should have left you. I should have been there. I let myself get caught up—"

"David, listen to me."

"I don't know what I would've done." He punctuated the statement with a kiss that effectively silenced my efforts to speak. Echoes of his deep need stirred within me and I tangled my hands in his hair pressing him closer. "I love you, Charline. I should have told you every single day. You're my world." The next kiss held all of the tenderness of his words and plucked at my heart.

Fear clouded his face when I broke the kiss and pushed him away. "I have to tell you something. It's about Victoria."

Rage burned in his eyes for the briefest instant, then extinguished. "What about her?"

I'd expected him to cut me off with some comment about how it was in the past, not encourage me and it took a moment to gather my thoughts. I took a deep breath and said as calmly as I could, "I almost killed her."

"The others would have stopped you if they believed she was in real danger."

"Not in real danger? I almost tore her apart!"

He shook his head and I stiffened. "She deserved everything she got. Pack justice is tough, but fair. An eye for an eye. She...she almost killed you," he added in a whisper that floated on the breeze and filled his eyes with sadness.

"You don't understand. If you hadn't shown up... I *would* have killed her," I insisted, recalling how her stomach had quivered beneath my jaws and how easily my teeth had pierced her flesh.

"No, you wouldn't have. That's not who you are." His breath mingled with mine as he brushed my cheek with the back of his knuckles.

"You don't know how I felt. I *wanted* to hurt her. It was

the only coherent thought I had. I'm not in control. What if next time I..."

What if next time it isn't Victoria. What if next time I go too far?

"I still feel it," I whispered.

The light of understanding shone in his eyes. "Oh my beautiful fox, you're not going mad. The first transition is hard and yours was particularly rough. That feeling is the moon still burning hot in your veins." He looked up to where I could just make out the delicate white sphere through the canopy, its bright light spilling across the night sky.

I felt a pull deep down as if my soul itself wanted to reach out and touch it.

"Stay with me, baby. It's too soon for another change, little fox."

"Wolf," I said, dropping my gaze back to him. "I'm a wolf now."

He smiled, giving me a lingering kiss. "You'll always be my beautiful fox."

It didn't matter that the moon was the only light to be found. I could clearly see the love shining in David's eyes, feel it as surely as I felt the moon glowing beneath my skin. I curled a hand around the back of his neck and brought him down for another kiss. He moaned and dropped his hands to my hips. His fingers dug into the soft flesh and pulled me tighter against him as he deepened the kiss with a ferocity that bordered on desperate.

I pulled away with a gasp, but didn't let go of him. David coasted his hands along my sides while his growing arousal pressed into my belly. I shuddered at the onslaught of sensation wreaking havoc on my body.

"What do you need?" David's low voice was a husky purr

that caressed my fevered skin every bit as much as his hands.

Need?

I considered the question for a moment while I stared into eyes I shouldn't have been able to see were blue. What *did* I need? Then, out of the whirlwind of emotion raging around my heart, the answer became clear. I'd almost *died*. I needed to feel alive.

Without a second thought, I mashed our mouths back together hard enough to bruise. In near perfect sync, David used his grip on my hips to lift me and I jumped to wrap my legs around his waist. His growl vibrated through my chest as I wiggled until his swollen head teased my already aching entrance. I arched into him and tightened my fingers in his short hair as I continued to dominate his mouth like it was my only source of air.

David's fingers dug into the globes of my ass, earning him a growl and a nip on the lip. Then he thrust up, burying his length inside my heat. I threw my head back and gasped out a cry of ecstasy at being so perfectly claimed. Only when I dropped it back to meet his penetrating gaze, though, did he start to move. I tightened my legs around his waist and rolled into each flex of his hips.

With every stroke I raced closer and closer to the edge. It started as a flutter and grew until I feared I'd explode. Then I did. I cried out my release as David emptied himself into me. He made a couple more shallow thrusts and slipped free. We panted for air while a welcome summer breeze cooled our sweat-soaked bodies.

Mid-pant, a laugh caught in my throat that turned into a fountain of giggles that left me gasping for air and shaking in David's arms. "Holy shit. That was... That was..." That was the fucking bee's knees was what that had been, but I couldn't grab enough breath to say so.

David let out a long sigh that seemed to melt us together. He placed a soft kiss on my shoulder then buried his face against my neck. "Full moon at midnight, I missed you," he mumbled against me.

I let out a happy sigh and rested my cheek on the top of his head. "Couldn't agree more."

20

MATED PAIRS

A kaleidoscope of sounds and smells accompanied us as we made our way back to David's stash of clothes. I paused in the small clearing where my own change had taken place and wrinkled my nose at the distinct odor of sickness tainted with something darker. The idea that only a few hours ago I'd almost died in this very spot seemed foreign and intangible. I remembered the fever and snippets of pain, but they didn't sync with how healthy I felt now.

David returned a few minutes later and handed me his shirt. "I know it won't cover everything super well, but it should be long enough." He followed my gaze to the turned earth and tucked a finger under my chin to lift it up. "You're okay now. Come on, let's get out of here." He laced our fingers and led us away from the clearing and the awful smell.

The trees thinned as we walked through the woods, our bare feet barely making a sound on the blanketed floor. Light glimmered between the trunks and the clean burn of woodsmoke curled in my nose. We cleared the pines and sound hit me like a wall as we emerged into a clearing at least fifty yards across with an enormous bonfire dead center.

People and shifted wolves filled the perfectly nestled space, the firelight dancing in their laughter. All eyes turned toward us as we stepped into the ring. A cheer rose up complete with clapping and howling. David's arm tightened around my waist, threatening to pull the shirt higher than was decent. I tugged it down for all the good it did and gave a shy wave. The raucous greeting died down and a figure separated from the crowd to race toward us. I took a hesitant step back, unable to make out their identity against the back light of the fire.

"Heads up," David said. I turned back to face the racing figure and let out an oof as they slammed bodily into me.

"Charline!" The petite body clinging to me squealed. "Oh my God. We were late getting out of town and I didn't find out until we got here a couple hours ago. No one would let me see you. Thank god you're okay." I tentatively hugged the woman back and a faint smell like daisies in spring drifted up.

"Sara?" I glanced behind her as another familiar figure joined us. "Michael?"

She immediately punched him in the arm. "See, I told you she'd be fine *and* she remembers."

"Oh, Sara," I cried as I wrapped her in a hug tight enough to make her wheeze.

"Easy," she wheezed. "You're stronger now, remember?"

I quickly released her. "Right. Sorry."

"Don't be sorry," she said with a smile. "It's new and I'm made of pretty tough stuff myself." I dropped my gaze to the ground and Sara placed a gentle hand on my arm. "At least you changed back the same night. As I see it, you're doing great." She held up a double OK as David laughed and

Michael rolled his eyes. My own smile finally stretched across my face. I'd missed her.

Michael grasped David's forearm and pulled him into a hug. "Thank the stars you're alright. I was worried when you didn't join the pack. That fight was nasty."

David squeezed him back and they separated. "Tell me about it."

Michael shook his head. "You shouldn't have waited so long to change."

"I know," David said as he ran a hand through his hair and let out a heavy sigh. Michael's weighty stare bored into him as if he wanted to say more. I glanced between the two of them, the sensation of missing something tingling across my skin.

Finally Michael blinked and turned to Sara. "Let's give Charline some space. This is a lot to take in."

"But..."

"Come on. You can catch up later." She looked back as he steered her away, leaving David and me once more on our own.

I sighed, content in seeing them, but relieved I didn't need to keep interacting. "They look good. I totally forgot about the Solstice party. You guys don't mess around. And this," I indicated his long plain tee hanging off of me, "is not what I'd planned to wear." I quirked an eyebrow at him, but couldn't hold the serious expression and it melted into a smile.

His eyes caught the light as he smiled back. "Damn I've missed that."

"What?"

His thumb traced the curve of my mouth while his other arm circled around my waist. "This. I can't remember the last time I saw you smile."

It slipped a bit. "There's been a lot going on..."

"I know," he whispered, leaning in and planting a soft kiss.

"Jeez, get a thicket!"

I twisted in David's arm to face the voice's owner. "Hey, Xander."

"Happy Solstice, Charline. I'm glad to see you're doing better." His gaze flicked past me to David then redirected to take in the rambunctious crowd."Now is this a party or what? But you're missing the best part." He held up two mason jars of mysterious liquid.

I grabbed the proffered glass, we exchanged a few more pleasantries, then he continued on his way, greeting and laughing with everyone he came in contact with.

"What is this?" I asked David when he'd gone.

"What else would it be? Moonshine." He gave me a crooked smile and knocked back half of it in one go. "Might want to hold your breath when you drink. Xander can put all the mint he wants in this stuff, but this shit is no joke."

I eyed the glass dubiously then took a tentative sip and immediately coughed. "Why is it so strong?"

"Let's just say our tolerance makes it difficult to truly appreciate having a drunken bonfire."

We polished off our thousand proof liquor, then David twirled us into the mix of music and revelry. I laughed at the sheer freedom filling the air and humming pleasantly through my veins. Eventually we bumped back into Michael and Sara and together we danced and drank until dawn.

Hours later, we stumbled into David's room and stripped down between bursts of laughter.

"That," I began, "was positively wild." I landed with a thud on the bed next to David.

He laughed and pulled me close. "You should see us when there's a blue moon," he said as he kissed my shoulder.

I spun to face him. "Is it really blue?" His laughter shook the bed and I pushed against his chest. "What? What's so funny?"

"I was joking. The blue moon is just the second full moon in the same month. Aside from falling within a designated time frame, it's nothing special."

"Oh." I giggled and nestled into the soft down of his chest. We lay like that for a while, letting the high of the night fade. Even suped-up moonshine couldn't hold for long against a werewolf metabolism.

"Charline," David whispered in the darkness that wrapped around us, "why didn't you tell me?"

"Tell you what?"

"Why didn't you tell me you were pregnant?" His voice was so soft, I almost didn't hear him.

My heart sank. "I...I wasn't sure. I'd started to wonder after visiting the doctor. I was going to take a test...when I got back home." His arm tightened around my shoulders. "How did you find out?"

"Dr. Fitz is also the pack doctor."

"Oh."

His questions and insistence on blood work made more sense now. He would have discovered the pregnancy when he was looking for the *were* gene. "It's...I'm not now, am I?" I wasn't sure why I asked. I already knew the answer.

"No."

My chest constricted as it absorbed all the sadness of that one word, how close I'd come without even knowing. I curled into him as an entirely different pain lapped at my heart. His arms held me tightly in the cocoon of his embrace and I let the tide pull me away, but after weeks of wracking sobs, all I could muster were silent tears.

"I love you, David," I whispered after a while.

He tilted my face up, gently kissing away the tears. "I love you too, Charline."

David's hand trailed along my waist as he passed behind me. I glanced over my shoulder at him, my smile undeniable and my heart finally at peace. There was still a lot to be said, but after my recent brush with death, I was content to enjoy the moment.

"Why have we never cooked together before?" I asked as he started chopping vegetables for the omelets, his cuts confident and precise. "You obviously know what you're doing."

He finished the mushrooms and green onions in quick succession before moving onto the peppers. "No offense, dear, but you can be a little terrifying in the kitchen." Merriment danced in his eyes and I gave him a light shove. "Hey, watch it," he admonished. "I have a knife."

"I feel like you've been holding out on me," I said with a pout.

Peppers complete, he grabbed a piece and popped it in my mouth. "I will never hold anything back from you again."

I barely had a chance to finish chewing and swallow before his lips found mine. The sweet kiss grew legs when his tongue boldly stroked across my bottom lip and I opened up for him. He wrapped his hands around my waist and pressed me hard against him, swallowing down my moan as he deepened the kiss.

"Thank the moon you two have finally made up."

We pulled apart like guilty teenagers, our lips swollen and our cheeks flushed. I fanned myself as I turned to greet the intruder with their still steaming mug of what smelled like Irish Breakfast. "Good morning, Maria."

"It is indeed. It's so hard to watch mated pairs fight," she mused aloud as she took a generous sip.

David's eyes went wide. I cocked my head to the side in confusion at the same time he whispered a harsh, "Maria!"

She glanced over the rim of her mug then let out a nervous laugh as she inched out the door. "Oops. Uh, I think I'll enjoy my tea in the front room." She stepped back into the hall with barely a rustle of her pink robe and vanished.

Still confused, I turned to look at David.

"I don't suppose there's any way we can talk about this *after* breakfast?" he asked hopefully.

In direct opposition to the words sitting on my lips, my stomach let out a massive growl. I narrowed my eyes. "Fine, breakfast first."

When we finished, we cleaned and dried the dishes together, then headed to the orchard sans shoes at David's insistence. It took all of one step in the thick, luscious blades curling softly around my feet to understand why. We meandered through the trees, the brilliance of the day rivaling anything I'd ever experienced before.

David's easy smile warmed my heart. I smiled back and appreciated the sensory experience of a normal day in the life of a werewolf. A twinge of sadness punctured my joy at the realization that it had taken nearly dying and being turned for David to finally see that his friend had been driving us apart.

David's smile crinkled with worry. "You okay?"

I nodded. What was done was done. Mama had always said I never could hold a proper grudge. I doubted I would ever truly forgive Victoria, but dwelling on the past would only spoil the future.

"I'm fine, but no more stalling." I plucked a leaf free

from a branch over head and it bounced hard showering us with even more loose items. "Out with it, mister," I said as I tossed the culprit aside to the backdrop of David's laughter. "What did Maria mean by mated pairs?"

He took a deep breath and let it out audibly. "You've heard about soul mates." He didn't pose it as a question, so I didn't answer it. "Well, *weres* have a similar ideology. Not everyone believes in a true mate, but..."

"Maria does, and so do you." It wasn't much of a stretch considering how close they were. Besides, I'd seen firsthand the level of intimacy that existed between her and Alexander. If that was what it was to be a mated pair, then I was definitely interested.

"I do. But mated pairs are more than just what you would consider the typical soul mate. Wolves mate for life. 'Til death do us part falls short of the reality and it's not optional: you either *are* true mates or you aren't."

"Okay...I think I'm following." His comments early on about not taking dating lightly took on a new weight, as did his mannerisms. The possessiveness, the need to have me near, the anger when I pushed him away. Another piece fell into place as I thought back to our first time. "So a lifetime ago when we...and you hesitated..."

"That wasn't just making love for me. Sex cements the bond." He paused, his gaze fixated on a twig as he pulled it apart. "I know I should have used protection, it was wrong of me to continue, especially without talking to you. But Charline, I don't think wild horses could have stopped me."

My head spun as I fought to make sense of everything. "What would protection have done?"

"Delayed the process," he admitted, guilt stamped across his face. "I don't know how to explain the drive to complete the bond. It's like the pull of the moon. You can ignore it for a little while, but the longer you go, the harder it is. I'm still sorry I didn't talk to you about it first, you deserved to know the truth. I just..." He trailed off and looked up at the sky, his shoulders sagging. "I hadn't seen you in almost two weeks. Having you close again, being able to hold you, smell you... I wasn't thinking clearly. But that doesn't excuse my behavior." His gaze fell back to me, remorse written in every line of his body. "I should have told you."

I shook my head, because no shit he should have talked to me about something so monumental, but arguing about it now would accomplish nothing. "How come I don't feel that drive?"

His cheeks darkened. "Because, we...uh already..."

I rolled my eyes and mentally smacked myself. Because we'd had sex beneath the full moon almost the second I'd changed back. We walked a little further in silence. "When did you know?"

He chuckled to himself. "I knew the first moment I saw you. There was this feeling deep inside that said I'd do anything to be near you. I'd been searching so long for that feeling and there you were, out of nowhere, when I least expected it."

I let that staggering information sink in. "Why didn't you say anything?"

He rubbed the back of his neck. "I've been told numerous times that my—beliefs—are a little intense, bordering on manic. I didn't want to scare you off."

I considered that for a second. Everyone wanted to believe in the kind of love that lasts forever and I was no exception, but that didn't mean I would've accepted it out of the blue. The more I contemplated his words, the more the overwhelming stimulus of the world fell away to reveal a light blossoming in my chest like an enormous sunflower, radiant, pure, and completely undeniable.

"Oh." Last night and this morning I'd assumed the

intense joy pulsing inside of me was because I wasn't dead and David and I had reconciled.

His gaze followed my fingers as they circled around my heart. "Yeah."

"You felt like this the whole time?" I asked softly as my hand hovered over the miniature sun pulsing in my chest. Its light washed over me like the warmest spring, carrying with it the knowledge that I was tethered to David in every way imaginable.

"Only since that first night." He stuffed his hands into his pockets and shrugged like it wasn't the most mind-boggling thing ever.

"Well shit. I kind of get why you didn't understand my insecurity now." He opened his mouth undoubtedly to apologize again and I held up a hand. "Don't. I've already wasted too much energy on what happened. I'm moving forward."

A smile softened his face and he tugged me close. "How did I get so lucky to find such an incredible mate?"

"You crashed a girls-only day," I said without missing a beat.

He chuckled and I looped my arms around his neck. He tipped my nose then sealed our lips with a kiss that sent tingles all the way to my toes and made the light pulsing inside me burn that much brighter.

"Damn," I whispered when he pulled away.

"I know it's a lot late to be asking, but are you okay with this?"

This. The small word held so many options. Okay with making up? Okay with being a werewolf. Okay with being committed to someone I barely knew for the rest of my life? The slew of possibilities made my chest spasm. I took a steadying breath and let it out slowly. Did I think we were moving too fast? Yes. Was there a damn thing that could be done about it? Nope.

"Not really optional, is it?" I finally said. Sadness immediately clouded David's eyes and I reached out to cup his cheek. "I love you. It'll take some adjusting, but I don't resent turning or this incredible connection we now have."

"I'm still so sorry about everything."

"What did I say? No more apologies. At least not right now." I stepped away from him and looked around at the precise rows of trunks.

"What are you thinking, my little fox?"

I spared him a grin that had led to more mischief than Georgia had peaches and took another step away.

"Don't do it," David cautioned, which only made me grin wider. "Charline..."

I spun on the soft grass and took off. Green blurred beneath my feet as I ran as fast as my legs could carry me with David hot on my heels. Laughter bubbled out of me and I pushed harder, angling for the line of darker trees north of the orchard. Unfortunately, leaving the apple trees behind also meant leaving softer ground. My steps faltered on the new terrain and I lost my lead. Without warning, David barreled into me and we crashed into the ground.

He laughed above me. "I told you not to run."

"Where's the fun in that?" I rolled us so that he was pinned beneath me instead. "Besides, then you wouldn't have caught me."

He let out a primal growl and yanked me down for a searing kiss. I moaned into him and clawed my fingers in his shirt. In the blink of an eye, we traded positions again. David leaned back to pull his shirt over his head then set about ditching his pants.

Eager to join the nakedness, my fingers fumbled at my hem while he tugged my jeans down. Finally liberated, I sat forward and wrapped a hand around his length.

Another growl rolled out of him as he looked at me with

such intensity my skin burned. I tightened my grip and managed to stroke twice before he removed my hand and yanked me into his lap. His fingers dug into my hips as I sank onto him.

"You're so fucking beautiful," he said, nipping at my neck. "And mine. All mine," he added, thrusting up hard.

I threaded my fingers in his hair and yanked his head back so I could drown in his intense gaze while I rode him just as hard. He kept one hand on my hip while he used the other to brush my hair back and massage my breasts, rubbing a calloused thumb over a nipple.

Sensation rioted through me as our punishing pace continued without slowing. Our breath mingled in panted puffs of warm air that ghosted over fevered skin. An unbearable ache tightened inside me as I sprinted toward a finish guaranteed to have stars.

David curled his arm around me and pressed me harder down with a grunt. I cried out as every nerve lit up, then exploded in a wave of euphoria. He held me tight as I milked out everything he had to offer and sagged against him. I whimpered with loss when he pulled free and gently lay me back on the padded leaves, too boneless too move. We lay quietly for a while, the sweat cooling on our skin as we stared up through the canopy at the spots of blue above.

"How do you feel?" David asked, rolling on his side to face me.

"I feel great." He gave a throaty chuckle as I turned to face him. "And it's not just the sex. All of me feels amazing."

Sadness filled his eyes once more as he trailed a finger along my cheek. "I don't know what I would've done if I'd lost you."

I grabbed his hand, kissing the palm. "You didn't." My gaze flicked to the marks on his arms that eerily mirrored my own scars. "Can I ask you a question?"

"I'll tell you anything you want to know."

"What happened?" My fingers brushed across his bicep. "Michael mentioned a fight."

He sighed and placed a tender hand on my hip. "After I brought you back to the House there was absolute chaos. I was sitting with you when someone came and told me a fight had broken out on the grounds between the townspeople and some of the pack. I left. All I could think was that they were going to try and take you away." He used his hold to pull me close and buried his face in my neck.

"Why would you think that?" I asked as I smoothed his hair.

"The kid at the B&B wasn't happy that I took you. I feared he might have riled up the others and they were on some misguided rescue mission. Them showing up here would *not* go over well. I don't know how I thought my going would help. When I got to where the fight was supposed to be though, there were only people from the pack. They demanded I take you back; said you were just going to die anyway." His grip tightened as he winced. "I didn't handle that well."

"Were there ever any villagers?"

"Actually, yes. Turns out Alexander was handling them as best he could. If Dr. Fitz hadn't shown up, though, I'm not sure what would've happened. You've made quite a few loyal friends, my little fox. I think that kid might even be in love with you." He scowled at the mention of who I assumed must be Jimmy.

"David, why did you come that day?" I asked.

"I..." His face burned crimson. "I was led to believe that you were seeing someone in the village. I had to see for myself. I thought maybe that's why you were ignoring me."

I raised an eyebrow. "Couldn't have anything to do with how mad I was at you."

He grimaced. "That would've given you more reason to move on to someone else."

"You should know me better than that."

"You're right. But I wasn't thinking clearly and being apart from you was not helping that."

"You know what I think?" I tossed out as I propped up on my elbows.

"What?"

"I think we were set up." His brow furrowed in confusion. "Hear me out. I think someone has been using our relationship to create a rift between the town and the pack."

"Vi—"

I narrowed my eyes and he wisely didn't finish. "I know she's involved, but I seriously doubt she's the mastermind. She's not exactly the brightest crayon in the box, if you know what I mean." I twisted my hair over my shoulder as I continued to think out loud. "No, someone else is pulling the strings. But who would want to divide the pack like that?"

"Someone who doesn't want Xander to take over or me to be his Beta." I watched as he put pieces together about the things that had been happening both at the House and at the village. "That would explain the ambush. If I was injured, I wouldn't be able to pursue the role and..."

"And if I died, you would have tried to kill everyone you thought was involved," I finished for him. "You'd have started a war."

He flopped onto his back. "Full moon at midnight, we've totally been played."

21

CONSPIRACY THEORY

I got my first real indicator of the state of affairs in the House when David and I stumbled over who to tell our theory to first. While I'd only been exposed to pack dynamics for a short while, even I could recognize that wasn't normal. If David wasn't sure who to address as reigning authority, then it was no wonder the rest of the pack was in such upheaval.

Ultimately we decided to tell Alexander, since he technically still held the title of Alpha. The real hurdle would be conveying my myriad assortment of knowledge into something resembling a solid theory. I didn't have a shred of evidence to back up any of my suspicions, only hearsay and gossip, though there had been the attempt on my life.

"Alexander, we need a word with you," David said as we walked into the study.

Alexander glanced up from taking notes on his reading. "I'm pleased to see both of you are doing so well. I would have checked in sooner, but..." He was busy trying to prevent the whole pack from going to hell in a handbasket. "But I wanted to give the two of you space. There's no telling what would've happened if you hadn't recovered." It was unclear which of us "you" was referring to.

I swallowed my sudden rush of nerves and stepped forward. "I have a few ideas about what might really be going on." He nodded sagely and put away his notes without a word.

"Alpha, you really should hear her out, it explains—"

Alexander held up a hand and David went silent. "I think we should go for a walk, don't you?"

"But—" David began. It took half a second longer than it should have, but I realized what he was trying to do. I nudged David none too gently in the ribs.

"I think that sounds like an excellent idea. Perhaps we could venture towards the northern woods?" David gave me a quizzical look, and I added, "I hear it's quiet up there since most of the others tend to stray more east and linger in the orchard." Understanding dawned on David's face and he vacated the room without another word.

We walked in almost perfect silence with only the crunch of fallen twigs to betray our steps. David very intentionally veered us away from where we'd spent a rather eventful day.

"I appreciate you recognizing the sensitivity of the situation, Charline," Alexander said when the shadow of trees blanketed the path. "David will make an excellent Beta with you by his side." My cheeks burned at the high praise.

"Alpha, we think we know what's really been going on, why the pack's been so uneasy," David began.

Alexander nodded. "People are taking advantage of the unusual situation to sow insurrection. I only wish I knew who was at the heart of it. Who could possibly know about the old town agreement? *I* haven't even read the thing."

"Edith Sharp."

His gaze swiveled around to spear me in place and I

nearly swallowed my tongue. "How do you know that name?" Even David was looking at me like I'd grown a second head.

"She's head of the City Council and she's the one leading the development project. Spend a lot of time in town, you hear things," I said with a shrug, though I wasn't sure how he'd feel about me knowing they used to be an item.

"You don't suppose she learned of it while..." Alexander's eyes narrowed dangerously and David trailed off.

I quickly spoke up before David could dig himself in any further. "Johnny. She learned about the agreement from him. I would even go so far as to say he probably has the copy everyone's been looking for."

Alexander's glare transferred to me and I instantly wished I'd kept my mouth shut, it also solidified my belief that I was on the right track. "Why would you say that?" The menacing undercurrent of the question gave me pause.

"I...overheard her talking on the phone in town." My gaze darted between Alexander and David. "Why? Who's Johnny?"

Alexander rubbed a hand over his face like he couldn't believe what he was hearing while David stared at him in confusion. "There's no way. He'd *never* work with Edith. It couldn't be him."

"Oh yes, it could be." A muscle in Alexander's jaw twitched. "As for Edith, he doesn't have to like her to work with her."

I held up a hand. "Not to be dense, but he who?"

Alexander's gaze glittered darkly as he looked at me. "Jonathan, the current Beta of the North Carolina Pack."

My eyes widened and I was now immensely glad that this was a conversation we were having away from the prying ears of the House. "What? No. But, David, you said—"

"Clearly I was wrong."

I shook my head. Every new instinct I had shouted that none of this made sense. "I don't understand, why would Johnathan want to hurt the pack?"

"What else did you hear?" Alexander asked so low goosebumps broke out on my arms.

"Um, there were some kids causing trouble. They were talking to a man, but I never learned his name. I don't know if they're the same person or not, but it seems like too much of a coincidence."

Alexander pinched the bridge of his nose and I stopped talking.

"Why didn't you mention any of this before?" David asked. I shot him a withering glare and he swallowed audibly. "Right." He turned back to Alexander. "What do you want to do, Alpha?"

In response, Alexander let out a savage growl as his fist made contact with the nearest tree. The bark cracked beneath the force and the whole thing shook. "I knew Johnny was less than pleased about my plans to retire, but this? And Edie of all people. To think, this whole time..."

It didn't seem like he was addressing anyone in particular, so I kept my peace and placed a placating hand on David's arm to encourage him to do the same. Alexander needed time to process.

Eventually he straightened up, his expression every bit the seasoned general I'd thought him when I first arrived. "Now that I know what I'm really up against, we should stand a better chance. The difficulty is that we don't have any evidence."

David crossed his arms over his barrel chest and frowned. "What about the agreement?"

"That would be great, except we don't have it," I pointed out.

"Johnathan will have it." The flat way Alexander spoke made the hairs on the back of my neck stand up.

David's frown deepened. "Except no one has seen him since spring."

"I think I might know of someone who could find him."

Two pairs of curious eyes turned to face me.

"He'll have insisted on meeting Edie in public places. Even with this subterfuge, I doubt he's given up his prejudices," Alexander said, leaving little room to doubt where humans ranked on Johnathan's list of acceptable acquaintances.

"I wasn't talking about her," I said and David's brow angled into a V. "There's not a doubt in my mind that Victoria has been doing his bidding this whole time. Who better to set us up?" I gestured between David and myself.

Alexander looked pensive for a moment then nodded. "The pack needs to know that I'm still in control. It's past time she received punishment for her actions. Let's see how loyal she is when it's her neck on the chopping block."

A chill slithered down my spine at the ominous statement.

"You can't mean..." David began, all of the color draining from his face.

"Is it any different than what you would've done had that night gone any differently?"

"No, but Char already..."

"Yes, Miss Montgomery exacted her pound of flesh for the crimes committed against her. However, there are several other grievous acts for which Victoria is culpable, all of which amount to treason. The punishment for that is clear. There are only two options, and if this plan is going to yield any fruit, then the most final will have to be the one we pursue."

My blood turned to ice at the cold steel in Alexander's

voice. He glanced purposefully at David, then began the long walk back towards the House. David and I trailed after him, maintaining a respectful distance.

"What does he mean when he says final?" I whispered. The effort was likely pointless, since Alexander could probably hear us anyway. Still, I didn't want to seem like I was questioning his judgment.

"He's going to execute Vicky." David's resolve was both frightening and heart-breaking. They'd grown up together, been friends. She might be an awful person who'd done inexplicable things, but that didn't make the betrayal hurt any less. And despite Alexander's assertion that David would have done much the same if left to his own devices, he still wasn't the kind of person that wanted to see his childhood friend executed.

"For biting me? For turning me?" I couldn't wrap my head around such a harsh sentence. It didn't even sound like there'd be a trial.

"No, you already made her pay for that," David said with a subtle note of pride. "This sentence would be for other crimes."

"Like what?" Why I was so hell bent on saving her life was beyond me, but it didn't stop me from offering up protests.

"She attacked you in broad daylight. In the middle of town." He gave me a pointed look. "There were witnesses."

"Oh, you found some of those, did you?" The snarky reply came unbidden. He passed me a look and I snapped my traitorous trap shut.

"She could have exposed the pack. Those at least will be the headliners. I doubt Alexander will share the gravity of her crimes at the sentencing with the rest of the pack though."

"What do you mean?"

"Insurrections are not tolerated in packs, Charline. Any *were* willing to mutiny under an established Alpha better hope they have backed the right wolf."

I clapped a hand over my mouth to stifle a gasp. "He's going to use her to smoke out Johnathan."

"Either that or she'll roll over and betray him. One way or another, Johnathan will be exposed and Vicky won't live to regret her mistakes."

I stopped. David only made it a couple steps before he did as well. "Will he really?" Yes, I hated Victoria and what she'd put us through, but outright execution?

The sad look David gave me tore at my insides. "It's either that or banishment. Most *weres* would consider death a mercy rather than be banished. Werewolf law is strict, even in a progressive pack, there are some rules that must be followed. There can be no forgiving what she's done. Johnathan will face the same once he's found and proven guilty."

"Proven?" I asked, still reeling.

"Yes." Alexander's firm assertion cut through our whispered conversation and I swiveled to face him, his face a mask of stoic resignation. "We'll need proof that Johnathan has been conspiring with the town. He still holds enough sway that simply finding and killing him could spark the very civil war I'm trying to avoid."

"There you are." The unexpected voice intruded on our exceptionally serious moment. We all turned to find Xander with his hands on his knees puffing for breath. "I've been looking everywhere for you."

"What is it, son?"

"A letter arrived from the Town Council. They're planning a meeting at the end of next week."

"What of it?" David asked.

"They're going to have lawyers there to go over the agreement."

Alexander let out a heavy sigh. I could understand why he was so eager to retire; running a pack seemed exhausting. And poor Xander was all ready to step up and take his father's place. I mentally shook my head. What sorts of burdens would his young shoulders have to bear? What hurdles would he have to overcome to keep the pack from falling apart?

"Then we need to make sure they do not have an agreement to review."

"Dad?" Xander seemed confused.

"There have been some—insights." At his unique choice of words I realized we were now in view of the House. "Gather everything you have about the real estate laws and codes. David, I need you to determine who's still loyal. And Charline, find out as much as you can about what the council already has and what their plans are."

"Yes, sir," the guys echoed at receiving their marching orders.

Alexander looked at me and I said two words that I never in a million lifetimes would have ever thought would pass my lips. "Yes, Alpha." He gave a sharp nod and walked towards the House, his son trailing after. David stayed behind with me.

"How are you doing, Char?"

"I'll be better once all of this is over."

"I suspect the townsfolk will be relieved to see that you're alright, especially after the scene I made getting you out of there."

"Don't worry, I'll apologize to poor Jimmy for you," I said with a playful smile.

"That isn't quite what I meant."

"I know, love, but this whole thing is about more than

just pack politics. The town is involved now too. If the pack is going to survive this, then you need to stop treating the townsfolk like unwanted guests. They're your neighbors and will likely remain so for many years to come. Relations with the village are as important as the ones within the pack." Logic might not have been what he wanted, but it was definitely what the whole pack needed.

Unexpectedly, he pulled me in close and claimed me with a kiss that stole my breath. "Have I told you how smart you are?"

"Constantly," I replied breathlessly. "Now you go take care of the pack, and leave the village to me."

He stole another kiss before releasing me. I didn't mind one bit.

22

DAMAGE CONTROL

With David and Xander pursuing their respective goals, I set out to marshal my own forces. Gathering information and assuaging the villagers' concerns was all well and good, but a few things at the House needed tending to first. It would do none of our efforts any good if the pack saw me going back into the village as running away. If I was going to be successful in mending bridges, then I would have to start at the foundation—within the pack.

I quickly ran through my options as I made my way back to the House and came up with a disheartening total of two people who might be amenable to giving me a hand. Marissa, Rosie's mother, definitely liked me. Her concern for what the village might do, however, could outweigh her desire to support my efforts to rectify the damage Victoria had done. Then there was Isabel who'd already stood up to Victoria...once.

I groaned and pushed down my reservations. Mama always said quitters never win and winners never quit, and Mama didn't raise no quitter. Shoulders back and head held high, I marched forward to achieve the impossible.

I'd scarcely walked through the back door when I spied

one of the people on my quest. Isabel stood in the sun room speaking with Kaleb. He said something I didn't quite catch and laughed as she rolled her eyes. I twiddled my thumbs in the hall until he finally left. He gave me a good natured nod that I returned with a wave, then I ducked into the room.

"Hey, Isabel," I said before she could wander out the other entrance.

She spun around at the sound of my voice, a look of terror plastered on her face. "Charline. Uh, hi."

"Do you have a minute?" I asked, stepping closer.

Her eyes widened even more and she held up her hands in a defensive gesture. "I swear I didn't know. I had nothing to do with what happened. If I'd known what she had planned I would've told Alexander. Please, Charline, don't hurt me," she finished, cringing in anticipation of retribution.

It took a moment to find my words through the shock. Finally, I shook my head. "Isabel, I don't think you had anything to do with Victoria's nasty schemes."

She ventured a peek from behind her defensive wall. "You don't?"

"Should I?"

"No, no, no," she said, waving her hands emphatically. "I would never."

"Good. Now that we've gotten that out of the way, I need your help."

"My help?" she echoed, straightening up. I bit back a sigh of frustration. This was going to be a very long conversation if I was going to have to repeat everything I said.

"Well, your support really." I quickly held up my hand before she could repeat me and her mouth closed with an audible snap.

"What can I do?"

"This whole changing of the guard business," I ventured, "it's some pretty complicated stuff."

"Not really. Pack tradition will have the contenders fight for the honor when the time comes."

"Be that as it may, I'm sure it hasn't escaped your notice that there's quite a bit of politics at play as well. It's not just about winning a fight. Who you support and who supports you matters."

"And you want to build support for David." She paused a moment before adding, "And Xander."

I nodded. "What do you say? Are you up for it?"

She twirled a curl of hair as she studied the floor and I feared I'd made a gross error in judgment. If I couldn't win over Isabel, I didn't like my chances with anyone else in the pack.

Suddenly, her head snapped up, her brown eyes glowing with a fierceness I'd never seen from her before. "Tell me what you need."

I tried and failed miserably to suppress my smile. "First things first, we can't accomplish much with just the two of us. We'll need more help. Also, I'm tired of being treated like some interloper. We'll need to address that as well."

"That's easy."

"How so?" I asked, hard pressed to imagine overcoming Victoria's toxic gossip would be anything as outrageous as easy.

"You're pack now," Isabel clarified with a shrug.

I looked back absolutely dumbfounded. These people were worse than that cult my cousin had accidentally joined.

Isabel gave me a funny look and pressed on. "As far as people, who did you have in mind?"

"Well, Marissa for starters. I think I've ingratiated myself enough with her and Rosie to be confident in her support."

Isabel nodded along. "I might have a few others as well. You're not the only one tired of Vicky and her cronies' bullying."

I was a little taken aback at the ferocity of her words. Had they simply been waiting around for someone with the brass to put them down?

"Let's see," Isabel mused aloud. "I'll start with Sandy, then there's Karen, and of course Michelle. I bet Julia and Nina could be brought around. And..."

"Before you get too caught up, I don't suppose you know where I could find Marissa?"

"I think it's Rosie's nap time. She's probably upstairs with her right now." At my questioning look, Isabel elaborated. "Second hallway, fifth door down. Stop when you smell baby powder and lavender."

"Got it. I want to talk to her before I leave."

"Leave. Where are you going?"

"I'm going into town." A tense second passed and I could see Isabel wavering in her decision to support me. "Look, someone has to get a handle on that situation. I already have an in. There's no reason I shouldn't exploit that for the benefit of the pack." At the mention of the pack, she visibly relaxed and I mentally shook my head. That kind of thinking was undoubtedly what had led to this mess in the first place.

I left Isabel to her growing list of names and went in search of Marissa. I'd lost track of doors when the smell of powdered lavender caught my attention. I stopped dead in front of a white door that looked identical to all of the others and tested the air again, amazed at the detail of the fine scents.

With exaggerated slowness, I turned the knob and pushed the door open. Marissa glanced up at the soft sound. Sure enough, both Rosie and her older brother Oscar were asleep. I gestured her over to join me in the hallway. If this went like I hoped, she could be my in with the other moms.

Marissa carefully extricated herself from the rocking chair and slipped into the hall, coaxing the door closed to minimize any sound that might wake up her two young ones. A pain stabbed through my heart as I realized how close I'd come to having my own budding angel. I willed the ache in my chest to ease and the sting in my eyes to dry as I took a deep breath. Even though I'd only suspected for a short time, having a family was something I'd always wanted. But before I could work on building a future filled with baby giggles, I needed to stop my new world from imploding.

"Hey, Charline, what's up?" Marissa asked, pulling me back to the present.

"I have a favor to ask of you and I'm hoping it's not too much."

"Sure thing, anything I can do to help Rosie's living princess."

"What?" I asked, taken aback.

She gave a quiet chuckle. "All she ever does is talk about Princess Foxy. I can't even begin to imagine how much more she'll adore you when she realizes you're like her now."

"Oh," I said, unable to prevent the heat from creeping across my face.

Marissa winced. "I'm sorry. She just completely idolizes you. As I'm sure you've noticed, you're not really like most pack girls."

"I've noticed."

"Sweet moon," she cried and clapped her hands over her mouth. "How thoughtless of me. I didn't mean to bring up unpleasantness. I know we're all relieved to see you're okay. Even Oscar has been asking after you." She glanced back at the closed door with an adoring smile. "Between you and me, I think Rosie's getting to him. Of course, you are popular with most of the pups." She gave me a conspiratorial wink and I chuckled at the idea of my own tiny fan club. "Now what can I help you with?"

"First off, I have a strange and potentially prying question."

"Trust me, you haven't *seen* strange until you see your nine-year-old son suddenly sprout a tail. Shoot."

"Who do you support for the next Alpha?" I blurted, abandoning propriety.

"I was wondering when you'd get around to that."

"What do you mean?"

"You're a very take-charge sort of woman. *Were* or not, it was only a matter of time before you decided to lead the campaign for David yourself. He's a wonderful man, but maybe not so great with words."

I laughed. "Tell me about it."

"To answer your first question, I think David would make an excellent Beta. And as far as Xander is concerned, he certainly has the smarts for the job. Though why anyone that young would want to take on so much responsibility is beyond me."

"That was my thought. But I confess, he's far more mature than anyone else I've ever encountered his age."

Marissa shook her head. "The mother in me believes he should enjoy being a kid while he can, but the wolf in me recognizes that he's more than up for the task. He may be young, but he's capable." She glanced back towards her own youngins again. "Plus, I know he'd keep them safe. Xander spends all the time he can with the children and I know David would lay down his own life to protect the pack's pups. He's going to make a great dad."

"Yes, he will," I echoed even as my heart twinged for our loss.

"They certainly have my support, but I don't see how that matters much."

"Well...I'm not just looking for yours." She gave me a curious look. "I want you to talk to the other moms. This whole shift has got the pack feeling out of sorts. It's time we found ourselves some unity. Alexander is still Alpha."

Marissa nodded and I fought the urge to squeal with victory. A small sound filtered through the door and Marissa gave me an apologetic smile. "Duty calls."

"I understand. Thank you for speaking with me."

To my surprise, Marissa stepped forward and wrapped me in a quick hug. "Anytime. I'll do everything I can to help. Not just for him or the pack though. For you too, Charline. You've found your way into more than just a couple tiny hearts." She flashed me another encouraging grin before closing the door quietly.

I clutched my hands over my heart and fought a different surge of tears. There was no way Marissa could possibly know how much such a statement would mean to me. I quickly brushed away a few renegade drops and made my way to David's room to grab the truck keys.

Now for the real moment of truth—I was leaving the House. Eyes followed me as the cab door closed and the keys turned in the ignition. My nerves rumbled in time with the engine. I let out a steadying breath, sent up a silent prayer that too many rumors wouldn't sprout as to why I was leaving, and shifted the gear into reverse.

Rocks crunched beneath the heavy duty tires as the front door burst open to reveal Lucia. I hit the brakes as she ran towards the truck and stopped in the middle of the lawn, unsure of what I should do.

She cupped her hands around her mouth and hollered, "Are you sure you don't want some help getting your things from town?"

I stared at her in open confusion, then took in all of the other curious faces around her and couldn't help but smile. Isabel hadn't wasted a minute. I put the truck in park and called back, "No thanks, Lucia. I'm only getting a little bit tonight. I'd love the help next time, though, when I get the larger things."

"Great, I'll be sure to let Mitch know. Be careful, alright?"

"You got it!"

She waved as I continued my exit. It was absolutely genius and I couldn't believe I hadn't thought of it first. What was even more surprising than the bold ploy to make sure everyone witnessing knew that I was coming back, was that I barely even knew Lucia and I knew even less about Mitch. I had no idea if he was her father, brother, or boyfriend, but it didn't matter—in a handful of seconds, she'd effectively shown that I was supported not only by women within the pack but men as well.

My burgeoning optimism stayed with me as I rolled down the drive, yet as the town came into focus, my anxiety returned. These people had looked after me, taken care of me when no one else would. And now, I had to tell them everything was flipped around again. It was a shame I hadn't bottled that hope while I'd felt it.

The sidewalk was clear as I pulled into a vacant spot in front of the B&B and cut the engine. When I went to open the door, however, an angry mob had formed, led by none other than Jimmy.

"Alright, you, we want Miss Montgomery back," Jimmy demanded as they closed in on the vehicle, clearly unable to see through the heavily tinted windows. "If you take her to the hospital now, we won't press charges." There was a lot of "we" in there and I wasn't really sure they had a leg to stand on as far as charges went. I bit back a smile, touched by their protectiveness.

This should be interesting.

I pushed open the door, my explanation for my miraculous recovery already queued up. "Good evening, Jimmy. Carly. I trust you've kept my things safe?"

Jimmy's mouth fell open and Carly plain keeled over backwards into the gentleman behind her. "M-Miss Montgomery, you... you're..." Jimmy stuttered in disbelief.

"So...it turns out I was having a severe reaction to some contaminated pills. Not to worry though, Dr. Fitz got me all fixed up. Amazing what a shot can do for you. Right?" No way would anyone in my own family buy that hogwash, but I mentally crossed my fingers anyway and hoped for the best.

"What about that?" Jimmy asked, indicating the truck.

"Oh, yeah...um, we reconciled..." I trailed off. His face twisted into a scowl and I floundered. "If we could all go inside, I'd be happy to explain."

The motley crew of townsfolk and B&B employees shuffled inside, keeping a watchful eye on me. I used the precious few minutes to devise what on Earth to say to these wonderful people so concerned about my welfare that might actually convince them. At the last second, I settled on the truth, or as much of it as I dared.

"Okay, Miss Montgomery, spill. The last I saw you, you were in no state to be going anywhere and that...that..." Jimmy's face mottled with indignant outrage as he choked on all the things he wanted to say.

"David. His name is David and he probably saved my life."

"I don't understand, Miss Montgomery, if he was actually helping, then why didn't you go with him any of the other dozen times he was here for you?" Carly asked, back up and conscious.

I let out a sigh and didn't have to fake the embarrassment burning across my face. "Do y'all remember the girl I got in a fight with on White Oak?" Several heads nodded. Right, silly question. "Anyway—gosh this going to sound awful—we were basically fighting over David."

Disbelief dominated the blank faces staring back at me.

This is going to be harder than I thought.

"So, *she* thought she had a right to him because she knew him first and knew him longer. I, obviously, disagreed."

"That doesn't really answer the question, Miss Montgomery," Jimmy insisted. "You were adamant about keeping him away."

"You're right. He wasn't handling the situation very well and it made me believe that he thought he'd be better off with her." The explanation sounded confusing out loud even to my ears. I caught some distinct scoffs. "I'm not excusing his behavior...or mine. I just want you to know that I'm fine and that we're back together. Despite David's flaws, I do love him. In fact, I've never been more in love with someone."

"I don't know..." Jimmy glanced at the others.

I laid what I hoped was a comforting hand on his arm. "Trust me, everything is okay. I just came to get a few of my things and let everyone know I was all right. I'll be back soon to collect the rest."

"But, Miss Montgomery, in the room, there was a lot of—"

"Sick," I cut him off. He was like a damn dog with a bone. But, bless his heart, I needed him to stop digging. "And I'm so sorry you had to see that. Thank goodness David got there when he did. Now, I don't suppose I could get a hand?"

Carly immediately stepped up. "I'll help."

"Thank you, sweetheart. Like I said, I'm not getting

much today. I'll be back with help." She frowned. "Don't worry, I won't be a stranger. I love this place too much not to visit often."

That seemed to restore her spirits, though Jimmy didn't look quite convinced.

23

EDITH SHARP

"Hey, little fox," David purred as he slid an arm around my waist.

I let out a contented sigh and snuggled closer, pressing my back into his chest. "Question for you."

"Lay it on me."

"Why do you still call me little fox?"

He nuzzled deeper into my hair to get to my neck. "Oh, Char, you'll always be my little fox. As for *why* I call you that, because you're a total and complete fox." I snorted a laugh even as my chest filled with warmth. "Of course, it doesn't hurt that you look like one too when you change," he added with a playful nip.

"I do not."

"You absolutely do. Granted, you're an intimidating four times their usual size, but you're the spitting image of a mischievous fox, green eyes and all."

"Not all foxes have green eyes," I countered, spinning around in his arms to face him.

"This one does." He squeezed me to him and stole a kiss.

I giggled and pushed against his chest. "Cad."

"Maybe," he replied cheekily as his hand ventured down to cup my bottom. He gave it a good squeeze and kissed the tip of my nose. "Tell me how things are going in the village."

I let out a heavy sigh and leaned forward to rest my head on his chest. David's hand immediately shifted to rub my back.

"What's the matter?"

"Things could definitely be going better."

"How so?"

"Half the village still doesn't seem to buy my inexplicable illness story or my miraculous recovery. Not that I blame them. Plus, there's still a good sized camp that's convinced you're the devil."

"The devil, huh?" he asked with a chuckle.

"It's not funny." I sat up. He followed suit, shifting to lean against the headboard beside me. I glanced over at him, miraculously clear in the darkness, and let out a huff of frustration. "I have no idea how to convince any of them that you're not the villain they think. I thought for sure winning the pack over would be the hard part, but now I'm not so sure."

David wrapped his fingers around my hand and pulled it up for a kiss before resting it in his lap. "You're right. I behaved terribly. The town has absolutely no reason to like me and I sure as the moon didn't give *you* any reason to believe in me."

"We don't have to do this now."

"Yeah, actually, I think we do." He gave my hand a gentle squeeze. "I'm so immensely sorry, Charline. I took for granted my connection to you and didn't offer you the reassurance you deserved that nothing and no one would ever come between us. I let myself get caught up in politics, which—let's face it—I suck at." I snorted and he gave me a lopsided grin. "Exactly. But I let myself get blinded to what you needed and your worries. It shouldn't matter if I saw what Vicky was doing to you or not, *you're* the love of my life and I should have supported you. I messed up big time and I almost lost you because of it. For as long as I live, I plan on doing everything in my power to make that up to you."

I used my free hand to wipe away the sudden well of tears that sprung free. "Thanks. I...I needed that." We sat in silence for a few moments resting against each other. "What's going to happen to her?" I whispered at last.

"I'm not entirely sure," he responded just as quietly. "I know what Alexander said about making an example of her, but he's not the kind of person not to look at a problem from every side."

I pressed a kiss to his temple and tightened my fingers around his. "I'm sure he will."

David offered me a wan smile then shook himself. "Okay, onto things we can immediately affect. How can I help with the town?"

"Hell if I know. Most of them still cringe when I pull up in your truck. You may have to get a new one."

"That's not happening," he deadpanned and if I hadn't been so stressed, I would have laughed. "What we need is for the pack and the town to stop treating each other like hostiles."

"They call the people who live in the House wolves. Did you know that?"

"No." He ran a hand over his face and the shadow of worry grew. "It seems we have our work cut out for us. Alpha is going to be livid. Whatever game Johnathan is playing at is a dangerous one. Risking exposing the pack with rumors like that—even if it *is* just name calling... It's more important than ever that we get the village and the pack on the same page."

"And how do you plan to accomplish that?"

David angled his head to the side and gave me an appraising look. "What would you say to a community fundraiser?"

"Come again."

"A fundraiser. One that would involve both the town and the pack. It was actually Xander's idea."

"But what would the fundraiser be for?"

David shifted to face me more directly, excited energy radiating off of him. "You'll love this." He paused for effect.

"Well, out with it."

"The children. We'll all work together to raise money for the schools. It's something that benefits everyone *and* it avoids conversation around developing that land."

"Unless of course they propose a park or playground," I pointed out and his enthusiasm fell into a frown.

"Well aren't you a Negative Nancy."

"Assuming the best, what kind of fundraiser did you have in mind?"

"I was thinking a bake sale, but I wanted to talk to you about it before pitching it to Xander," he suggested tentatively. "You being the resident culinary genius, I thought you could take the lead."

"Pastry genius," I corrected.

"You're an everything genius," he said with a grin. "So, what do you say? You up for taking point on this? I'll be with you every step of the way, whatever you need."

I bit my lip and fought to keep my bubbling excitement under control. Where I'd grown up, organizing the annual bake sale was a coveted honor. While I wasn't sure if that's quite how things worked here, it didn't mitigate the prestige in my eyes. "I'd love to."

The following morning found me bright eyed and bushy tailed, ready to conquer the day. I swiped David with a quick kiss then headed straight for town, already on the phone with the Secretary of Community Affairs. Typically a bake sale of this magnitude would take months to prepare, which meant I had to make every minute of the next week count.

I tapped on the steering wheel in time with my mental list of things that needed doing as I drove down Main Street after obtaining the permit for the event. In a stroke of inspiration, I veered into a vacant spot in front of the butcher shop and hopped out.

The door dinged overhead as I stepped inside. Darren looked up from the order he was filling and waved, then despite his numerous customers, walked around the counter and swung me up in a hug.

"Well, hello to you too," I said once he set me down as I straightened my dress.

"They said you were better, but I could hardly believe it. Seeing you now, I'm still not sure I do." He gave me a less than subtle appraisal that brought a rush of heat to my cheeks. "I've been meaning to call on you at the B&B, but as you can see," he gestured to the impatient line and his poor apprentice struggling to keep up with shouted orders.

"Well, it wouldn't have done you much good to call on me there," I said in an attempt to get this visit back on track.

"What?"

"I'm surprised you haven't heard. I'm back at the House now. I'm also back with David." It seemed best to go ahead and get that out there lest we revisit another display of exuberance.

His face fell, but he quickly schooled his features into a forced smile. "That's nice."

"Go ahead and help your customers. I'll talk with you when you're caught up."

"Um, sure," he said before disappearing back around the counter.

I located a vacant seat and settled in to wait. It took

longer than expected, but eventually his apron fell unceremoniously across the back of a matching chair as he finally joined me.

"How have you been?" I asked in an attempt to keep things light, though the hopes of my favor being granted had diminished significantly in the face of his obvious disappointment.

Darren shrugged noncommittally. "It's good to see you're doing better. I know you had several people quite worried. Lance for sure," he said, gesturing to the oblivious assistant. "What did you want to talk to me about?"

"A couple things actually. For starters, I'm assuming you've heard about the fundraiser the Wolfsbanes are sponsoring." It was a bit of a long shot, but gossip worked funny in small towns. If Darren already knew about it, then half the battle of getting the word out was already won.

"Yeah, it's for the schools right?"

I mentally whooped with victory. "Yep. It's going to be a bake sale."

"Really now?" he asked with a smile, clearly intrigued despite his previous cold demeanor.

"And yours truly is heading it up." His face soured again. I barely contained my exasperation. There wasn't enough time in the day to deal with the fragile male ego. "I was wondering if you knew if it would be possible to use the bakery next door for the event."

He gaped at me. "That old thing? No one's baked in there for over a decade. I doubt it's fit to cook in."

"There's one way to find out. Who would I need to talk to?"

"You'd have to go through Councilwoman Sharp. She used to run all of the real estate in the area and just sort of kept it up over the years. Far as I know, it never sold. If anyone can grant you access, then it would probably be her."

"Thank you, Darren." I popped up from my seat, eager to tackle this latest obstacle in my quest.

"Wait, that was it? You just wanted to know about the bakery?"

"Well, I mean unless you have any thoughts about how to worm my way into Miss Sharp's good graces?"

He flashed a devious smile. "As a matter of fact, I do."

As it turned out, Edith Sharp had a notorious sweet tooth. More specifically, anything with apple. Small wonder where that had come from if she'd dated Alexander for as long as everyone said, though I couldn't help but wonder if she loved apples before or after.

I conquered what other errands I could and the next day I dug deep to make the best apple fritter of my life, using freshly plucked apples from the orchard. Now all I had to do was find the elusive Miss Sharp.

"Oh hey, Miss Charline," Misha called in greeting as I entered Silver Linings Boutique, literally the only place I'd ever actually seen Edith Sharp.

"Funny question for you. I don't suppose you've seen Councilwoman Sharp lately or know where I could find her?" I asked, shifting the sizable Tupperware to my other hip. She gave me a conspiratorial grin after noting the contents, effectively confirming my suspicion that Darren was absolutely the town gossip.

"You actually just missed her. Sounded like she was headed back to the town hall, though I don't know how long she'll be there. If you hurry, I bet you could catch her." I thanked her and passed her a spare fritter. It always paid to reward your informants.

As quickly as my parcel would allow, I hot-footed it over to the hall, relieved to find Edith's signature sporty red car still parked out front. I scurried inside and gave my name to the receptionist. He encouraged me to have a seat with a friendly smile and said he'd let the Councilwoman know I was here. I smiled back and chose a chair beside her door.

I'd just finished settling when the muffled sound of voices drifted through the door. I glanced back at the receptionist who hadn't mentioned anything about her being in another meeting. My fingers tapped a nervous rhythm on the container in my lap. Much as I wanted to use the bakery for the event, I didn't have time to wait around for God knew how long.

I cast another furtive glance at the receptionist paying me no mind, then closed my eyes and focused on the voices. Maybe if I knew what the meeting was about, then I could gauge whether or not it was worth waiting. Words leapt to perfect clarity in an instant and I nearly dropped the fritters. Werewolf hearing really was something else.

"I don't give a damn what you're dealing with. You promised me that land. Produce the agreement or the deal is off. You can pursue whatever vendetta you have on your own." The high pitched voice definitely belonged to Edith Sharp.

"Like I'm the only one pursuing retribution," a decidedly masculine voice responded. "It has been decades, Edith. He chose someone else. A *better* someone else. All you ever were was a distraction to him."

"That's a lie and you know it. You never did like me. Ironic now, considering you need my help."

"I don't need anything of yours."

"Then why are you here?" Edith paused, then snickered. "Yeah, that's what I thought. Last warning, Johnny, that agreement better be at the meeting next week or else I'm bulldozing the whole place and putting up a Godforsaken strip mall."

Something heavy hit the wall followed by the approach of footsteps. I quickly ducked my head as a man easily the size of David stormed out of the office without a backward glance. One look at him and there wasn't a doubt in my mind that he was the North Carolina Beta.

"What do you want?"

I startled at the terse question and jumped to my feet. "Good afternoon, Councilwoman Sharp. I'm Charline Montgomery. I'm here about the fundraiser this weekend."

She gave a curt nod, eying the container and waved me into her office. I followed behind her and hoped my offering would be enough to assuage her bad mood. She stopped by her desk, foot already tapping with impatience and I immediately set down the container and popped the lid. Instantly the smell of fresh baked apples curled with seductive hints of cinnamon filled the room.

"As you no doubt already know, the fundraiser is to be a bake sale. They do seem so appropriate for children, don't you think?" I began, laying on the southern accent as thick as I could. Mama did always say you could catch more flies with honey than vinegar and a little twang never hurt nobody neither. Edith appraised the generously stacked morsels, but didn't take one. Not the best start so far. "Anywho...I heard you were the woman to talk to about unused properties."

She glanced up at me and I winced inwardly at my poor choice of words. "Kindly get to the point, I have a very busy schedule today."

"Mimi's Bakery. You wouldn't happen to know if it's fully equipped still or if the previous owners took the ovens with them?"

"Why are you asking? What does this have to do with the fundraiser?" I watched as she gingerly picked up what I hoped was a still warm fritter.

"Quite frankly, I'm thinking of buying the place and wanted to give it a trial run by using it to make the treats for the sale." It seemed plausible enough. The village had to be desperate by this point. Fifteen years was a long time to have a vacant storefront. As a sitting member of the council *and* a previous real estate broker, Edith would be more than motivated to see the prime location occupied.

"You're a baker, I take it," she said before taking a tentative bite.

"Yes ma'am," I replied as modestly as I could.

"These are quite good." Pride surged in my breast at the compliment. Before I could thank her, she said, "I will see what I can do. While the town does hold a vested interest, there are some legal complications with the previous owners."

"I thought the owner died." The sudden absence of a deep southern accent certainly got her attention. I quickly back-pedaled and twanged it up extra. "I mean, that's what that handsome butcher says at least."

"Yes, Darren does tend to over share. The principal owner passed, but there were contingencies. To my knowledge, the equipment was left there. As for what state it's in, I can't make any promises. I'll have it inspected and let you know. Don't let it be said that the town council does not support today's youth or small business owners," she said, guiding me toward the door. I very intentionally did not move to retrieve the container of goodies.

"Thank you so much, Councilwoman Sharp. I promise to make something extra special just for you."

She glanced back at the still heaped platter. "I think I would like that quite a bit."

It took an active force of will to contain my excitement until I was out of sight of the town hall. Not only would I have a better space to prepare the goods for the sale, I would finally get to see the inside of Mimi's Bakery. It was literally the only historic location I hadn't explored and that fact was killing me. My two-fold victory was starting to go to my head, then a sudden thought minimized my mounting enthusiasm—I had to tell David.

24

FUTURE PLANS

Edith Sharp was one hundred percent a woman scorned, but she was also maybe not as bad as everyone believed. Though what on Earth possessed me to say I had any intention of buying the bakery, I had no clue. Sure, owning my own bakery would be a dream come true, except this wasn't any old empty shop waiting to be filled with sweet treats. It was David's mom's. Even the fantastic news that not only was the bakery viable, but the Council would be paying to have it cleaned and stocked for the fundraiser as their contribution, couldn't diminish my reticence to broach the topic with David.

I pushed away my persistent concern and forced myself to focus as Marissa filled me on her progress with the mothers of the pack. Things were definitely looking up on that front and I couldn't help but be impressed at how many people she and Isabel had spoken with in such a short amount of time. Out of the corner of my eye I caught sight of David. I debated filling him in on the news later when he didn't appear quite so busy, then reminded myself what that kind of thinking had led to before. I waffled another moment as his silhouette got farther away, then finally caved. Now was as good a time as any.

"Excuse me, Marissa, I need to have a word with David."

"Alright, I'll touch base with you later. And Charline?" she called after me as I began to follow him. "Thank you for organizing all of this. It's been ages since we did anything like this with the people of Stone Creek."

I smiled and shook my head. "Don't thank me. It was all Xander's idea." Her face lit with surprise then softened into a grin. I left her to her revelation and raced after the last place I'd seen David only to find an empty hall. Then a hint of fresh cut cedar and sunshine tickled my nose. I followed the scent as it wove between countless others through the House until it suddenly vanished.

Frustrated, I retraced my last few steps and came to the same conclusion. David's scent said he should be right here, and yet, he wasn't. "Where in Sam Hill did you go?" I growled to myself. Without warning, a hand circled around my wrist and yanked me into an adjoining room where a pair of eager lips mashed against mine.

"I'm surprised I lost you. You were doing an excellent job of following me," David said with a sexy grin and a hint of pride.

I glowered and smacked him in the chest.

"Ow. What was that for?"

"Are you trying to get yourself killed?" I hissed. "You can't just go around grabbing people from hallways. You scared me half to death."

"Yeah, but you realized it was me, right?"

"No, I just randomly go around letting just anyone kiss me."

David raised an eyebrow. "You mean like the butcher?"

I blanched. It hadn't even occurred to me that Darren's

scent might linger after that rather unexpected hug. "Nothing happened."

"I know," he said, pressing into me. "Still doesn't change the way he looks at you or the fact that he touched you in the first place." Goosebumps pebbled on my skin as he laid a trail of teasing kisses along my neck.

"Are you always going to be this possessive?" I quipped while I fought my body's response to his proximity. I was on a mission damn it.

"Yes."

The sultry reply stoked my desire and I clung with a white knuckle hold to my original purpose for seeking him out. "Before you get too carried away, I need to tell you a few things."

He mumbled some sort of acknowledgment and his calloused hands slid beneath my shirt.

"About the fundraiser and Edith Sharp."

David gave a low groan of disappointment and removed the heated touch, though the deafening pounding of my heart didn't relent so easily. "What have you found?"

"Let's go up to the room where we're less likely to be disturbed."

"*That* I can certainly agree with," he said with a wolfish grin.

I rolled my eyes and let him lead me up the stairs. Relatively safe in the confines of his bedroom, I relaxed a little.

"So what is it? Is something wrong with the plans for the fundraiser?" David asked quietly after closing the door. Just because we were in a private space, didn't mean our conversation would stay that way.

"No. Nothing like that. Actually, things are going quite well. Marissa was just telling me how all the moms plan to pitch in and how some of the ones that live in town have already buddied up with moms from Stone Creek."

"That's great news!" David's smile stretched from ear to ear as he stepped close and wrapped his arms around my waist. "I knew you could do this. You're incredible, Char." He leaned down and captured me with an all consuming kiss.

I quickly pushed him to arms length. "Like I was saying, things are going along swimmingly."

"Is that what you wanted to tell me?" he asked, dropping his voice down to a delicious purr as he leaned in to suck out a bruise on my neck.

"Y-yes. I mean no. There's more."

He chuckled and straightened up. "Well, let's hear it."

"I got permission to use the old bakery," I said in a rush before he could distract me again. "If that's okay with you, that is," I added even as his face went blank. "I know your mother used to run Mimi's Bakery."

"Who told you that? Maria?" He released his hold on me and stepped back, his gaze falling to the floor.

"The butcher." His shoulders tensed and I quickly went on. "But I wish you had. David, if we're going to work, I need you to be open with me. I understand that it's a sensitive subject, but don't you think this is one of those things you should share?"

He sagged on the bed as if the weight of years pressed him down. "You're right. I know you're right."

I quietly sat beside him and waited until he let out a sigh that seemed to fill the whole room.

"I already told you about my dad. I think my mom knew long before being told of his passing." His vacant gaze fixed on the floor as he clasped his hands together in his lap. "She just stopped eating one day. No matter what I did, she wouldn't laugh or smile. With each passing day, she got colder. Not just distant colder, but literally, physically colder, like her inner fire was going out."

He tilted his head back and stared up at the ceiling.

"When the official news finally came it got so much worse. She cried for days. Maria tried to get her to hang on, but in the end nothing could stop the inevitable. Not even living for her only child. She made it a few years before she finally faded. But she was empty."

"That's awful," I whispered as I wrapped an arm around his shoulders. He leaned into me and my heart broke for him. "But I'm not sure I understand. From what I've gathered, you get your heart from her. I can't imagine that she would just leave you."

"My mother was a wonderful woman, bright and full of life, but when my father died, he took that with him." He turned sad eyes on me and trailed a light finger down my cheek. "That's the curse of finding your mated pair."

I mentally went back over everything that had happened. How he'd said he'd known it was me from the beginning, the flashes of memory that showed him looking worn beyond belief. At the time I'd believed it was the weight of keeping the pack together, but this provided a new perspective.

"Mated pairs can't live without each other," I said quietly. He nodded and dropped his hand. "I'm so sorry, David." I squeezed him as tightly as I could, which was substantially more now that I had werewolf strength. He let out a grunt and looked at me. "Two more questions about your past if you're up for them." He didn't nod, but he didn't say no either. "Who's the boy in the picture?" He glanced up towards the shelf.

"That's Nyle. He's my cousin on my father's side. Maria tried to keep in touch with that side of the family after my mother's passing, even going so far as inviting him to come spend summers with me." He shrugged, his expression forlorn. "In the end, it was too much. I had my first change and it became progressively harder to maintain the pack's secrets around a curious human boy." He paused after finishing. "I miss him sometimes. We used to spend a lot of time together. It helped when Michael came to the House. We were close in age and had so much in common from losing our parents, I suppose our friendship was inevitable."

"You two are like brothers," I said with a smile for how warmly he spoke about his friend.

"Yeah. Now what was your other question?"

I took a deep breath and let it out slowly. "Are you okay with me using the bakery?"

He cupped my cheek while a broad grin split his face. "I think it would be great. My mom would love to see someone as passionate about cooking as she was using the place to bring joy to the whole community."

"You really think she'd approve?"

"Know so." He used his hold to pull me in for a kiss. "I love you, Char."

"I love you too." I stole the next kiss, deepening it from tame to needy and burying my fingers in his golden locks.

He pulled away long enough to make sure the door was locked and yank his shirt over his head. I immediately placed my hand on his bare chest, reveling in the heat that emanated off of him.

"How long do you think we have?" I asked, my voice rough with want.

"Thirty minutes maybe, an hour if we're lucky." He tugged at my clothes while he snatched hungrily at my lips. "We'll have to be quiet though."

I bit back a moan as his fingers pushed aside my panties and curled inside. He kissed his way down my neck and torso until he snared a beaded nipple. My hand flew to my mouth to stifle a gasp as I arched off the bed. He rubbed a calloused thumb over my clit and my entire body shuddered. Then his fingers were gone. He stood and used my thighs to pull me to the edge of the bed. Despite his assessment that we had little uninterrupted time available, he seemed in no rush.

My fingers clawed into the sheets as he teased the ache to unbearable heights. Finally, he took mercy and drove deep in one smooth slide. I instantly tightened around him and he sealed his mouth back over mine, capturing my whimper. My arms curled under his shoulders to keep him close. Somehow I'd become completely wrapped up in this man. He'd stolen my heart and I was in no hurry to get it back.

He broke the kiss as he picked up the pace, driving us both towards a desperate pinnacle. I wrapped my legs around him and met each thrust. The edge of release pulsed hotly between us. David's fingers dug into my hips with bruising force as he pumped harder. I bit down on his shoulder and cried out my release as he grunted and lost his rhythm.

We clung to each other, panting through the post orgasmic high, a thin sheen of sweat glistening on our mostly naked bodies. I whimpered again as he slipped free and bent to retrieve a discarded towel to clean us up.

"I hate having to rush." He tossed the towel aside and brushed a delicate kiss across my lips. "A body like this," he said as he caressed my sides and ample hips, "deserves to be worshiped."

Heat burned fiercely across my cheeks and chest. "You spoil me."

He grinned and helped me sit up. "You deserve to be spoiled." I shook my head at a loss for what to say and set about putting myself back to rights. Once more presentable, I spared the locked door a disdainful glare.

"We really do need to get a place of our own." I turned to

find David giving me the broadest grin I think I'd ever seen. "What?"

"You said 'We'."

"Well, yeah. I think it's been made abundantly clear that I'm not going anywhere." He continued to give me that goofy smile as he wrapped his arms around me once more. I gave an exasperated sigh that quickly turned to a giggle as he nuzzled my neck.

"What about your job?" The low whisper turned my insides to jelly.

"I'm sure I can find something in town."

"You know, you don't have to work at all," he said as his hands resumed their roaming.

"You and I both know I'd be bored out of my mind." He laughed deep in his throat, setting all the butterflies inside to flapping at once. "David," I said in a breathy whisper.

"And your house? I know how much you love your little yellow cottage."

"I-I'll rent it out," I stammered as his arduous attentions progressed. His smile pressed against my flushed neck right before the barest scrape of teeth. My breath caught and I struggled to keep focused. Definitely needed our own place.

"Are you sure?" he asked, a note of doubt creeping in. His eyes widened with surprise when I promptly smacked him in the chest.

"Of course, I'm sure. I don't casually just decide to uproot my whole life for just anyone, you know."

His warm smile crinkled his eyes. "There is nothing casual about you, Charline Montgomery."

"Are you calling me high maintenance?"

"I'm calling you perfect," he said, capturing me with a kiss that had my toes curling in the carpet. I pressed into him, longing for more, but not trusting myself to stay as quiet a second time.

"*Really* need our own place."

"Char, I will build you the house of your dreams," he said with an entirely different promise in his eyes.

I blinked back at him in shock, I'd never heard anything more romantic in my entire life. All of my attempts to prevent us from falling back into a heated ardor fell by the wayside. Without preamble, I wrapped my arms around his neck and hopped up to straddle his hips. He let out a guttural growl as my legs tightened around him and I conquered him with a kiss that he enthusiastically returned.

"God, werewolf stamina is incredible," I gasped as he claimed my body for the second time.

"Speak for yourself. One of these days you're gonna wear me out."

"I'll do my best," I said, wiggling for good measure.

He gave another groan that sent delicious vibrations rippling through me and all thoughts of being overheard went up in smoke.

25

BAKE SALE

I bolted out of bed the morning of the bake sale excited, nervous, and already running late. "Drat that man," I grumbled to myself as I pulled on the dress I'd set out the night before. "What part of 'still have a laundry list of boxes to check' says let me sleep in?" I whipped my rebellious curls into a high ponytail, having no time for anything else, grabbed my overstuffed bag, and zipped out the door.

At the bottom of the stairs, I ran into Michelle and Isabel. "Morning, Charline," they chimed together.

"Thank goodness you're already here. Have you seen David? I can't find the keys for the truck."

"He's already left for town," Michelle said.

My hands fell from their flurry of conquering stray hairs. "He did what!"

Isabel laughed and looped an arm through mine as Melissa relieved me of my bag. "Don't worry. My car is all set with the last minute supplies. There should be just enough room to squeeze the rest of us in there."

I sagged with relief. "That's not funny," I said as they dragged me through the front door, laughing anyway. We'd almost made it to Isabel's compact, which really was near full to bursting, when a familiar voice sent a river of ice down my spine.

"You think you've won."

I froze and turned to look at Victoria. She looked like shit. Dark hollows circled her sunken eyes, making her sallow features appear even more gaunt. Faint silver scars criss-crossed her face and upper torso. Distantly, I registered that I'd caused those and realized the reason I hadn't seen her around was because she'd been recovering from the fight.

A sneer twisted her face as she took in my contrasting health. "It would have been better if you'd died."

"How can you say that?" I said, taking a step toward her. "I understand you hate me, but it would've killed David too."

She scoffed and rolled her eyes. "Don't tell me you're buying into that whole 'mated pairs' crap."

I recoiled at the vehemence of the statement and finally accepted the truth. She'd never had any real machinations on David. We'd merely been pawns in a much larger game. Childhood friend or no, this woman had absolutely no idea who David was.

"You don't care about David at all."

"Me, someone else, doesn't matter. *Anyone* but you. He deserves a real wolf, not some cheap imitation." My ruff instantly went up and I bared my teeth, but before I could unleash, Isabel and Michelle came to my defense.

"She *is* a real wolf, Vicky," Isabel said, stepping up beside me, her arms crossed over her chest.

"And she's more pack than you'll ever be," Michelle added, not to be left out. "Charline may be bitten, but she handled your scrawny ass well enough. Or did you need a refresher?" Isabel arched an eyebrow and Victoria darted an anxious look between the three of us.

She licked her lips as she searched the yard for any sign of support. While there were plenty of people milling about in anticipation of the event later in the day, no one made a move to come to Victoria's aid. She was alone. For the first time, I truly understood the gravity of what it would mean to be exiled, to have your entire pack and support system completely disown you. Victoria might not have been officially banished, but she'd burned a lot of bridges when she bit me.

"Come on, ladies," I said, turning back to the car. "We don't have time for this. Let her lick her wounds in private." Both Isabel and Michelle spared her one last scathing look then moved to join me.

"I can't believe you're on her side," Victoria hissed, grabbing Isabel's arm and pulling her up short.

Isabel glared daggers at her former friend and yanked her arm away. "You're half the wolf she is. Don't touch me or mine ever again."

The last door of the sedan shut with a hollow thud that echoed eerily in the stuffed car. Michelle leaned forward from the back seat to rest her forearms on the center console. "Well, that was awkward."

Isabel cracked a smile and I released a nervous laugh. "Come on, those treats won't cook themselves."

Isabel shifted the car into gear. As we made our way down the drive toward town I made a concerted effort to put the confrontation behind me. Tomorrow, I could stress about the blow karma would deal Victoria. Today, I was baking in a bona fide bakery for the benefit of the whole community.

We pulled up to a storefront and it took me a hot second

to recognize the old bakery. "Wow," I said, staring in open-mouthed wonder at the pristine glass.

Michelle tsked impatiently and grabbed my arm to drag me inside. A cute little bell above the door chimed and I refocused on the people crowding the interior.

"Oh. Um, hi." I offered a little wave to all of the people now staring at me.

A mop of blond hair followed by broad shoulders poked out from the back. "Good, the girls got you here," David said as he walked around the counter. He snagged a wrapped parcel from one of the long tables set up around the room and walked up to me.

"David, I...what... Who *are* all of these people?" I floundered.

He glanced over his shoulder at the cluster of people milling about and gave me a cheeky grin. "Some of them are Edith's, some of them are mine. All of them are here to help."

"Oh my heavens." I pressed a hand to my chest in a vain attempt to temper the gratitude threatening to overwhelm me.

"Hey." David tucked a finger under my chin and turned my gaze to his. "We're here to offer as much or as little support as you need. But before you give your marching orders, I wanted you to have this." He held out the brown wrapped parcel, that could have just as easily been a cut of meat from the butcher as anything else.

I blinked away the sudden sting of tears as I unwrapped it with shaking hands. The twine holding it together fell free to reveal a beautiful floral pattern. David crumpled the paper while I held it up to get a better look. My fingers tightened on the soft yet sturdy fabric as I took in every detail of a sharply pressed apron complete with all the pockets and loops I loved.

"What do you think?"

I tore my gaze from the outrageously thoughtful gift to find David grinning like a schoolboy. "It's perfect." My eyes burned again and I fanned them to cool the tears threatening to spill over.

He gently took the apron from me, looped it over my head, then stepped behind me to tie the strings around my waist. His lips brushed a kiss on my jaw as his fingers dug softly into my hips. "There, now you're ready. Go get 'em, little fox."

I took a bracing breath and stepped deeper into the room beneath the watchful gaze of the expectant gathering. "First off, I'd like to thank you all for coming out to help. This place looks absolutely amazing. No matter how today goes, know that you are the best part of this community."

Carly smiled at one of the young teens from the pack helping her to polish the display case. Behind them more people emerged from the kitchen, equal parts pack and townsfolk. Joy at seeing everyone coming together briefly overrode what I'd intended to say, then Isabel gave a discreet cough.

"Right," I laughed. "As I was saying, I appreciate the thoughtfulness, but as I'm sure we've all heard, there can be such a thing as too many cooks in the kitchen." They gave a collective laugh. "I'll happily take all the help I can get, but maybe not here. Anyone without baking experience is welcome to help David Bringer with the rest of the set up in the park."

David clapped his hands together. "Alright, you heard the lady. I'll be working on the play area for the children, but there's plenty of more work to go around for willing hands. And who knows, maybe the lovely baker will have some extra treats for all of the hardworking volunteers," he added, giving me a wink.

"Thanks for the extra work," I said under my breath as people began vacating the bakery, knowing full well David could hear me.

"It's nothing you can't handle. You've got this, love." He planted a wet kiss on my cheek then smacked my ass. "Knock 'em dead." He waved for the last volunteers to follow him, leaving me in a room full of people who at least thought they could bake.

It quickly became apparent that not all of them could. However, that didn't mean I lacked work to give them. Displays were just as important as the actual baking, not to mention they were fully capable of refreshing supplies as we went. In hardly any time at all, we became a well oiled machine.

My brief stint using the Lunar Cafe's kitchen had prepped me somewhat for the chaos of extra bodies in a space I normally dominated by myself. But cooking a lunch was one thing; baked goods were an art. Luckily, there were several artists in the village, the most impressive of whom was Elise. The older woman had all the know-how of my grandmother and was in no way shy about whipping my helpers into shape.

I fell into an easy rhythm as we turned out trays upon trays of cookies, brownies, cupcakes, fritters, and sweet treats. A timer dinged and I spun around with a tray of hot scones to place them on the cooling rack. It wasn't until I caught Elise and several others giving me a strange look that I realized I'd done it without a protective mitt.

Apparently there were several things on the list of things to be careful of when you suddenly found yourself a were-wolf. I gave them a nervous smile and shrugged as if to say it was nothing. And it wasn't. My hand was barely even warm from the burning metal.

Note to self: beware excessive shows of strength, appetite, and endurance.

A hair more conscious of my newfound abilities, I returned to baking, even making sure to set aside a few extras of everything for the volunteers and a special plate for Miss Sharp herself. Who knew, maybe I could get her past this whole land dispute by winning over her stomach. Wouldn't be the first time I'd charmed someone with food. I laughed to myself as I dusted the last of the flour off and headed outside.

"What's so funny, Miss Montgomery?" Jimmy asked, surprising me.

My small smile instantly morphed into a full blown grin. "You made it after all! That's wonderful. As for what's funny, nothing really. Just enjoying working in the bakery."

"Why don't you buy the place then? I've already heard several of the volunteers talking about how nice it is to have it open again."

"You don't say." Truth be told, aside from my ploy with Miss Sharp, it hadn't really occurred to me to actually follow through.

"Hello, little fox," David said, walking up to join us. He wiped what assumed was probably renegade flour from my cheek and replaced it with a kiss. "Hi, Jimmy."

"Hello, Mr. Bringer," Jimmy replied by rote.

David smiled warmly at him and extended a hand. Jimmy looked at it skeptically before accepting it. "Please, call me David. I don't think I ever properly introduced myself or apologized for my behavior. Thank you for taking such great care of Char, especially when I wasn't doing such a bang up job of it myself." I flinched at his unfortunate choice of words. However, to my infinite surprise, Jimmy shook his hand and smiled.

"It's no trouble, David. Miss Montgomery has really

brightened this town and all of us would be more than willing to help in any way we can."

"I can see that. From what I understand, you're responsible for the repairs on the gazebo in the square. Am I right? That was excellent work."

Jimmy ducked his head and I caught the hint of a blush. "Yes sir."

David clapped him on the shoulder nearly knocking the poor boy over. "Have you ever considered pursuing a career in construction?"

I shook my head as he steered Jimmy toward the main area, talking shop. With the majority of the treats taken care of and setup nearly complete, all that was left was to find Miss Sharp and thank her personally. After a bit of searching, I spied her amidst a group of overly serious faces, one of which I suspected to be the mayor himself.

"Good afternoon," I said by way of interruption. All eyes turned on me, though Edith's instantly sought out the tray I bore. "If you'll please excuse me, I just wanted to have a quick word with Councilwoman Sharp." I just barely remembered to include the southern twang. Curious faces stepped aside to let me pass. Now to really sell it.

"Miss Sharp, I just wanted to thank you again *so* much for all of your efforts. This is turning out to be a wonderful success and none of it would have been possible without your help."

Edith stopped just shy of openly preening at the lavish praise. I presented her with the assortment of apple pastries all conveniently bite-sized with a flourish that captured the attention of her companions.

"Oh," I simpered sweetly, "I'm so sorry. I promised Councilwoman Sharp that I'd bring a sample of the goods to thank her for everything she's done to make today a success.

I know everyone is immensely grateful." If I laid it on any thicker, I was going to get a cavity.

Edith stole another minute to bask in the praise, then finally addressed the others gathered. "Of course I would be happy to share. It will help whet their appetite for the actual sale." She graciously accepted the platter and held it out for the others to retrieve their own miniature sample. While she was at it, she casually introduced me to her cohorts, including Mayor Hawthorne. He seemed exceptionally impressed by the voracious Miss Sharp, though, personally I thought he should be a tad more concerned about his own position.

After the niceties were out of the way, I surreptitiously stepped into the background, but stayed in sight. My play wasn't over just yet. At last, Miss Sharp laughed and excused herself, leaving the tray of goodies behind.

"Well played, Miss Montgomery," she said quietly as she stepped up beside me without making eye contact.

"Us women of ambition have to stick together, do we not?" I said as I casually produced a full-sized apple tart.

"Oh, you are good," she said as she accepted the treat. "I don't suppose you're actually interested in purchasing that little bakery? The village could benefit from someone of your skills, especially during tourist season."

"Funny you should mention that. I was going to inquire about the previous owners and these mysterious legal complications. It would do me no good to try and purchase a place that's already spoken for."

Edith turned slightly and arched an eyebrow. "I believe you're already intimately familiar with the legal complications." I frowned, assuming she must mean David, but when she continued, I realized I couldn't have been more wrong. "Maria Wolfsbane is the only one standing between you and baker's bliss. She's refused countless offers over the years.

And as the sole trustee of the Trust that holds the bakery, the village hasn't been able to force a sale. To be frank, I was surprised she agreed to let it be used today."

I shoved my surprise down and took my cue. "In that case, I propose we set up a meeting to discuss price."

Her face lit up with borderline manic glee. "I'd be happy to act as your agent. I'll arrange the paperwork and get the information about purchasing the property to you as soon as possible."

"That sounds lovely. You'll find my contact information on a card tucked in the napkin." Edith almost broke the ruse by fully turning to look at me.

"You *are* a crafty one."

I don't know what possessed me to ask, but I couldn't help but press my luck. "Is the village often faced with legally complicated properties?"

She took another bite and slid a sidelong look my way. "They do crop up from time to time, although nothing that can't quickly be resolved. Honestly, the bakery has been the biggest obstacle the village has faced in recent years."

She paused to flick away some fallen crumbs, then added, "I'm sure you've heard the rumors to develop the land south of the Wolfsbane mansion. While it would be nice to have the added public recreational space, the town really doesn't need it. In any event, it will all be settled at the Council meeting next week. It's open to the public if you're interested." I gave a barely perceptible nod and tried to hide my smile. She popped the last of the tart in her mouth and took a step forward. "I'll be sure to get you that information. In the meantime, it looks like I'm back to schmoozing."

Before she could go too far, I whispered, "I think you'd make an excellent mayor."

A suspiciously smug smile twitched on her lips as she rejoined her colleagues. I tucked my hands in my dress pockets and sauntered off to give David the good news. Not only did Edith not sound motivated to acquire the disputed property, she'd all but admitted a legal issue didn't actually exist.

I couldn't help but wonder if she ever would've caused such a fuss if it hadn't been for Johnathan's interference.

26

ST. MARIA

I peered out the window at the people milling about outside enjoying the perfect summer day and twirled a loose lock of hair as the phone rang. My gaze dropped to the pages stacked neatly on the desk, pages I'd never thought I'd need.

"Come on, Sara. Pick up, pick up, pick up."

"Hey you."

I let out a breath I hadn't realized I'd been holding. "It's about time."

She snorted and I caught the faint squeak of the chair as she leaned back. "Some of us didn't take a three month sabbatical."

"Shit. Right. Work." I smacked my forehead, bumping the desk and the papers. I absently reached out to straighten them. "Sorry. I suppose it can wait until after five." Except it really couldn't.

"I'm just giving you a hard time. I've got a few minutes. What's up?"

My tongue froze. Now that the moment had finally come, I couldn't seem to push the rehearsed words past my teeth.

"Charline? Is this about what's going on with the pack?

Michael filled me in on the details. I still can't believe it. I mean, Johnathan? And don't even get me started about Vicky. Insurrection on top of what she did to you? She deserves more than the beating you dealt."

The pack. Of course, right, that's why she would think I was calling. I glanced back at the locked door, conscious of prying ears that might or might not be eavesdropping on purpose.

"Heard the bake sale was a spectacular success..." Sara ventured.

"I'm selling my house," I blurted.

She barked a forced laugh. "Umm....what? I don't think I heard you right. It sounded like you said you're selling your house."

"I did."

"But, Charline, you love that house! Adorable white shutters, little flowerbeds, custom kitchen?"

"I know. I *know*. But I can't really maintain any of that when I'm never there, certainly not if I plan on staying here to build a life with David."

Sara's squeal split the air and I yanked the piercing sound away from my ear. "Shit," she hissed. "Sorry."

"Are you apologizing to me or your coworkers?" I asked, daring to bring the phone close once more.

"Both, but mostly them. Just had to reassure Bob that I haven't had a psychotic break."

"How are things going with the boss, anyway?"

"Oh no you don't. I want details. Did David propose?" I could practically see her hunched over her desk in her new private office vibrating with excitement.

I ran my fingers lightly over the crisp pages and smiled, reaffirmed in my decision. "Not yet, but I don't expect it's far off. We're bonded, after all."

The chair squeaked alarmingly on the other end of the

line and Sara let out a giant whoosh of air. "Holy shit. Really?"

"Yeah, really."

"How...how do you know?"

The fact that she had to ask at all answered the question I hadn't wanted to pose to her. "First off, I'm absolutely in love with the goof. And second...I can feel it, like the first rays of dawn on a spring morning or the scent of fresh blueberry muffins curling in your nose and reminding you of home. It fills me up and I just *know*."

"Oh. That's...that's really beautiful, Charline. I'm so happy for you," she said with a touch of sadness.

"This doesn't mean what you and Mike have is any less! I've never seen two people more suited for each other. Michael adores you and I'm pretty sure if Bob hadn't promoted you after that miracle you did with the Sanderson project, he would have eaten him."

She laughed. "You're probably right. We've talked about it, you know. He said he doesn't care about the bond, just me. Now that things are right with him and the pack, he plans on loving me until I can't stand him any more." She laughed again. "I threatened to sic Tom on him if he got too out of hand."

A smile tugged at my lips. I'd finally had the pleasure of meeting Sara's adoptive parents, Tom and Peter. The two were adorably in love and fiercely protective of their daughter. "Tom is plenty threat for anyone."

"Michael made dinner *and* did the laundry for a week after that."

I chuckled and shook my head. "Living the dream. Anyway, back to my big news. I was kinda hoping you could help me out."

"Of course, what do you need?"

"I have some papers for you to sign. You can have the

office notary help you out. They grant you power of attorney so you can act in my stead for the house prep and sale. Assuming that you're okay with that?" I held my breath.

"More than okay. I still owe you for taking such great care of me while I was recovering from the attack."

"How many times do I have to tell you, you don't owe me anything. You're my best friend. That's what besties do."

"Exactly, so accept the gratitude and tell me when to expect the fax."

I chuckled and shook my head. "I should be able to get them to you later this afternoon. I'll pop into town and use the B&B's fax machine. And since you're feeling so generous, you won't mind helping the movers pack up my stuff and the real estate agent show the house."

"I take it back. I don't wanna help and you're not allowed to sell your house."

"Thanks, Sara," I said sincerely despite the jest.

"That's what besties are for. I'll keep an eye out for those papers and keep you up to date."

We disconnected and I sagged with relief. One hurdle down, one more to go. I placed the papers I'd prepared in my bag and set it by the door, then went downstairs in search of Maria. On the way, I seemed to pass half the pack. I returned each of the enthusiastic waves and greetings, curious if I'd missed some memo.

Several more bodies passed by me as they exited the front room. I glanced back at their retreating forms and wondered if I should postpone my quest in favor of figuring out why everyone seemed to be moving around with such purpose.

"You're looking casual today."

I spun back around to find Maria exiting the front room as well. A smile quirked my lips as I plucked at my t-shirt. "Yeah, I don't seem to have as many dresses as I used to."

She grinned broadly and did a flourish that took in her own understated ensemble.

"Dresses are pretty, but you can run in pants."

"You can run plenty well in dresses!" I countered, though my mother would be scandalized to hear such a remark. "Do you have a minute? I was wanting to talk to you about something." She glanced behind me and I followed her gaze. "Is something going on? I would have expected the House to be emptier after the Solstice."

Maria shrugged. "Generally once people arrive they tend to stay the full summer. As for what's going on, it'll keep another few minutes. Why don't we go to the kitchen for some tea? I have a feeling I know what you want to talk about."

"Really?" I asked, but Maria was already making her way down the hall. I scrambled to catch up and arrived in time to take over preparing the tea. She pulled up a seat as I poured water heated from the microwave over our favorite blend of Earl Grey with dried orange peel. I grabbed a spoon and saucer, then joined her.

"What did you want to talk to me about?" she asked as I stared into the steeping tea.

I took a deep breath and slowly raised my head to meet her speculative gaze. Like all the other times I'd been one on one with the woman, she reminded me strongly of my own mother with her serene composure and no-nonsense attitude. "Why didn't you tell me that David's mother owned Mimi's Bakery?"

She sighed and sat back. "I suspected as much."

"That would've helped a lot," I pushed.

"I'm sure it would have, but that was David's story to tell."

"I hate to tell you this, but I pretty much heard everything from everyone who *wasn't* David."

She winced as she blew on the steaming liquid then took a sip. "That man. I swear sometimes he's still just a boy." While I wholeheartedly agreed, this wasn't the time.

"I also know that she left it to you." Maria paused mid sip and her gaze flicked up to me. "You could have said something when I got permission to use the bakery for the fundraiser. How *did* that happen anyway? Did Sharp actually talk to you?" Knowing their history, I found that hard to believe.

"Yes. She came several days ago to badger me about selling so the town could finally see the property occupied. While she asks every year, she's never done so in person."

"Wait. She came *here*?" How had I not heard about this? It should have been the talk of the House.

"She did. Sat right where you are now." Maria nodded toward me and where my jaw was currently sitting on the table in shock.

"How did you manage that?"

"I told everyone to get out. That I had a private meeting to attend to and they could return in an hour." I shook my head unable to absorb the casual way she said she'd simply asked dozens of werewolves to get lost. Even more unbelievably, they'd apparently done it.

"What happened?"

"First, I let her yell herself out. That took quite a while. I gave her some tea. She yelled some more, spouting all kinds of accusations about how I stole her man and that Alexander had wronged her. Then I gave her some more tea with a little something extra. Girl needed a drink after all of that." Maria sat her now empty mug on the table.

"And...?"

"And I told her she was right." My jaw bypassed the table to smack on the floor. Maria merely shrugged. "Alexander *did* treat her horribly. It was wrong how he handled things.

Hard as it may be to believe, he was not always as diplomatic as he is now."

"How...how could you possibly tell her that?"

"Because it was what she needed to hear. She's waited years to have her feelings be validated. All this hate and anger has been weighing her down, pushing her to lash out at anything to do with Alexander, including the pack. Yelling at me gave her the chance to finally get it out. Telling her that her feelings were justified simply helped her let them go.

"Edith never did anything to deserve what happened. She just happened to fall for a werewolf who ended up bonding with someone else." Maria toyed with the handle of her mug. "That being said, Alexander definitely could have handled that situation better. But what's done is done. Now that she's finally said her piece, I think all of us can finally move past this."

I sat in stunned silence. Hands down, this was why Maria was so revered—woman was a damn saint. She'd accomplished in under an hour what Alexander had failed to do in over ten years.

Maria glanced up at me and winked. "And of course you can have the bakery, my dear. It will be so nice to be able to keep it in the family. I don't suppose you've thought of any new names yet?"

It took me a moment to come back to the present. "Wha —? No, I assumed I would just keep the same name."

She waved away the idea. "Stars no, you need to make the place your own. It hasn't been Mimi's in fifteen years. Personally, I think it's past time it got an update. Don't you?"

I smiled back at her. I'd actually quite liked some of the more retro out-fittings, it made the place feel more authentic.

"Maria, Charline, what are you still doing here?" Sandy asked, nearly skidding past the entryway to the kitchen.

"We're coming. I thought we had a little more time. If you see Alexander, let him know we're on our way."

Sandy gave a quick nod and resumed her brisk pace.

I stood as Maria did and passed her a curious look. "So, something *is* going on. What is it?" I asked, trepidation trickling through my veins.

"Alexander has called a pack meeting. Everyone's to be there. He can be so melodramatic sometimes. Men, always aiming to make a big show of everything," she scoffed as she led the way. Maria looked back at me when I suddenly stopped dead in the middle of the now vacant hallway. "What is it dear?"

"Maria, do you know what's happening at this meeting?" My voice shook as I connected the last of the dots.

Her gaze turned harder than granite. "Of course I do. Now, we should get going. Neither one of us can afford to be late."

I nodded numbly and followed her out the back door into a crowd of *weres*.

27

WOLF IN SHEEP'S CLOTHING

A distinct air of expectation thickened the air and weighed heavily on the entirety of the pack gathered on the back lawn

"What do we do now?" I whispered to Maria.

"First off, we can't exactly stand back here." As if on cue, the people in front of us parted silently to let us pass.

I followed in Maria's wake, sticking close. Countless pairs of curious eyes passed over us, though none seemed to hold the level of anxiety currently brewing in the pit of my stomach. Suddenly, I caught the sharp scent of ginger and violets. I glanced up to find Victoria glaring at me, not two feet away.

My surprise at seeing her must have been clearly written across my face, because her own clouded over in confusion. I quickly ducked my head before I could do something that I would regret. For some reason, I wanted to warn her, tell her to run while she still could.

A firm hand landed on my arm. I tore my focus from the weathered grass to meet Maria's stern gaze. She gave the smallest shake of her head as if she knew the track of my wayward thoughts and my heart landed with an uncomfortable squelch in my stomach. It would seem that not even Saint Maria could forgive everyone.

We finally reached our destination beside a modest platform that definitely hadn't been there earlier. I took up a place just off to the side and behind David. He spared me the briefest glance then returned his attention to the man at the center of it all.

Alexander stood at the forefront of the gathering elevated enough to be seen by all, conversing with his son. A couple more minutes ticked by in silence filled with the fidgets of people who had no idea what was happening. Eventually, Alexander lifted his head and passed a considering gaze over the crowd. Whatever he saw seemed to satisfy him and he stepped away from Xander.

"As you all know, this summer has been unusually trying for the pack. The announcement of my retirement seems to have generated a level of uncertainty among you. It saddens my heart to see that some took advantage of this difficult time to sow discord."

A rustle of sound rolled through the crowd. My unease ratcheted up another notch and I fought the impulse to scan the crowd for Victoria. He wouldn't. Not here in front of everyone. Would he?

"I would like to say that this has been the act of a child lashing out. However, the betrayal goes much deeper." The rustle became a murmuring wave as people turned to look at their neighbors. "The current predicament surrounding the east running grounds was brought about by none other than one of our own."

Shocked gasps floated up and my chest tightened. *No, no, no. Please don't.* I stared at the back of David's head for any hint that I could be wrong, but the stiff set of his shoulders said that wasn't the case.

"What's more, an even more heinous crime has been committed. Someone threatened to expose the pack."

A shout came from the middle of the gathering, followed by a screech of indignant rage. "Let go of me!"

The mass of people twisted as one to seek out the source. I didn't have to. My voice stuck painfully in my throat as Victoria was forcibly escorted by two substantially larger men. Bodies parted before them, eyeing her with an alarming mix of scorn, hatred, and worst of all, skepticism. When they reached the raised area where Alexander stood, they released her, but didn't step away. Rather than run or at least try to, she stood boldly in front of Alexander and glared daggers.

"You have no right! That cunt already took a bite out of me." She pointed an accusatory finger at me, briefly transferring her seething rage. Pure shock kept me from physically recoiling at the vitriol.

"You are correct, Miss Everfrost," Alexander said, as unflappable as ever. "Charline has indeed exacted her own retribution, as is her right under pack law."

Victoria stood there with a smug smirk, completely oblivious to her fate. It was like watching the Titanic sail right towards the iceberg. I closed my eyes, unwilling to watch the fatal crash. Suddenly, a tiny hand slipped into mine. I let out a small gasp and looked down to see little Rosie. My stomach lurched sideways. The children were here?

I quickly raised my head to search for her mother. Rosie had no business witnessing any of this. Across the way, Maria speared me with a look that halted all of my movements to remove Rosie from the situation. I swallowed thickly and tightened my hold on her tiny hand. However, she'd come here, neither of us were leaving now.

"Then I guess we're done." Victoria flipped her hair and

turned to leave. Alexander let her get three paces before his icy words pulled her to a halt.

"We would be, except the biting of Charline Montgomery is not what you stand accused of."

Confused shock exploded across her doll-like features as she turned in slow motion to face the Alpha she'd dismissed. "What?"

Without warning, her earlier escorts grabbed her arms and forced her to her knees. Alexander stepped forward, his dark eyes hollow and ruthless. "For the crimes of exposing the pack to the human village you are hereby sentenced to death."

Victoria screamed in outrage, pulling futilely at her retainers. "You can't do this to me! You have no right!"

Silence undermined by my thundering heart descended in the aftermath of her outburst. No one moved. No one breathed. Not so much as a whisper could be heard in the eerie quiet that enveloped the pack.

Horror crept up my spine as it sank in that no one would question this judgment. There would be no trial, no witnesses, no evidence brought forward to condemn her—Alpha's word was law, and it was final. A fierce need to do something burned in my veins. This was wrong. You couldn't just sentence someone to death like this. I took half a step forward when the weight of a small hand pulled me up short. Rosie blinked up at me with wide, innocent eyes and suddenly I knew she wasn't here by accident.

She was here to keep me from interfering.

People glanced between myself and Victoria, an equal mix of curious and judgmental. But they didn't compare to the scathing looks directed solely at Victoria. She'd jeopardized their way of life, had put their children in danger. I'd only known the pack a short time and actually been part of it less, but even I knew they had no forgiveness for such things.

A small eternity passed between Alexander's proclamation and the crushing silence. "What do you have to say for yourself?" he finally asked, looking down at Victoria kneeling before him.

Her chest heaved as she hung limp between her captors. She'd given up fighting and streaks of silent tears ran down her face. "Don't do this, Alexander," she pleaded. Steel flashed in his eyes as she realized her mistake a second too late. "Alpha. Please, have mercy."

"Give me one good reason why I should extend mercy to someone determined to see this pack brought to its knees?" The irony of the statement reflected in Victoria's eyes as she stared up at him helplessly.

I glanced at David, amazed at his calm, but upon closer inspection, I realized tension lined his shoulders and corded his neck. My heart went out to him. Despite the fact that she'd turned on the pack and him, she'd still been his friend. My fingers hovered inches from comforting him when Victoria's response froze them in their tracks.

"Because it wasn't me. This was Johnathan's doing!"

Her words had all the effect of dropping a hornet's nest in the middle of a Fourth of July picnic. The quiet crowd erupted into chaos. Shouts of disbelief followed cries of outrage and demands to know where Johnathan was. Only four people remained unaffected—Alexander, Maria, David, and me. Alexander gazed calmly back at Victoria and her shoulders slumped with the realization that he already knew about Johnathan.

She wiggled in her hold and attempted to inch closer to the man staring at her with cold disdain. "Wait. You have to listen. It was his plan all along. He stole the agreement and gave it to Edith Sharp. He told her what to do to get the biggest reaction. He led the surveying team to the East grounds. It was his idea to stir up trouble in the town. I was only following orders. I—"

Alexander held up a hand to stop the flood of confession. Her mouth snapped shut and she began to sob in earnest. Those closest shrank back while the rest shifted with uncertainty. He stared down at her with the full weight of judgment. "Is there anything else you'd like to add?"

She swallowed and nodded.

"Let's hear it."

"I know where he is," she whispered quietly, defeat etched into the sag of her shoulders.

"For your honesty and cooperation," Alexander said, addressing the pack at large, "you shall be spared execution."

She visibly drooped as she cried softly, "Thank you, Alpha. Thank you."

Alexander's cold gaze fixed back on her. "However, the severity of your crimes cannot go wholly unpunished."

Victoria looked back up at him, tears staining her porcelain face, her eyes wide with fear. Rosie scooted closer, sensing the tension in the air. My own confusion had me pulling her close and inching toward David. The pack held a collective breath as we all stared at Alexander in anticipation.

"Instead of execution, you will face banishment." He'd barely finished the word before her howl of despair rose up. Where the casual sentence of death had met with no clear reaction from the pack, this sent a ripple of unease to the farthest reaches.

"Alpha, no. Please!" Victoria begged, fighting even harder than she had before. "I beg of you. Give me death. Anything else. Maim me. Take a leg or an eye. Take both! Anything but that. Alpha, please!"

Her cries fell on deaf ears. Alexander turned away from her and began exiting the impromptu stage. He gave a wave and guards started to drag Victoria away.

Shocked stillness dominated the crowd, the only sound Victoria's continued shouts for death. My gaze sought out David once more. His hands balled into fists at his sides and he squeezed his eyes shut as if it could somehow block out the desperate cries for mercy.

The crowd parted to allow the guards to continue escorting the damned unhindered, though they seemed to be carrying her more now. When her sobbing form disappeared into the House, David finally turned away. He joined Alexander at the bottom of the impromptu stage along with Xander.

David's statement that banishment was the worse punishment rang in my ears as I joined them. At the time it had felt like a platitude, but now I wasn't so certain. Clearly being a werewolf and understanding how the *were* community actually operated were two very different things.

"That's a good girl, Rosie, you can run along to your mama now." The dulcet tones of Maria's voice snapped me out of my carnival of horror. She took one look at my face and nodded. "I see David was right. Even after everything that woman has done to you, you still would've stood for her life."

"David put you up to this?" I asked in disbelief as I watched little Rosie scamper off with barely a care in the world to the mother I'd been unable to locate not ten minutes before.

"Not in so many words. He simply said that being so new to this way of life, you might not be prepared. The punishments may seem harsh, but it's by necessity. Everyone here is capable of being lethal. Without a strict legal system, chaos would rule and the pack would never survive. This world cannot handle hundreds of lone wolves who answer to nothing but their own basest instincts."

I unwittingly flashed to the monster that was Ted. Even imagining a dozen of him running loose and unchecked was enough to make me quake. I nodded numbly.

"I'm sorry if you feel that my having Rosie keep you steady was too much. There were really only three guarantees that you wouldn't interfere. David couldn't very well be seen having to hold you back and we all know you have a soft spot for the children."

"What was the third option?" I asked, although admittedly I wasn't sure I really wanted to know.

"Keep you in the House." The steel in her eyes as she said it reminded of the same unforgiving way in which Alexander had proclaimed Victoria's betrayal and subsequent punishment.

Yes, on the surface, all of these people were nice and well adjusted, but not nearly deep enough lurked the potential to be a killer.

It was with no small amount of terror that I realized, I now made that list.

<hr>

"What now?" I asked into the darkness. I could understand now why most *weres* forgot to turn on lights. The dark was not full of terrors, it was a lover's embrace, a friend holding your hand, and quite frankly, it wasn't nearly as obscuring as it used to be.

A hand touched mine and I barely didn't flinch from it. David had disappeared after the spectacle and this was the first time we'd been alone together. Despite the long day and late hour, I wasn't tired. I also still hadn't decided how I felt about his role in all of this.

"Now we wait."

Unease bubbled in the pit of my stomach. "Would he really...would Alexander really have executed her right there in front of everyone if she hadn't spoken out about Johnathan?"

He shrugged and sat on the bed to remove his boots. "Who can really say? But I doubt it, not with all of the children present." Relief flooded me to hear that David shared my concerns about the youngins.

"What about the other?"

He looked up at me, confused by the vague question.

"I know you said that banishment was a harsher punishment, but would she really prefer death?" I elaborated.

Sadness clouded his features. I hated asking these questions, but if I was going to be a part of this pack then I needed to understand. He let out a heavy sigh and pulled me close. My fingers threaded through his hair as he rested his head against my stomach.

"I realize that accepting these things is difficult for you and it may not seem to make much sense. Being exiled is like being totally and completely disowned by your entire community. For a pack *were,* it's almost impossible to move past that. Everyone you ever knew or loved turns away from you. No matter what happens in your life, no one will ever come to help. Do you remember how much Michael changed after we got back from the House?"

"Yeah."

"Michael was what you would call a lone wolf." The way he said that made it sound like a deadly disease.

"I don't know what that's supposed to mean. It sounds bad, but that's all I've got."

"Lone wolves aren't capable of meshing with the pack and they pose a threat to the natural order. Typically when one is identified, they're put out of their misery."

"You mean killed?" I gasped. "But Michael is such a good person. He would never do anything to harm anyone." Granted I hadn't really known him all that long and before that my knowledge stemmed purely from gossip. Even then, I was confident in my assessment.

"Michael was an exception. He grew up pack and Alexander identified the signs early enough that he was able to create a unique arrangement outside of normal pack law."

"I still don't understand why it would've been necessary to kill him," I insisted, looking down at David. His intense gaze seemed to slice through all of my doubt to reach my soul.

"Werewolves require harmony and absolute obedience to the Alpha. You may not realize it yet, but pack *weres* instinctively obey the Alpha. It's literally ingrained. That's part of why it's so important to have an Alpha that truly has the pack's best interests at heart. Mutinies in packs are incredibly uncommon. This whole year has been against almost everything that the pack has ever known." He sat up and rubbed his face. "Lone wolves don't have that piece and that makes them very dangerous. They don't know how to act as one unit, nor are they capable of putting anyone's needs above their own. There are some who believe that lone wolves are actually broken."

"If that's the case, then why the special deal with Michael?"

"Because Alexander was practically a father to him and me. We were like brothers. We'd both already lost so much, he couldn't bear to add to that. Maria believes Michael's dissociation was brought about by the death of his parents. That he simply lost the meaning of pack and as he got older it became more apparent. You can't fake pack—you either are or you aren't."

"Okay," I responded dazedly as I moved to sit on his knee. His arm wrapped comfortingly around my waist. "What changed?"

"Sara. He found pack in Sara. Before I saw him at the House, I was actually a little afraid that he would break the agreement and try to run off with her."

"What would've been so wrong with that?"

"It would've been a rival pack."

"But what if they went far enough?"

He shook his head. "It wouldn't have mattered and it would've put her on the chopping block as well."

My eyes went wide. Sweet Sara executed for nothing more than falling in love and eloping? It was outrageous.

David sighed and tucked a stray curl behind my ear. "You still don't get it. Werewolves are extremely territorial. The nearest pack is over six hundred miles away. And even if they'd gone that far, then they'd be encroaching on the territory of a far less forgiving Alpha. Most likely, they would've reacted as if it was a breach of territory and attacked our pack for violating the boundaries."

"But what about the exchange program?" I argued, recalling him mentioning what a big deal that had been.

Once more he shook his head. "It has to be agreed upon by *both* Alphas, and only one at a time. No pack is willing to run the risk of an insurrection."

"Damn, this stuff is complicated. And here I thought I was in a house full of adorable fluffies that ran around and howled at the moon when they weren't at their day jobs."

He chuckled, which helped bring some levity back to the serious conversation. "I love you, Charline," he said as he stroked my cheek. I'd like to think that I managed to maintain a perfectly sultry expression, but I wasn't fooling anyone. It felt like the moon itself was radiating out of me and my smile simply couldn't be contained.

"I love you too, you big fluffy."

His laughter rang out and I found myself unexpectedly toppled onto the bed. "Come here, my little fox."

I giggled and squirmed as he tried to bring me closer. His throaty growl turned my insides to jelly and it became harder to fight him off. Eventually, I let him win and he snared me with a kiss, then promptly worked his way across my jaw and down my neck. The world was awash with sensation. Sara had never mentioned anything about how phenomenal lovemaking was when you had heightened senses.

"Have you changed your perfume?" he asked suddenly, catching me off guard. The question was quickly followed by yet another kiss.

"What? No. I don't even know the last time I wore perfume. Why?"

"You smell a little different. Still you, but different."

"Is that gonna be a problem?" I quipped.

"Not in the least," he responded huskily, then promptly rolled me to lie atop him. There, he stole my breath and my top.

"David," I scolded once I acquired enough air.

"What?" he asked, completely undeterred. I arched into him as his hands caressed my back and ventured lower to cup my ass and grind me against him.

"What about prying ears?"

"Did I forget to mention? Most of the House has gone to town," he said with a smirk. "It seems your efforts to mend bridges have really paid off. There's some sort of community event or other."

I smacked him in the chest. "David!"

"Ow," he laughed, sending delicious tingles spiraling through me where the thin material of my night shorts pressed against the heat of his erection.

"You definitely did not mention that at all. And why aren't you there? You're supposed to be schmoozing."

"I'd rather be schmoozing you," he replied heatedly and pulled me back down.

It took a minute to extricate myself from the embrace. When I did, I sat up. "Since we seem to have the whole place to ourselves..." I trailed off and tightened my thighs around his hips for emphasis. He let out a delicious groan and I pressed down harder, the flimsy material between us arousing in its friction and infuriating in its persistence.

"Char," he moaned breathlessly. "*More.*"

28

THE NATURAL ORDER

"Sara, I just, I can't...I don't even know what I'm trying to say." I massaged my forehead as I paced the empty bedroom. The House had been eerily quiet in the wake of Victoria's confession, the laughter and chaos that normally filled the halls now shut away in their respective rooms.

"I know what you mean," Sara sighed on the other end of the line. "Intense doesn't really seem to cover it."

"It all seems so abrupt and unforgiving, no trial, no jury —just the judge. And before you decide to give me a lecture, I already got one from David."

"I get that this is new for you. To be honest it's pretty stark for me too. But can you honestly say that you don't think she's a threat?"

"Well, no," I conceded. "But surely there's some other punishment."

"Can you think of one?"

"Community service?" I suggested without conviction.

"Really, Charline? Forget half the other crap she's done. If she'd bitten one of the townsfolk, this would be a very different story. They don't have mercy for *weres* with that sort of behavior. For the bitten sure, but not for the culprit," Sara said passionately. After all, it was how her own maker had come to be. "Add to that the fact that she was willing to do it in broad daylight, in the middle of town—"

"I know, I know," I grumbled. She was right, they were *all* right, but that didn't make the harsh sentence any easier to swallow. "You should have seen it though, Sara. No one raised a finger to help her. Hell, no one even reacted until she pointed the finger at Johnathan."

"Johnathan is a respected member of the community and as the Beta, the idea that he could be the one responsible for putting the pack in such peril is unthinkable."

"You're missing the point. No one. Not her friends, not any family, not even a lone voice of doubt. They all stood there and quietly accepted it."

"What would you have had them do?"

I threw my hands up in frustration, nearly dropping the phone. "I don't know, *something*. Look nervous at least. And I don't believe for a minute that it was just the two of them. Others had to be involved."

"You wouldn't honestly expect them to risk exposing themselves after such a sentencing would you?"

"Not when you put it like that. Who asked you to be all logical anyway?"

"Pretty sure you did, otherwise you wouldn't have called," Sara pointed out and I grumbled half-hearted agreement. "When do you think it will happen?"

"They have to find him first. David and a few others left hours ago. Assuming Victoria's information is right, I can't imagine it will take long."

"I'm gonna tell Michael to pack our things, if he hasn't already. If I wasn't running so lean on personal days, I'd have insisted we stay longer rather than come back right away."

"Why?" I asked at the unexpected turn in conversation.

"Because I imagine everyone will be called to the House bear witness."

My stomach sank and I followed it, sitting down hard on the edge of the bed. "I don't know if that's brilliant or a really, *really* bad idea."

"How do you mean?"

"On the one hand, it definitely asserts the Alpha's authority, but on the other, just how many people does Johnathan have in his pocket? I'm telling you, Victoria is not an isolated supporter." I glanced at the closed door and lowered my voice. "You were here for a day, you can't possibly understand what the atmosphere has been like. Plenty of people are uneasy with his decision to step down. Admittedly, the longer I'm here, the more I feel like it's... it's..." I struggled to find the right words to describe the uncertainty.

"Unnatural?"

"Something like that," I admitted begrudgingly.

Sara's heavy sigh drifted through the line. "I'm so sorry, Charline. If I'd taken your concerns about everything more seriously, maybe some of this could be avoided."

"Stop it, you can't blame yourself. It's done and that's all there is to it. Let's focus on today's problems."

"How do you do that?" she asked with a hint of awe.

"Do what?"

"Move past everything so easily? I mean, I only recently started to move past my childhood issues. And let's not even get started with the ones I developed as an adult or what happened earlier this year."

"I just do. Sure it hurts, but I refuse to let that hold me back from living my life. I can't enjoy what I do have if I'm stuck obsessing over what I've lost or never had to begin with."

"You're a miracle of nature," she said with a laugh.

I shook my head. It wasn't anything special, it was simply how I was raised. You have to conquer what's in front of you to move forward and if something you wanted was behind you, it got there for a reason.

"I'll let you get to your anticipatory packing."

"Ugh," she groaned. "I *so* don't have enough sick days to be a werewolf."

I laughed and bid her goodbye. The phone found its way back to the nightstand, then I flopped back on the bed. How had everything become such a mess? I was on the cusp of drifting off when the front door slamming downstairs had me bolting upright.

David.

Without a second thought, I zipped into the hall and went straight for the banister to peer over the railing. Sure enough, David and Xander stood in the foyer. They looked a little worse for wear, but at least they were in one piece. The anxiety I'd been nursing that Victoria had actually led them into a trap eased.

As if by some sixth sense, David looked up to meet my gaze. He angled his chin in a slight nod, then turned to whisper something to Xander. He gave a clipped nod in return and strode out of sight without another word. David glanced at me once more, then followed after.

I stepped back from the railing, a strange mix of relief and trepidation swirling inside me. It was done. They had him.

The quiet of the House suddenly seemed unbearably loud. I looked around and found several pairs of anxious eyes peering back at me from cracked doors. I took a bracing breath and strode back down the hall, but didn't return to David's room.

As I walked, doors opened wider and their inhabitants ventured out to join me. When I finally stopped, nearly everyone had emerged. I took in their expectant faces and a sudden wave of paranoia surged up within me. How many of these curious faces belonged to traitors?

"What did they say?" Lucia asked, stepping ahead of her boyfriend.

"They didn't actually say anything, at least not to me, but I gather he's been found. I suspect Maria or Alexander will be filling the rest of us in shortly with the details." Or so I hoped. "Until then, dinner still needs to be made. Can I get any volunteers?" At the mention of food, almost everyone visibly relaxed. Food always made things better. Immediately two tiny bodies burst into the hall.

"We can help, Miss Foxy," Rosie said, taking her thumb out only long enough to volunteer.

"Hey, I was gonna say that," Oscar whined beside her. She removed her thumb once more to stick her tongue out at her older brother. He scowled and I reached out to ruffle his already unkempt hair. Leave it to children to lighten the mood.

"Now children, I suspect Miss Charline was in search of slightly older helpers," Marisa said as she stepped up behind her little ones.

"Quite the contrary," I said, bending down to be on their level, "I have some very special jobs for two of my best helpers. Especially this young man." Oscar puffed out his chest and preened. I held back a giggle and added with a serious look, "That is, of course, if you're up to the task. It won't be easy."

"I can do it. You'll see," he proudly proclaimed.

"What about me, Miss Foxy?" Rosie asked with sad eyes and a slight warble.

"Don't I always have something extra special for you?" I asked, and she immediately brightened.

"And what exactly will these three superior chefs be making tonight?" their mother asked them. They shared a look, then turned lost expressions on me.

A smile stretched across my lips as I straightened up and put my hands on my hips. "What do you say we have another go at spaghetti?" They both nodded enthusiastically as I rubbed my hands together. "Alright my champions, I don't know about you, but I'm ravenous."

"What does r-ravnus mean?" Rosie asked, struggling with the word.

"It means," I said, leaning back down and tickling her, "extra, extra hungry." She squealed with delight while her brother laughed at what he deemed her misfortune. The sound of children's laughter effectively dispelled the last of the melancholy lingering in the hall.

"We'll make a run to the store to make sure you have enough," Mitch said, stepping forward and taking Lucia's hand.

I spared them a grateful smile. "That would be lovely, thank you. The rest of us will go make sure the kitchen is in tip top shape for when you return with all of the goodies."

"Cleaning," Oscar groaned in utter dismay.

"Yes, cleaning. It's important to care for the area you use to make delicious treats. And who knows, maybe while we wait for Mitch and Lucia to get back, we might make some delicious treats of our own. What would you say to that?"

Oscar and Rosie's eyes went wide with hopeful anticipation. In the blink of an eye, they both spun around and proceeded to race each other to the kitchen.

"No running, you two!" Marissa called after them to no avail. "I swear you're gonna spoil them rotten with sweets. They're going to end up looking like overfed house pets."

"Eh," I said, waving away her concerns, "they'll run it off."

She laughed and walked with me down the stairs towards the kitchen where no doubt, my eager helpers had already begun simultaneously cleaning and taking out every pan they could find.

A week, a whole freaking, impossibly long, excruciatingly slow week went by before the pack was informed that Johnathan was being held. Even David had somehow managed to keep the details from me. The most I'd gotten from him was that first barely perceptible nod, followed by a whole lot of "I'm not at liberty to say."

Okay, maybe a week was a bit of an exaggeration, but the days separating Sunday and Wednesday certainly felt like one.

My phone rang and I squinted down at Edith Sharp's name flashing across the screen for the millionth time. While I had a strong interest in speaking with the woman, I also seriously doubted my ability to maintain my composure.

With a grimace, I reached for the phone before it could stop ringing. "Good afternoon, Councilwoman Sharp."

"Ah, Miss Montgomery, I was beginning to fear that you'd changed your mind regarding the purchase of the bakery."

"Not at all, Miss Sharp. Things have just been...busy around here of late," I skirted, toeing a leaf in the grass.

"Apologies if I'm interrupting anything pressing. I simply wanted to follow up about the proposal I emailed you. It's a very generous offer given the prime location, so I can't imagine that those terms will linger very long."

It took an active force of will not to call her out on the spot. There wasn't a snowball's chance in hell that those terms were going anywhere, nor was it in any way "generous." Edith clearly had no idea how close I was with Maria or she never would have had the brass to present such an inflated offer. Unfortunately there was no time to set her down politely or otherwise.

"Understood, Councilwoman. I will review the terms with my lawyer and get back to you as soon as possible." Not that I had legal counsel. But perhaps with all of the studying Xander had put in, he'd be willing to take a gander. And it was possible the pack's construction company had one on retainer. Then I could counter with a legitimate fair market value.

"I'm glad to see you are taking this seriously." Edith cleared her throat and added, "The village really would benefit from having an artist of your caliber taking up the shop."

"You're too kind, Miss Sharp," I replied sweeter than honey to the over-the-top veneration. "While I have you on the phone, the information you sent made no mention of the meeting this Friday. Is that still happening?"

She hesitated a moment before saying, "Yes, the meeting is still being held. However, there has been discussion of closing it to all non-involved parties."

I couldn't help but wonder if this recent development had to do with the fact that Johnathan was MIA with the agreement that *they* needed. "That is indeed a shame."

"I do apologize for the inconvenience. I hope this won't affect your interest in the bakery?"

I smiled, smelling buying power. "Of course not. Why should it?" Properly reassured, we exchanged a few more pleasantries and ended the call.

That out of the way, I zipped back into the House to

make sure David and the others knew of this sudden change in plans. The council was wavering and that was nothing but good news for us. My excitement died, however, when I ran into an exceptionally serious Alexander as he exited his study.

"Miss Montgomery, I feel that you are old enough to know better about running in the halls."

I swallowed and looked into his haggard and gaunt face. Poor man looked like he'd been dragged through a knothole backwards. "Sorry, Alpha," I replied meekly and he softened ever so slightly.

"Was there something you wanted to share?"

I shuffled my feet, still feeling remarkably cowed. How did he do that? I felt like I was five years old again and had gotten caught trying to sneak out of the kitchen by my Great Aunt Shirley.

"I've just gotten off the phone with Edith Sharp." He raised his eyebrow at the name and I blazed on before I could inexplicably lose my nerve. "It seems as though the meeting set for Friday afternoon will no longer be public; only interested parties need attend."

"It's about time she realized she was fighting a losing battle. Thank you, Charline." He gestured back into the study. "You'll find David inside. Best tell him and Xander the good news." A glance behind him showed the aforementioned deep in conversation, looking even more melancholy than Alexander. I nodded and moved to let him pass.

"What was all that about?" I asked, stepping into the study. David looked up and I noticed the circles under his eyes had gotten deeper. Even Xander looked far older than his meager nineteen. "What's wrong?"

"Tomorrow morning, with the entire pack in attendance, Johnathan will face sentencing." The hardness in Xander's eyes as David gave the dire news made my blood run cold.

I'd seen that look before in his father, right before he banished Victoria.

"So soon?" All my impatience about being kept out of the loop vanished in a puff of smoke. Why the rush? We had the agreement—didn't we?

On cue, Xander pulled out an old parchment and carefully unrolled it on the table. "The longer we wait, the greater the odds the rift will continue to grow. Now that the pack knows we have Johnathan, there will be unease until it's dealt with. Even then…"

He didn't have to finish. We were all painfully aware the pack balanced on the tip of a knife. Tomorrow morning would be the event that pushed it one way or the other. I prayed that the chips would fall in our favor.

"At least we were finally able to get a look at this thing. Had it hidden quite well," David said, looking over at Xander as he hunched over the aged paper

"What does it say? Do they actually have a claim to the land?" I asked, dreading the answer.

He let out a burdened sigh. "Yes and no. This part here," he pointed towards the top, "clearly states that the land is communal property to be shared by the people of the village. Yet this part says that that can be revoked at any time if the land is bought, sold, or otherwise allocated."

"But who would have the right to do that?" I asked, craning to get a better look. "Surely that land has been passed around so many times it would be impossible to find the true owners."

"You would be right…if I hadn't found this in the town archive earlier this week," Xander said with a smirk as he held up an impressively old ledger. "It details the bills of sale for almost all of the properties in relation to the town."

"That's wonderful!" I exclaimed.

Xander's smirk grew to a half smile. "It will be as long as

they don't produce another such record showing that the land got resold to a town family."

"Oh." My enthusiasm shriveled at the reality check. "How can we know it wasn't?"

"Honestly, as far as that goes, the only assurance we have is the fact that no one has built on it in the last hundred years."

"That seems a bit iffy," I said skeptically.

"It's all we have," David said as he wrapped an arm around my shoulders. It felt like such a flimsy hope beside all that we'd faced.

"If you don't mind, I'd like some space to study this," Xander said without looking up. "I don't have much time to put together an argument before the meeting." He took a seat as David steered me out of the room.

"Do you think it will be enough?" I whispered as we made our exit.

"Mother of the moon, I hope so."

We drifted outside, making our way towards the woods in heavy silence. When the trees completely surrounded us, David cleared his throat. I looked at him askance and he gave me a grim smile that fell well short of being reassuring.

"About tomorrow..."

"You are *not* telling me I'm not going." I stepped away from him and planted my hands firmly on my hips.

"What? No." He looked at me like I'd grown a second head. "Everyone will be there, it's not optional. I've already called Michael."

That took the wind right out of my sails; seemed Sara was right after all. "Oh, well, then what?"

He took a deep breath. "You're going to see a side of pack justice you haven't been exposed to yet."

"I don't need a pep talk, David. I'm a grown woman, I can handle it."

"Still, I wanted to talk to you about what will be expected." He gave me a sidelong look. "I know that the episode with Victoria upset you."

"That's because I wasn't expecting it. I know now." Not that I thought knowing would make it any easier. His gaze slid away from me and I frowned. "What?"

"This will be different."

"What do you mean?"

"Alexander is not just going to march him up there and denounce him in front of the pack. There can be no delay once he's been seen."

"Wait, so he's just gonna... Right in front of everyone?" I asked in disbelief. "That's barbaric."

"That's pack law. Justice is swift and there's no room for mercy. Victoria will also be made to bear her punishment as well."

"So tomorrow morning there will be a banishment *and* an execution?" I asked, my voice bordering on a screech. "What about the children? They won't be there this time, will they?" The guilty look on David's face said it all. "You can't be serious. Children have no business being exposed to any of that."

"The whole pack means the whole pack, Charline. I'm sorry if you don't agree with the mechanics of it, but that's just the way it is."

"The mechanics!" I shouted at him. He flinched and I realized he'd anticipated this reaction. "Why on earth would the children need to be there? If it's a matter of someone having to miss the meeting to watch them, then get some of the villagers to do it."

"It's more than that."

"How could there possibly be more?" I asked.

"They need to see pack law being upheld first hand. It's important that they understand no one is above the law, not even the Beta."

"Rosie isn't even old enough to know what day of the week it is, let alone understand something as complicated as pack politics," I argued.

"You'd be surprised."

"I doubt it."

"You can't honestly tell me that you haven't felt the subtleties in the pack," he said, a note of fear creeping in.

"Of course I do," I quickly said, "but I'm an adult and can recognize these things."

"No, you're a werewolf and you *know* these things." The look he gave me said it was better not to argue this point. As I stared back, I had to concede that he was right—I had no idea how I knew some of the things I did about the pack. I just did, and I certainly hadn't before I was bitten.

"I just...the children. It doesn't seem right. Such a harsh lesson to learn so early in life."

"I know, but it's the way it has to be. Werewolf pups cannot afford to live sheltered lives."

"And what? He'll be executed in the morning and everyone will just traipse off to the council meeting to finish dealing with the land dispute?" I glanced at David out of the corner of my eye. He looked haggard and beaten. This summer hadn't gone the way either of us had expected.

"Ideally, yes." His response made it sound like there were contingencies in place. I shuddered to think what those could be considering tomorrow's main goal. "Just promise me that you won't do anything, no matter how much you disagree with what's happening." The beseeching look he gave me broke my heart. "The pack is still so fragile and tomorrow will put everyone's loyalties to the test."

I took a deep breath and let it out. I could disagree about how this was being handled until kingdom come, but that wouldn't change a damn thing. "What do you need me to do?"

His relief flowed off of him and he caught me in a hug that made my ribs creak in protest. "Nothing," he whispered. "Absolutely nothing."

29

THE RECKONING

Friday morning brought with it a sour stomach and a cold bed. I stared at the empty side a moment longer than necessary, then rolled out of bed and got dressed in a daze. Mostly presentable, I trudged down the stairs in search of something to settle my stomach. I'd almost made it to the kitchen when someone shouted at me.

"Holy shit!"

I looked up to find Sara staring at me in utter disbelief. Concern eclipsed my joy at seeing her as I looked around for the source of the expletive. When I found none, I asked, "What?"

"You're wearing jeans."

I looked down. Sure enough, denim bedecked my legs. I frowned at her.

"Don't look at me like that," she said. "In the three years I've known you, the only non-dress thing I've seen you wear was slacks."

"Today didn't really seem to be a primp kind of day."

Her smile slipped, all of my own doubts reflected in her eyes. She took a step forward and we wrapped each other in a hug. "How are you holding up?" she asked quietly, stepping back.

I shrugged. "About as well as can be expected, I guess."

She followed me into the kitchen and leaned against the counter while I put together an exceptionally humble breakfast of bacon and eggs. A few minutes passed in silence while I got organized and she made herself some coffee.

"When did you get in?" I asked, pushing the eggs around in the skillet.

"Actually, about five seconds before you came down the stairs."

"Y'all must have gotten up wicked early."

"Isn't that the truth. We would've left last night, but I got held up finishing a project for Bob." She rolled her eyes. Robert Hargrave had to be the most incompetent department head. How Sara didn't already have his job was anyone's guess. "Anyway, I was so beat that I completely passed out when I got home and Michael didn't have the heart to wake me. So here we are. Any idea when this whole thing is supposed to start?"

"No."

"David talk to you about it?"

"Michael talk to you?"

She mirrored my nod. We shared a silent moment and returned our attention to our plates. What was there to say? We were literally sitting around waiting to watch someone die.

I lost track of how long we sat there pretending to eat breakfast. When Maria suddenly appeared without a sound in the doorway, Sara and I exchanged a knowing look and abandoned our plates to trail after her out the back of the House.

To my surprise, we veered towards where the bonfire

had taken place. I suppose the backyard couldn't really accommodate the entire pack and we wouldn't want any uninvited parties stumbling across the grisly scene. The knots in my stomach twisted tighter.

I can do this. I can hold my tongue and do nothing.

Part of me knew that was the right thing, but another very human part simply could not come to terms with what was about to happen.

The muffled sound of too many voices gathered in one space floated between the thick trees. Then, just like when I'd arrived in the clearing after my first change, the trees fell away without warning and I was met by countless curious eyes. This time though, they barely spared me a glance, instead following Maria as if waiting for some kind of sign.

We paused at the fringes of the crowd and I looked to Maria for guidance, silently praying that she wouldn't have me go up to the front again. Without actually saying anything, she left me to my own devices at the back. I let out a sigh of relief that I wouldn't be forced to take a front row seat to this event and turned to ask Sara if she was okay waiting in the back, only to find her gone.

I frantically searched the crowd until I saw her off to the side with Michael. Well that wasn't fair in the least. I certainly didn't want to stand by myself. Against my better judgment, I began searching for a sympathetic face.

I'd just spotted Marissa when a ripple went through the crowd and all eyes turned back to where we'd come in. Reflexively, I followed suit and had to step aside as a pair of burly *weres* stepped into the clearing leading a trussed up Victoria. My stomach rolled uncomfortably as I took in her uncombed hair and the tear tracks streaking down her cheeks from bloodshot eyes. Was what she'd done really so bad?

Deep in my heart, I knew the answer was yes, even if I hated it. Victoria was getting exactly what she deserved.

I watched in silence as the depressing caravan made their way past. She never so much as glanced in my direction despite walking right by me.

This time, I felt the shift and was prepared for yet more people to join the gathering. The guards leading Victoria pulled stopped to watch as none other than Johnathan himself strode into the clearing, arms manacled before him, flanked by two guards as well as Alexander and David. Unlike Victoria, Johnathan marched with his head held high, not an iota of shame or remorse on his proud face.

He paused too close for comfort and surveyed the crowd. His haughty expression soured when his gaze landed on Victoria a few feet away. "It was you?" His lip curled with distaste.

Victoria squealed with terror and miraculously broke free of her escorts to make a run for it. Before anyone had a chance to react, Johnathan surged forward and grabbed her, spinning around with her like she was a hostage. I watched in horror as not a soul moved to intervene, even Victoria held perfectly still, silent tears streaming from bulging eyes that pleaded with someone, anyone, to do something.

Johnathan raised a withering gaze to Alexander and snapped her neck. The crack of sound hit the barrier of trees and doubled back, filling the clearing with a discordant echo as Victoria's lifeless body hit the ground. I slammed a hand over my mouth to stifle a gasp. No one moved as Johnathan quietly resumed his position between his own pair of guards.

"Are we going to get this over with or not?" he asked, like he hadn't just killed someone in cold blood.

Still no one stirred. I imagined everyone, like myself, was paralyzed with shock. But someone had to do something.

We couldn't just leave her like that. Before I could convince my limbs to move, a warm hand blanketed my arm. I looked up into David's eyes, dark with sadness. He glanced at the now empty husk of his childhood friend and back at me, the silent command clear: don't touch her. I gave the tiniest nod and he silently retook his post beside Alexander.

No one spared Victoria's body a second glance as they followed the morbid parade's progress to the front of the gathering. I, on the other hand, couldn't seem to take my eyes off of her. The unnatural angle of her head. Her lifeless eyes staring up at the summer sun. The way she looked more like a doll than ever splayed on the ground.

Bile rose up my throat and I forced it back down. I couldn't stay here. As I made my way around the edge of the crowd, I caught whispers of unsettled disbelief that Johnathan bore chains. The sick feeling in my stomach resurged with a vengeance. Not so much as a mention of the fate that had befallen Vitoria.

Eventually I found a position that afforded me a good view of everyone, including another makeshift stage, this one significantly larger than the one that had been used for Victoria's sentencing. I scarcely dared breathe as Johnathan walked smugly up the steps and took his position center stage.

The discontented voices went silent as Alexander stepped up beside his former friend. Alexander's eyes were pure stone as he looked at the man who had betrayed both him and his pack. This was not the kind man who had smiled and laughed at a dinner table surrounded by a family he loved. This was a man who'd been hardened by a life of difficult choices, once more facing another. Johnathan stared ahead, ignoring him, while those gathered shifted uneasily.

"Johnathan Scott, you stand accused and found guilty of

treason. You are to be executed before those you have betrayed. Do you have any final words?"

"As a matter of fact, I do." A smirk twisted the former Beta's lips. "Jerry, Paula, Clint, Valerie, Roland, Ian, Laurence, Harriet, Nicole, Terri, Corey, Lyle, Trevor—"

"What are you doing?"

Johnathan raised an eyebrow and spared Alexander a condescending look. "I figured you'd want the names of my supporters. Leslie, Agnes—"

Absolute chaos erupted. People pushed and shoved, eyeing their neighbors with distrust while others whose names had already been called tried to make a break for it, only to be hindered by their packmates.

"...Toni, Derek, Alvin..."

Infighting sprouted up as brothers and sisters turned on each other. Former friends grappled in the grass as more and more names were added to the list.

"Irene, Camille, Mercy, Leroy, Blake, Horace..."

Shouts and curses filled the air, nearly drowning the condemning litany. Johnathan's menacing laughter rolled out in direct contrast to his imprisoned state.

"That's. Enough." The firm voice sliced through the din.

Everyone froze. I looked back at the stage to see none other than Xander standing front and center.

"This is what he wants. Can't you see that? Release them," he demanded, gesturing to those who had been restrained. Dubious faces looked back at Xander, though whether it was because they doubted his authority or his order was anyone's guess. "*All* of them." The hard edge of his voice rang with an authority that rippled through the air like heat waves.

Slowly, the guards who still had hold of people let them go. Nervous looks passed between the recently freed and those whose names had not been called.

Xander shook his head. "This pack has been through too much to meet its end at the hands of one spiteful man."

"What would you know?" Johnathan snarled. "You've grown up with a silver spoon in your mouth. This whole affair is an affront to nature. There's no such thing as succession among wolves."

Xander turned fierce eyes on him. "You're right. Pack law is pack law. Only the strongest can lead." His eyes narrowed and his lip curled in disgust. "*You*, however, will not be here to witness the pack herald a new age. Your treachery knows no bounds. Selling out your supporters in a final attempt to tear apart the pack is low, even for you. But we're stronger than that, stronger than *you*. Today, you take your final howl, but the rest of us will go on." Xander paused in his furious rebuke to look back at his father. "Alpha."

Alexander didn't say a word, but Xander took a step back nonetheless, leaving the path to a now fuming Johnathan clear.

"You think you've won, old friend?" Johnathan spat. "The pack will not stand idly by while you systematically destroy all of our traditions, replacing them with a mockery of progress. This isn't the end. I'm not the only one who disagrees with these *improvements*. Others will rise."

His bitter words had no visible effect on Alexander as he stepped forward. Johnathan bared his teeth and pulled at his chains when the Alpha stopped not even a foot in front of him. Tension strained the air, the end of everything a mere snap away. Then, without warning, Johnathan spoke again, his voice clear enough to carry across the hushed crowd.

"I challenge you to a reckoning."

Gasps echoed through the pack.

"Done." Alexander ordered. He gestured to the guards who had initially escorted Johnathan. "Remove his chains."

A sense of foreboding crawled along my skin. I had no idea what this was, but I already knew I didn't like it.

"I'm impressed that you'd face me yourself, old man. You've never been able to take me before."

"And I don't plan to now." Confusion passed across Johnathan's face as Alexander stepped back. Then to my complete and utter horror, David stepped forward.

I wanted to shout, to demand he stop, but fear held my tongue. "Do nothing" was the only thing David had asked of me. Had he known this was in the cards the whole time? Was that why he'd made me promise?

Alexander's voice rang out clear across the gathering. "It is the Alpha's right to choose a champion. As the Beta, you should know that better than anyone."

David embodied calm as he waited for Johnathan to be released. My fingers clutched my throat as terror gripped my heart.

"I should have known Alexander wouldn't have the brass to face me himself," Johnathan said with a sneer as he sized David up.

"A wise leader knows when to fight and when to let others do the fighting." David squared his shoulders. "You want this pack? Come and take it."

One moment, Johnathan stood there rubbing his wrists. The next he'd barreled into David, nearly forcing him from the stage. I finally found my voice in the form of a strangled cry and immediately clamped a hand over my mouth. David couldn't afford any distractions and I'd be damned if I was the reason he got hurt.

Crimson blossomed on David's shirt as he found his footing at the edge of the stage. With a savage growl that turned my stomach he pushed back. Johnathan stumbled only a step before regaining his composure and the two locked. David was easily among the largest *weres* in the pack, but Johnathan was equally imposing with a height and bulk that rivaled David's.

Their faces twisted as they snarled at each other, struggling for the upper hand. Suddenly, I realized the reason their teeth looked so sharp was because they'd partially changed. I winced at the dual growls as they broke apart and came together again and again, each rejoining bringing more red and slicking the stage. Already, David's shredded shirt hung from his heaving frame and blood painted Johnathan's clawed hands.

Without warning, David slammed against Johnathan with a sickening thud, sending both of them crashing to the ground. The sound of splintering wood accompanied their savage growls. They rolled unhindered across the abused stage, the two forms indistinguishable amidst the blur of limbs. Suddenly, David was kicked loose. He flew a good twenty feet and slammed into a tree that butted up against the stage. I jumped at the loud crack.

He stumbled a few feet and shook his head. Fear clawed at my heart. David might have youth on his side, but Johnathan had experience, desperation, and nothing to lose. David regained his bearings just in time to meet the fresh assault. Johnathan slammed into him once more, and David's legs buckled beneath the force.

The horrific scene swam before me as Johnathan moved to take advantage of the weakness. He stood over David's fallen form, victory clear on his face. Johnathan took one more fateful step forward and David surged up, his claws raking across Johnathan's chest.

Johnathan staggered back, pain and shock clear on his face. He scrambled to defend as David advanced on him, having officially gained the upper hand. My heart soared to see that the move hadn't been the result of a serious injury, but merely a ploy to lure Johnathan. I wanted to cheer at the turn in events, but the eerie silence held as everyone waited with bated breath for the outcome.

David landed another blow and Johnathan let out a howl of pain-filled rage. He swiped wildly at David who easily danced out of the way. Despite his series of victories, David hadn't escaped unscathed. Blood dripped in thick streaks down his torso and back. Suddenly, I didn't care that David wanted to be Beta or how important this fight was. I didn't want him to have any part of it. I just wanted him to live and I refused to stand here and watch him die.

People shot me angry looks as I forced my way to the stage. Only one person attempted to stop me. I couldn't focus well enough to even name them, let alone determine if they were friend or foe. It didn't matter, they took one look at my face and let me pass. Pack politics be damned; this was barbaric.

I briefly lost sight of the stage in the press of bodies. The sound of a strangled oath rose, and I redoubled my efforts, forcibly moving people who didn't react quickly enough. I had to get to David, had to stop this nonsense. How could Alexander let David take his place? This wasn't his fight.

A break opened in the crowd and I looked up in time to see David rip Johnathan off of his back. The move left yet more deep rents that flooded red. Fear paralyzed my limbs and terror froze my heart. Then Johnathan ran back into David who caught him head on. My feet once again found their motivation. The last line of people gave way and I stood there confronted with more unadulterated violence than I'd ever seen in my life, and that included when Sara had torn Ted apart.

The sharp, metallic smell of fresh blood permeated the air. My stomach churned as I recognized most of it as belonging to David. The two circled each other, looking for an opening. My mad dash to stop this disaster stalled out at seeing the brutality up close. If I tried to intervene, it would more than likely result in David getting hurt, or worse, killed. Much as it pained me, I held to my promise—and did nothing.

Johnathan gave an experimental swipe and David lunged, leaving a fresh smear of blood in his wake. Somehow David managed to get behind Johnathan. The muscles in his arms bulged as he tightened his grip around the former Beta's neck. Determined ferocity colored David's eyes a disturbing dark gray. I held my breath as David snarled and used his other hand to tighten the vise he'd made. Johnathan tore lines of red into David's arm, but his hold didn't loosen.

A loud crack punched through the air and Johnathan stilled. His vacant eyes looked out over the crowd he'd sought to turn on itself. David released him to fall face first on the stage where he lay unmoving. David's scored chest heaved from exertion while blood continued to pool beneath him. Shocked silence dominated the large clearing.

"Insurrection will not be tolerated," Alexander said as he stepped forward. "The world is changing and we *will* change with it." Those who'd been called out before shuffled nervously. "If you disagree with how things are being run, please, by all means, face me yourself." When no one moved he added. "I will take no champion. I will have no aid."

Maria gasped and Xander moved to restrain her. Still no one moved.

"What? No one? Is there not a single *were* who would stand and face me?" He let the challenge hover and his gaze sharpened once more. "*I* am your Alpha. From today forward, we are one pack, no matter if your name was called or not. Remember that we are a family, a unit that runs as one."

His words faded off until not even the whisper of an

echo could be heard. Then a howl rose up. First one voice, followed by another and another, until the entire clearing rang with one pure note. Despite the uniform show of support, Alexander didn't look relieved. He looked *tired*.

Gradually, the voices died out and people began slipping away into the forest. Johnathan's body vanished, and I suspected Victoria's had equally been spirited away. I inched my way through the dispersing crowd to join everyone at the stage, except when I got there, David had disappeared.

"Are you out of your mind!" Maria shouted as she stabbed a finger into Alexander's chest. "No support? Just invite the whole damn rebellion on stage to tear you apart? *That* was your grand master plan? That's a hell of a gamble."

"And one that needed to be made," Alexander said, resting his hand on her shoulder. She still looked beyond livid, but the move silenced her. "Xander, my son, I fear I have not made the next leg of your journey any easier. You will undoubtedly face more opposition than originally anticipated in the coming months."

Xander shrugged. "It's okay, Dad. I want to do things right. More competition just gives me more opportunity to show I'm worthy of being our pack's next Alpha."

"That's my boy," Alexander said, pride in his eyes as he ruffled his hair.

"Dad," Xander griped, laughing as he pushed him away.

"Hey, you're still my son and until *you* are Alpha, I can do as I damn well please." He embraced Xander and the last of the anger in Maria's face melted away.

"There you are," David said, appearing out of nowhere. He swept me up in his own bone-crushing hug, effectively covering me in blood. I didn't give a rat's ass. He was alive, that was all that mattered. "I was worried when I couldn't find you. Thank the stars you're okay."

"Me? What about you?" I asked, pushing back to try and get a look at him.

"I'll be fine."

"Fine?" I repeated. "Are you out of your fucking mind! Look at you."

"Char, please."

"Don't Char me. You knew about this from the start. And *you*—" I rounded on Alexander who simply raised an eyebrow and my rebuke fizzled out.

"David did me and the pack great service today. Johnathan was right when he said I've never been able to best him. If he'd wanted to be Alpha all those years ago, he could've been." Alexander shook his head sadly. "I just wish he'd come to me with his concerns instead of...this." He gestured vaguely to the blood-soaked stage around us.

"I was so worried," David said again. There was something in that and I gave him a curious look. He glanced at Alexander before leaning in close to whisper, "Those called out are being watched. Anyone caught trying to stir up trouble or leave the pack will quietly be detained and stopped."

"Stopped?" I echoed.

"Permanently."

I swallowed. "And why would you be worried about me?"

He brushed gentle fingers across my cheek. "What if they'd wanted a hostage?"

Tears pricked my eyes and I buried my face in his shoulder. "Please tell me all of this is over."

"Not quite," Xander said. He glanced down at his phone. "If we don't leave soon, we'll be late for the meeting with the Village Council."

30

CITY PLANNING

I rushed to the House, gathered the tin of sweets I'd prepared the day before, snagged a fresh shirt to replace my blood-stained one, and emerged on the front loawn just in time to stop David from getting in his truck.

"You are *not* coming," I said, reaching for the keys.

"I have every right to be there."

"Look at you! You're in no condition for polite society. If I didn't have to go and make sure Sharp is properly buttered up, I'd stay here and doctor you myself."

David scoffed. "I'm perfectly fine."

"You're still dripping blood!" I howled as I waved the tin of bribery in the air.

"All I need is a new shirt."

I barely reined in my emphatic arm-waving in time not to clock Alexander as he joined us. "I understand you want to be there, David, but I need your help here. A blanket pardon does not always yield the desired outcome." He glanced around at the sprinkling of people wandering the lawn as if lost. "Today has been stressful for the entire pack. See to your wounds and make sure the others know their orders."

"Yes, Alpha," David said a little deflated, then spun around and began barking orders to the meandering zombies. "Martin, Zack, give me a hand would you? We need to get the others. And someone get me a shirt."

Alexander shook his head as David made his way toward the House, then turned to Maria. She held up a hand to stall him and looked at me. "I'll see that he's taken care of. The last thing we need is one of those marks getting infected." She turned back to Alexander and kissed his cheek. "You can tell me all about it when you return. Try not to rile up the villagers too much." He gave her a wolfish grin and I could almost imagine what they must've been like when they were young. "Xander, keep an eye on your father. You know how he gets," Maria added, shifting her attention to their impatient son. Xander rolled his eyes, earning him a smack upside the head. "Oh, and Charline, you tell them that offer is far too high. Even if I did want top dollar for the old place, it still needs a ton of work."

"Thanks, Maria." I gave her a hug. "And thank you for looking after David for me."

"Stubborn bear is all he is."

"This is a lovely chat," Xander interrupted, "but we really do need to get going."

"Right." I spared one last look at David's receding back and tossed Xander the keys. Alexander took the passenger seat and I slid into the back, cradling the tin of sweets in my lap. The tires skidded in the loose gravel and we tore off towards town.

"Do we know where we're going?" Alexander asked calmly. There was a moment of hesitation where the only sound was the wind rushing past the windows as we sped down the narrow road.

"It's at the town hall," Xander finally supplied.

"No it's not."

Xander jerked the wheel and the truck swerved as they both turned to look at me. He quickly re-devoted his focus to keeping the truck on the road.

I released my death grip on what my mother lovingly referred to as the "oh shit bar" and double checked that I hadn't damaged anything. "When we spoke the other day, she said the meeting was being moved to a more private setting."

"Did she say exactly which private setting?" Alexander stared at me in the rearview mirror.

"Uh…" I searched my memory for a clue. Truth be told, I hadn't really been paying attention by that point and she'd only mentioned the change in passing. Barely even a blip. Alexander still hadn't blinked. I swallowed hard, squeezing the tin in my lap and wilting beneath the intense scrutiny. Then it came to me, like the last bubble of air being released from cake batter. "The Planning Committee Office!"

"Shit. That's clear across town." Xander slammed on the brakes and immediately altered our course. He glanced at his father while the truck picked up speed.

Alexander's face pinched like he'd swallowed a lemon tart whole. "Seems Edie still has a few tricks up her sleeve."

"Good thing she still thinks you're a townie," Xander said as he glanced back at me.

We careened around the final bend and stopped dead in front of the appropriate building. The world seemed to freeze for a moment as we sat there and stared at the door. The paper sign taped to it very clearly read "Private Meeting".

"Do we have everything?" Xander asked into the quiet.

"I sure hope so." Alexander opened his door and we simultaneously tumbled out of the truck to follow after him. Xander tucked the rolled agreement under his arm along with several folders. Compared to that, I felt poorly armed with my tin of baked goods.

Several faces turned as we entered. Edith looked surprised to see me. But when her gaze fell on Alexander, barely contained rage flashed in her eyes. Whatever Maria had said to her might have eased her resentment of Maria, but her animosity towards Alexander was still very much alive.

All of the hope that had propelled us here seemed to shrink until it was nothing more than a tiny, fluttering bird struggling for flight. *Please, please, please let it be enough.* Truth be told, I had little information about the particulars of this whole disaster; I'd been a little preoccupied minding my own crumbling universe. Now that I was here, even I was beginning to wonder why Alexander had me tag along.

As we made our way to some open seats, I nodded to the other council members who I'd gotten to know. They each smiled in return and spared anticipatory glances towards the tin in my hands. Then it hit me—I was the ambassador, the link between the town and the House. These people knew me, or at least thought they did, and were comfortable around me. Alexander, on the other hand, had been an enigma to them for years, and I seriously doubted whether anyone knew Xander since he'd been away for school.

"Miss Montgomery, I do believe I said that this was to be a private meeting. Do you mind explaining your presence?" Edith's tone barely managed to be professional and there was nothing to be done about the daggers she now divided between Alexander and me.

In light of my epiphany, I had no idea how to respond. I looked to Alexander for help. She noted the deference and fury marched across her face.

"Miss Montgomery is here as my guest and liaison with the town. I understand that she has come to know the area quite well during her brief stay and I trust her opinion in these matters," Alexander said, smooth as silk.

"And the boy?" Edith asked, finally deigning to shift her penetrating gaze to Xander.

A warm smile spread across Alexander's face. "The young man is my son Xander. He's been doing extensive research on the real estate laws in the area."

Her expression went from sickening recognition to snide doubt. "Fine, these two can stay, but I hope you don't plan on marching in anyone else to aid in your hopeless quest."

Alexander raised his hands. "I promise none of the other interested parties will be in attendance."

Nervous glances passed around the room. Even after decades of harmony, they still had no idea what went on up at the House. Small wonder Johnathan had managed to drive a wedge between the two so easily. I flashed to the memory of David breaking his neck and nearly dropped the tin. Edith's fierce gaze snapped back to me.

"Sorry," I fumbled. "Perhaps it would be best if I went ahead and passed these around before they meet an untimely end." I instantly regretted my word choice and was glad that no one seemed to notice my sudden blanch.

"This is hardly the time for cookies, Miss Montgomery." Edith's words were instantly contradicted by the numerous pairs of hands that eagerly reached for the small container.

I obligingly opened it and began distributing the contents. "Last time I checked, a few sweets never hurt any deal." She looked like she'd swallowed an under ripe fig.

"Yes, and as for 'hopeless quest'..." Alexander interjected as he snagged a cookie for himself. "I think you may find it's not so hopeless after all. Xander, if you will." He gestured for his son to take center stage where there was a table laden with all sorts of papers. He took another bite and turned to me. "Divine as always, Charline."

My mouth opened and closed several times before I finally managed a stuttering, "Th-thank you." It wasn't like Alexander had never complimented my culinary skills before, but something about the compliment hit harder now. I felt like the first time my nana had said my peach turnovers were better than hers. Alexander winked as if he knew exactly what was going on and returned his attention to Xander. Released from his focus, my wits returned. I shook my head to clear the last of the cobwebs. This Alpha business was heady stuff.

Xander stretched the aged parchment out on the table. "As you can see, we've located our copy of the agreement." Alexander reached back to me and I helpfully offered the tin as a paperweight. "According to this," Xander circled a section with his index finger, "the land clearly belongs to the House. Unless, of course, your copy says something different?"

The challenging look he leveled at Edith spoke volumes. He'd done his research and was prepared for whatever she could throw at him. He was calm, confident. It was easy to see why David put his faith in him to be the next Alpha. His father had taught him well.

"You are welcome to review it yourself." Xander waved broadly at the anchored page and took a step back.

Edith took a halting step forward and leaned down to begin her perusal. After my previous conversation with David and Xander, I knew there were several vagaries and could clearly see when she found each of them by the smug grin that spread across her face. She straightened back up, but before she could get a word out, Xander interrupted.

"Oh, I nearly forgot. You'll also be wanting these. I'll save you the hassle of deciphering the flowery text. They are bills of sale that eliminate any claim the town ever had to that land. Seems your shopping mall will have to go elsewhere, Miss Sharp."

While Xander was the essence of cool victory, Edith looked like she was having a stroke. "Kirkland, review the documents, I—I need to make a call."

Edith quickly moved aside to allow who I assumed must be Kirkland and several others to step forward and make their own assessments. Xander naturally stayed to help guide their focus while she retreated to a far corner of the room to undoubtedly call Johnathan. She was going to be sorely disappointed. He wouldn't be taking anyone's calls ever again.

My stomach turned. How many people had he hurt in his mission to tear the pack away from Alexander? He'd hurt me and likely hadn't given two thoughts about the human casualties. And David, the way Johnathan had set him up to be ambushed. Or the incident in the meadow with the kids.

A raised voice snatched me away from the troubling thoughts. "Sharp, is this the same document you reviewed before?"

"What?" she responded absently, still fussing with her phone.

"Miss Sharp."

That got her attention. I shifted around to see who was addressing her so harshly.

Oh snap, it's the mayor.

"Is this the agreement you read before?" Mayor Hawthorne repeated.

The blood drained from her face. "Well, I...I only got the barest look at them before," she floundered. "How was I supposed to know?"

"Because it's your job. And what about these?" He held

up the bills of sale that reduced the town's claim to barely more than a friendly agreement between neighbors.

"Are they even valid?" she argued. "I mean, do they have the proper seals or filing? Where did he find those things? They could be entirely fabricated for all we know."

"Oh, I'm positive they're legitimate."

"How can you be so sure?" she insisted, stepping back up to take a closer look.

Mayor Hawthorne's dire demeanor morphed into a full on scowl. "Because the most recent one has *your* signature on it."

Edith froze, the papers in hand. First she looked to Xander who was maybe a tad too smug for the occasion—not that I could blame him—then onto Alexander.

"I believe this meeting is at an end." Alexander would have been well within his rights to address Edith with scorn, but he didn't. Instead he was the essence of propriety, going so far as to extend a hand.

"I concur," Mayor Hawthorne added. "And I would like to humbly apologize for the inconvenience and any harm that may have resulted from this misunderstanding. If there's anything we can do to help make amends, please be sure to let the council know. As for Councilwoman Sharp, I feel that her resignation is in order. Should you desire a seat on the council, I would be happy to add your name to the ballot."

"That won't be necessary, Mayor. And there's no damage so great that we cannot recover. This has been quite the learning experience for us as well. Needless to say, we'll be keeping much better records in regards to the estate from now on." Alexander had already begun to turn away when he abruptly spun back to face the man. "There is one thing you could be of assistance with."

"Name it and I will do whatever is in my power to see it done."

"The abandoned bakery, it's my understanding that the town is rather eager to see it occupied. However, the 'generous proposal' that Miss Sharp sent, didn't strike me as the least bit generous and seemed to include an egregious amount of fees. Perhaps you could see that the quote is revisited with more of an accurate representation for the property's worth."

Mayor Hawthorne looked borderline apoplectic as he glared at Edith Sharp. She withered beneath his gaze as did any hope of her becoming mayor herself one day. "The proposal will be revisited and on your desk by tomorrow morning."

"Oh, I'm not buying it." The mayor frowned in confusion. "She is." Alexander pointed at me. I gave a shy wave just before Mayor Hawthorne rounded back on Edith.

"Miss Sharp. A word?"

31

BETA

I rode back to the House in a stupor, flabbergasted as to how we'd managed to win the land dispute *and* get Edith Sharp fired. The trees gave way and the ancient plantation home came into view, its lawn littered with people eagerly awaiting the outcome of the meeting. Xander parked the truck and looked at his dad. Alexander gave a slight nod and began getting out. I followed suit and closed the door just in time to see Xander swing on top of the truck to stand on the roof. Quiet descended as all eyes riveted on him.

"The Council of Stone Creek has very graciously decided to drop their claim on the land." Shouts and shrill whistles of joy pierced the air. Xander held up his hands, barely containing his laughter. "Turns out, they don't have one." Howls erupted across the yard and I slipped around the truck to steal a word with Alexander.

"Hello, Charline. I hope you don't think it was too bold of me to speak on your behalf to the council."

"What? No, quite the contrary. I wanted to thank you. Though you didn't need to; I'd have figured something out."

He smiled. "Charline, even if you weren't formally a

member of this pack, you're still family. We look after our own."

Tears stung my eyes. "Would it be weird if I hugged you? Because I really wanna hug you right now."

His eyes crinkled with the same happiness I'd seen when I'd first arrived at the House as he held his arms open and I stepped into them. It felt like a lifetime ago with its fair share of ups and downs, but the longer I held onto Alexander, the more a sense of peace and acceptance filled me. I could see now that being the Alpha wasn't all about being the boss, there was something else about Alexander. It inspired trust and loyalty. I knew without a doubt that he'd die to keep me safe, to keep all of us safe, and I'd do the same for him.

I let out a shaky breath and wiped away a renegade tear when he released me. "Thanks."

Alexander smiled again and gently squeezed my shoulder. "Any time." He gazed up at his son howling in triumph with the rest of the pack and chuckled. "As for the bakery, if that new proposal isn't up to snuff, Xander's already put together a counterproposal."

I fanned my stinging eyes. "Stop, you're gonna make me cry and I've already done enough crying to last a lifetime."

"Welcome to the family, Charline." Alexander glanced back up at his son, who was for once acting like his age."

"He's not going to go into real estate now is he?" I joked.

"Stars, I hope not." He shook his head, turning his gaze from his exuberant son back to me. "I confess, I was rather pleased to hear that you're planning to make this a more permanent stay. What will you do about your life in Raleigh?"

I'd been expecting the question to come up eventually and wasn't surprised that Alexander was the one to voice it. "Quite frankly, aside from Sara, this summer has shown me that I don't really have much of a life there. Sure, I had friends, but they were more judgy acquaintances than anything, and my job is going nowhere in a hurry." I rolled my eyes and he laughed.

"Have you always wanted to own a bakery?" he prodded as we meandered toward the House amidst well wishers and various whoops of joy.

"Well, no. I mean Sara has suggested it on more than one occasion, but it never occurred to me that it could be a reality, let alone *my* reality."

He nodded in understanding. "I'm not sure what your plans were for purchasing the property, but if you need anything, you have the full support of the pack and my resources at your disposal."

I pressed a hand to my breast, overwhelmed by the open-ended offer. "Alexander, I couldn't, that's far too generous." He opened his mouth, no doubt to remind me of the benefits of being part of this wolfy family, and I cut him off. "Besides, I'm planning to sell my cottage in Raleigh and use the proceeds to buy the bakery. Sara's actually helping me with that."

"What is Sara helping with?" David asked as he joined us.

I smacked him in the arm. "What are you doing out of bed? You're supposed to be resting."

"Ow. Werewolf strength, remember?"

I immediately snatched my hand back, much to Alexander's amusement.

"Charline is planning to buy Mimi's Bakery."

David's face was a mix of surprise and disbelief. "You're really buying mom's bakery? I know we sort of talked about it, but..."

"Is that alright?" I asked, suddenly anxious.

"Alright? Of course it's alright!" David wrapped me in a

hug that defied the injuries I knew to be lurking beneath his fresh shirt. "I love you, little fox."

"I love you too, you big lug. Now put me down before you start bleeding again."

He did as I asked and gazed back at me, all the love in the world shining in his baby blues. "It'd be worth it, it was all worth it, just to have you," he said, tucking a wave of hair behind my ear.

In that moment, I knew he would've given up everything, all of it—pack, job, the chance to be Beta—everything, just to be with me. I squeezed him in a tight hug, forgetting for a moment about the fierce marks that decorated his torso. I'd never known a love like his and I knew without a doubt that I never would again.

"Great, you're bleeding again. I just finished cleaning you up," Maria scolded as she stepped up beside her mate.

Alexander slipped an arm around her waist and planted a kiss atop her dark hair. "Forgive them, Maria, young pairs are so easily moved, the passion is like moonlight in the blood."

"I remember," she said with a fond smile. "But those wounds will need quite a bit of time and cleaning to make sure they don't get infected."

"I trust Miss Montgomery is up to the task."

I beamed at Alexander and loosened my grip on poor David. Now seemed as good a time as any to spring the idea I'd been nursing right alongside owning the bakery. "Alpha, is it common for the Betas to live in the House?"

Alexander cocked his head to the side and considered me.

"What I mean is, is it required?" I added.

He gave me a knowing smile. "No, though it does tend to happen more often than not."

"Suppose there was a more appropriate place for the Beta to live..."

"You mean like in town?" Maria asked while David seemed a bit dubious at this sudden line of query.

"I was thinking a bit closer," I tip-toed, shooting David a wary glance.

"But Char, I thought you wanted to build a house of our own." Bless his heart, he still had no idea where I was going with this.

"I do. It just seems like it would make more sense if the Beta was still fairly close as in...right next door?"

Alexander's eyes widened with surprise while David looked absolutely pole stricken.

"I mean it wouldn't be anything nearly as grand, just some-where *not* the House. A private space away from the hustle and bustle of everyday pack life," I finished in a rush. Alexander blinked back at me, surprise still plain in his dark brown eyes.

"Alpha, please don't be—" David began once he found his voice.

"No, no," Alexander cut him off, "it's not that. I'm actu-ally wondering why no one's ever thought of it before." David's stricken look returned as Alexander shook his head and laughed to himself. "While the pack may not have need of guest houses, it stands to reason that the Beta should have their own residence. Of course, it would be the *Beta* residence in the same way that the House is intended for the residing Alpha." Alexander looked at me.

Message received loud and clear—while the idea of a separate house had merit, it would not be *my* house, at least not permanently. Despite the reality check, I couldn't suppress my excitement. There wasn't a doubt in my mind that David would win the battle for Beta now. He not only had the backing of most of the pack, but he'd also defeated the current Beta unaided. Abruptly, I realized that blood was not only seeping through his shirt but mine as well.

"I think Maria's right, I better tend to these again before he bleeds out on the front lawn," I said as I attempted to steer David back towards the House. A pointless endeavor. No one moved someone like David unless he wanted to be moved. I let out an 'Oof' and gave it up.

He flashed me a grin, that he then shifted to Alexander. "If that's something you really want to pursue, Alpha, I can get the crew on it as soon as we're finished remodeling the bakery."

"Why would you remodel the bakery?" I asked, glancing between David and Alexander. "It's perfectly fine."

"It's stuck in another decade, my dear," Maria offered kindly.

"I like it," I grumbled, crossing my arms beneath my breasts.

David laughed, pulling me into a side hug and planting a wet smack on my temple. "But you need to make it your own. I appreciate that you're inclined to leave my mother's old bakery the way it is, but it hasn't been her bakery for a very long time." Sadness briefly clouded his eyes then just as suddenly disappeared, burned away by his usual sunny demeanor. "Have you decided what to name it?"

"What is it with you people and changing everything?"

"The change is part of our nature," Alexander replied stoically.

I barked out a laugh then another and another while everyone stared at me like I was off my rocker, with the exception of Alexander, whose eyes twinkled with pleased mischief. Sure, werewolf puns were a dime a dozen, but never did I expect to hear one come from Alexander.

"So... Now that she's officially snapped, I think it's time I let her clean me up," David said as he gently took hold of my shaking shoulders. "Let me know when you want to go over plans, Alpha."

I let him steer me away, more focused on seeing the ground beneath my feet through the tears of laughter. Maybe my cheese was a little off the cracker. But who could blame me? I'd been in the worst cat fight of my life, nearly died, turned into a werewolf, witnessed two executions, and helped save the day. Far as I saw it, it was a miracle I hadn't cracked sooner.

"I cannot believe you did that," David said as we stepped into the House and veered for the stairs.

"Did what?" I asked, assuming he meant the impromptu giggle fit, which again, earned.

He glanced over at me as we hit the landing. "Just up and asked about building a house on pack property."

"Alexander thought it was a good idea," I said with a shrug and followed him into the room. "Besides, it does make sense."

He shook his head, chuckling to himself and calmly removed his shirt. The move had the unfortunate side effect of escalating the bleeding.

"Oh David!" I gasped. It had been nearly impossible to see the true extent of the damage Johnathan had wrought earlier, but the glaring fluorescents painted a stark reality. Claw marks raked from behind his shoulders and across his chest to finish on his side with a couple other sets dominating his middle and back.

He caught my staring. "Hey, it's not that…"

"I swear by all things holy, if you try to tell me it's not as bad as it looks, I'm going to smack you into next week. And don't forget, I have werewolf strength now, so it's entirely doable." My threat didn't seem to hold much water as he simply laughed over it and my scowl, but at least he stopped talking. "Would changing help?" I asked, using the recently removed shirt to try and stem the latest rivulets.

He let out a deep sigh, which didn't bode well. "This *is* after the change."

"David."

"Please don't fuss too much. I'm okay—mostly—and I *will* heal. Sure, they'll leave scars, but I hear strong women like scars." He gave me a crooked grin and I frowned. "Now back to what we were talking about."

"You mean about Alexander thinking I'm a genius for suggesting the Beta's house be next door?"

"Yes," he said with a laugh. "I love how you go for things." His eyes shone with love while I devoted my attention to a particularly stubborn stream. "The mothers adore you and it's obvious you have the pack's best interests at heart in everything you do. You truly are a wonderful woman." I ducked my head to hide the burning in my cheeks at the profuse praise. "You're going to make an amazing Beta female," he added.

I looked up sharply. "Beg your pardon?"

"Comes with the territory, little fox. If I'm Beta, so are you. Consider it a perk of being mated." He wiggled his eyebrows and I couldn't help but laugh at the not so subtle implication of other "perks" as he put it.

"David Bringer, way to put the cart before the horse," I scolded as I carefully straddled him.

His face clouded with doubt and I struggled to keep a straight face. "I mean, I know the Beta business isn't a hundred percent settled, but I feel..."

"Oh, I'm right behind you on that," I cut in. "This pack has gotten to see numerous times how qualified you are. That's not what I'm talking about."

His brows snapped together. "Then what?"

"You haven't even asked me to marry you yet." Try as I might, I slipped and smiled at the end.

"You beautiful, moon-kissed vixen," he growled, flipping us. I let out a squeal of delight and giggled until he silenced the laughter with a demanding kiss. Once he'd stolen all my breath, he pulled back and looked down at me. "I still can't believe I found you."

EPILOGUE

A solid six months later, my little yellow cottage finally sold. I couldn't help but think it might have sold faster and for a better price if I'd gotten the likes of Edith Sharp to head up the sale. But after the scene with the planning committee, no one had seen hide nor hair of her. My little birdies told me she'd turned in her notice and promptly left town, thankfully without making a big to-do of it.

The real mercy however, was that no one inquired as to Johnathan's whereabouts. Apparently, his dislike of the townsfolk had been stark enough to limit what exposure they did have with him and I seriously suspected that anyone even realized he was missing. All the same, the entire pack had been briefed on what to say in the unlikely event that someone ask.

I wiped down the new marble counters while my mind continued to play over the events of the last few months. Things had finally settled down with the town and everyone was as friendly as ever, only now it wasn't just with me. I smiled to myself. Even poor Jeffrey seemed to have warmed up to David *and* he'd finally asked out Carly which was a miracle in and of itself.

My own resignation from the HR department of Raleigh Marketing had been accepted with minimal kerfuffle. Much to my amazement, there'd been no shortage of sad faces and not all of them from my own department. Sara I'd expected, and maybe even Laurie, but definitely not the slew of well-wishers and flowers from virtually every department. Even some of Ted's old buddies turned out to send me off with a friendly wave on my last day. All this time I'd thought everyone believed I was nothing more than the office gossip in a dress.

"Are you sure it needs to be pink?" David asked, effectively startling me out of my reverie.

"Bakeries are pink, that's just the way it is."

"It wasn't pink before," he grumbled under his breath as he made his way past with a box overflowing with paint cans.

"Hey, you're the one who wanted me to make this place my own," I said, waving my rag at him as I trailed after. He set the box down amidst the other myriad collection of materials and laborers. I peered around at the dusty mess and wondered how I would ever manage to get this place clean enough to serve food.

David chuckled and wrapped an arm around my waist. "What are you scowling about?"

"I'm going to end up as big as a house surrounded by all of these sweets."

He waved his hand dismissing my concerns. "Not with that metabolism, you won't."

"But look at me! I already look like I've cleaned the place out," I whined, not convinced that a werewolf metabolism would magically protect me from the dangers of confections.

"You are absolutely radiant, my love," he said sincerely before stealing a kiss that was not appropriate given our audience. I was about to fuss some more when he headed me off. "Are you ready to see the sign?"

"Is it up?" All of my insecurities vanished in the wake of my enthusiasm.

"Sure is," he said with a grin. He grabbed my hand and led me back outside. "Wait, wait, wait. Close your eyes."

"David, I already know what it's supposed to look like. I did help design it."

"Would you just indulge me? You don't have to be stubborn about *everything*, you know."

I obediently closed my eyes and placed my hands over them for good measure. From my cocoon of darkness, I stuck my tongue out.

"Hey, no peeking," David admonished.

"I'm not." I sealed my fingers more firmly together, lest I be tempted to do so as he carefully guided me until I was sure we were standing on the sidewalk.

"You ready?"

"You already know the answer to that."

"Okay, open them." The infectious joy in his voice had me smiling by the time I removed my hands. And damn it all if he wasn't right, seeing it hung up and everything was a far cry from a sketch on paper. My breath caught in my throat and I placed a hand on my stomach as if I could somehow encourage my body to draw breath again.

"Oh David, it's perfect!" I didn't even bother to stop the tears that welled up from falling. *Foxy's Treats* proudly graced the storefront in elegant swirls complete with a fox tail underlining the script. Little Rosie had actually been the one to give me the idea, and although I'd had my reservations, seeing it firsthand convinced me. "I never dreamed..." I stopped mid-sentence and gasped.

"What?" David rushed to my side, his eyes full of concern.

"Give me your hand." He dutifully held it out and I delicately placed the calloused hand of a man who believed in hard work on my belly. "Do you feel that?" His face filled with wonder as he looked up at me and I mirrored his broad grin. "She's gonna be a feisty one."

"Just like her mama." He pulled me into an embrace and I didn't care who was watching as he kissed me thoroughly enough to make my own mama blush.

"Shouldn't be much longer now."

"Then I guess I better hurry up with that house so you can finally get your hands on the nursery," he said, nuzzling my neck.

"I'm sure Maria wouldn't oppose a baby in the House." I grinned as his hand slid possessively around the belly that was at once a source of frustration and of pride.

"Just please promise me the nursery won't be pink too." His low chuckle sent goosebumps cascading across my skin despite the perfect spring weather.

"And what color would you paint it?"

"Yellow, like the sunlight you've brought to my life."

I couldn't help but giggle. "It's hard to argue with that. Fine, you win, yellow it is. Now about names..."

David let out a put upon groan. Then the love of my life guided us back inside, where townsfolk and packmates alike were working tirelessly to get the bakery open before our bundle of joy could steal the last of my focus.

If you enjoyed *Sara's Moon*, you'll love the next book in...
Moons of Mystery

Book One: *Sara's Moon*

Book Two: *Charline's Solstice*
All Charline wanted was happily ever after. Instead,
werewolf politics might tear her and David apart forever.

Book Three: *Diana's Eclipse*
Coming soon!
Keep reading for a sneak preview.

View the series here!
BooksbySBolanos.com/moons-of-mystery

Keep up as the adventure continues...
Want to stay in the loop with all the latest and greatest? Get
announcements and specials by subscribing to my
newsletter. Sign up now to receive a sneak peek at my
current WIP and maybe a few other treats from my
paranormal lovelies.

BooksBySBolanos.com/newsletter

Like on FB:
facebook.com/BooksBySBolanos

Follow on Twitter:
twitter.com/BooksBySBolanos

Follow on Instagram:
Instagram.com/SBolanosBooks

Check out the Playlist:
bit.ly/CharlinesSolsticePlaylist

DIANA'S ECLIPSE: SNEAK PREVIEW
DEAD BODY ON CAMPUS

I neglected the massive ornate doors in favor of the modest and far more accessible push bar. Beyond the glass door, swaths of orange and magenta colored the thickening twilight, lending the campus an ethereal quality. Mercifully, the heat of the day had started to cool, bringing Blackwell Hollow to a comfortable seventy degrees and nowhere near cold enough to warrant the light sweater still gracing my shoulders.

"Are you sure we can't convince you to come out with us?" Millie's voice chased after me.

I spun on my heel and walked backwards a few steps. Unsurprisingly, earnest hope shone in hazel eyes set in a fawn-colored face surrounded by brown ringlets. Behind her, I could make out two other young women attempting to crowd through the small door all at once.

Millie's eyes widened comically as she mouthed "Please."

I held back my laughter and shook my head, causing my forever straight black hair to swing dramatically. Without thinking, I snagged a hairband from my wrist and pulled it back. "Not tonight ladies. Still have to read those three chapters for Poli-Sci."

The collective groan of two of the women was cut short by the third pushing her way to the forefront. Hyacinth Van Helsing stood boldly before the main school library with her arms crossed and a stubborn set to her mouth. The yellow light pouring out from behind her made her dark skin glow even as the building mist curled at her feet. Hyacinth had been indomitable since she was three. Not much had changed in the nearly twenty years I'd known her.

"Seriously, Ana?" Kora huffed and mimicked Hyacinth's stance. "Stop being such an overachiever. It's only the second week of classes." She rolled her blue eyes set in an overly tanned face.

I shrugged and hiked my bag higher up my shoulder. The strap dug mercilessly down with the weight of too many books. Just then a light rain started up. I glanced up at the sky and back at my friends. "Looks like I'll have to take a rain check."

The trio of women retreated under the relative safety of the library entrance, faces plastered with varying degrees of disappointment. Hyacinth's scowl deepened, but she allowed herself to be pulled deeper beneath the awning.

"Promise, next time." I swiveled to face front before I could slip on the increasingly wet ground and waved goodbye.

Hyacinth's deep voice filled the deepening twilight. "I'm gonna hold you to that, Diana Harker."

I winced at my full name even as my wave turned into an overzealous thumbs up. Hye had a unique gift of making anything she said sound like a threat. Our families had been friends for as long as I could remember and while Hyacinth wasn't exactly a bully, she was very used to getting her way. I quickened my pace in case she decided to come after me anyway. Thankfully, my apartment wasn't all that far and I was confident I could make it before she decided whether or not I was worth the trouble.

It wasn't until I crossed the quad veering North-West that I let out a relieved breath. Hyacinth was nothing if not persistent. I glanced around at the red brick buildings, some of which had stood for nearly a hundred-fifty years. Blackwell Hollow University may not have been the most prestigious school or even the largest, but it was nice in its own way, namely that it was far away from my overbearing and demanding parents. I grimaced to myself as I sloshed through a tiny puddle. It had not been a great surprise to learn that Hyacinth had also decided to attend.

Not that I expect her to stay.

I gave it three months tops before my childhood friend opted to transfer to another school. BHU was simply too small and quiet to entertain someone like her for long.

Unless she's here to keep an eye on me...

I forcibly shoved down the persistent paranoia and returned my focus to the path. To my alarm, the mist had thickened into a full-on fog that nearly obscured the distant Administration Hall. A slight breeze stirred the few leaves that had given up their summer perches in anticipation of an early fall. I pulled my sweater tighter as a chill crawled across my skin, suddenly glad that I hadn't bothered to remove it before leaving the library.

A faint howl rose up in the distance and I came to an abrupt halt. The sudden shift in motion had my backpack sliding free of its precarious perch. I struggled to maintain my hold on the heavy bag even as my heart slammed an irrational rhythm against the inside of my ribs.

Take it easy. There are no wolves in Blackwell.

Another shrill cry rose up into the night sending a

cascade of goosebumps erupting on my flesh. I spun in a circle in a desperate search of the unlikely sound that was impossibly closer. My breath came in harsh pants as I fought to get control over my spiraling fear.

You're just imagining things. It's probably just the Iota Nus torturing a fresh batch of pledges.

Determined not to panic, I reoriented myself in the direction of my apartment. I'd only gone ten feet when the crystal notes of a hunting call climbed into the night to be joined by two other voices—one of which was in front of me.

Adrenaline shot through my veins. I purposefully adjusted my trajectory and willed myself not to break into a sprint. Even knowing running was a terrible idea, my pace quickened as the haunting lilts continued to dog my heels. I swallowed down increasing terror as the sounds got closer. But for every turn I made, I only seemed to be getting nearer to their source, not farther.

I caught sight of a blue light shining six feet off the ground and made a beeline for it. How the feeble light had managed to penetrate the intense fog was beyond me. My hand was inches from the panic button, when a heart-stopping howl echoed loudly through the night. I smashed the button and bolted, searching the darkness for the next station. Police would follow the trail of panic to find me, hopefully *before* I became someone's dinner.

My feet pounded on the concrete path as I blasted through fog, the sharp smack of my shoes betraying my location. Air burned in my lungs even as I hit the next button and kept going. Yips accompanied the howls in a cacophony that drowned out all other sound. I hit the latest pole and veered off the sidewalk, my feet sliding on the damp grass.

I strained to catch the sound of pursuit as I ran full tilt.

The thick fog was like an impassable wall that only gave way to patches of thinner mist gradually soaking my clothes, but never broke enough to see.

A yip off to my left sent me swiveling right with barely a pause. I skidded on the slick ground, the weight of my bag slowing me down. By some miracle, I kept my footing. There was a loud yelp that just barely registered as I dropped the dead weight in pursuit of speed and agility. Without the books weighing me down, I surged forward and right into a wall.

I bit back a curse as the obstacle came into view too late to be avoided. Coarse bricks raked scratches on my arms as I just barely prevented my face from meeting the unforgiving surface. I pushed off the wall that had materialized without warning and spun to keep moving. The chorus of yips and howls swirled around me with no identifiable source, every-where and nowhere all at once.

The stitch in my side begged me to slow down, a painful reminder to the harsh physical regimen I had pointedly abandoned upon enrollment. I resisted the urge to clutch at my heaving ribs and stumbled deeper into chaos, the sound of my own breathing threatening to mask the cries surrounding me.

All of a sudden there was a sharp twang. The eerily familiar sound of an arrow being loosed. The fog was too dense to hear it whistle on its path, but it did nothing to stop the pained yelp that followed. A moment of dead silence descended. I froze, unwilling to betray my location by so much as a breath. Only the focus that comes with years of practice enabled me to slow my thundering heart to some-thing less audible.

No sooner did I dare breathe again than howls rose up in a keening wail. A menacing snarl drifted out of the fog from my right. There wasn't time to second guess my direction as I launched myself through swirling gray in the opposite direction, my efforts at calm evaporating faster than I could run. My foot caught on a large bulge in the ground and I went sprawling onto cobblestones. I glanced back to see what it was.

For a fraction of a second, the fog swirled where I had disturbed it, then dispersed into the tiny vacuum I'd created. I choked back a scream and scrambled backwards from the body. My hand slipped on the slick ground and I pitched backwards.

The back of my skull made contact with the fountain with a resounding crack that hit the dense fog and bounced back. The world swam as I blinked away a myriad of brightly colored spots. I let out a groan as I reached back to carefully inspect the point of impact. That's when my gaze lit on the body once more. The naked, *dead* body of a young man with an arrow sticking out of his chest.

<hr>

"I've already told you: I. Don't. Know." The ache at the back of my head had quickly been replaced by a pounding at my temples. I'd only managed a few yards before disorientation and what was likely a concussion had forced me to sit. Then the cops had shown up...finally.

The officer referenced his pad again where he'd written nothing but gibberish as far as I could tell. "Wolves, you said?" He scratched his head with the back of his pen, ignoring my exasperated groan. "McGuinness!" the man called to the partner that had arrived with him twenty minutes ago.

"Yeah?" the guy called back from where he was helping the coroner load the body onto a gurney.

"We get any reports of wolves lately?"

His partner snickered. "Nah man. But those fraternities are gonna catch hell for terrorizing the student body again."

My guy turned back to me. "See? Couldn't be wolves. Now let's try this again." I bristled at the underlying implication that I was likely drunk, high, or both.

"Officer Hatchet."

Hatchet flinched back from the authoritative voice. "Yes sir."

A man in a long coat designed to keep out both the chill and the wet disentangled himself from his inspection of the sheet-covered body to walk over. He may have been younger than Officer Hatchet, but it was obvious he had more clout. "If you're finished harassing my witness, I'd like a word with Miss—"

"Harker," I filled in.

"Harker as in the Harkers of Bethany?" The newcomer's eyebrow arched up in curious disbelief.

"One and the same," I said, barely managing not to grumble.

"Wouldn't have thought they'd let one of their own attend such a modest university."

"Yeah, well, a name isn't everything." I crossed my arms and met the man's level look.

"Don't be so sure, Miss Harker. A name may not be everything, but it has a power in its own right." He let the mild admonishment sit a moment then shifted gears. "I'm Detective Takashi and I'd appreciate it if you could tell me what happened. Did you know the young man?"

My face went cold as I recalled lifeless brown eyes staring back at me.

"In your own time," the detective encouraged.

I clenched my jaw and let out a frustrated breath. "Like I already told Officer Hatchet. I left the library around eight."

"Were you with anyone?" Detective Takashi interrupted.

"Yes, I was with friends."

"And their names?"

I glared at him and he clicked his pen as if eagerly awaiting my response. "Millicent Roberts, Hyacinth Van Helsing, and Kora Laskaris."

He scribbled each name and made another note before gesturing for me to continue.

"I was walking to my apartment when I heard howling." I paused for him to discount my tale as Officer Hatchet had, but Takashi waited patiently for me to continue. "It was coming from everywhere like it was chasing me."

"That's when you hit the Emergency Call."

"Yes. I didn't feel safe waiting for help though, so I kept running." The detective nodded along, continuing to take notes. I eyed his notepad, but kept going. "I got turned around in the fog, but when I heard the bow, I stopped."

"Did you say bow? As in bow and arrow?"

"Yes. But I didn't get a good look at the arrow. It seemed safer to get as far away as I could. Clearly," I indicated our general vicinity, "I didn't get far. It may have been a long bow, but it could have just as easily been a short or a crossbow."

"And where did this arrow go, Miss Harker?"

I gave the detective an incredulous look. "What do you mean 'where did it go?' It was sticking out of his chest." I gestured at where I'd stumbled over the body where now the only evidence was a dark stain on the grass.

Detective Takashi met my gaze. "There was no arrow."

Before I could ask him what the hell his idiot officers had done with the damn thing, Officer McGuinness walked up. "Everything has been collected, Detective, and the coroner has the body. Did you need anything else?"

Takashi clicked his pen and slid it into his front pocket. "No.

Now we just need to get a handle on this before the student press decides this is a killing spree." At his words, several flashes went off where students and professional journalists alike had gathered. Takashi took out a card and held it out to me. "If you remember anything else, Miss Harker, don't hesitate to call."

I opened my mouth to say I remembered plenty if he would just listen, but he was already walking away.

"Hey, Ana."

I swiveled around and stared in shock. "Jenny. What are you doing here?" I glanced past her where more officers, including my two, were diligently working to control and disperse the clamoring crowd. "How did you get past the tape?"

Jennifer Brightburn glanced over her shoulder where the yellow "Crime Scene" tape was strung with abandon. "I was walking to the dining hall when I saw all of the lights. I came to investigate. When I saw you, I just waited 'til no one was looking and slipped through. Terrible perimeter by the way." She gestured with her thumb at the chaos behind her, causing her long, dark hair to sway.

Unlike Hyacinth and the others I'd left at the library, Jenny was substantially more grounded when it came to studies and life in general. I appreciated our fast friendship more than I could express and the fact that she was here now sent a ripple of relief through me.

"—you okay?"

"What?" I asked, having missed everything else.

"I saw the coroner. Are you okay? What happened?"

I reached up to tenderly touch the back of my head. Yep, definite goose egg, maybe even some blood. In my frustration to deal with the police, I'd declined medical attention. A decision I was coming to regret. "I'm well enough. Mostly just got spooked. Ran around like a dizzy fruit fly after I heard wolves calling until I tripped over the body and smacked my head on the fountain."

"Wolves?" Jenny echoed.

I rolled my eyes and flapped my hand. "The cops are saying it was the Iota Nus getting out of hand with pledges again."

Jenny's gaze slanted over to where the grass was still bent in the shape of a body. "Seems a little more extreme to me than that. Are you sure you're alright?"

"I'll be—"

Before I could finish, a young man bounded up to join us. His dark hair was a shiny black beneath the spotlights erected by the responders while his body was lithe and bordering on gangly. The fresh look on his face and overeager smile betrayed him as the underclassman he was. First guess would put him as a Sophomore if not a Freshman.

"Hey, Jen. Good, you found her. This must be yours." He held out my backpack.

Jenny stared at the bag a moment then seemed to shake herself. "Oh right. Ana, this is my cousin, Alexander Wolfsbane the Second."

View the series here!
BooksbySBolanos.com/moons-of-mystery

364

ACKNOWLEDGMENTS

As always, there are too many people to thank individually. Charline's Solstice was a little closer to home than some of my other stories and writing her journey was far from easy. There's a delicate balance in fiction between pulling from real life and and a story intended for escape.

I want to thank my family for being there and supporting me through the real life parts of this adventure and the writing community for helping me make it a story that could offer catharsis. I'd also like to extend a special thank you to the incredible author, Skye Kilaen, who helped make Charline's Solstice so much more. I know it wasn't easy, but I couldn't have done it without you.

ABOUT THE AUTHOR

A genderqueer author, S (she/they) enjoys creating worlds that feel as real as they are fantastical, and doesn't shy away from the darkness that makes the light so much brighter. Her passion for fantasy and the supernatural has given rise to stories where the mystery is just as riveting as the romance.

S is of Cuban-American descent; born in Miami, FL, raised in Mobile, AL. They currently live in Texas, a startling eight miles from everything, as the saying goes. Their two Labradors keep them company (whether they want company or not), and their supportive husband is invaluable when it comes to working out sticky plot points.

Their characters are lively, well-rounded, and reflect the conflicts we all face, albeit with a supernatural twist. Readers can look forward to many stories within the same universe that reach into the past and stretch all the way to the future. Welcome to the adventure!

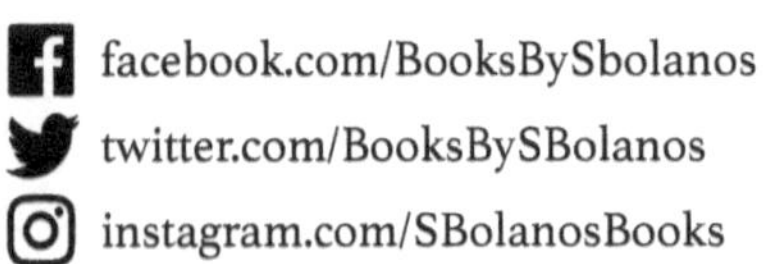

facebook.com/BooksBySbolanos

twitter.com/BooksBySBolanos

instagram.com/SBolanosBooks